HOPE DARES *to* BLOSSOM

HOPE DARES
to BLOSSOM

Elisabeth Conway

atmosphere press

For my mentor and friend
Jayne Woodhouse

"Words spoken between true friends
are as sweet as the perfume of orchids."

- (I-Ching)

The title of **Hope Dares to Blossom** comes from the poem
"Hope Knows No Fear" by Sri Chimoy

"Hope knows no fear.
Hope dares to blossom.
Even inside the abysmal abyss.
Hope secretly feeds and strengthens promise."

SRI CHIMOY, "HOPE KNOWS NO FEAR"

PROLOGUE
Leaving Cape Town Behind, June 1824

The breeze filled her sails and hastened her passage; the *Mariner* was leaving Cape Town behind. Stamford Raffles stood on the deck, staring at the eastern horizon. This was the point where he put his previous life behind him and turned to face his future back in England. It wasn't easy; he'd lived in the Orient for the greater part of seventeen years. It was only his own poor state of health that was now forcing him to return home.

It was already twelve months since he left Singapore, but he knew it was unlikely that he'd come this way again. He paced the deck, looking longingly towards the Indian Ocean, thinking about the people he'd left behind – Dick, Chin Ming and Wing Yee. It was Dick, his adopted son, over whom he'd agonised the most, of course. He'd always known that one day, the young Papuan would no longer need his protection, but nevertheless, it had come as a surprise when Dick revealed his intention to stay in Singapore. Raffles knew it would be difficult for the young man to develop his artistic talents in England, whereas the wealthier merchants in the Settlement had already begun to seek him out. This knowledge made him feel better, and he was glad that Dick was now making his name as a portrait artist.

As the ship changed direction and set its course in a north-westerly direction, he shivered and the melancholy returned.

Raffles' major regret was not being able to help Chin Ming establish the truth about her father's disappearance. The letter he'd sent to Guangzhou to investigate the rumours about Li Soong Heng's abduction had never received a response. He knew that Chin Ming would continue to believe that he was alive, but the likelihood of that being true faded as each month passed. The young woman was obviously a survivor; she was already occupied in helping to make the fledgling school a success. Wing Yee too had overcome severe anguish; her personality was strong and she'd seized the opportunity to build on her extensive knowledge of traditional medicine. Nevertheless, Raffles worried about what would become of them all in the long run.

The wind increased, filling the sails to full capacity, speeding the ship away from the past and forcing him to focus on what lay ahead. In an effort to improve his mood, he reminded himself that his last year in the East hadn't been easy. Since leaving Singapore, it felt as if his life had been blighted. He and Sophia had been obliged to return to Sumatra to pack up their belongings, but it served only to remind them of the three children they had buried there; then the new baby – Flora – had lived only two short months. Sophia's own health had suffered and his headaches had returned; it was almost too much to bear. They'd lost most of their possessions when, on an earlier voyage, fire broke out; even this journey had been alarming at times. During the violent storms in the Indian Ocean, he'd begun to think they were destined never to reach England.

However, the three weeks spent in Cape Town had restored his health and now he looked up to see a clear blue sky; the weather was set fair and the *Mariner* should reach St Helena within a few days. After that they would head towards Plymouth; he was beginning to feel less morose, and this walk on deck was helping to drive away the last remaining strands of disappointment. Raffles took a deep breath and decided to go below so that he could inspect his collection of animals and plants.

He was pleased to see that the livestock – a beautiful cinnamon-coloured langur, a pair of civets and a comical-looking tapir – all appeared healthy. The deckhand who had been put in charge of them may not have been the brightest star in the sky, but he certainly had a soft spot for these creatures. He'd cared for them and he'd made sure their cages held fast, even when the ship was pitching around in the storm.

Throughout the voyage, Raffles had checked on the safety of his precious cargo at regular intervals, the last time being only a few days ago. There were thirty barrels holding all but one of the plant specimens that local guides had collected for him in recent months. People chosen for the task were familiar with the terrain and knew what plants to find in the mangrove swamps, the rainforest and the mountains. The containers were still lashed firmly together and their contents looked good. The sweet scent of jasmine pervaded the air, competing for attention with the musky smell of cloves.

He took a few more paces to the place where he'd hidden the *Paphiopedilum superbiens*. He'd chosen the spot, trying to mimic the orchid's shady habitat, but it was nowhere to be seen – someone must have moved it.

Raffles checked all the other barrels, carefully at first, but then more urgently. He questioned the deckhand, but he didn't understand what all the fuss was about. Raffles searched again, but the orchid was definitely not there; he rushed up on deck to question other members of the crew. He emerged into a melee of excitement; something was agitating his fellow passengers. He saw members of the crew trying to instil a sense of calm, but it was useless. He looked for Sophia and found her eventually amongst a small cluster of people who had gathered at the side of the ship. Some had their hands lifted to protect their eyes from the strong sunlight, others pointed towards a smudge on the horizon – the port they'd now left far behind.

'What's happening?' Raffles asked when he reached his wife. 'I've just been below and I can't find the orchid – it's quite rare and ...,' his voice trailed off as he saw the expression on his wife's face.

'Oh,' she gasped, as she turned away from the others. She clenched her hands together and her voice sounded odd as she said, 'your orchid is not the only thing to go missing!'

Raffles' eyes widened as he waited for her to continue.

'That Frenchman – the one who seemed so interested in your plant collections – well, I'm afraid he's gone missing too! Someone saw him go ashore about an hour before the anchor was raised – he hasn't been seen since.'

CHAPTER 1
Singapore, 15th January 1825

The track Chin Ming and Wing Yee had taken to the summit of Bukit Larangan was much less hazardous these days than when they had first arrived in Singapore over two years ago. Nevertheless, their progress had been slow and they had welcomed the shade provided by the majestic rain trees along the way. Today, when they reached the top of the path, the sun had already gained strength and they paused for a few moments to adjust to the bright light. Their gaze fell upon the house they'd shared with Raffles and Sophia; the site he had chosen because it was cool and quiet, away from the hustle and bustle of the town, but still providing a glorious view of the harbour. The bungalow was now occupied by John Crawfurd, the new Resident; but Dick, Chin Ming and Wing Yee had continued to meet nearby, in the area they always referred to as their *Talking Place*.

Dick leapt to his feet as soon as the two women approached. '*Saang jat faai lok*,' he said slowly and deliberately, looking to Wing Yee for reassurance. He smiled at Chin Ming and repeated the carefully rehearsed birthday greeting. She was dressed in a pale blue tunic, worn over a long skirt in a darker shade; both garments were embroidered with butterflies. She looked radiant, as always.

'How did you know the Cantonese for a birthday greeting?' Chin Ming said once she'd regained her composure.

'Wing Yee taught me, of course,' Dick replied. 'Did I get it right?'

'Perfect,' she said. 'But I had no idea ...'

'You know Dick teach me to speak Malay,' Wing Yee said. 'Sometime we swap, I help him learn Cantonese. He can get words in right order, but tones more difficult. He make special effort for you, today is special occasion.' Her use of English was improving all the time, but she continued to omit the occasional word.

'What a lovely surprise and it's good to have an excuse to spend some time here, with my best friends,' Chin Ming said, 'but apart from that it's no different to any other birthday.'

'Oh, but it is,' said Dick. 'At least, that's what Alexander Johnston says. You should ask him when you see him this evening.'

'I will,' she replied. 'In China, birthdays are only important when a child is one year old, and when an adult reaches sixty.'

'Baba Tan say same for Peranakans,' Wing Yee added. 'Just two days' worth celebrating – when child one month old and when sixty-one years; people then believe full life lived.'

They all laughed at what, in both cases, seemed a lifetime away.

'Well, Wing Yee and I thought we'd make today different,' said Dick. 'Just think of all the things that have happened to us since we first met. As well as your birthday, I think we should celebrate all the times we've enjoyed together – and to value our friendship.' He looked slightly embarrassed the moment he'd finished speaking; he wasn't used to making formal speeches, but Chin Ming knew exactly what he meant.

The idea for the birthday celebration had been Dick's alone, but Wing Yee had been glad to go along with it. She was looking forward to their time together. She'd also been told about the surprise Dick had planned; he'd made something special for Chin Ming and he wanted to present his gift amongst friends, in the privacy of this place on the crown of the hill.

Neither Dick nor Wing Yee noticed the fleeting shadow that crossed Chin Ming's face. For her, another birthday always brought back memories of the last time she'd seen her father. It was now three years since Papa had been swept away during the lunar new year celebrations. The image of his face remained very clear, but the detail was beginning to fade from her memory and the colourful shapes that were once so vivid were slipping into pastel shades that lacked focus.

Dick pulled a small package from the pocket of his shirt; he offered it to her. 'I made this for you,' he said. 'It's only very small, but there's something inside it that I thought you might like to have.'

Chin Ming looked at him and smiled. He was one of the kindest people she'd ever known, and she was grateful to him for this distraction.

'Am I to open it now?'

Dick nodded. The present was wrapped in a small piece of red velvet, tied together with a matching ribbon. Chin Ming took her time to explore the shape of the package with her fingers before opening it. She had no idea what was inside.

'Hurry,' said Wing Yee. 'Dick not tell me what he give you; cannot wait to see inside.'

Wing Yee squeezed Dick's hand as Chin Ming began to untie the ribbon. They were both anxious to see if the present gave her pleasure, but every movement she made seemed to be in slow motion. When the last fold of the velvet was turned back, it revealed a small locket. She lifted it away from the material to examine it more closely.

'You made this yourself?' she asked, and Dick nodded. She held the small oval object in one hand and stroked its surface with the other. It was made of wood, onto which Dick had carved an intricate pattern. The central panel remained plain and was polished, whilst around the edge there was a delicate rattan frame with a piece of red ribbon threaded through it to form a long loop. There was a tiny hinge on one side and a clasp on the other. She had never seen anything quite like it. 'It's exquisite,' she said.

'Before you put it around your neck,' Dick began, 'I'd like you to open it up. There's something inside that I hope you will like.'

Chin Ming was intrigued. Dick showed her how the clasp worked, and then left her to open the locket herself. She gasped. 'Is it the same thread?' she asked.

'Yes,' he replied. 'Raffles sent the letter your father wrote to Calcutta. It was an important part of the evidence against the Dutchman, but he gave me the gold thread that held it together. He thought you might like to have it one day and I've been thinking, for a long time, of making something for you that will keep it safe.'

Chin Ming carefully closed the locket and held it tight. She averted her eyes, trying to hold back the tears. She swallowed hard, then put it to her lips before hanging it around her neck. 'Thank you, thank you so much,' she whispered. 'It's all I have left of Papa now and your beautiful gift will protect it always.'

'That's what I had in mind,' Dick said. He'd enjoyed the challenge of making the locket, but now wondered if it was perhaps too personal a gift; he hoped she wouldn't read too much into the gesture.

Wing Yee smiled to herself. Everyone knew Dick was artistic; his ability to produce striking portraits had prospered in the last two years, but she had no idea that his talent extended to making such a beautiful piece of jewellery. She knew Chin Ming would treasure it.

They moved further into the shade and Wing Yee spread a piece of cloth in front of them. The women had brought freshly made *otak otak puteh* and a selection of *kueh*; Dick added rambutans, papaya and bananas. He was always hungry, but after his birthday speech he now felt quite parched. He'd found a green coconut earlier on and he hurried to split it open with his *parang*, providing them with a cooling drink. Tonight, there was to be a special dinner, to which more of their friends had been invited, but for now they were content to share a leisurely lunch and spend the next few hours catching up with each other's news.

*****

Just after dusk, Dick arrived at Baba Tan's house accompanied by his new guardian, Alexander Johnston. Raffles had settled an allowance on Dick when he left Singapore, and his close friend Johnston had been glad to offer Dick a home.

Red and gold lanterns were strung across the doorway and images of Chin Ming's birth sign were apparent in every corner of the house. Before she met Wing Yee, Chin Ming had never paid much attention to the signs of the zodiac. Her father had encouraged her to learn about art and literature, languages and science, but he had avoided anything to do with superstition and what he considered to be fortune-telling. Wing Yee, however, set great store by ancient astrology and its relationship with long life, happiness and good fortune. Today, Chin Ming was content to go along with her friend's beliefs.

Dick was keen to know the significance of Chin Ming's birth sign and what good fortune she might expect. He listened carefully as Wing Yee explained the supposed qualities and characteristics attributed to the Year of the Pig.

'It's possible that I share the same sign,' he said 'I don't know the exact date of my birth, but I was twelve when Raffles came to Bali and rescued me from my slave master. That was nine years ago, so we must have been born in the same year.'

'But remember, calendar years not same as lunar years,' Wing Yee said. 'If you born after spring festival then you born in Year of Rat, not Pig.'

'If that's the case,' Chin Ming added cheekily, 'it would also mean that you are younger than me.'

Dick was sure she was only teasing, but he couldn't help feeling quashed; he wasn't sure how to respond.

She saw his downcast expression and was immediately apologetic. 'It's not important, you know,' she said. 'After Wing Yee, you are my dearest friend, that's all that really matters.'

He envied her sophistication; her ability to describe how she valued their friendship. He thought she was exactly the sort of person he would like to have had as a sister. She smiled at him. He was still struggling with a response when the discomfort he felt was broken by Wing Yee, who called them over to join the others around the table.

Baba Tan sat at one end and Alexander Johnston at the other. They'd been joined by Abdullah, who was no longer required to perform secretarial duties for the new Resident as he had done for Raffles. Instead, he was working with Chin Ming at the fledgling school. Baba Tan's wife, Yan Lau, who had a small child in her arms, was the last person to sit down. The events that had brought the seven of them together two years ago had forged a closeness that continued to grow stronger every day; they shared an understanding that made them feel like a proper family. They were comfortable with each other, and Chin Ming looked forward to their present contentment continuing to grow. It had nothing at all to do with the year of her birth.

The dishes served that evening had their roots in the culture Baba Tan and Yan Lau had brought with them from Malacca, a fusion of Malay and Chinese cuisine. Their cook appeared as soon as everyone was seated; he carried a large bowl of *bakwan kepiting* and placed it in front of Baba Tan. The aroma of the crab meatballs infused the air as he filled seven small bowls with the soup and passed them to each of his guests. The next dish to be served was *ayam buah keluak*. Yan Lau had obviously planned the meal carefully, with the least spicy dishes being served first. Chin Ming imagined Alexander Johnston had lived in Singapore long enough for his palate to be used to eating all sorts of food, but thought it was kind of Baba Tan's wife to take into account their European guest. A warmth travelled through Chin Ming's body, and she smiled quietly to herself as she reached for a piece of chicken with her chopsticks; it was good to see everyone chatting to each other and enjoying the feast. The meal ended with a large platter of freshly sliced pineapple to cool their mouths after the final dish of fiery *laksa*.

Baba Tan pushed back his chair and stood up. 'Friends,' he said, 'we are here this evening to celebrate this important birthday of a very special young lady.' He turned towards Chin Ming and smiled, then he raised his glass and invited everyone to join him in a toast.

'Chin Ming,' he said, 'we wish you much happiness on this, your twenty-first birthday, and good fortune for the future.'

'To Chin Ming,' they all chorused.

She swallowed hard, knowing that her face had turned pink; then she managed to smile and thank them for their good wishes. 'But I still don't understand why you think being twenty-one is so important,' she said. 'Mr Johnston, Dick told me you would be able to explain.'

'Oh dear,' Johnston said, 'I have to confess that when Dick told me how old you would be today, I did say it was important. You may not know,' he said, 'but the idea of celebrating birthdays began in Persia. As other cultures adopted the practice, they all made their own decision about the age at which a young person became an adult; twenty-one is the age chosen in England, that's all.'

'But why that particular number?' Chin Ming said, not entirely satisfied with his explanation.

Johnston laughed. 'It's all to do with becoming a knight,' he said.

At this point, it was not only Chin Ming who had her eyebrows raised. Johnston now had the attention of everyone sitting around the table; they were all equally puzzled. He began to explain about the three stages of knighthood developed during medieval times. 'They're all set seven years apart, ending with young men achieving knighthood on their twenty-first birthday, providing they'd successfully completed the tasks required of them at the age of seven and fourteen.'

'So, does that mean I'm now a knight?' Chin Ming asked as an amused grin spread across her face.

Johnston opened his mouth to explain about knighthood, then realised she was teasing. He relaxed, then simply said, 'Let's just say you have successfully come of age!'

She touched the pendant Dick had made for her, held her breath and let her thoughts drift to her father – what would he think of her if he saw her now? The spell was broken when she realised everyone was gazing in her direction; she smiled to cover her embarrassment and thanked them once again for their good wishes.

*****

The following week, life had returned to its usual pattern. Chin Ming was to be found with Abdullah in the small school; their intention was to prepare their young pupils for the time when Raffles' dreams for the Singapore Institute would be fulfilled.

Wing Yee climbed the stairs each day to the place in Baba Tan's warehouse where she ground together medicinal herbs; then she combined them to make salves and tinctures to relieve the common ailments which often beset people in the Settlement. Dick was putting the finishing touches to a family portrait.

Muhammad Aljunied had arrived in Singapore in 1819 from Palembang in Sumatra. He was joined shortly afterwards by his nephew and together they had built a prosperous business. As soon as he learned about Dick's artistic capabilities, the Arab merchant was keen to have not merely a portrait of himself, but an image that would encapsulate his whole family, with himself seated at its centre.

The task had been quite tricky. One of the women had been reticent about having her likeness recorded, believing that it took away something that could never be replaced. One of the younger nephews was constantly fidgeting until Dick asked him to hold a small, highly decorated box. The object was, in fact, completely empty, but Dick had made the boy believe that it was a treasured possession and must be kept completely still.

The babies seemed to be in constant need of attention, which meant their mothers often wandered off. In the end, Dick had managed by drawing an outline of the whole scene, making notes about who was sitting where, the details to be filled in later. He made individual sketches of the different faces and then spent time with each one of the adults to make sure their garments were correct and displayed to their best advantage.

*****

When Raffles left Singapore to conclude his responsibilities in Bencoolen, Dick had initially been at a loose end. It was Wing Yee who had encouraged him to develop his skills as an artist. Alexander Johnston had been glad to support the enterprise and had even introduced him to some of the more prosperous merchants who wanted to have their portraits painted.

Since then, hardly a day had gone by when he wasn't busy capturing the likeness of some merchant or another – those who were beginning to make a name for themselves.

*****

Now, Dick sat in front of the Aljunied portrait with his arms resting on his knees and his hands clasped together; his nose was resting against them whilst he scrutinised his work. He knew that it was an accurate record of the scene, but he needed to make sure the work reflected the vivacity he'd felt during the time he'd spent with this particular family. His concentration was so intense that he didn't hear the squeaky stair as Alexander Johnston climbed up to his attic studio.

'We both have letters,' the Scot proclaimed, waving two fat envelopes in Dick's direction as he approached. 'An Indiaman anchored in the harbour yesterday; they say it departed from England almost four months ago so it's reached here in record time.'

Dick recognised the writing immediately; it was from Raffles. He turned his head to one side and scrutinised the package.

He'd received many notes and some lengthier missives during the nineteen months since he'd said his goodbyes to Raffles and Sophia, but he'd never before received an actual letter folded within an extra piece of paper – an envelope.

His heart began to race and his mouth was dry. Johnston noted the wide grin that spread across his face and the sparkle that had returned to his eyes. 'I'll leave you to read your letter in peace,' he said. 'I'll take mine down to the office, and I'll be there if there's anything you want to discuss with me later.'

Dick appreciated the privacy. As soon as Johnston had

reached the lower floor, he took himself to the corner of the studio and sat cross-legged on the floor. Very carefully, as if it was made of gossamer, he opened the envelope and began to read.

CHAPTER 2
Singapore, 21st January 1825

Cheltenham – 21st September 1824

My Dear Dick,
　　We reached Plymouth just over one month ago and spent the first night nearby. Then we hastened to this place where Sophia's parents have been looking after our darling daughter. I have not written at any length before this time because I wanted you to settle into the new life with Mr Johnston, but now it is time to bring you up to date on our news.

Raffles proceeded to describe the highlights of their voyage and the days they'd spent in Cape Town to recuperate from rough seas in the Indian Ocean. No mention was made about the theft of the orchid – there was little point. He described the brief stop at St Helena, hoping Dick would remember visiting the island with him several years ago. The reunion with Ella, their only surviving child, had been difficult at first as the little girl didn't recognise them. He said they'd now rented a house not far from Sophia's parents, but would travel to London very soon. Raffles needed to meet with the directors of the East India Company to discuss his pension and negotiate what money was owed to him following the loss of his possessions when the *Fame* caught fire. Finally, he told Dick, they planned to move to London permanently.

Initially, they would rent a house in the centre of town; it would provide a base for him to visit the Company offices and enable him to accept the many invitations he'd received to speak at various functions. Eventually, he hoped to purchase a property in the countryside where he could get away from the hustle and bustle; he would become a farmer. The letter continued in this vein, describing various visits he planned, people he hoped to meet, and so on. He did not mention the state of his health. Finally, the missive drew to a close.

I will let you know our address in London as soon as I am able to do so.
  Your loving Uncle,
  Stamford Raffle

Dick read and re-read the letter again. He couldn't quite believe that Raffles was finally back home, on the other side of the world. He longed for the next letter, when he might be given a permanent address to which he could respond. He wanted to tell Raffles about his own news, his growing reputation as a portrait artist. Right now, however, he needed to find Chin Ming and share the news with her and Wing Yee.

*****

Today, Chin Ming had insisted that Abdullah leave her to walk home alone. He had been called to a meeting with the Temenggong and she'd told him she needed to stay a little longer to prepare for tomorrow's lessons. Abdullah took his duties as her escort extremely seriously, but she felt perfectly capable of retracing her steps the short distance back to Baba Tan's home by herself. Abdullah had tutted loudly, obviously not approving; he believed that respectable young women should not be out on the streets alone.

'When I stayed at the mission in Guangzhou,' she told him,

19

'I used to go out on errands for Father John almost every day. Singapore is tiny compared with such a large city. There is no need to worry.'

Finally, Abdullah had been obliged to give in to her, otherwise he would be late for his meeting with the Temenggong. When it was over, he resolved to retrace his steps so that he could check the school building and make sure that all was well. It would only be a slight diversion from the route he usually took to his own house.

*****

Chin Ming loved working alongside the gifted Malay teacher, but she was pleased to have some time to herself. She smoothed the front of her tunic and smiled, then wandered around the schoolroom, unhurried and relaxed. She cleaned the children's slates and returned them to the cupboard, along with the chalk and the charts she always used to help the children learn. Two new children had joined her only this week, extending the class to ten, ranging in age from six to twelve; the school was becoming more popular as more and more of the merchants wanted their young families to understand figures and be able to read.

Instead of packing up her belongings, she sat down at the table and took a sheet of paper from the drawer. It was now well over a year since she'd received her last letter from Father John in Guangzhou. He'd responded quickly when she first wrote to tell him about the time she'd spent with Raffles and her subsequent decision to remain in Singapore when he left for Sumatra and eventually England. She'd told him about her friendship with Wing Yee, but had mentioned nothing of the traumas they'd endured at the hands of the towkay and the Dutchman. She'd told him, too, about the efforts Raffles had made to discover what had happened to her father – and that all his investigations had come to nothing.

The priest had made no comment in his reply, but had been sympathetic to her decision to remain in Singapore and take on a teaching role at the fledgling school. He had promised to visit her if ever he had reason to visit the Settlement. There had occasionally been notes since then, but the last time he wrote to her, she got the feeling that he was preoccupied with the many instances of unrest happening all across Guangzhou. She'd not responded immediately because she thought he had enough to deal with, but now she felt she owed him an explanation.

She sat quite still, reflecting on the event that continued to haunt her – the crush of the crowd, Papa handing her the scroll, and the blur as he disappeared from her sight – all now colourless phantoms from three years ago.

During the last few weeks, she had begun to admit to herself that she needed to face the fact that she would probably never know what had happened that day. When Raffles had interrogated the Dutchman, he'd admitted the men who had arranged his own escape from Guangzhou were the same people who had snatched Papa from the crowd while she watched the Lion Dance at the lunar new year.

Chin Ming shuddered. The memory of the man who had tricked Wing Yee and herself, locked them into his remote dwelling on the edge of the jungle and raped her friend filled her with loathing.

He'd said the conspirators had taken Papa to Amoy and put him on board the *Tek Sing*. She remembered Father John telling her about a junk that foundered somewhere in the South China Sea; the name matched and the timing was right. She knew deep down that the evidence was overwhelming. She just didn't want to admit it. When her friends had insisted on celebrating her coming of age only a few days ago, she realised that now might be the time to face the truth.

She had shared these thoughts with no-one, had talked to no-one, not even Wing Yee. Her first step would be to write to Father John; she would tell him that maybe he'd been correct about Papa's disappearance after all.

*****

When Dick reached the schoolhouse, he thought that Chin Ming had already left for the day. There was no sign of her, Abdullah, or any of their pupils. It was unusual to see the place empty so early in the afternoon, and he decided to check for himself that nothing was amiss. He strolled up the path, brushing aside the distinctive fishtail-shaped fronds of the tronok palm, and took a deep breath to enjoy the sweet fragrance floating down to him from a frangipani vine. He made a mental note to come back here with his sketchpad very soon; he would draw these plants and indeed the schoolhouse itself. They would look very well in the new collection of images he intended to send to Raffles.

He didn't notice Chin Ming until he was almost parallel with the small *attap* building that served as the schoolroom. Its windows were flung wide open and he could see her now, seated at a desk on the far side of the room. She was unaware of his presence and appeared to be completely self-absorbed. There were several sheets of paper spread in front of her and he noticed that her hand was poised, holding a pen, as if about to write. She had a far-away expression on her face and he was anxious not to disturb her reverie. He slumped down onto his haunches, content to watch and to wait.

Since the day of their first meeting, he had always been slightly in awe of her. Once she had recovered from the terrifying experience of being incarcerated by the Dutchman, she had gradually regained a natural poise and confidence. One day soon, he intended to paint her portrait, but he knew her well enough to know that she would not readily agree to such an idea. Her long, black hair fell over her face and she instinctively used the fingers of her left hand to comb through it and sweep it behind her ears. She appeared to be staring into space, but then he became aware of a low murmur and realised she was talking to herself. She looked up, tensed her shoulders, and sighed. He thought he saw tears in her eyes and wondered what was disturbing her. He was hesitant to rush forward and intrude into her privacy; it might upset her more to know that he'd been watching. He decided to stay quiet a little while longer, biding his time. He would make himself known when she was ready to leave.

When he looked again, she had picked up the pen and was scribbling furiously. Every so often, she dipped the nib into the pot of ink, continuing to scribble as if her life depended on it. Then, quite suddenly, she put the pen down, blotted the missive, folded the paper in half and took a long, deep breath.

When he thought she'd had time to recover, Dick started to whistle so that she would recognise his approach. She looked up and smiled.

'Did Abdullah send you?' she asked.

'I haven't seen him today,' Dick said. 'What made you think that he'd asked me to call round?'

'We finished school early because he had a meeting with the Temenggong, but he wasn't happy about me staying on here to walk home by myself.'

'Well, you know how courteous he always is. Besides, a lot of people still consider it improper for young ladies to be out on the streets without a chaperone.'

'I am not most young ladies,' Chin Ming retorted. 'I would not be here, teaching the children, if I was like the delicate flowers that are kept at home until they are ready to marry. I told Abdullah that I was perfectly capable of walking the short distance back to Baba Tan's house.'

'Well, you need not worry, I didn't come specially to escort you home – though now I'm here, we may as well walk back together? I've had a letter from Raffles – it was written just after they arrived in England. I thought you'd like to hear all the news. I wanted you to be the first person I shared it with, then I want to show it to Wing Yee and Baba Tan, too.'

'I am honoured,' she said. 'It's good to know they've arrived safely, especially after all the troubles they've had since leaving here.'

Dick gave a resumé of his letter. They exchanged ideas about the life Raffles and Sophia now planned to lead. Chin Ming asked him to tell her about the time when he'd lived with Raffles in Sumatra – before coming to Singapore – and about baby Ella. He responded with great enthusiasm. Halfway along the path, she put her hand on his arm.

'I know you talk to Wing Yee a great deal,' she said, 'but do you ever discuss how you felt when Raffles and Sophia first left here?'

'What do you mean?'

'It must have been far harder for you than it was for Wing Yee and me.'

Dick raised an eyebrow.

'I mean, moving from the house on the hill into Mr Johnston's house. You came here as the son of the Tuan; I've always thought that made you special, I suppose?'

'The adopted son,' Dick added, anxious, as always, to emphasise the difference.

'Yes, but everyone recognised you when you walked around the town. When you stepped into the Company office, when you visited the Temenggong in the kampong, when you walked along the quay – everyone knew ...' she paused so that her words would reflect what she had been keen to make clear, '...the young man who was known as the son of Stamford Raffles!'

24

'At first, I wasn't aware that anyone took any notice,' he said. 'It became more obvious when everyone knew that Raffles was leaving and I planned to stay behind. Very few of the Europeans thought I'd be able to survive, but I've proved them wrong. I told Raffles I wanted to stand on my own feet, and that is exactly what I've done. It all began during the time I was searching for you and Wing Yee, of course, and the sketching I did for Raffles made me realise how much I enjoyed making pictures.'

She laughed. 'But it's different now, isn't it?'

She noticed a wistful expression flit across his face; it was there for only a moment, but once again it made her wonder whether he ever regretted his decision to remain in Singapore.

'It was strange at first,' he admitted, 'but once I'd made the decision to take up drawing portraits, it was far easier. I think Raffles thought I might settle to becoming a merchant alongside Mr Johnston, but it doesn't interest me. If Mr Coleman ever returns here, I might think about learning to design buildings, but for the time being, I'm quite content.'

Chin Ming looked quizzical.

'Honestly,' Dick said, 'I really enjoy what I'm doing right now. I enjoy talking to Mr Johnston in the evenings – did I tell you; he asked me to call him Alexander? He says calling him Mr Johnston when we are alone is far too formal!'

'I'm sure that's right, but you need to feel comfortable with that. Anyway, you now have news from Raffles,' she said, deciding not to pursue the subject any further.

'Yes, that does make me feel better, I must admit. Not knowing where he was, whether the *Mariner* was making good progress or had hit rocks along the way – that was hard. I'm sure it won't be long before they find a house in London and when they are settled in their own home, I'll be able to write to them all the time. I know it takes months for letters to travel back and forth, but that doesn't matter; it makes it all the more exciting when they do arrive.'

He was glad that they were able to talk like this, to share their memories of the time they had spent together with Raffles and Sophia, and to discuss their hopes for the future. Despite their different backgrounds, they had become like brother and sister; he would always be there for her and now, he realised, she would always be ready to listen to him.

Chin Ming gave him an understanding glance, and then a smile lit up her whole face. 'Maybe the next letter you receive will tell you all about life in London,' she said.

CHAPTER 3
London, May 1825

Sophia looked up from her sewing to see her husband gazing out of the sitting room window. Even with his back towards her, she could recognise the tension in his shoulders. She put the needlework down and walked quietly to his side. Raffles gazed at the buildings that lined the other side of Grosvenor Street. Immediately opposite, each house had a white painted stucco façade and a black front door framed by two white columns. They were, in fact, mirror-images of the house he and Sophia had moved into nearly three months ago.

'You look pensive, my dear,' she said as she touched his arm. 'Is anything troubling you?'

'I was just thinking how solid all these houses look and wondering how long some of our neighbours have been living here,' he said.

'You still miss the wonderful view over the harbour from Bukit Larangan,' she replied, looking for signs of sadness in his face.

Raffles took his wife by the shoulders and gently turned her towards him. 'I do miss it, you're right,' he said. 'I miss seeing ships from all over the Orient jostling for position in the harbour. I miss the smell of frangipani as soon as I step out of the house; I miss the sound of crickets and the humid warmth of the sun on my face, but most of all I miss Dick. I regret that I will not see him grow from a young man who is just beginning to find his way in the world into ...'

'Into whoever he chooses to be,' Sophia said. 'Dick may no longer be the shy youngster you adopted all those years ago in Bali, but there will always be a special bond between the two of you. He had his reasons for remaining in Singapore when we left, but think of the fondness expressed in the way he writes to you; remember the portfolio he sent. He must have gone to a lot of trouble to replace the drawings that went down with the *Fame*. I think you should be proud of the way he's turned out.'

'I'm sorry, you're right,' Raffles replied. 'It's all this business with the Company that's getting me down. I can't understand why they are taking so long to sort out my pension and the compensation for everything we lost in the sea.'

'Well, at least the weather has improved – no more dank autumn days or shivering through the darkness of winter. We're here in the centre of London for the season and your presence is in great demand. Seldom a day goes by without us being invited to some engagement or another.'

*****

Raffles took his appointment as chair of the Zoological Society very seriously and had been busy raising funds since the end of February. Every time he was invited to attend a dinner party – which was often – he made it his business to gain more support. He already had one hundred names on his list of subscribers. Despite the fact that he had hardly any time to himself, he enjoyed these occasions and the opportunity to engage in intellectual debate. During the many years he'd spent in the East, there had been many projects to champion, but only a few opportunities to discuss his ideas with anyone other than those with a vested interest in his vision.

There was a fascination now, amongst dinner party

guests, to hear about his life in Sumatra and Singapore; the people he'd met, the food he'd eaten, as well as the animals and plants he'd come across. Just over a week ago, he'd been introduced to two brothers who had been anxious to meet him before they left for a plant-collecting trip to China. They were remarkable young men, and both displayed a thirst for knowledge, but it was the younger one, Edmund, who had interested him the most. Now, they were about to meet again; Sophia had invited Edmund Beaumont and his brother James to join them for dinner this very evening. There would be no other guests, so they would be able to get to know them better and find out more about the proposed expedition.

*****

'Slow down, you're walking too fast,' James Beaumont said to his brother. 'The invitation is for seven-thirty and it would be impolite to arrive any earlier than that.'

'I still can't quite believe that we are to dine with Sir Stamford Raffles,' Edmund replied. 'I'm just eager to see him again, that's all.'

James smiled to himself; it was refreshing that his brother, at the age of almost twenty-six, was still capable of such excitement. 'I believe we are the only guests this evening,' he said, 'so there'll be plenty of time for you to talk to him.'

'There are so many questions I want to ask about the various trips he embarked upon in Java and Sumatra,' Edmund continued, 'but I'm afraid they will all go out of my head the moment I see him. I've heard that he's invited to dinner all over London; he's a regular guest of the Duchess of Somerset and is friends with so many important people. I can't believe our luck.'

'Well, you obviously impressed him when we met him at Bowood, but I imagine it's the fact that we will be passing through Singapore on our way to China that interests him most.'

*****

Edmund need not have worried. Raffles had spent the majority of his adult years mixing with people from all walks of life. He was equally at home with sultans, fishermen, botanists, merchants and duchesses. Only three people had ever caused him any upset; two of them were soldiers, and the other was the Dutchman he'd sent to trial in Calcutta shortly before he left Singapore. The Company had eventually supported his actions over the criticisms made against him by both Major Gillespie in Java and by Colonel Farquhar in Singapore. As far as the Dutchman was concerned, Raffles had received news only last week, informing him that Pieter Steffens had been found guilty of smuggling, perjury and assault. The sentence he'd been given was transportation to Australia and Raffles was satisfied that he would get his just desserts.

*****

Once the pleasantries were out of the way, they settled down to talk about the plant-collecting trip the two brothers were about to embark upon.

'I seem to remember, when we met last week, you told me that your interest in plants developed during your time at Oxford,' Raffles said, addressing Edmund. 'Is that correct?'

'I had rooms overlooking the Physic Garden,' the younger Beaumont replied. 'I'm afraid I was never really suited to a classical education, but being the son of a clergyman, I didn't have much choice in the matter.' Edmund glanced in his brother's direction and received an affirmative smile. 'There are some elements of my studies which have, however, proved to be useful. I'm sure it's easier to remember the Latin names of plants, for instance, when you have a grounding in the language. And now that we're going to China, I'm looking forward to finding out about the art and culture of the places we visit.'

'What about you, James?' Sophia said. 'Did you also rebel against a classical education?'

'I was at Jesus, not Magdalen,' he said. 'My rooms were in Turl Street, so I didn't have the same distractions as my brother. Besides, I tend to be the conformer in the family; I was content to return home to Great Bedwyn when I finished my degree. I was fortunate enough to inherit a farm from my aunt – our mother's sister – when I was in my early twenties and I married my cousin, Margaret, two years later.' He coughed before continuing. 'My wife died in childbirth last year,' he said. 'She gave birth to twins. The boy followed his mother three days later, but the girl survived; she is being cared for by my parents.'

'I'm so very sorry,' said Sophia in a hushed voice.

Everyone remained silent for a while. Sophia and Raffles had lost four children of their own during infancy; they knew only too well the heartache of child mortality

'My apologies,' said James, 'I didn't mean to put a dampener on such a pleasant evening.'

'It is I who should apologise,' said Sophia. 'I should not have asked about your personal life.'

'You were not to know,' said James. 'Besides, since my little brother persuaded me to accompany him to China, I now have a great deal to look forward to and I am fortunate that I don't have to worry about my daughter.'

During the course of the meal, the four of them discussed the journey the brothers were about to embark upon. Their father had contacted one of his friends – a missionary turned botanist – who lived in Guangdong Province; the man had been happy to help organise their visit. He would meet them when they arrived in Guangzhou and then he would spend the next four months accompanying them on a plant-collecting trip. Raffles was aware that many people in England had recently become obsessed with gardens and gardening; this, he suspected, had much to do with the Physic Garden in Oxford being so keen to sponsor the expedition. Edmund had been given the task of acquiring new plants to add to the University's collection.

The candles had burned low when they rose from the table. Sophia invited them to move into the sitting room so they could all enjoy a glass of Madeira. It was all very informal and they made themselves comfortable. Almost immediately, Edmund began to ask questions about the flora and fauna his host had seen in Java and Sumatra.

Raffles responded with his usual gusto. He began by telling them about the time, many years ago, when he sent a small group of men into the jungle that surrounded Malacca.

'I sent one man to look for various types of leaves, flowers and fungi,' he said. 'Another was charged with finding worms, different kinds of butterflies, beetles and so on. A third was despatched with a basket to get coral and shells and finally, the fourth went out to catch wild animals – birds, deer and small quadrupeds.'

Sophia coughed quietly. She knew how easy it was for her enthusiastic husband to get carried away, and she didn't want him to bore their guests. She need not have worried; Raffles was with young men who were as hungry for knowledge as he'd been himself when he first went out East.

All the same, Edmund and James were surprised at what they'd heard. They knew Raffles had a reputation for being interested in botany, but they had no idea that his curiosity about the natural world was so extensive.

'What did you do with the specimens the men brought

back to you?' James asked.

'I pressed the leaves and flowers between pages of a book I kept just for that purpose, but I gave the fruit and flowers to a Chinese artist from Macau. He made drawings of them for me.'

'So, would you say you are as interested in the world of animals as you are in plants?' James asked.

'When we were in Bencoolen,' Sophia interjected, 'we had a Malayan Sun Bear, which was brought up in the nursery along with the children.'

James raised his eyebrows in astonishment and Edmund burst out laughing.

'We sometimes allowed it to sit at the table,' Raffles told them. 'It had a particular liking for champagne, I seem to remember!'

The brothers sat like two small children, listening to the stories Raffles and Sophia had to tell. It all sounded like a fairy tale, an enchanted world which they themselves were about to enter. By the end of the evening all four of them had become intoxicated with the magic of it all. The spell was broken only when the clock struck ten.

Forever the practical one, James was the first to react. He rose to his feet. 'Sir, regretfully I'm afraid it is late, and it's time for us to make our departure. Lady Raffles,' he said, turning to Sophia, 'please accept our thanks for a most delightful and entertaining evening. I must apologise if we have remained too long and outstayed our welcome.'

'Not at all,' said Raffles, getting to his feet. 'It is so encouraging to find two young men so interested in the East, so eager to explore the delights of nature. There's so much more I would like to discuss with you. I hope we'll see you again before you depart?'

*****

It was just over a week later when Raffles saw the brothers again. He was keen to show them the house he had bought near the village of Hendon, to the north of the metropolis. He wanted them to tell Dick and all his friends in Singapore all about his new home and the plans he had for the future. He arranged to meet Edmund and James at the beginning of Edgware Road, so that they could share a chaise together.

'What a pity Lady Sophia wasn't able to join us today,' James said. 'It's such lovely weather for a carriage ride and a day in the countryside.'

'My wife sends her regrets,' Raffles said. 'Our little girl has been having nightmares again, so Sophia felt she needed to stay close by. Having lost our other children, Ella is very special, you see.'

James swallowed hard and offered an understanding smile.

Only Edmund noticed his brother wince. Though James rarely talked about Margaret, he knew any reminder of his own loss, which was still quite raw, often caused him pain.

'How old is Ella?' Edmund asked in an effort to draw attention away from his brother.

'She is just over three,' Raffles said, 'and as bright as a button. She wasn't even twelve months old when we sent her back home to England with Nanny Grimes. We were so eager to see her when we first arrived, but it took her a little while to get to know us again. Now, she has bad dreams which often seem to be about my wife and I letting go of her hand.'

'Poor little mite,' James said. He had regained his composure now, but was grateful to his brother for taking charge of the conversation.

Their progress along Edgware Road was slow at first; the thoroughfare was busy with people on horseback and men pushing overloaded carts. 'No doubt there will be many occasions such as this when you get to Guangzhou,' said Raffles.

'The port area is full of activity and I believe the streets are always busy; this is a good lesson in patience.'

'It looks as if the journey might prepare us for our trip in other ways, too.' Edmund laughed as he glanced at the crowd. 'I never knew the streets of London entertained so many different nationalities – look, James, there is even a Hindoostani gentleman selling food on that street corner.'

'That's another thing the East India Company is responsible for,' Raffles said.

'How is that?' James asked, looking curious.

'Men who have worked out East and developed a taste for spicy food – men who come back to England and retire from the Company – they find themselves missing the flavours and the dishes they've grown to enjoy. It's the same with the Jews and the Huguenots who have settled in this area. Mark my words, the days of bully beef are numbered; one day we'll all be enjoying dishes from many countries other than our own.'

After a bumpy ride of about eight miles, over a road surface made rough by the constant flow of carriages, they reached Edgware village. Then, they turned right and continued for another three miles along a country lane. It was a pleasant May morning; the trees displayed the bright green leaves of early summer and birdsong wafted through the air.

'This is so lovely,' James said. 'My brother enjoys the hustle and bustle of the city, but I must admit, I much prefer the countryside.'

Edmund was glad that his brother was enjoying himself. It had been a hard year since the death of Margaret and their son; the baby girl only served as a reminder of his loss. The close bond he and James had enjoyed as children had inevitably diminished as they became adults, and Edmund had felt powerless when unable to prevent his brother's heartache. Now he'd been able to persuade James to accompany him on his plant-collecting trip, he hoped it would help re-establish their relationship as well as enable James to overcome his grief.

As soon as they reached Highwood House, Raffles leapt down from the chaise; Edmund and James followed close behind. The house was currently empty, awaiting decoration, but Raffles had bought the property and its surrounding acres as a going concern. It was fully stocked and planted, and would continue to be maintained by the farmhands until Raffles and Sophia were ready to take up residence in another couple of months. The three of them crossed the lawn in front of the house and walked around to one of the barns at the back, where Raffles introduced his visitors to George White, the estate manager. They talked about the livestock for a while, but when George had no more to report, they left him to continue with his work. Raffles suggested a walk across the fields. He told Edmund and James about his plans to lay out the estate and how pleased he was to have his friend, William Wilberforce, as his neighbour.

When they reached the boundary of the farm, he turned to Edmund. 'Now tell me every detail about your expedition,' he said. 'If your ship is blessed with good weather, I daresay you'll arrive in Singapore around the middle of September.'

'That's what we've been told,' James said, 'and we should get to Guangzhou by early November.'

'Will you spend any time in Singapore on your return?'

'We've been talking about that,' Edmund said. 'Since we had dinner with you last week, we've decided to include a visit to either Java or Sumatra, maybe both if time allows. The length of time we spend there will depend on how long our funds last, but we'd definitely like to spend some days at leisure in Singapore before returning to England.'

'Maybe you can bring back one or two shrubs that I could plant here at Highwood?'

'That would be our pleasure,' Edmund said.

James nodded enthusiastically. 'I believe there is also something you'd like us to do for you on the outward journey?'

Raffles had drafted several letters addressed to the people in Singapore for whom he had the greatest affection; he asked the brothers if they would be kind enough to deliver them to his friend, Alexander Johnston, for distribution. They agreed willingly and then bombarded their host with yet more questions. They wanted to know as much as possible about the thriving Settlement.

'The Resident is John Crawfurd,' Raffles told them. 'He's a bit of a dour Scot, but he's a good administrator and that's what the place needs. You should make sure you introduce yourselves to him as soon as you arrive.' Whilst what he said out loud remained true, he remained tight-lipped about his private thoughts. Both he and Crawfurd had published books on the Indian Archipelago, and each had criticised the work of the other.

'Who else should we make sure to meet?' Edmund asked.

'Johnston will introduce you to Baba Tan and Dick, of course,' he said. 'It's a pity you can't take Dick with you on the trip. He's an extremely good artist and was responsible for the majority of my botanical sketches. If you come across any plants that are too delicate to transport, his skills would be useful and you could show his pictures to your sponsors.'

'Does Dick speak Cantonese?' James asked, thinking that it sounded like a good idea.

'He is fluent in English and Malay but has not learned enough Cantonese to be helpful. You would need Chin Ming or Wing Yee for that task.'

Both brothers were intrigued. They turned their head in a manner that invited more information. Their curiosity had been roused, but James was content to wait for Raffles to enlighten them further. Unlike his brother, Edmund was impatient to know more.

'Who are these people? Where are we likely to find them? Do you think they would be interested in joining us?'

Raffles smiled. Edmund reminded him of his younger self. He'd been twenty-three when he left England for Penang in 1805; he was as full of hope and ambition then as Edmund was now. Part of him couldn't help being a little envious of the young man.

'They are two remarkable young women,' Raffles replied, 'but unfortunately, it would not be thought appropriate for them to accompany you to Guangzhou; besides, neither of them is interested in returning to China.'

A torrent of questions followed. Raffles spent the next hour telling Edmund and James a little about the women. They learned how both women had come to Singapore seeking answers to their individual questions, only to have their hopes shattered by one unfortunate event after another. He omitted to tell them any of the details concerning Chin Ming's and Wing Yee's personal stories; neither did he say anything about Dick's role in their rescue. He thought it unnecessary to provide such detail. After all, it was unlikely that any of them would spend a great deal of time together.

CHAPTER 4
Singapore, 18th August 1825

The harbour was busy today, but that in itself was not unusual. Trade was, after all, the *raison d'être* for Britain establishing a settlement here. Since Raffles first set foot on the island, the waterfront had been transformed and it was now a central port-of-call for sailing vessels of all nationalities. But it wasn't the activity within the harbour itself that particularly interested Dick this morning; it was the crowd of people who had gathered along the whole length of Boat Quay. His curiosity grew the nearer he got to the seething crush of bodies; he gazed intently but recognised none of his friends amongst them. He asked first one person and then another what all the fuss was about, but no-one offered an answer, other than to point in the direction of the multitude of sails fluttering across the entire breadth of the harbour.

Dick's appointment, this morning, was with one of Baba Tan's neighbours, but he had plenty of time, and he was sure his old friend would know the cause of all the excitement. Somehow, he managed to squeeze past the assembly and get into the open space further along the river.

When he entered the warehouse, he was surprised by the lack of activity; it appeared to be completely deserted. He remembered the very first time he'd entered this space. Alexander Johnston had brought him here to introduce him to the Peranakan merchant who was now one of his closest friends.

Dick remembered seeing the rolls of brightly coloured fabrics for the first time; being mesmerised by the bales of silks, piled high upon the shelves and the fine muslins and ribbons spread out on the lower levels. Baba Tan's business had expanded in the last three years; first of all, bringing in tea and porcelain from China and more recently, herbs and spices from all over the Orient. Nevertheless, it was still the vast kaleidoscope of textiles, dyed every shade from palest pink to deepest purple, that continued to draw his attention.

Today, everything seemed to be as usual – except for the silence. Dick called out and listened for a response, but the whole of the go-down remained quiet. Puzzled, he turned back towards the door. He was just about to step out onto the quay when a shaft of sunlight enveloped him. He raised his forearm to shield his eyes and then looked up at the small balcony above the main floor. A door had opened and there stood a figure, swathed in a golden halo. As soon as his eyes adjusted, he could make out the European garments, favoured by the Peranakan merchant when he was at work. Baba Tan beckoned him to climb the flight of stairs, at the top of which was the room now used by Wing Yee to produce her medicinal tinctures and salves. Dick assumed he was being invited to greet her.

He climbed the steps two at a time, full of energy and enthusiasm. Baba Tan took him by the arm and led him to the edge of the balustrade. 'Have you seen the crowd on the quayside this morning?' he asked.

'I couldn't fail to see them,' Dick said. 'I came here to ask if you knew what was happening. Mr Johnston didn't mention anything last night – and he left before I was awake this morning.'

'A ship has arrived from India. It's the *Bengal Merchant*, a private trading ship that has recently been licensed by the Honourable Company.'

Dick was amused by his friend's use of the informal title, favoured by Europeans. Most of the Chinese merchants referred to the British East India Company in a way that fell between awe and trepidation, but Baba Tan's mixed-race background and his business partnership with Alexander Johnston meant that he was completely at ease with the idiosyncrasies of the English language.

'But why all the fuss?' Dick asked. 'We get lots of ships from India all the time.'

'She's carrying convicts,' Baba Tan said. 'This is the first consignment to come to Singapore. Up until now, the men who are generally well-behaved have always been sent to Bencoolen, but now they are to come here instead. I'm told they will be used to clear the land; to help drain the swamps and begin to build proper roads.'

'Are they not needed in Bencoolen?'

'Bencoolen is no longer a British settlement; it was handed back to the Netherlands in exchange for Malacca, if you remember. Maybe the notion of bringing convicts here was part of the bargain Mr Crawfurd made with the Dutch before he signed the treaty; everyone knows he is keen to get the recla--mation work completed so that more buildings can be started.'

'Baba Tan, why are you whispering?' Dick asked.

'Wing Yee is in her workroom. She's heard about these new arrivals – and as you might imagine, it's made her feel uneasy.'

'You mean,' Dick said, suddenly feeling more than a little alarmed himself, 'that one of them could be the man who assaulted her?'

'I think it is almost impossible,' Baba Tan replied. 'These prisoners are more likely to be Indian convicts – and I don't even know which port the ship sailed from. If you could stay with Wing Yee, I will go to the harbour to ask for more information?'

'Gladly,' Dick said, 'but I'm due to call in on your neighbour – about his family portrait – I think I ought to explain why I will be delayed.

'I will do that on my way out,' Baba Tan said. 'You go and see Wing Yee. Try to keep her calm. I'm sure there is nothing to worry about, but it is best to know the exact details. In that way, we can reassure her that there is nothing at all to worry about.'

It was nearly an hour before Baba Tan returned. Dick had tried his best to distract Wing Yee, asking her questions about the dried herbs that were hanging in bunches around the room and what was hidden in the various containers – all different colours, shapes and sizes.

She knew Dick had been sent to distract her, and he was doing his best, but it was still hard for her to concentrate. When she'd stood beside him at the top of Bukit Larangan a couple of years ago watching the vessel, in which Pieter Steffens was imprisoned, fade from view, both she and Chin Ming had believed he was out of their lives for ever. Now, she was not so sure.

At last, Baba Tan came bustling up the stairs. 'Good news,' he exclaimed. 'The *Bengal Merchant* sailed from Madras, not Bengal. There are eighty convicts on board, seventy-nine men and one woman; they are all Indian.'

'That's good to hear. You see, I told you there was nothing to worry about,' Dick said, giving Wing Yee a reassuring hug. Gradually, the colour began to return to her cheeks.

*****

Six weeks later, all the initial speculation had died down and seeing the Indian arrivals labouring away was now common-place. Both Alexander Johnston and Dick were looking forward to the arrival of the next Indiaman from England. With any luck, the *Charles Grant* would bring the consignment of books Johnston was expecting, and hopefully there would be another letter from Raffles.

Johnston had been to the harbour master's office almost every day for the last week and today, he'd learned that the *Charles Grant* would arrive within the week. It had been delayed by an early seasonal storm. He hurried back to the house that evening, anxious to share the news with Dick. He found him on the balcony, looking at the sketches that had occupied him for the last few days.

'It was apparently blown off course towards the Carimon Islands, where I believe it suffered some damage,' Johnston said as he shared his news. 'I got talking to one of the Bugis traders at the harbour; he was telling the tale to anyone who was willing to listen.'

'Does that mean it will be here for a while?' Dick said.

'That might depend on the extent of the damage, I suppose, but I imagine the captain will want to be sure the vessel is seaworthy before he proceeds to Guangzhou.'

They only had to wait another three days, before news came that the Indiaman had been sighted on the horizon. A crowd, comprising both local and European merchants, flocked to the quay as soon as the information had been widely broadcast. Several bumboats were already preparing to leave when Dick arrived. As usual, he was eager to see any visitors who might decide to come ashore and to hear the news they brought from England.

*****

Many of the passengers who had no previous experience of long sea voyages couldn't wait to walk on dry land again – especially after the recent storm. By the time the official from the harbour master's office completed his paperwork, their patience was wearing thin. A riot almost broke out when a Frenchman, who had joined the ship in Cape Town, pushed his way to the front of the queue to secure a place in the first bumboat. A missionary sought to intervene when a man from Kent tried to challenge such audacity. Edmund and James smiled quietly to themselves and moved away from the discord. It was understandable that tempers were frayed, but they had no wish to get involved.

Another hour had passed by the time the brothers joined one of the last bumboats to depart for the harbour. 'A penny for your thoughts,' James said, as he noticed the look of concentration on his brother's face.

'It's just like a painting, don't you think?' Edmund replied. 'It reminds me of a watercolour I once saw in the house of a friend, in Oxford.'

They both turned their attention to the distant shore. The vista, from this distance, was indeed similar to an English landscape, but as James pointed out, the colours, the types of building and the vegetation they could now begin to identify was entirely different. A soft green fringe of trees stood behind and beyond the simple wooden and attap houses, making the infant town seem more like a village set between the hills and the sea. Behind the trees, a series of small, golden hills stretched as far as they could see in both directions and above them was a vast, cloudless blue sky.

Edmund pointed to the hill that dominated the scene. 'That must be the house where Raffles lived,' he said, 'the one beside the flagstaff!'

A member of the crew, who was sitting close by told them they were looking at Government Hill – where the Resident now lived and where a flag is hoisted whenever a ship enters the harbour, to inform the merchants of its arrival.

The Malay lighterman, who stood up in the stern, rowed with great skill, manoeuvring his crossed oars to steer a passage through an incredible number of vessels of various kinds from all over the world. The small craft threaded its way between Chinese junks with their characteristic horseshoe-shaped sterns, heavy Cochin vessels, tub-like boats from Siam and a scattering of Bugis prahus with their single mast and low sails made from matting. To Edmund and James, all the lively activity within the harbour was almost hypnotic; it felt like entering a magic grotto.

The oarsman guided his boat to a place along the quay where the passengers could safely disembark. Six others climbed the steps ahead of the Beaumont brothers, giving them time to discretely examine the people who had gathered to witness their arrival. Hordes of coolies scurried to and fro, claiming sacks of rice and other cargo on behalf of their employers, while merchants threaded their way between the piled-up sacks anxious to inspect their newly arrived merchandise.

'I bet there wasn't any of this frenzied commotion in your sombre English landscape,' James said.

'What did you say?' Edmund asked. They found themselves surrounded by noise – chains pulling the heavier crates, incomprehensible dialects being exchanged all around them, and other boatmen vying for business. James decided there was little point in repeating his question; he would just have to shout louder if he wanted his brother to understand him. He was about to try again, wanting to comment on the colourful tapestry that surrounded them and all the different nationalities he could identify, when Edmund tugged at his sleeve.

'Do you see the young man at the end of the quay?' he shouted. 'The one sitting slightly apart, with a sketchpad open in front of him?'

James shaded his eyes and looked in the direction that his brother was pointing. He realised immediately what Edmund was thinking. 'Well, would you believe it?' he said. 'He matches the description that Raffles gave us exactly; it must be him.'

'Let's go and ask,' Edmund replied.

As they approached, their shadow fell across Dick's drawing; he looked up. He had assumed all the passengers had disembarked from the Indiaman long ago, but there was no other place these two European gentlemen could have come from. One of them was probably not much older than him; he had dark, curly hair that had been ruffled by the breeze on the journey across the harbour. The other one was slightly shorter, with sandy-coloured hair and much paler skin; they were both grinning at him. He didn't feel particularly intimidated by their proximity, but he stood up anyway so that they were all at the same level. He was just about to introduce himself when the dark-haired one said, 'You must be Dick.'

James stepped forward to make the introductions. 'Please forgive my brother,' he said. 'He gets ahead of himself sometimes. I am James Beaumont and this is my brother Edmund. We met Raffles in London and he told us all about you – in fact, we have letters to deliver on his behalf, and one of them has your name on it.'

Dick couldn't believe his ears. He'd hoped, of course, that the vessel might be carrying news from England, but he'd never dreamt of it being personally delivered by someone who had recently spent time with Raffles. Countless questions leapt into his mind, but his mouth was dry and it was impossible to voice any of them right now. Eventually, he gathered his wits and offered his hand. 'Yes,' he said, 'I am Dick, welcome to Singapore.'

'I can't believe we found you so easily,' Edmund said. 'We'd planned to ask for directions to the Company office and then enquire how to find you, but here you are – almost as if you were sitting, waiting for us to arrive.'

'Singapore is a small town, but I'm glad I stayed to finish my sketch, otherwise we would have missed each other,' Dick said. 'Usually, the mail is taken straight to the Company Office and we collect it from there. It often takes a while for every-thing to be sorted. I was hoping to receive a letter from Raffles – he promised to send his London address so that I can write to him again, but his last letter mentioned nothing about entertaining guests.'

'It all happened quite suddenly,' Edmund said. 'There wasn't time to inform you beforehand. We are on our way to China to collect plants for the botanical garden where I work. About three weeks before we were due to depart, we had the good fortune to attend a dinner given by a friend of our father – and Raffles was the guest of honour. We met him only briefly on that occasion, but he was interested in our plans and invited us to his home the following week.'

'They have settled in London then?' Dick asked.

Edmund nodded. 'We spent an evening with Raffles and Sophia at a house they have rented in Grosvenor Street – that's right in the centre – but he also took us to visit the house he is in the process of buying – it's in the country – and they have probably moved in by now. He wanted us to go there so that we could tell you all about it, but I'm sure he will explain everything in the letter.'

'I imagine that one of the letters you have is for Alexander Johnston – he is one of Raffles' closest friends and when I decided to stay in Singapore, he offered me a home. He'll probably be busy at his warehouse right now, but I could show you around the town and then take you to meet him if you would like that?'

The two brothers needed no more encouragement; they were anxious to see as much of this fascinating place as they could and to meet anyone who was a friend of Raffles. Dick walked between the visitors, guiding them between groups of newly arrived Bugis traders, all busily unloading baskets containing striped and checked cotton cloth, rice, cedarwood, tortoiseshell and colourful birds in cages. Occasionally, they stopped to gaze more intently, to take in the smells, the sounds, the heat, the sheer difference between this place and anything they had ever encountered before. They bombarded Dick with question after question, so he had to be content to wait to hear all the things he longed to ask about the man he missed more than he was prepared to admit to anyone – even to Chin Ming and Wing Yee.

CHAPTER 5
Singapore, Late September 1825

When they reached an area further along the quay that was less busy, Dick suggested it might be best to visit the Company office before they went anywhere else. 'Nearly all Europeans go there first,' he said. 'Mr Crawfurd likes to know everything about visitors to the Settlement ahead of anyone else.'

'What's he like?' Edmund asked.

'I don't know a great deal about him,' Dick said. 'He doesn't entertain much, so apart from those he works with, not many people have got to know him. I've heard him referred to as a dour Scot, but I'm not sure what that means?'

Edmund caught James' eye and smiled before saying anything further. This was exactly how Raffles had described the man.

'It could mean a number of things,' James said. 'Maybe he's someone who shows resolve or someone who has a stern character. On the other hand, he might just be a gloomy person or even unfriendly.'

'Well, whichever description is correct, I'm sure he'll be interested in hearing all about your expedition,' Dick said.

*****

When they reached the building in High Street, which housed the East India Company base, they found John Crawfurd bent over his desk, writing furiously. Dick made the introductions and told the Resident that Edmund and James had met Raffles in London. He was polite enough and showed some curiosity in the trip the brothers were about to embark upon, but nothing further. Edmund told him how spending time with Raffles had inspired them to continue on to Sumatra once their work in China was completed.

'My knowledge of the archipelago is largely connected with Java,' Crawfurd said.

'Sir Stamford told us about the years he spent there,' Edmund continued. 'The animals and plants he sent back home during his years in the East has gained him quite a reputation and his interest in natural history is much admired in London.'

Crawfurd nodded politely, but the muscles in his face tightened. Dick thought he looked irritated, but maybe he was anxious to get back to his papers.

'He's been appointed chairman of the new Zoological Society,' James added, sounding as enthusiastic as his brother and completely ignoring Crawfurd's hard smile. 'Raffles is a frequent guest at dinner parties, which provides him with many opportunities to approach all his friends to support the idea. When we left England, he'd collected well over one hundred names – all of whom are willing to subscribe to the organisation.'

Crawfurd remembered only too well Raffles' persuasive powers and his passion for things he cared about, but he had no wish to continue the conversation. His own talents lay in being a good administrator and an able academic, but he was uncomfortable with emotional outbursts – especially where the name of Raffles was concerned.

Unaware of any embarrassment, Edmund continued. 'People in England are eager to know about discoveries from all around the world. Many have become obsessed with anything exotic, particularly when it concerns gardens and gardening.

However, I'm only interested in collecting plants that can be studied.'

'Then you should talk to Wing Yee,' Dick said, trying to change the subject. The expression on John Crawfurd's face told him that he had given them enough of his time. 'She knows a great deal about the plants native to China.'

Instantly, both the brothers wanted to know more. Edmund recalled the conversation they'd had with Raffles about two Chinese women whom they might meet when they visited the Settlement, but their names had slipped into the recesses of his mind. However, as soon as one of their names was mentioned he was reminded of that discussion. He decided, as soon as they had said their goodbyes to John Crawfurd, he would ask Dick if it was possible for him to make the arrangements to meet Wing Yee; someone with such specialist knowledge could be invaluable.

*****

It was late afternoon by the time Dick had shown the brothers the full extent of the ever-expanding town. There was no time, on that occasion, to escort them to the Spice Gardens or to trek to the top of Bukit Larangan; he promised that excursion for another day and hopefully in the company of Wing Yee. They approached a warehouse with the name *A. L. Johnston & Co* written in large letters along the whole length of the building. At the moment of their arrival, a moderate wooden door cut into the large entrance gates opened and Alexander Johnston stepped out onto the pavement. The brothers introduced themselves, and Dick explained what they had been doing for the last few hours.

'Then I daresay you are extremely hungry,' Johnston said. 'Why not come back to my house for an early supper? I can't let Dick monopolise you completely – besides, I want to hear all the news about Raffles and Sophia.'

It took only a short while to reach the house. Compared with the other European dwellings, Johnston's home was quite modest. James and Edmund followed Johnston from the unpretentious entrance on Beach Road around to the side which faced the sea. When he saw them gazing at the huge overhanging roof, supported by slender white pillars, Johnston explained that its design provided shelter from the rain during the monsoon season and at other times, shade from the scalding midday sun. They entered through a central door, framed by a delicate white trellis which led to a large room furnished with a mixture of rattan chairs, some heavy wooden loungers, several small tables and a scattering of colourful floor cushions.

Edmund handed the letters he'd brought from Raffles to Johnston and Dick, but rather than read them straight away they both decided to save them for later. Now it was the turn of Edmund and James to be bombarded with questions. Over the next two hours, they enjoyed refreshing drinks and a number of local dishes served with rice, *sambals* and other accompaniments. They talked non-stop about Raffles' various enterprises, his health, his plans for the future, and his family. None of them noticed the time speeding by until finally, a platter containing fresh pineapple, papaya, lychees and jack-fruit was placed in the middle of the table by the cook.

'It is far too late for you to return to the ship,' Johnston said, 'Why don't I have beds made up for you here – in fact,' he added, 'why don't you stay with us for the whole of your visit?'

'That is very generous of you, sir,' Edmund responded. 'I must say, it will be good to sleep on dry land again.' He turned to James, who readily agreed to the arrangement – and so it was settled.

'And please refrain from calling me sir,' Johnston said.

'Alexander will do nicely. I keep asking Dick to do the same, but he seems reluctant to do so. Maybe your being here will encourage him to feel more comfortable about it.'

*****

The following morning, after collecting a fresh supply of clothing and other necessities from the ship, Dick took Edmund and James to meet Baba Tan. The Peranakan merchant was also keen to hear news of Raffles, but when that conversation had been exhausted, they began to talk about the plant-collecting trip the brothers were about to embark upon.

'You will begin your journey in Guangzhou. Is that correct?' Baba Tan said.

'That was the original plan,' Edmund replied, 'but when we visited the Resident yesterday afternoon, he handed us a letter from William Lawrence – he's the man with whom I have corresponded and who has arranged everything concerning the expedition once we reach China. The letter instructs us to disembark in Macau, where he says he will be waiting for us.'

'Do you know why the arrangements have changed?'

'He didn't say,' Edmund said. 'Initially we thought it was quite mysterious, but all I can think of is that he has business to conduct in Macau and it's simply a matter of convenience.'

'There are some very well-known gardens in Macau,' Baba Tan said. 'Maybe your Mr Lawrence wants to take you there before you set out on your travels. I believe it's easy enough to travel from there along the Pearl River delta,' he added. 'There are many tributaries into the mountains that will provide a rich variety of plants for you to examine. Maybe that's what Mr Lawrence has in mind.'

Edmund and James soon learned that Baba Tan's knowledge of the area came from tales told to him by the various merchants he dealt with; the people who brought bales of silk, baskets packed with delicate porcelain and chests full of tea.

Dick told the brothers about the first time he had visited Baba Tan's warehouse, when the vast array of silks, ranging from palest ivory to deepest purple, had made his head spin. All four men continued with their discussion and no-one noticed a door on the balcony above them open, nor did they feel the slight movement of air as Wing Yee descended the stairs.

When she realised Baba Tan was entertaining visitors, her instinct was to return to her workroom. She could see the head and shoulders of two men; the garments they wore identified them as European, and she had no desire to engage in conversation with them. She lifted the hem of her sarong, but as she turned to retrace her steps, Dick looked up and waved his hand.

'Excellent timing,' he said. 'These gentlemen arrived from England only yesterday. They spent some time with Raffles before they left and have brought letters with his latest news. This is Edmund and this is his brother, James,' Dick continued, indicating which brother was which with his hand. 'Mr Johnston invited them to stay with us until their ship leaves for Guangzhou.'

Hearing the word Raffles in association with the visitors made her pause; she continued down the remaining steps, slowly. Both men bowed politely to acknowledge her arrival; she was glad they neither rushed forward to shake her hand as she had seen other European men do when they greeted each other. When they raised their heads, their kind eyes and friendly smiles made her feel more relaxed. One had dark, unruly hair; the other man, who looked nearer her own age, had more orderly, sandy-coloured locks.

Neither James nor Edmund had met a Chinese woman before, let alone had the opportunity to engage in conversation. Edmund had already worked out that this must be the woman Dick had already referred to as there was traces of soil on her hands and the lingering perfume of dried herbs on her clothes. He couldn't wait to ask her questions. James, usually the practical one of the two, was taken aback by her height; he had imagined Chinese women to be shorter. Her figure was masked by a loose-fitting shirt and long skirt, but he could tell that she was slim and elegant. She looked shy and yet there was something noble about her. She wore her shoulder-length hair tied back with a red ribbon. He tried not to stare, but he found her intriguing.

'You go to Guangzhou?' Wing Yee said quietly, still not overly confident when speaking English to strangers.

'That was our original destination,' Edmund said. He explained about the change of plan and the purpose of their trip. 'Do you know that part of China?'

'I born nearby,' she said. 'Spend many year in Guangzhou before I come Singapore.'

'This is Wing Yee, the young lady I told you about,' Dick joined in. 'She knows everything about the healing qualities of plants; that room up at the top of the stairs is where she works her magic; she makes various concoctions from different types of leaves – herbs and other things.'

Wing Yee felt the colour rising in her cheeks. She wanted to explain that the methods she used to make her salves and tinctures had been learned from her father, that they had been used in China for many generations; but her English failed her, so she smiled politely and said nothing.

Before they left Baba Tan, it had been agreed that Dick would collect Wing Yee the following morning and together they would introduce Edmund and James to the delights of Bukit Larangan and the Spice Garden.

*****

There was a good deal of gossip amongst the Settlement's permanent residents regarding their most recent visitors. It became common knowledge that it would take five days for the *Charles Grant* to be repaired, which meant there would be five days of rumour-mongering and speculation.

Likewise, the passengers were curious about the Settlement and many came ashore during the hours of daylight. There were two European ladies – always accompanied by two European gentlemen. They tiptoed between the hawker stalls, holding handkerchiefs to their delicate noses. Chin Ming witnessed such a scene one day on her way to the schoolhouse and wondered how such people would fare when they found themselves amongst the hurly-burly of places such as Macao and Guangzhou.

A few of the gentlemen were said to have visited the more prominent merchants in town, and one or two had expressed an interest in the growing prosperity of the port. On the whole, however, the visitors showed little interest in the Settlement, returning to the ship once the novelty of inspecting the town had worn off. Only Edmund and James remained ashore, having gladly accepted the hospitality offered by Alexander Johnston.

*****

On the morning of their third day in Singapore, the two brothers accompanied Dick on the short walk to Baba Tan's home; they presented themselves early as arranged, ready to join Wing Yee on a botanical expedition. Bukit Larangan was a place both she and Dick frequented regularly; she to plant delicate new specimens and he to sketch the trees, ferns and flowers that had occupied the hill for centuries – long before the Javanese princes occupied the island then known as Temasek and certainly long before the British arrived.

Wing Yee was waiting in the courtyard when they arrived. Today, she'd chosen to wear a dark grey shift and coolie trousers. They were not unlike the garments Chin Ming had worn when they first met over three years ago. Under her arm, she had a conical hat, which she placed firmly on her head as soon as they left the house. She pulled it down over her hair and tied the long black ribbons beneath her chin. It was a very practical choice for the gardening she intended to do, but it also meant that she could walk alongside the three men and be completely ignored by any bystanders. All her adult life she'd been scrutinised, particularly by men; nowadays even the slightest glance from a stranger often made her feel uneasy.

'You not draw today?' she asked Dick, noticing that for once he was not carrying a sketchpad.

'I'm going to inspect the cloves and the nutmegs,' he replied. 'The saplings are quite sturdy now, and I'm keeping an eye on them so that I can draw them once they start to produce some fruit.'

Wing Yee nodded, smiling quietly to herself. It gave her a great deal of pleasure to see Dick so full of energy, so full of enthusiasm. She knew he still missed Raffles and supposed, as far as he was concerned, the presence of these two young men who had recently spent some time in his company was almost as good as seeing the man himself.

'What about you?' he said. 'What have you brought along to plant today?'

Wing Yee pulled back the waxed paper that was covering the contents of her basket.

'Turmeric roots. Baba Tan arrange for one trader to bring from China. I have them for few days, but they still good. I hope they survive in new home.'

'Dick told me that your father taught you how to use plants to make medicine,' James said. 'Do you plan to bring in more herbs that are popular in China – those used back in your village, perhaps?'

'Soil here – very poor, many thing not grow.' Her vocabulary was continuing to improve, but she occasionally faltered over words that she seldom used. 'Baba Tan – he make plan to im-port many herbs. Some now arrive, so we make more medicine.'

'I'm sure any plants you look after will grow strong,' James said. 'We are looking forward to seeing your garden and hearing about the various remedies you produce from them.'

She didn't know how to respond to such praise, especially from a stranger. She smiled gratefully and pointed in the direction of the path they were about to take. It was the original path that led from High Street to the summit of Bukit Larangan.

'I used to come this way every day when we first arrived in Singapore,' Dick said. 'We lived with Raffles' sister, Mary Ann, before the bungalow was built. There are certain plants I used as markers until I was familiar with the route. There's one in particular I think you might be interested in.'

He found the kapok tree first. 'Be careful,' he said, 'don't trip over those great roots.' The plant he was seeking wasn't far away. He pointed to the flowers, each supported by a long, slender, leafless stem. Some were fully open, showing off their large, red bracts; others remained discreetly shy, exposing only their pink buds. One of the plants was as tall as Dick; its leaves, arranged alternately in two opposite vertical rows, were huge.

'In China, we have plant like this,' Wing Yee said, turning towards the visitors, 'but smaller.'

'The English name is torch ginger lily,' Dick said, 'but in Malay, they call it *kantan*; its fruit is used to treat earache.'

'In China, we use ginger to chase cold out of body – also good for headache.'

'I remember you making ginger tea for Raffles,' Dick said.

'Ginger also good for pregnant ladies, when feel sick in morning. Sophia also drink my ginger tea.'

The four of them continued along the path; led by Dick, they followed a trail that enabled them to skirt around the side of the hill towards the Spice Garden. Wing Yee stayed close to Dick with James not far behind and finally, Edmund brought up the rear.

The heat of the day was already becoming intense when they reached the open space of the garden. Wing Yee pulled her hat down further to protect her face and made her way to a patch of shade so that she could concentrate on planting her turmeric. Meanwhile, Dick led Edmund and James towards several rows of aromatic shrubs; he pointed out the minute detail of each bunch of the cream-coloured cloves, just coming into bloom. James gazed at them intently, marvelling at the profusion of tiny buds which hung in clusters, reminding him of elderflowers in an English spring.

'Those buds will change to green soon, then bright red,' Dick told them. 'That's when they're ready to harvest and spread out to dry in the sun. They'll look exactly the same as the dark brown buds you've seen piled up in sacks outside the warehouses down by the quay.'

'These good for toothache,' Wing Yee said.

A short while later, Dick led them all towards a row of nutmeg trees. Most were still in flower with their delicate fragrance teasing the occasional blue butterfly in mid-flight. These trees, being still quite young, had not yet reached their full height. Dick stretched between the pointed, dark green leaves and pulled a branch towards him, so that Edmund could inspect the pale yellow, bell-shaped flowers. As soon as he let the branch spring back again, two ochre-coloured, oval-shaped fruit fell at his feet. One of them split in half, revealing a purplish-brown seed swathed in a bright-red cloak.

James knelt down and quickly scooped them up with his hands. It had never occurred to him to spend time examining the seeds that spiralled around his head every autumn when he walked across his land back home, but now he felt compelled to scrutinise every small detail of trees he had never seen before. He put a couple of the seeds in his pocket and handed the others to his brother.

'How old these trees?' Wing Yee asked.

'They are probably some of the first saplings that Raffles sent to Colonel Farquhar, from Sumatra. I remember, when we arrived here a couple of years later, his friend Mr Wallich told me that it takes between five to seven years for them to bear fruit; this might be their first harvest.'

'That must be the same Nathaniel Wallich who Sir Stamford told us about when we all travelled out to Hendon,' Edmund said. 'We considered visiting him ourselves when the ship reached Calcutta, but we discovered he was away, helping another plant collector who was planning a trip in the Himalayas.'

Dick realised that Wing Yee might not know who they were talking about, so he relayed the tale of the Danish doctor-turned-botanist, who Raffles had asked to come to Singapore and design an experimental spice garden on these slopes.

'Why I not meet him?' she asked.

'He came here in November 1822; I think he'd been unwell and used the visit as an excuse to recover. He and Raffles had been friends for a long time, but once the design was complete and the initial planting established, Mr Wallich had to return to Calcutta. He already had an important job there, you see, at the Royal Botanical Gardens; once his health improved, he had no excuse to stay. It all happened a few months before you and I first met.'

*****

At the end of their visit, all three of the men insisted on accompanying Wing Yee back home. They had just finished saying goodbye when Baba Tan came scurrying out of the house with a hastily scribbled note in his hand.

'Please give this to Mr Johnston,' he said to Dick. 'We are very happy to accept his invitation tomorrow night.'

Dick looked puzzled, but took the note from his friend and tucked it into his pocket. Edmund and James thanked Wing Yee for all the things she had told them about the plants they'd seen, what they might expect to find in China, and the minor ailments they could cure. She smiled politely and left them to talk to Baba Tan. Surprisingly, however, he quickly excused himself, explaining that whilst they had been away, he had received a visitor and now there was something he needed to tell Wing Yee.

CHAPTER 6
Singapore, 4th October 1825

As soon as Dick returned home with Edmund and James, he discovered why Baba Tan had been anxious for his response to Johnston's invitation to be delivered quickly; his whole household had been invited to join them for dinner the following evening.

'After all,' Alexander Johnston said to the brothers, 'it will be your last evening with us and you haven't yet met Chin Ming.'

'That is most kind,' James said, 'but there really is no need. You have been more than generous already.'

'But there is every need,' Johnston said. 'We must wish you luck for your grand adventure – and besides, Dick tells me that in two days' time young Edmund here will be twenty-six years old. By then, of course, you will be on the high seas and it may not be easy to celebrate such an event on board ship; the seas between here and Macau can be very rough!'

*****

The brothers rose later than usual the following morning. Dick was just finishing breakfast and was about to depart when they appeared at his side. He looked up to see Edmund standing unusually close, with a wide grin on his face. James paced about behind his brother; they exchanged a knowing look, nodded and then Edmund took a deep breath.

'We have a proposition to put to you,' he said.

Dick pushed his chair away from the table so that he could take a good look at the brothers. What on earth had happened to make them behave like a couple of excited puppies?

James held his breath and smiled, but said nothing. This was Edmund's idea, and it was he who must convince Dick it was one worth pursuing.

Edmund took the chair to Dick's left; his eyes sparkled. He shifted to the edge of the seat and clutched his hands together before embarking upon the words he'd practised in advance. They came out in a torrent of high-pitched incoherence.

Dick moved his chair back even further and put his head on one side. 'Sorry, I'm not sure what you mean. You said something about a proposition?'

Edmund took another deep breath before continuing. This time, he spoke slowly and deliberately.

'We'd like you to come with us to China!'

'What? Why?'

'Because,' said Edmund, 'you are obviously a very talented artist. We know there will be some plants that are too delicate to transport, but you could solve that problem for us.'

'How? I know very little about plants. I've learned a few things from Wing Yee, that's all.'

'But you can draw them – anything that is either too fragile or too rare – I would not want to take. Those that are in abundance will provide a rich assortment of plants to propagate, and your drawings will enable us to show people in England all the other wonderful varieties that grow in this part of the world without having to remove them from their native habitat.'

'I'm flattered,' Dick said, 'but it's impossible, I'm afraid.'

'Why?' said Edmund instantly.

'Maybe you can find a local artist when you get there,' Dick said. He didn't want to cause offence, but apart from the time when he'd been abducted as a child, all the travelling he'd done to date had been with Raffles; he wasn't sure that he was ready to leave the security of this place he now called home.

'But we've got to know you in the last few days. We get along so well – and we thought you might even enjoy the adventure! And China won't be our only destination – after we've finished in Macau and Guangzhou we're planning to go on to Sumatra. I know that's where you began your drawings for Raffles – we thought you might like to see your old home again?'

Dick listened to what they had to say, but he hardly knew these two young men. True, during their short time together they had enjoyed each other's company, but spending months with them away from home was a different matter. He had come across other Europeans who wanted help with their hairbrained schemes – proposals that were not sufficiently thought through.

'You would be doing us a great favour,' Edmund said. 'I don't have a great deal of money, but there is sufficient to pay your passage. Your accommodation and food will also be covered, of course, but I'm afraid I can't offer much of a fee at present.'

Dick was running out of excuses and Edmund was being honest enough, but there was no way he could embark upon such an expedition even if he was warming to the idea. 'You leave tomorrow,' he said. 'Even if I agreed to join you, it would be impossible to arrange everything in time.'

'We've got all day to arrange your passage, and we're sure William Lawrence won't mind an extra member of the expedition,' Edmund said. 'All you have to do is gather together a few possessions and your drawing materials,' James added.

'Please come,' said Edmund, who had now set his heart on the idea of Raffles' adopted son being part of their expedition.

'Like James says, we'll make all the arrangements. All you have to do is pack up your things!'

It took another couple of hours before the brothers finally convinced Dick that the idea was feasible. He had to admit that the timing was perfect; he'd delivered his latest portrait on the morning the *Charles Grant* had dropped anchor; he'd already decided to spend a little time sketching the rapidly growing town and its environs rather than embark upon more portraits, so he would not be letting anyone down. Nevertheless, he insisted on consulting Alexander Johnston before making a final decision. His guardian thought it was an excellent idea, so with no more excuses left, he remained at the warehouse making lists and deciding what he should take with him while James and Edmund went down to the harbour to arrange his passage.

*****

Baba Tan was looking forward to the dinner party, but he thought it might be difficult to persuade Yan Lau to accompany him. She was a good wife and a wonderful mother, and she could speak English well enough, but she was sometimes ill at ease in the company of strangers.

'Of course, we must all attend,' Chin Ming said when she heard about the invitation. 'It would be impolite to refuse.' The gentle art of persuasion triumphed when, with Wing Yee, they convinced Yan Lau that they needed her to come along as their chaperone. Wing Yee smiled to herself afterwards. After all, Yan Lau was not yet thirty, but as a married woman she had more status than either Chin Ming or herself. Besides, even though she had enjoyed meeting the two visitors and showing them the plants, she too lacked confidence in her own ability to converse in their language for a whole evening. By the end of the discussion, Chin Ming had managed to convince both

Wing Yee and Yan Lau that they wouldn't have to worry as long as Dick was around; he always had plenty of things to talk about.

*****

Before the guests arrived, and whilst everyone else was still dressing, Dick stood alone on the veranda wondering what he had let himself in for. He was overwhelmed, as always, by the magnificence of the setting, with its splendid views over the water. A slender line of silver, drawn across the horizon, separated the darkness of the ocean from the indigo sky. A finer brush, dipped in pitch, outlined the shape of the ships in the harbour, making them look like small toys on a glittering pond. He could have stood admiring the scene, taking in the scent of frangipani blossom all night, but then he became aware of the hand of Alexander Johnston under his elbow, gently guiding him back into the house.

'Our other guests will be arriving soon,' he said. 'I need you to help me welcome them and introduce them to Edmund and James.'

'But haven't they all met already?'

'You told me that Yan Lau was not at the warehouse the day you took Edmund and James to meet Baba Tan – and neither have they been introduced to Chin Ming.'

'No, of course not,' Dick said. 'Sorry, I'd quite forgotten.'

At that point, James arrived looking very smart in formal evening dress; he was followed moments later by Edmund, similarly attired. All four men were engaged in animated conversation when their guests arrived.

Baba Tan led his wife towards Alexander Johnston, believing Chin Ming and Wing Yee were following behind. Instead, the two young women remained on the path, surveying the scene in front of them. When they reached the edge of the veranda, they could see Dick clearly. He had his face towards them and he was grinning from ear to ear. His dark eyes were shining and his gaze constantly flitted between two men who were standing with their backs towards the women. All three were engrossed in animated conversation, oblivious to anyone else.

Chin Ming was in no hurry and took her time to study the scene. Wing Yee was content to remain close by her side.

'It's hard to tell their ages from here,' Chin Ming whispered in her friend's ear, 'but from the way they're behaving I think they can't be much older than me.'

Wing Yee remained silent. She hadn't really considered their ages when they'd spent the day together; as far as she was concerned, it was their curiosity about the medicinal properties of plants that made them interesting.

Both women continued to examine the two visitors, one slightly taller than the other.

'I thought you said they were brothers,' Chin Ming continued, 'but they appear not to be at all alike – the colour of their hair is quite different; you didn't even mention that when you told me about their visit to your garden.'

'It seem not important,' Wing Yee said, 'but think coat they wear tonight very hot,' she added, keeping her voice very low.

'It must be the fashion in Europe,' Chin Ming replied, 'but I agree, they are not suitable for this climate.'

Both men wore dark coats with tall collars. There were small, shiny buttons at their waist, on their cuffs and along the tails that tapered towards their knees. The buttons all sparkled in the light from the oil lamps whenever the conversation became more animated and the men raised their arms or tossed their heads back.

'What are they getting so excited about?' Chin Ming said. 'Look, even Dick is joining in.' Neither woman could stop herself from laughing quietly at the sight of them.

Wing Yee took a step closer to Chin Ming and was about to whisper to her when the two guests, having picked up on their mirth, became conscious of being observed. James and Edmund swung round to face them. Dick too was now aware of their presence, but he only had time to briefly introduce Chin Ming when a gong was heard and Alexander Johnston announced that dinner was about to be served.

Dick was delighted to find himself seated between his two friends, and although Wing Yee would have preferred to have been the one seated in the middle, she did begin to relax a little when she realised that it was James, the quieter of the two brothers, who was on her right. Her comfort was eased further when she saw Yan Lau sitting directly opposite. If conversation with the Englishman ran dry, then she could always chat to Baba Tan's wife. Chin Ming found herself seated directly opposite Edmund Beaumont and wished there had been more time to be properly introduced.

For once in his life, Edmund was stumped for words. He had given little thought to the other young woman Raffles had told them about, his only consideration being that she might be something like Wing Yee.

Now, he found himself transfixed; he had never seen anyone as truly beautiful as Chin Ming, with her lustrous black hair cascading down over a red silk tunic, intricately embroidered with gold thread. There was a small spray of flowers in her hair and she wore a strange pendant around her neck, which she occasionally fondled, like a child with a favourite toy.

To avoid further embarrassment, he asked her questions about the school and the pupils she taught. She surprised him with her answers, showing a great deal of passion. She told him about Raffles' ambition to establish a larger school for older pupils and her disappointment that the Singapore Institute, as it was to be called, still showed no sign of being started.

'But meanwhile, you're preparing the younger children – and by the time the Institution is built, those you are teaching now will be ready to move on,' Edmund said. 'I'm sure Raffles will be glad to know that – and you obviously enjoy the work. I would love to see your school. Maybe I could visit when we return to Singapore?'

'When is that likely to be?' she said.

'We leave on tomorrow's tide,' he replied. 'With luck, we should reach Macau in about three weeks' time.'

'Wing Yee told me that you plan to collect some of our native plants and send them back to England. Will you be looking for anything special?'

'Everything we collect will be special,' he said, 'but we'll only collect the plants that grow in profusion. I have no intention of taking anything that is extremely rare.'

'Unlike the visitor I had yesterday,' said Baba Tan, who had overheard Edmund's declaration.

All eyes turned to him; everyone around the table waited for him to continue.

'While the three of you were at the Spice Garden with Wing Yee, a young man arrived at my warehouse. He was anxious to tell me he'd heard that I supplied traditional medicines; he bombarded me with questions about the plants being used and where they came from. But I'm afraid I became suspicious when he failed to tell me anything about himself – when he arrived in Singapore, how long he intended to stay, even his name.'

'What did he want?' James asked.

'He asked if I was interested in purchasing any rare items. He used words that made me think he must be French – he said he could obtain anything considered to be *exotique, peu abundant, extraordinaire.*'

'That's odd,' James said. 'There was a Frenchman who joined the *Charles Grant* in Cape Town.'

'And when we arrived here, he caused such a commotion,' Edmund added. 'He insisted on boarding the first bumboat to come ashore; he almost started a riot. I wonder if it's the same man?'

'This same man you tell me about?' Wing Yee said.

'Yes. I was worried that he might approach Wing Yee directly,' Baba Tan explained to the others. 'I told him I wasn't interested in anything dubious or illegal and I asked him to leave. Fortunately, there has been no sign of him since. It is good to know,' he added, turning to Edmund, 'that you, my friend, are only interested in collecting specimens that are plentiful.'

'Luckily, my brother has powers of persuasion that will allow us to capture anything that is rare in an entirely different manner,' James said.

'What you mean?' Wing Yee asked.

Now the attention swung round to Edmund. Johnston smiled to himself knowing what was about to be revealed, and a deep crimson flush crept across Dick's cheeks.

'Dick has agreed to come with us,' Edmund said. 'He will sketch all the plants that are too delicate to transport, plus anything we come across that is noteworthy or unusual.'

There was an audible intake of breath from both Wing Yee and Chin Ming. 'You didn't tell us,' Chin Ming said.

'The suggestion was only made this morning,' Dick said hastily. 'It took me a while to agree and ever since then I've been busy getting everything ready.'

'He tried to convince us there would be someone we could hire once we got to our destination,' Edmund told them, 'but then I told him we planned to visit Sumatra as well as China.'

'I'm sorry,' Dick said, addressing first Chin Ming and then Wing Yee. 'You are my very best friends, but it has all happened so quickly. Actually, one of the things that finally changed my mind,' he said, 'was when it occurred to me that I would be visiting the country where you were both born. You see, I have no idea about the places you lived before you came here. I could make some sketches for you to have as a reminder – if you would like that?' As usual, he now felt uncomfortable having made a passionate speech. 'It will also be good to see how Sumatra has changed,' he added to cover his embarrassment.

Nothing else was said, and any further awkwardness was overcome by the arrival of a Malay servant holding a platter high above his head. All heads turned to follow as he slowly walked the length of the room carrying something which was just beyond their line of vision. Johnston looked slightly nervous, willing the man to reach his destination without mishap. Others caught his mood and held their breath. At the far end of the table, the plate was lowered with great ceremony and a large cake was placed immediately in front of Edmund.

Johnston rose to his feet. 'Ladies and gentlemen, we have much to celebrate tonight. First and foremost, I would like you to join me in wishing young Edmund here a very happy twenty-sixth birthday in two days' time.'

Everyone raised their glass and repeated the words *happy birthday*.

'Next, I hope you will want to join me in wishing *bon voyage* to our friends, both old and new, who are about to embark upon a great adventure. We wish you well and look forward to welcoming you all back to the Settlement in about six months from now.'

A chorus of voices was heard saying *bon voyage* and *happy birthday* in English, Cantonese and Hokkien, as slices of the cake were passed around the table.

Edmund rose to his feet, looking slightly awkward. He thanked his host and his fellow guests for their kind thoughts and good wishes.

'Both James and I consider ourselves extremely fortunate, first of all, to have met Raffles in London and now to have received such a warm welcome from his friends here in Singapore.'

James said, 'Here, here,' and nodded in agreement.

Edmund looked around the assembly before he continued. When his glance fell upon Chin Ming, she was fingering the pendant which he'd noticed earlier. As she raised her eyes to look at him, a slight breeze caused one of the candles to flicker, bathing her in a ribbon of light. Not for the first time that evening, he was lost for words.

He heard a faint cough from the other side of the table and when he turned, James was staring at him with an eyebrow raised. He pulled himself together.

'We have indeed made new friends during our short time here,' he said. 'During the course of this evening, however, I've realised that Dick's decision to join us came as a great shock to you and that he will be greatly missed. Let me reassure you that we will do our best to make sure he comes to no harm, and I hope we'll be able to tell you all about our various experiences when we return. I'm sure I speak for my brother as well as myself when I say that we are very much looking forward to renewing our acquaintance with you all.'

Once the cake was consumed, the evening drew to a close, and Baba Tan gathered his family together to thank their host and say their farewells.

*****

With Chin Ming's help, Wing Yee spent the remainder of the evening making a few notes about some of the plants the young men might want to look out for when they reached China.

Chin Ming joked with her about this unexpected enthusiasm, using it as an excuse to avoid voicing her disappointment that Dick would not be around for the next few months.

'I notice James look sad some time,' she said. 'I think he sad about his wife. It only one year since she die. He tell me Edmund say to visit new places might make bad memories go. He easy to talk to and he ask me about some plants to look for in China.'

'So, you thought you'd give him extra information?' Chin Ming said.

'What is wrong?' Wing Yee said.

'Nothing, nothing at all,' replied Chin Ming, smiling to herself.

*****

The following day, Wing Yee asked Baba Tan to accompany her to the quay. It would be frowned upon to go there alone and Chin Ming had already left to welcome a new pupil to the schoolhouse. He was pleased that she felt able to share some of her knowledge with someone else, especially with a European gentleman. Perhaps the memory of her assailant was beginning to fade at last. He was pleased to escort her.

They reached the quay in good time. A group of coolies, who were busy loading one of the bumboats with supplies for the Indiaman, told them that the two gentlemen who had been staying with Mr Johnston were yet to arrive. A few minutes later, they heard the noise of horse's hooves and carriage wheels rolling over the cobblestones. Johnston had seen fit to load the vehicle with the small amount of luggage the Beaumont brothers had brought ashore alongside the various packages Dick had chosen to take with him. James was the first to descend, followed by Edmund; Dick handed the luggage down to them, then jumped down onto the cobblestones himself. Johnston was in the process of shaking them all by the hand when Baba Tan arrived, accompanied by Wing Yee.

'Well, this is a surprise,' said James as he saw them approach.

'Wing Yee has made some notes that might help you when you're in China,' Baba Tan explained.

'Chin Ming help,' she said as she handed them to James. 'My English, not good for writing.'

'What a very kind gesture,' James said. 'Look, Edmund, no excuse now. We'll know exactly what to look out for.'

Edmund added his thanks, bowing politely to Wing Yee and shaking Baba Tan's hand enthusiastically. Wing Yee was pleased that her efforts were well received, but thought Edmund looked slightly distracted. Dick fidgeted a great deal, first picking up one parcel, then putting it down in favour of another; his eyes flitted along the quay and back again. Maybe they were both disappointed there was no sign of Chin Ming.

'She send greeting,' Wing Yee said, looking first at Dick, then at Edmund. 'She in schoolroom already. You find her, you go there – when you return.'

CHAPTER 7
Macau, 17th November 1825

Edmund rose early. Today, they were due to arrive in Macau and he couldn't contain his excitement any longer. The note they'd received from William Lawrence, telling them to join him in the Portuguese settlement rather than in Guangzhou as originally arranged intrigued him. Lawrence had given no hint about the change of mind or any detail about the new location.

'Could you not sleep?' Dick said as he approached the younger Beaumont brother.

'I'm eager to see what the place looks like, that's all,' Edmund replied. 'James and I made it our business to find out all we could about Guangzhou before we left England and now we find ourselves going to a place we know very little about.'

'That makes us equally ignorant then,' Dick said, as a broad smile crept across his face. 'I noticed you talking to Chin Ming for a long time during that last evening in Singapore. I thought you might have asked for her advice?'

Edmund felt colour warming his cheeks. He wanted his response to be casual and relaxed, but he feared the tone of his voice might indicate a more than insouciant response to the mention of Chin Ming's name. He took his time before saying, 'Both Wing Yee and Chin Ming gave us some valuable information; we were fortunate to meet them when we did. Their most recent memories are from Guangzhou, of course, but quite a lot of what they told us relates to the whole of this region. Anyway, if Baba Tan was correct in his assumptions, we're likely to end our trip in that city. I was thinking that we might try to find the mission that looked after Chin Ming when her father disappeared; maybe someone there will have some news we could take back to her.'

'I think Chin Ming clings to her memories because they are almost all she has left of her father. She never stops thinking about him and goes over and over what she remembers of their life together. It's a good idea to see if we can contact the mission, but you do know that Raffles tried to get in touch. There was no response. Maybe the person in charge has moved on. I'm afraid it's already too long ago and we'll never be able to discover what really happened.'

Edmund nodded. He was glad that Dick hadn't noticed his unease when Chin Ming's name was first mentioned. He still had no idea whether Dick was in love with her himself, let alone what she thought of the young man who had been responsible for rescuing both herself and Wing Yee from the clutches of the infamous Dutchman.

'And Wing Yee is so knowledgeable,' he added, trying to change the focus, 'about plants and their medicinal properties, I mean. It seems such a pity that she is unable to be recognised for all the work she does for Baba Tan – just because she's a woman.'

'Would it be so different in England?' Dick said. 'I didn't meet many women who were able to do exactly as they pleased – when I was there with Raffles – unless they were very wealthy, of course.'

'Even then, it is not easy for women to do as they please,' Edmund said. 'But in England, those women who are very clever quickly learn to make us men think some of the ideas they have, some of the things they want to do, are actually our notions, and so they get what they want, anyway.'

Dick began to laugh; then Edmund joined in when he realised how amusing his explanation must sound. To change the subject, Edmund asked Dick to tell him about the time he'd spent in England with Raffles. It was almost ten years ago, but Dick still retained some unpleasant memories of the climate and the hostility he encountered from a few people when Raffles was out of sight. Edmund was outraged that his countrymen could behave so badly. He and Dick were still deep in conversation when the older Beaumont brother arrived by their side.

'I thought you came aloft to get the first sighting of land,' James said.

'That's right,' Edmund said, 'and Dick had the same idea.'

'Well, I'm sorry to tell you, that's you've both missed the moment. One of the officers knocked on our cabin door about fifteen minutes ago to say that the coast had been spied through a telescope – and look, that grey smudge on the horizon is probably what he was talking about.'

Dick and Edmund swung round to gaze in the direction of James' index finger. All three stared at the slender, grey brushstroke that outlined the place from which they would start the next part of their journey. Gradually, the mirage turned into a broad stretch of grey-green coastline, which encompassed and cocooned an enormous bay. Close to the shoreline, they began to make out the shape of buildings – proud, white, and similar in design to those Edmund and James had seen when they visited Lisbon. How clever the Chinese had been, James thought, to let the Portuguese build a small trading settlement here back in the sixteenth century and then use them as agents to exchange goods in the countries they were not allowed to travel to themselves. He'd been told by the ship's captain that the place was not as glorious now as it had been back then; but in his eyes, it was still impressive.

*****

77

A tall man in a limp shirt, shabby brown trousers and big, sturdy boots waited at the end of the quay. William Lawrence wasn't a botanist by training, but he was definitely one by nature. He'd come out to China as a missionary fifteen years ago; the work had always been hard and seldom satisfying. The government had only allowed foreigners to travel short distances from Guangzhou and Macau, and many of the local converts to Christianity found themselves being persecuted. Instead of returning to England at the end of his contract, he'd decided to remain in China. William now concentrated on collecting plants rather than souls, but until the Franciscans had been asked to leave, he'd always enjoyed the company of a friend based at the mission in Guangzhou.

During their acquaintance, Father John had told William about the journeys to the interior undertaken by French Jesuits in the previous century, and how successful they had been in transporting significant numbers of plants and seeds to France. Despite the fact that his own travels had been limited to Guangdong Province, William took every opportunity to explore as much as possible, and it was during these trips that he'd discovered many varieties of plants never seen in Europe.

Twelve months ago, he'd received a letter from a friend he'd met at theological college, telling him that his youngest son was in the process of arranging a plant-collecting trip to China. Richard Beaumont had asked for his advice.

William had replied by return. He relished the idea of an official expedition and had been in correspondence first with Richard and then with his son. Edmund's last letter was received in June; it told him that his brother would also be joining the trip. They had booked passages on the *Charles Grant*, which was due to arrive in Guangzhou towards the end of November.

A few weeks after that letter arrived, William learned about a particularly unpleasant incident in Guangzhou involving a foreigner. One of the rumours claimed that the man concerned had stolen some seeds from the Temple of Six Banyan Trees, whilst another one maintained he was involved in piracy, including the illegal transportation of rare plants. Whether or not either tale was true, it caused William to re-think the journey he was arranging for the Beaumont broth-ers. Fortunately, he knew the *Charles Grant* would call in at Singapore. He wrote a hasty note to the brothers, suggesting a change of plan, which involved starting their journey in Macau. Now he was here to meet them.

*****

There was no resemblance between the person who stood waving a red handkerchief in their direction and the only other missionary Dick had ever met. A fleeting image of an austere-looking man, who had passed through Singapore a few years ago, came to mind for a moment or two. That man had worn heavy black robes, even in the heat of the midday sun. He'd harangued the crowd who had stood before him; they had all listened patiently because it was Christmas Day. This man looked nothing at all like that.

*****

As the three of them carried their luggage along the length of the quay, James remembered some of the visitors his father had entertained at the parsonage back home; many had been missionaries, but they bore no similarity to the man now walking towards them. Edmund, who had no preconceived ideas to distract him, thought the person approaching them looked friendly and welcoming. Uppermost in his mind was the sheer delight of arriving at their destination and the anticipated pleasure of what lay ahead.

William greeted them warmly and took them to the lodg-ings he had rented. There had been no time to inform him about Dick and the fact that he would be joining the expedition, but it made no difference to their host; he was always glad to welcome visitors. Once they had time to sort out their belongings, William suggested a walk around the town. 'It's a while since I embarked upon a long sea voyage,' he said, 'but I do remember how good it was to have the freedom to walk beyond the limits of the deck.'

The first place they visited was an eating-house; William ordered a dish that they could all share. Neither Edmund nor James spoke any Cantonese; Dick knew only a few phrases, so they were surprised when a huge bowl of soup was placed in the centre of the table. Edmund recognised some of the ingredients immediately – prawns, mushrooms maybe, and the herb he now knew to be coriander. He had no idea about the pale, shiny parcels floating in the deep brown liquid. The aroma teased everyone's nostrils and made them realise how hungry they felt. An old Chinese man, wearing a long vest over a colourful sarong, shuffled towards them. He placed a small white bowl decorated with a blue fish in front of each of them; then he traipsed to the back of the room. When he returned, he handed them all a matching spoon and a pair of chopsticks.

William served the soup, making sure that everyone received a share of all the ingredients; Dick, who had enjoyed such meals as this for as long as he could remember, began to eat straight away. William looked across at the brothers; James had picked up his spoon and Edmund was struggling to position his chopsticks. 'I'm afraid you'll need to learn to use them,' William said, 'otherwise you'll starve.'

Dick stopped eating immediately, feeling slightly guilty that he'd rushed ahead and given no thought to the fact that Edmund and James may never have had to use chopsticks before. He realised now that during their brief stay in Singapore, they had always been given spoons and forks. He turned to Edmund and showed him how to position his chopsticks so that they sat comfortably between his thumb and index finger. Then, he demonstrated how to manoeuvre the upper stick and gain control over what he wanted to eat. James received a similar demonstration from William. The brothers managed to pick up the prawns quite easily, but mushrooms and the oddly shaped parcels, called wontons, provided great entertainment. By the end of the meal, however, their skill had improved considerably; the spoon enabled them to drain the last drops of tasty liquid from their bowl, and they felt replete.

*****

During the two hundred or so years since the Portuguese first arrived in Macau, they had built luxurious villas overlooking the Praia Grande and splendid baroque churches – all paid for with the wealth accumulated from their monopoly on the trade between China and Japan. Nevertheless, the size of the metropolis came as something of a surprise to the Beaumont brothers. Their amazement grew when they discovered the early seventeenth-century church of St Paul was now being used to house a military battalion. William told them that the church had been abandoned shortly before the Jesuits departed. He pointed out two carved flowers beside a figure of the Virgin Mary and told them that the peony represented China and the chrysanthemum Japan. It was typical, Edmund thought, that a botanist would choose to point out these small details from amongst all the other sculptures and stone carvings that remained on the front of the building.

During that first evening, and throughout the next day, William escorted his three visitors to different parts of the town; they saw traders, craftspeople, hawkers and labourers. In the old city, they viewed traditional clan houses and humble, one or two-storey homes. James loved the names given to the streets – Rua das Estalagens, Rua de Madeira and Rua dos

Mercadores, but Edmund's favourite was the Ru da Felicidade, which William told him meant Street of Happiness. At no point did William say why he'd asked them to disembark in Macau.

At the end of the second morning, Dick wanted to be left at the foreshore, from where he could begin to make some rough sketches of the bay. He outlined the rolling hills behind the broad sweep of impressive white buildings, and then began to capture the shapes of the many sampans bobbing about in the water. It reminded him of Singapore, and his thoughts drifted to Chin Ming and Wing Yee. He wondered what they were doing right now.

'Where did you learn to draw like that?' an unknown voice asked. Dick turned round to see a serious-looking middle-aged man; his speech and his dress led Dick to believe that he was most probably English. He had short, light-coloured hair and bushy eyebrows. He wore spectacles on the end of his large nose and his bright-red lips were pouting. More significantly, he was carrying an easel and a bag from which protruded a number of slender brushes.

'My name is Chinnery – George Chinnery,' he said.

Dick wondered if he was supposed to know the name. He held out his hand to the man and said, 'I'm Dick. I don't really have another name – not one that I was born with, anyway.' He'd completely forgotten that he could have given his adoptive name, but then thought the better of it. 'Are you a painter?' he asked.

'I am indeed – and I can see that you have quite a talent, too. How long have you been in Macau?'

'We arrived two days ago,' Dick said. 'I'm here with two brothers who have come out from England to collect plants. They're talking about their plans with Mr Lawrence – he's going to take them to Foshan – and then on to Guangzhou. I'm here to sketch some of the plants that are not suitable to transport. We'll be leaving tomorrow.'

'That's a pity,' Chinnery said. 'I would like to show you some of my own work. I've painted almost this exact scene in oils. I'd like to know what you think of it.'

'I'd like that,' Dick said, 'and I've almost finished. The detail can be filled in later. Do you live far from here? I could come now, if that's convenient.'

Dick spent the rest of the afternoon with George Chinnery. He'd never painted in oils himself, but he liked the idea of the texture and depth of colour that it was possible to create. Chinnery told him about a young Chinese artist who painted in a very similar style. He said that Lam Qua would be glad to see him when he reached Guangzhou and before they parted, he gave him an address where the young man could be found.

*****

The next day, the four men left their lodgings early and stepped out into swirling ribbons of thick, white mist. Dick walked with William down to the quay; Edmund and James followed behind. Their Chinese guide was already waiting beside his craft, eager to depart. It was just getting light when the small boat pulled away; it stirred up the silt which typified the delta, causing red-brown ripples and the stench of decay to mark its passage. They were all glad to leave the hustle and bustle of the busy town behind.

Instead of heading in the direction of the wide mouth of the delta, however, the vessel turned westwards, passing a number of offshore islands. The sail flapped above their heads and was then lowered as they turned into the Xi River. Once the course was set, William introduced their guide merely as Yong, a man with whom he had travelled on many previous occasions. Yong inclined his head and greeted them in Cantonese; he knew hardly any English.

Dick now lay back in the stern of the boat, completely spellbound by the magical shape of the mountains. Each one appeared to be clad in a rich velvet robe that fell in deep folds around its magnificent shoulders. They reminded him of pictures he'd seen in a book of fairy stories, sent to Raffles for his young family when they lived in Sumatra. He noticed William was now deep in conversation with James, no doubt explaining the route they would take into these same mountains in approximately two days. Edmund was sitting cross-legged under the canopy that provided shade in the centre of the boat. He roused himself and moved quietly towards Dick.

'What are you drawing?' he asked.

Dick continued sketching. 'The contours of the landscape are so fascinating,' he said. 'The sides of the mountain look so steep – almost as if they are completely upright – but they are beautiful. I just hope we won't be expected to climb too high when we start searching for your plants. I want to record the setting from this viewpoint – once we're walking amongst them that won't be so easy.'

'You're right, on both counts,' Edmund said. 'I've never seen mountains quite like them before, so sheer and mysterious-looking.'

'That's the other thing that's odd,' Dick replied. 'I've got a strange sort of feeling that I've seen something like them before, but it must have been a very long time ago. It couldn't have been in Sumatra; the mountain ranges there are enormous but not arranged in single peaks like these, rising from nowhere and reaching for the sky!'

Edmund told Dick about the wild mountain plants they hoped to find and William's preference for them over the cultivated specimens to be found in the nurseries around the cities. 'Some,' he said 'will be easy enough to transport, but I'm hoping there will be time for you to sketch any that are too fragile to ship back to England; your talent will be invaluable, and I'm so glad you agreed to join us.'

Meanwhile, James continued to listen to William and learn a little about the life he had lived for almost a decade. Still, nothing was said about their new route, but the whole experience was so new and exotic that James forgot to ask.

Each one of the men on board was now so engrossed in their own small tasks that no-one noticed another vessel – a sampan – that had slipped out of a small creek a few miles back. It had been following them at a discreet distance for several miles.

CHAPTER 8
China, 19th November 1825

They reached the shore as the light was beginning to fade. William had arranged for Edmund, James, and himself to stay the night with a friend of his, a retired carpenter who had moved away from the city to spend his days growing vegetables. It hadn't occurred to William, until now, that arriving with an additional guest might be something of an imposition. He need not have worried. Their host introduced himself as Freddie; he was the son of a European trader and a local Chinese woman, and he'd spent most of his life constantly on the move. Now, he was happy to stay put, providing an opportunity for him to welcome as many travellers who ventured in his direction as possible.

The evening meal was a leisurely affair, during which Edmund and James discovered the joys of eating chilli crab with their fingers. They asked Freddie how he'd first met William and was told about the years he'd spent working mainly for the foreign factories in Guangzhou. His favourite employer turned out to be a Franciscan priest at the mission based within the British compound.

This was the second time recently that Dick had heard Father John's name mentioned. 'Do you know what happened to those missionaries?' he asked. 'Did they all return to England when the mission closed?'

'Not all English,' Freddie said in the truncated manner

favoured by the Hong merchants and those of mixed race who had regular contact with Westerners. 'One man from France, one maybe from Portugal; Father John send all to Calcutta. There they join other missionaries.'

Dick turned his attention towards William. 'Is that where Father John has gone? Have you heard from him recently?'

William shook his head. 'I wasn't in Guangzhou when the missionaries were told to leave,' he said. 'But no, I haven't heard from him for a while. Freddie is right when he says arrangements were made for members of the mission to relocate to Calcutta. However, I have a feeling that Father John did not accompany the other members of his order.'

Dick moved closer to William. The others had started to discuss something entirely different, which gave him an opportunity to ask more questions. He told William about Chin Ming and her missing father; he related as much as he knew about the circumstances of her father's disappearance and the subsequent months when she had been cared for by the mission.

'You see,' he said, 'Chin Ming left here believing she might find her father in Singapore, but there was no trace of him. She left a note for Father John and has written to him from Singapore, but there has been no news for ages. I just wondered, if he didn't travel to Calcutta with the others, where might he go – and why?'

'I'm afraid I can't help.' William said. 'I remember him telling me about a certain Chinese teacher and the conversations they shared. I'm trying to remember his name.'

'Soon Heng – Li Soon Heng,' Dick offered.

'That's it! I discovered, afterwards, that the name meant a person with great endurance and I recall being thankful that I was simply William,' he laughed. 'But I'm sorry. I never actually met your friend's father.'

*****

The following morning, after breakfast, Freddie's guests made their way back to the river. Yong was nowhere to be seen, but as they finished buying provisions for their journey from the hawker stalls, he came hurrying into view. He bowed several times, apologising between each kowtow for his absence. William took him to one side; there was a brief conversation in Cantonese, after which William's brow creased into a series of parallel lines. He cast his eye along the length of the quay and then indicated that they should get on their way as quickly as possible.

'What do you think that was all about?' Edmund said to his brother in a hushed voice.

'I've no idea,' James replied. 'Maybe Yong has relatives hereabouts. Maybe he spent the night with them and simply got delayed. Maybe he was hoping William might employ more members of his family; he did look as if he was checking to see if there was anyone else around.'

'I thought they both looked uneasy, as if they were concerned about something,' Dick said.

'Do you think we have anything to worry about?' James said. 'After all, William has never explained why he wanted us to disembark in Macau instead of Guangzhou. Don't you think that's a bit strange?'

'I'm sure it's nothing deliberate. Remember, we've all been fairly busy for the last few days. I'll make a point of asking him though, if that would set your mind at rest.'

Dick and James both nodded, then Dick settled himself towards the prow of the vessel, sketchpad in hand. The brothers moved into a position where they had a good view of the passing scenery and could also take an interest in what Dick was drawing.

Today, they headed further north. The river divided at one point, melding together again after a diamond-shaped island. The boat progressed at a slow but steady state through a landscape dominated by padi fields, inevitably causing Dick and his companions to feel hypnotised by their uniformity; all three felt increasingly drowsy in the warmth of the sun and no-one noticed William reposition himself so that he was sitting very close to Yong.

They spoke in Cantonese. William asked a series of questions; Yong became agitated and waved his arms around a great deal. William pacified him, then continued with the questions, this time making an effort to modify his tone. Finally, he stood with his hand shielding his eyes so that he could scan the whole of the river in both directions.

Dick woke with a start. William turned towards him and pasted a smile across his face as the younger man grinned back at him. William was determined not to reveal the feeling of unease which was beginning to consume him; he would mention nothing to any of his guests until he was sure of his facts.

They reached their destination after another hour. This time, there were no hawkers plying for trade, no evidence of habitation. Yong steered the craft towards a wooden jetty; it protruded well out into the river but was nothing like any jetty they had seen before. The water reached almost to the top of the wooden piles, and on the platform, they could see four white pillars supporting a tiled roof.

William stood, scrutinising the river in both directions to make sure they hadn't been followed. The nausea he'd felt earlier was beginning to subside and his throat was no longer tight.

'There should be someone here to meet us,' he said as he leapt onto the wharf. He strode along under the canopy, climbed the six steps that took him onto a covered bridge, and once across, he continued down more steps to reach the small platform that led to the riverbank. Edmund, James, and Dick hesitated, not sure whether or not they were expected to follow. Eventually, Edmund's curiosity got the better of him and he too stepped onto the wharf. By the time he caught up, William was engrossed in conversation with two local men. He turned to Edmund to explain that the newcomers had been engaged as bearers; they would help carry their luggage and supplies, for this was the point from which they would begin their journey into the mountains.

When all their belongings had been offloaded, Yong took the boat and moored it under the elevated section of the jetty, tying it securely and removing the oars. Trees lined the entire length of the river at this point, but once they were clear of them, they could see the track that would lead towards the bold silhouette of low-slung hills that formed the horizon.

'I wonder what William's waiting for,' Edmund said. 'He keeps checking the river as if he's expecting someone else to join us.'

'Maybe he just wants to be sure the boat is secure,' Dick said. 'We have our two bearers; I would think that's more than enough.'

The first part of the journey took them through field after field of rice paddies. Until now, neither of the brothers had considered the cultivation of the familiar staple that accompanied nearly everything they ate. The path they followed was parched and cracked, as this was the beginning of the dry season; it skirted around fields flooded with water from the river and a young crop of green shoots that looked similar to the hay that grew in James' fields back home.

'Is it correct that the very first rice came from this part of China?' Dick asked.

'That's what everyone believes,' William said. 'There are lots of legends, of course, one of which involves the emperor who is also said to have discovered tea. But most Chinese people believe that rice is a gift from the animals. The legend says that long, long ago there was a disastrous flood and no food was available. One day, a dog ran through the fields to the people with rice seeds hanging from its tail. The people planted the seeds, the rice grew and hunger disappeared.'

They all laughed at William's version of the popular tale. Wherever they went in this part of the world, there was always a story to explain even the simplest of things; each one they heard fuelled Edmund's imagination and made him eager to learn as much as possible.

When they had trekked for a couple of hours, William paused while they watched a barefooted man work his way from one end of the flooded field to the other. 'This area has been recently harvested,' he said. 'Now, the man in the conical hat drives his water buffalo up and down the padi field, and that simple wooden plough churns up the mud and makes it ready for the next lot of seedlings.'

The heat of the day had subsided when they commenced the last part of their journey; this time, very little was said until some outbuildings came into view and then they cheered, grateful at last to reach the monastery where they would spend the next few nights.

*****

William was more relaxed now and for the next three days, Edmund, Dick and James followed him into the foothills to examine the rich variety of trees, shrubs and vines that grew there. He told them that when they reached Guangzhou, he would take them to the famous Fa-tee nursery on the outskirts of the town; but for now, he wanted them to have the opportunity of seeing wild varieties growing in their native habitat.

*****

One evening, when Edmund had finished discussing the details of the next stage of their journey with William, he decided to question him about the decision to start their journey in Macau instead of Guangzhou. William felt embarrassed that he'd not yet revealed his reasons and knew he owed Edmund an explanation. He rose from his chair, took Edmund's elbow and led him out onto the balcony. The evening was already cool; both men pulled their coats around them as they gazed into the darkness.

'Now we're here,' Edmund said, 'it makes lots of sense to begin the expedition in Macau. But, you see, the very first time I heard from you it was from your address in Guangzhou, so I assumed that is where we would commence our journey.'

'It was the original plan,' William said, 'and in many ways it would have been far simpler to arrange.'

'But surely, this way round, we'll complete the expedition in Guangzhou, which will enable us to load the plants onto the ship from there? When I wrote to you from England, I had so little knowledge of the areas we're allowed to travel in, no information at all about the terrain and ...'

'And no awareness of the rogues that operate in this part of the world,' William added.

Edmund raised an eyebrow. 'Raffles did warn us about pirates,' he said. 'On his journey back home last year, one of the specimens in his collection went missing. He didn't discover the theft until after the ship left Cape Town.'

'Did he tell you anything else?'

'The only thing I remember is something about a fellow passenger; a man who failed to re-join the ship, but I've forgotten the details, I'm afraid.'

'Did Raffles know where the absentee came from?'

Edmund tried to remember the conversation, searching his mind for the tiniest detail; it had taken place during their walk across the newly acquired land in Hendon. 'James might remember,' he said. 'Why it is important?'

The expression on William's face told him that it was, so

he went to find his brother. He located him in a corner of an inner courtyard, scribbling furiously in his notebook. Dick was close by, but had fallen asleep in his chair still clutching his sketchpad in one hand and a pencil in the other. Edmund quietly told his brother that William had something to ask him. He rose from his chair and together they tiptoed past Dick, saying nothing else until they reached the veranda.

'The man who Raffles talked about was French,' James said. 'I remember because when we reached Cape Town, a Frenchman came aboard the *Charles Grant* and I couldn't help wondering about the coincidence.'

'And when we reached Singapore,' Edmund now joined in, 'it was a Frenchman who made all the fuss about getting off the ship first.'

'And it seems possible that the same man approached one of the merchants we met in Singapore; he was offering to supply him with rare plants, but Baba Tan thought the man wasn't to be trusted and sent him packing.'

'Was this man on the *Charles Grant* when it brought you to Macau?' William asked.

'We didn't see him after we reached Singapore,' Edmund said. 'He upset some of the other passengers who also wanted to get ashore quickly, and a quarrel began. We moved away to another part of the deck. There was no sign of him by the time we arrived at the quay.'

'That's right,' James added. 'We didn't see him again.'

'Forgive me, William,' Edmund said, 'but I don't see what all this has to do with us disembarking in Macau?'

'I was about to come to that,' William replied.

James lowered himself onto the seat next to Edmund; William cleared his throat and looked them straight in the eye. 'On our first evening together,' he said, 'you spoke about the growing popularity of gardens and gardening in England.'

Edmund nodded.

'In essence, that's good; I approve of such things,' William said, 'but it concerns me that there are now too many people who come here to pillage and vandalise any plant they think will make them a quick profit. I'm afraid it's become a bit of an obsession of mine.'

'But our interests are purely scientific,' Edmund protested. 'All I want to do is take back a few samples that can be propagated and studied.'

'I'm aware of that, young man. I would not have agreed to accompany you on your expedition had I not believed you to be a collector of plants, rather than a hunter. However, there are many who are not so well-intentioned, and I suspect this Frenchman may be one of them.'

Edmund looked at James and then back towards William. They both remained silent while they waited for their host to continue.

'There are many rumours, as you might imagine. I've heard about a young man who makes it his business to find rare and expensive plants – often dishonestly – to order. He is thought to be French, but no-one is absolutely sure, and no-one knows his name. Do you remember the morning after we stayed with Freddie? When we reached the quay, there was no sign of Yong?'

'Yes, I remember,' said James. 'He seemed very apologetic. We thought that he might have been staying with relatives and forgotten the time!'

'Yong and I have travelled together on many occasions,' William said. 'As far as I know all his family live in Guangzhou. He spent that night on board the boat. But you're right, he was distressed that morning and I believe he had every reason to be. About an hour before we arrived, he was approached by a young man, a European.'

'What did he look like?' Edmund said. 'What made Yong think the man was European?'

'He'd noticed the man the previous evening. He said the man had walked past the mooring two or three times, but whenever Yong raised his head to ask him if he needed help, the man hurried away. Then, just after dawn, he saw him again. This time, the stranger started to ask all sorts of questions.'

'And Yong is sure it's the same person?' James said.

'The man is quite memorable,' William said. 'He has long, dark hair, tied together at the back but not plaited into a *queue*. He also has a scar over his left eye.'

'That sounds quite sinister.'

'Yong also said his clothes were unusual; dark blue breeches and a red cravat tucked into the neck of his shirt.'

'What did he want to know?' Edmund said. 'Was he speaking French? Is that what made you suspicious?'

'They spoke in Cantonese. He didn't offer a name or any personal information; he asked where we had come from and where we were headed. Initially, Yong thought the man was a stranger, maybe newly arrived in this part of the world. But when it became clear his Cantonese was fluent, he realised the man was not a recent arrival. Yong also thinks, because of the way he was dressed, that he was not English.'

'But neither can you be sure the man was French,' James said.

'No, I can't,' said William. 'Neither can I be certain that the young man I was warned about is French. But it concerns me that there is someone out there asking questions about the route we're taking; someone interested to know the purpose of our expedition. What reason could he have to ask these questions other than having an ulterior motive?'

'What did Yong tell him?'

'He told him that we were from Macau, but that was all. When pressed, he invited the visitor to wait so that he could ask me himself about our plans and where we might finish our journey. It's evident that the stranger made Yong feel uncomfortable. He said he couldn't pinpoint anything in particular, but there was something about the tone of the man's voice and his shifty manner that gave him reason to be cautious. He tried to give the impression that he was feeling disgruntled because I am always changing my mind and he never knew from one day to the next where we were headed.'

'That was clever.'

'Yes, it was. But I know the incident upset him. I've noticed that, since we left the mooring this morning, he is constantly looking over his shoulder. It's so unusual for Yong to be nervous; I'm worried that there is something else he may not yet have told me. Whoever the visitor was, he caused Yong to feel uneasy, and that's a good enough warning for me. From now on, I think we should all try to keep our wits about us.'

CHAPTER 9
China, November 1825

During the next few days, William led Edmund, Dick and James away from the monastery each morning. Bringing up the rear, and always a little way behind them, was Yong and the two bearers. Officially, their job was to carry equipment, care for any specimens and occasionally help William to remember their Chinese names. In reality, Yong and the bearers also took on the roles of scout and sentinel. Whilst the plant collectors searched the rocks and surrounding woodland, the three men bringing up the rear constantly searched for any other sign of human activity.

The first trip was nothing much more than a stroll through the forest followed by a gentle climb amongst the lower slopes of the mountains. William was anxious for his visitors to appreciate the plants in their natural habitat, to be aware of what grew in profusion and what was more unusual, uncommon or even scarce before they decided which specimens to collect.

At this time of year, almost none of the plants retained any of their flowers, but most displayed colourful fruit or seeds in abundance. On one occasion, Edmund cursed himself; maybe he should have planned the trip to arrive here in the spring so that it would have been easier to identify certain varieties by looking at their blossom and to appreciate their beauty.

'Yes, it's a real joy to see them at that time of year,' William said, 'but remember you would then be totally dependent on each of the samples surviving the journey back to England. We can collect small specimens now and we also have the advantage of being able to gather the seeds. This way, you have more than one chance of cultivating healthy examples of the flora from this part of China.'

Edmund knew this made sense, but he worried about Dick. He'd enticed the young man to join the expedition with the specific notion of recording anything that was delicate. In his head he'd imagined dainty buds, individual blooms and the occasional inflorescence. He hoped Dick would not get too bored and that the magnificent colours of late autumn would be enough to hold his interest.

*****

By the end of their first week, they had obtained an impressive collection. As was typical of this time of year, there had been no rain for over a month and the almost-dry river beds provided a useful means of getting from one location to the next. What water there was skimmed over their boots, providing a pleasant coolness to tired, aching feet. After several days spent trudging along in this manner, they had acquired a slender bamboo, several different types of fern and a deciduous sapling that William said could grow to over thirty feet tall.

'Be careful to protect its trunk,' he told them. 'If it gets damaged, it will exude an amber-coloured liquid oil which is combustible. Local people sometimes use it in their lamps – you might have noticed its strange aroma in the evening. It always reminds me of caramel.'

'That might be useful, if we get stranded in the forest at night,' James responded, and everyone laughed.

Their treks amongst forest glades filled their nostrils with the comforting earthy smell of decomposing leaves, where tiny insects waited to munch their way through all the decaying matter – centipedes, millipedes and beetles galore. Dick was always delighted when he came across toadstools or mushrooms clinging to branches, roots and rotting vegetation. The rest of the party often discovered he'd been left behind and would find him, crouched down on his haunches, rapidly sketching yet another cluster of colourful – and sometimes stinking – fungi.

For Edmund, the expedition yielded miniature varieties of white yew, laurel, and a whitebeam which, clad in its autumnal golden-pink cloak, was not to be ignored. He was pleased to observe Dick scribbling away at every opportunity. The strange shape of the rocks and the rich hues above his head, as well as the peculiar fungi that clung to fallen branches beneath his feet, provided a Pandora's box of artistic opportunity. Edmund need not have worried that he would become bored.

They collected seeds from different types of fern and a sago palm, in addition to those produced by a small collection of shrubs and trees. One of the evergreens, known locally as *pak muk huang*, produced a profusion of woody capsules covered in short, grey hairs. William scooped up a handful and split one of the pods open with his fingers. Inside, Edmund could see a silky thread winding from the base of each valve to hold a single seed at its tip. He took a deep breath and was straightaway reminded of their last night in Singapore. Johnston had lit incense sticks every evening to ward off mosquitos, but that evening there had been more of them than usual. He remembered the blue-grey smoke drifting slowly among the guests, twirling around their shoulders and leaving its musky aroma on their hair. An image of Chin Ming came into sharp focus and filled his thoughts.

Other seeds came from an acer which was flaunting the bright yellows, orange and reds of its remaining foliage and some from a fruit that was served after their evening meal. The brothers had never eaten soursop before embarking upon this expedition and due to its delicate, refreshing taste it soon became a favourite. Its seeds were carefully washed, dried and stored in an airtight tin.

At the end of each day, they discussed their finds and made lists. William always went to great lengths to describe how the trees would look when they reached maturity, when they would be expected to bloom, the shape and colour of their flowers and when they might produce fruit. James had been given the task of recording all this information. Everything was noted down according to its name, where it had been found, what aspect it favoured and how it should be nurtured.

*****

Their second location was similar to the first, but at a slightly higher elevation. They stopped briefly to admire the view across the valley where two rivers met. Tall poplars seemed to emerge from the blue water of a lake, shimmering in the heat and beyond that to a forested hillside where they could see a mysterious pagoda sitting amongst the trees. They were too far away to see any of the detail and for once, Dick had to forgo his instinct to start sketching. It occurred to him, however, that Yong was no longer constantly looking behind him. Perhaps this part of their route was more familiar and there was no need to check they were heading in the right direction.

Yong delighted everyone when he discovered a medium-sized dogwood called a dove tree. He found a small cluster of them, surrounded by several saplings which had already established a firm foothold. He revealed a toothless grin when he explained, with William providing a translation, that it had acquired this name because of the way its pure white petals fluttered in the wind, like doves' wings.

Another delight occurred when one of the bearers brought Edmund a small example of a *gutta-percha* tree. He recognised it immediately from his studies back in Oxford, where it was known as Mazer wood. He'd been told that it was used in the Malayan archipelago to make walking sticks and handles for knives; he remembered it had been discovered by John Tradescant back in the sixteen hundreds, but as far as he knew it hadn't yet been grown successfully in England. Edmund hoped this specimen might prove the exception to the rule.

*****

By the end of their second week, they were ready to move on to Shunde. They returned to the place where their boat was moored, grateful that it had not been tampered with. William now felt less need to continually look over his shoulder; there had been no sign of the man who had confronted Yong, nor any other strangers asking about their journey.

They left the main river behind after about an hour and turned into one of its many tributaries; their progress was slower now as the waterway was narrow and full of twists and turns. By the time they reached the town they had exhausted both conversation and themselves. William led Dick, James and Edmund to yet another monastery, but as this was a more urban setting, Yong and the bearers slept on board the boat. They were left in charge of the equipment and their growing collection of samples.

'I've given Yong and the others a couple of days rest,' William told his companions the following morning.

Edmund raised an eyebrow, asking a silent question of his host.

'I know what you're thinking,' William said as he steered Edmund away from the others. 'I've been checking to see if there has been any sign of the mysterious Frenchman ever since our stay with Freddie. Yong and the bearers have been keeping their eyes open too, but there has been nothing to see.

Hopefully, he has moved on to another unsuspecting traveller. But if he does turn up again, Yong has the bearers with him; one of them will come to find me the moment there is any sign of trouble. In the meantime, I think we too deserve a small break in our schedule.'

'What do you have in mind?' Edmund asked.

'There's a well-known garden that I think you should see. We might also visit one of the silk farms and then, just before we move on to Foshan there is an ancient temple that I think might interest you.'

'That all sounds wonderful,' said Edmund, 'and it will be good for Dick to see some cultivated plants – things that give him more scope for his talent.'

'Don't worry about me,' Dick said, who had wandered out to join them. 'I've enjoyed everything about the trip so far. We've been lucky that autumn is late this year. It's given us a chance to enjoy so many colours, shapes and textures. I love the dry freshness of the forests, the sound of leaves cracking beneath my feet and the musty aroma of everything getting ready to go to sleep. It was autumn when I arrived in England with Raffles. At least that's what he told me to call that time of the year, but all I can remember was dull, foggy days that enfolded everyone in their gloom.'

'To be fair, it's not always like that,' James added. 'An English autumn can be really beautiful – maybe not so late into November, but I can think of glorious sunsets touching the edges of woodland near my home, when the leaves are changing colour. It looks as if the whole place is on fire.'

'Maybe I should visit your part of England one day,' Dick said. 'That does sound more inviting.'

'Indeed, you should,' James and Edmund said in unison.

Their journey that morning was on foot and they kept getting distracted by all the unusual sights along the way. It took most of the morning to reach the Qinghui Garden on the opposite side of the town.

'I've never seen a garden like this before,' said James as they made their way between an extensive array of decorative pottery, statues, ornamental grasses, and carvings featuring trees, flowers, and birds from the southern part of China.

'It is typical of a classical garden,' William said. 'This one was first constructed well over two hundred years ago by the man who became an adviser to the last Ming emperor. Follow me and I'll show you.'

William led his guests through graceful pavilions, arbours and verandas, each of which was characterised by its robust construction. He pointed towards another building which he told them was called Chuan Ting. 'It means Boat Hall, literarily,' he said, 'but as you can see, that brightly coloured pleasure boat is sitting firmly on the land.'

They gazed at a two-storey building that was decorated with lifelike carvings of bamboo plants, snails and other designs. An undulating ribbon of waves formed a fringe at its edges, giving the illusion of a ship in the harbour. William told them that the garden held over a hundred different varieties, including purple bamboo, wisteria, Chinese holly, pine, larch and other species typical of a classical garden.

'Now I can see where the inspiration for the Great Pagoda built in the royal gardens at Kew came from,' Edmund said.

*****

Shunde was well known for its silk farms, but Dick found their visit to one of them not particularly interesting. Neither was he excited about the prospect of visiting an ancestral temple. He didn't want to upset anyone, but the truth was he was far more interested in ancient gardens, so he told his friends that he planned to make his way back to Qinghui. He wanted to sketch all the things that had captured his imagination a couple of days ago – rare stone formations clustered amongst the tranquil water, remarkable carvings, gingko trees as old as the garden itself and extraordinary plants that blended into the striking architecture.

He'd been there for about an hour when he had the distinct feeling that he was being watched. Just in front of the arch he was sketching, he could see two people; a man whom he assumed was a gardener and someone, sitting slightly apart from the others, who looked as if he had fallen asleep. The man with the trowel changed his position too frequently for Dick to capture his image, but the sleeping figure fitted perfectly into the drawing he was about to complete. The hat, worn over his long, dark hair, cast a strong shadow over his face, but Dick was sure there was a mark of some sort over one eye. He sketched it in faintly, believing it added a sense of mystery.

When he was satisfied with his efforts, Dick picked up his belongings and wandered away. He was looking for a particular pavilion that he remembered from his earlier visit. William had explained the significance of the different architectural features used in classical gardens, but it was the pavilions that interested Dick most because they provided such a perfect vista for the surrounding garden in all directions. The specific building he'd chosen was divided into two sections. Adjacent to the north-facing side was a lotus pond which provided cool air; this was the outlook designed for use in summer. The southern part was the side used in winter and it was this aspect, with a courtyard planted with pine trees that Dick was now facing. He recognised the bare skeletons of plum trees stretching skywards, even in their dormant state. How wonderful, he thought, it would be to see them in full blossom, heralding the arrival of spring.

He'd just finished outlining the shape of the ornate roof, with its curved ceramic tiles and splendidly coloured dragons, when a shadow fell across his sketchpad.

'You are very good,' the person standing behind him said in a measured voice.

Dick turned, but all he could see was a dark silhouette against the bright afternoon sunlight. He immediately thought of his encounter with George Chinnery, when he was painting the seascape in Macau, but although the nature of the comment was similar, this was not Mr C.

'You are not with your usual companions,' the man continued in his curiously precise manner.

'No,' Dick replied. 'We were here earlier in the week, but I wanted to come back so that I'd have time to capture all the details of the architecture.'

'You have a particular interest in buildings then?'

'I did once think I might like to train as an architect,' Dick said, 'but the person I'd hoped might teach me went away. I began by drawing plants, flowers mostly, but these days I mainly draw portraits for the successful merchants in Singapore. Fortunately, people seem to think I'm quite good at it, so there's always lots to do.'

'That is where you come from, then?'

'It is my home,' said Dick. 'What about you? Do you live here in Shunde?'

The man didn't answer directly. He shrugged. 'I live here and there,' he said. He asked Dick how long he and his friends would be in Shunde and about their next destination.

'We're leaving for Foshan in the morning,' Dick said. 'We've been enjoying a rest for the last few days, but tomorrow we'll go back to plant collecting.'

'Foshan has many nurseries,' the man said. 'It's a town, just like this one; perhaps your guide intends to stop off along the way?'

'I'm afraid I wouldn't know,' Dick said. 'I don't pay much attention to the details of the route. Why, is there somewhere that you would recommend?'

The two of them talked for a while about inconsequential things. Dick still had no idea about the man's identity or why he was interested in William, their expedition and the plants they intended to collect. Each time he tried to ask a question, the man avoided giving an answer. He did let slip that he knew William had come to China as a missionary and there was a brief reference to the plants collected by French missionaries in the last century, but as soon as Dick tried to find out more, the man clammed up completely. His resentful expression did not invite further questions. It was obvious that he had an interest in plants, so Dick asked him if he would like to come back to the monastery to meet his friends. The invitation was declined, the stranger saying that he must be on his way.

As he lifted his hat to bid farewell, Dick saw his face clearly for the first time. He realised that it was the same man he'd seen earlier in the day, sitting beside the arch. He was just about to comment and to ask the man's name when he bowed dramatically and said, '*Au revoir, mon ami.*' The mark Dick had lightly pencilled into his sketch was now quite clear; the man had a scar over his left eye.

CHAPTER 10
China, late November – early December
1825

William and the others had been back at the monastery for over two hours by the time Dick returned. Edmund was sitting on the wall, waiting for him.

'I'm so glad to see you. I was beginning to think that you'd got lost,' he said.

'Have I kept you waiting for supper?' Dick said. 'I'm sorry.' He was a little out of breath as he'd tried to run during the last part of the journey, but carrying his drawing materials had hampered his progress.

'Not at all. William has gone down to the boat to check on Yong and to agree on what time we need to depart in the morning. I'd expected you back earlier, that's all. You must have done a lot of drawings – may I look?'

Dick sat down on the wall beside Edmund and started to open his sketchbook. 'I got talking to someone this afternoon. That's what held me up. He was an odd sort of fellow. I'd seen him earlier on, but it wasn't until the afternoon, when I moved over to one of the pavilions on the far side of the garden, that he approached me and started to ask me lots of questions.'

'What sort of questions?'

Dick recounted as much of the conversation as he could remember. 'He gave me the impression that he was interested in our expedition,' he said. 'In fact, I asked him to come back with me to meet you all.'

'And what did he say?' said Edmund.

'He made some sort of excuse. I can't quite recall his exact words, but one thing I do remember is the strange way that he said goodbye.'

Edmund began to feel uneasy, but maybe he was over-reacting; he waited for Dick to continue.

'He used some words that Chin Ming sometimes says for fun. She says it means goodbye my friend, in French. Why would he do that?' Dick said.

'*Au revoir, mon ami?*'

'That's it,' said Dick.

Edmund's mouth felt dry and he swallowed hard. He had a sinking feeling in the pit of his stomach and wished William would hurry back soon. 'Did the man give his name?'

'No, I did ask but he changed the subject. I also asked him if he lived in Shunde, but he was evasive about that too. But he was keen to know how long we'd be here and where we planned to travel next.'

Edmund went pale and Dick now noticed the change in his friend's behaviour. 'Stay there,' Edmund said. 'Don't move an inch. I need to find William to tell him about this man.'

Dick was puzzled; why was Edmund so agitated? The man he'd spoken to was slightly odd, but he wasn't sure why William needed to be told about him so urgently. However, he didn't have long to wait before he found out.

*****

William was approaching the gates of the monastery when Edmund almost collided with him. He blurted out his suspicions about Dick's mysterious contact and together they hurried back to the bench where Dick had been asked to remain. The story was repeated to William – and then again when James decided to join them. Dick didn't understand why they all looked so concerned. Finally, he told them about the scar on the man's face; simultaneously they threw up their hands in horror and started to pace around on the veranda.

'Dick, I owe you an apology as well as an explanation,' William said. He took a deep breath before continuing. 'The morning after we stayed with my friend Freddie, there was an incident; I told Edmund and James about my concerns at the time, but I'd completely forgotten that you hadn't been part of that conversation. It was not my intention to exclude you, but the incident upset me gravely and I'm afraid I've been a little preoccupied ever since. Please forgive me.'

Dick had no idea what William was talking about and why everyone was behaving so strangely.

William then proceeded to tell him about the man who had engaged Yong in conversation and the questions he'd asked. Dick recognised them immediately; they were almost identical to the questions put to him only a short while ago. Edmund and James joined in the conversation, telling Dick about the man who'd joined their ship in Cape Town and the possible connection with a number of suspicious episodes, one of which involved the theft of an orchid from Raffles' collection – also in Cape Town.

'And you think this is the same man?'

'From the description you've given and the questions he asked, I think it is extremely likely,' William said.

'Do you think he's dangerous?'

'All I know,' said William, 'is that he makes it his business to acquire rare specimens for people who aren't fussy about their provenance. How he comes by some of the animals and plants that he sells is another matter. That's all my friend in Guangzhou was able to tell me, but I think we all need to be extremely wary from now on.'

'I told him we planned to travel from here to Foshan,' Dick said. 'I'm sorry.'

William considered this information before replying. 'Actually, that piece of information might be extremely useful,' he said.

The eyes of all his companions turned towards him, interested in hearing what he had in mind. He pulled out an old map which had seen better days; it had torn edges and its many folds made it difficult to read. James fetched an additional lamp. William laid out the map on the floor, looked around to make sure they were completely alone, and then invited them to gather round. Dick sat on his haunches and the brothers hitched their breeches to make kneeling more comfortable. Some dry leaves fluttered in the draught and a small grey mouse scurried away to the safety of a pile of logs.

William pointed to a smudge in the middle of the chart. 'This is where we are,' he said. 'And this is the route to Foshan; now, keep your eyes on my finger.' All three edged a little closer. Instead of tracing a line along the river they had followed so far, William's hand moved towards a tributary that flowed eastwards and eventually led to the delta of the Pearl River. Edmund looked up and raised an eyebrow; no-one spoke.

'I think we might find that a more interesting route,' William said.

*****

When they set off the next morning, the air rippled with nervous energy. Neither William nor his three companions spoke as they made their way to the river where Yong and the bearers had already prepared to depart. William spoke to Yong in a hushed voice; the welcome smile disappeared and the colour drained from his cheeks. Together, they scanned the river for any other signs of activity, but no other travellers had yet ventured forth. Dick, with Edmund by his side, had been given the task of checking the wharf. Dick recognised no-one from amongst the scattering of early risers making their own preparations for the day ahead; he nodded to William. There was hardly a sound as Yong pushed the boat away from its mooring. He steered it slowly into the main stream of the river, then turned to the east, in the opposite direction from the one originally planned. The last strands of early morning mist burned off quickly, giving them clear sight of the way ahead.

They had yet to convince themselves that the Frenchman was not watching, making them more alert to their surroundings than usual. This landscape was much flatter than the mist-covered mountains they had grown used to; the waterway meandered slowly in leisurely loops, and at this early hour they encountered few other travellers along the way.

Towards the middle of the morning, they witnessed the rude awakening of a bird whose owner had decided to clean its cage in the river. Later, there was nothing but padi fields, stretching almost as far as they could see on both sides of the water. Occasionally they saw people working in the fields, and once they observed a couple of men pushing single-wheeled carts across a simple bamboo bridge. Low hills now formed the banks of the river, the high mountains affording only a blur on the horizon.

On the first evening after leaving Shunde behind, they stopped at a small village and decided to make it their base for the next few days. It meant sleeping on the boat rather than in a comfortable bed at a nearby monastery, but they could take it in turns to keep watch throughout the night, enabling everyone to get a little rest. Nevertheless, they remained tense and they no longer left the boat for long periods. William and Edmund continued to search for plants, taking either Yong or Dick with them and only one of the bearers. This meant there were always three people left behind to protect the plants gathered from the earlier part of the expedition, and each group had one person amongst them who could identify the Frenchman. When they continued on their journey almost a week later, they had added a red flowering plantain, two small hibiscus shrubs, and an unnamed tree that filled the air with the scent of oranges. William was pleased that Edmund's approach to collecting plants was similar to his own; taking only species that grew in abundance and never more than two examples. Even the plants that grew in profusion in the wild had to be carefully chosen.

*****

Panyu – 18th December 1825

'We've reached the very heart of the Pearl River delta,' William told his guests. 'If we continue by boat, we will be travelling first east, then north and finally west in order to reach Guang-zhou – almost three times as long as if we went due north.'

'But how would that be possible?' James asked. 'The river has no tributaries flowing in that direction.'

'In exactly one week, it will be Christmas. I would like to be home in time for the celebrations,' William said. 'If we travel overland, we will have plenty of time.'

'How do you propose we do that?' Edmund said. 'Surely it's not feasible, is it? We have no means of transporting all the plants other than by boat. We cannot possibly expect the bearers to carry our entire collection.'

'Of course not, but I've already asked Yong to make some enquiries,' William said. 'We can get a good price for the boat; Yong has found some fishermen who are interested in buying it. That will enable us to purchase at least three sturdy carts to carry the plants and all our equipment. We can take it in turns to push them along.'

'But will it be safe? How sure can we be that we've escaped

the interest of the Frenchman? How long would it take before he found out about our change of plan?'

'We couldn't have been more careful when we left Shunde,' William replied. 'I'm positive there was no-one watching us that day. Besides, I think the Frenchman would have already gone ahead, believing he would arrive in Foshan before us.'

'You say this man is known for obtaining rare plants for his so-called customers and his methods are underhand. I don't understand why he is interested in our expedition; we have been very careful not to take anything that is rare or even scarce,' James said. 'Do you think we may have been over-reacting?'

'I cannot answer your questions, James, but do you not think it strange that he has never introduced himself and has spoken only to Yong and Dick, both when they were alone?' William replied. 'From what I've heard, the man lacks all integrity and is often short of funds. He squanders any money he does have in the gambling dens and brothels of Macau and Guangzhou. Foshan has a reputation for attracting people who collect particularly rare plants; maybe he believes that's our reason for going there. He did ask Dick if we planned to visit anywhere along the way, remember. That in itself might be a good enough reason for him to be interested in where we go and what we do. If he went ahead, as I suspect, he would realise there had been a change of plan only when we failed to arrive in Foshan.'

'And by that time, he would have no means of finding out which route we have taken,' Dick said.

'That's correct,' said William. 'All he can do is speculate. This area is criss-crossed by so many streams that I doubt he will waste time trying to find us; better to await our arrival in Guangzhou. However, because we've taken a different route, we may have given him reason to think we do have something to hide, something he'd be interested in acquiring. That's another reason that I propose going by the overland route from now on; he will expect us to arrive in Guangzhou by boat, from the Pearl River delta, I'm sure.'

The conversation had drained them all of energy, but they had to agree William's plan made sense. One by one they rose to their feet and agreed it was time to think of having something to eat. They would be sleeping on the boat again, which meant visiting the nearby hawker stalls and bringing back a collection of dishes for everyone to share. Tonight, that task was given to Yong, James, and Edmund. Communication between the three of them was a mixture of words gleaned from each other's native language and an assortment of visual gestures, but somehow, they managed.

Since arriving in China five weeks ago, James and Edmund had learned a great deal about the characteristics of the cuisine they had grown to love, and the importance of creating a harmonious blend of colours, flavours, and texture. William had explained early on that dishes are created according to the principles of yin and yang – opposite but complementary qualities – dark and light, hot and cold, male and female. Despite understanding the importance of these beliefs, they both struggled when they reached the market, following Yong as he surveyed each of the hawker stalls in turn. Mostly, they were huts erected beside the road, but some balanced precariously in various nooks and crannies along the harbour wall. Wherever they looked, weather-worn men – wearing singlets and baggy trousers held together with pieces of rope – conjured up delicacies from whatever they had in front of them. The air was permeated with a rich aroma of garlic, steaming fish, hot chilli oil and sweat; Edmund felt lightheaded as pangs of hunger gnawed away in his stomach.

'*Chi fan le ma?*' The usual greeting asking if they had eaten already was on the lips of every stallholder. Before making any rash decisions, Yong responded politely, creating a mental note of what was being offered, by whom and at which stall. Edmund and James clutched the tiffin carriers they were holding close to their chests, longing for the moment when they would be full and the three of them ready to return to the boat. A few minutes later, Yong made his way back towards the first groups of stalls they'd seen and beckoned for Edmund and James to follow; they hoped another circuit would not be necessary

Yong pointed to a trio of sea bass; their skin crisp and slightly burnt from a recent encounter with very hot oil. Edmund nodded enthusiastically. His mouth watered as the stallholder scooped the fish into his tiffin carrier, adding a robust sauce made from tomatoes, chillies and kaffir lime leaves. The remaining compartments were subsequently filled with dishes comprising squid ears, mushrooms with green beans and lastly, fried wontons. Into the tiffin carrier held by James went sweet-sour pork and stir-fried water spinach with garlic; steaming rice was piled high into the two remaining sections to provide a final balance to the meal.

*****

Back on the boat, William waited with Dick. They sat in silence, listening to the irregular slap of water against the side of the vessel. Somewhere nearby, crickets tuned up for their regular evening overture and the muted cries of hawkers further along the quay provided a comforting chorus. Little by little, a musky aroma, which Dick associated with smouldering joss sticks, began to tease his nostrils; it was faint at first and then became much stronger; he couldn't understand where it was coming from. He stared into the darkness, but there was no moon and Yong had taken a couple of their lanterns to light the way to the market. Those that remained cast long shadows but provided little illumination.

William too became aware of the aromatic perfume. He got to his feet and peered over the side of the vessel into the inky blackness; Dick quickly joined him. A light autumnal breeze fuelled their nervousness as it lifted hidden clusters of dry leaves, gradually gathering momentum to perform a gavotte. Something else moved; a tall solid shape appeared to be drifting along the quay towards them – no detail was visible but the unmistakable fragrance of incense now filled the air.

'Mr Will'am,' a soft male voice whispered. 'I look for Mr Will'am.'

William grabbed one of the remaining lamps and raised it aloft; below, in the shadows, he could now see a young Buddhist monk, instantly recognisable by his saffron robes and closely shaved head. He studied the slender figure before him and wondered why he was seeking him out.

'I am Mr William,' he said. 'Where are you from? What do you want with me?'

'I come from Shengji Temple,' the young man said, slowly and carefully in English. 'Shi Jingsu send message for you.'

William recognised the name of his old friend, a monk he had met when he first arrived in China nearly ten years ago. He hurried across a rough plank they used to link the boat with the quay to greet the messenger. The young monk thrust a note into William's hand, but before anything further could be said and before William was able to read the contents of the letter, the yellow robes had already been consumed by the darkness and the visitor was gone.

CHAPTER 11
China, December 1825

William had just begun to examine the note when some small points of light he'd seen in the distance changed into large yellow moons held aloft by three young men looking very pleased with themselves. Yong led the way and the Beaumont brothers each clutched a tiffin carrier close to their chest. The fragrance of incense had been replaced with the enticing aromas of pork, fish and spices.

Dick sensed that nothing would be said of the visitor until they had eaten. It had been a long day and everyone was hungry. For the next half-hour, they sat on the deck, filling their bowls first with one dish, then another until all the food was gone. Dick kept his eyes on William who had now moved into the light at the stern to read his letter. Edmund and James sat quietly chatting to each other about the prospect of the overland journey, oblivious of the recent visitor.

'We must have no more secrets or misunderstandings,' William suddenly announced. 'I have some information here that I'd like to share with you all.' He relayed what had happened whilst the others had been at the market and whilst he and Dick had been keeping watch.

'A young monk came to see me from Shengji Temple,' he said. 'He handed me a letter written by an old friend of mine. Shi Jingsu is the spiritual master – a role similar to the abbot of a Christian monastery if you like.'

'How did he know where to find you?' James said, immediately suspicious.

'That, I cannot answer,' William said, 'but Panyu is a small place and the arrival of several Europeans is probably not that common. I'm afraid I had no idea Shi Jingsu was here; the last time I saw him was in Tsing Poo, just to the north of Guangzhou, about three years ago. He has asked me to meet with him tomorrow morning.'

Dick stood up, glancing first at William, then at Edmund. He sensed the brothers mistrusted the motives behind such an invitation. Indeed, Edmund in particular was feeling apprehensive; their earlier conversation about the Frenchman and William's decision to take the overland route now made him question anything out of the ordinary. What motive, he wondered, lay behind the request.

'I can understand why you are wary,' William said, 'but I cannot believe my old friend would be taken in by any trickery. The occasion to meet, if only for a short time, has presented itself and I welcome the opportunity to spend an hour or two with an old man whose knowledge and wisdom I very much respect.'

Edmund leant back in his chair, clasped his hands together and smiled to indicate he sympathised with the sentiment. The others remained quiet, but nodded in approval.

*****

The following morning, William asked Edmund if he would like to join him. It transpired that Shi Jingsu had suggested meeting not at the monastery, but beside the Temple of Lord Bao in a small garden being developed in Zini village on the fringes of Panyu. 'I imagine he's come across some plants that he wants me to identify,' William said.

After breakfast, Yong set off to finalise the purchase of the carts and James and Dick busied themselves with packing up their belongings and the plant collection, while Edmund and William set off through the maze of narrow streets. By mid-morning, they had arrived at their destination. William said they should make their way towards the lake, which turned out to be a series of inter-connected waterways with a number of bridges linking one to the other. Edmund found it difficult to keep up with William as he strode over the Purple Ribbon Bridge in the direction of the temple. He would have liked to stay and examine the multitude of carvings that decorated all nine of the arches.

'They each represent a famous Chinese story,' William said as he turned around to check why Edmund was lagging behind. 'We can look at them afterwards, if you like, but I don't want to keep Shi Jingsu waiting. Stay here, if you prefer; I'll come to find you after I've talked with him.'

'No, no, I'd like to meet him,' Edmund said. 'I've never had the chance to see a Buddhist monk before.'

They found Shi Jingsu sitting in the shadows of the temple courtyard. There was a stillness about this elderly monk, a serenity that radiated far beyond him which Edmund found appealing. As soon as Shi Jingsu recognised William, he rose. His entire body was clad in a simple, long robe with sleeves that fastened at the front in a shade somewhere between brown and grey; hints of the more familiar saffron showed beneath the hem. There was no obvious smile on his lips, but Edmund felt he was smiling from within. The monk placed both hands together with his fingertips almost touching his face; he bowed his head. William mirrored the greeting. Then, he spoke quietly to Shi Jingsu in Cantonese, turning after a few minutes towards Edmund. Shi Jingsu asked a question and William continued, finally waving Edmund forward to join them. Once again, Shi Jingsu placed his hands together and bowed his head.

'I've explained why I've brought you along and told him something about your expedition,' William said. 'He is happy for you to join us, but wants us to walk with him to somewhere more private.'

Shi Jingsu led them past a pond filled with lotus blossoms and into a hall decorated with elegant stone carvings and clay sculptures. At the far end, there was a giant rosewood screen with a statue of Lord Bao standing in front of it. Shi Jingsu hurried through the hall, ignoring all the beautiful decorations; when he reached the screen, he turned to William and whispered something in Cantonese.

'Would you mind remaining here while Shi Jingsu and I talk?' William said. 'I will explain everything later, but stay here and keep a lookout for anything untoward – especially anyone else attempting to come into this part of the garden.'

Edmund nodded, trying to hide his unease. He remembered what William had said about the behaviour of the young monk who delivered Shi Jingsu's message and he remained uncomfortable about the clandestine nature of this meeting. Instead of wandering off to further examine the architecture or to look more closely at some of the plants, he sat on a carved stone seat and pretended to read the notebook he always carried with him. Edmund had the distinct notion that Shi Jingsu was feeling anxious, but he couldn't pinpoint anything specific. Maybe William also felt uneasy; that would equate with being asked to stand guard, but he couldn't imagine what might have happened to upset the tranquillity which encompassed the elderly monk. Maybe he was letting his imagination run away with him.

He looked up from his book occasionally, but the courtyard remained empty. A sudden breeze flipped the pages of Edmund's book; he glanced around to see leaves lifting and twirling in an exotic dance. The birds had stopped singing and a pleasant earthy smell filled his nostrils; a warm blanket of damp air wrapped itself all around him just before the first fat drops of rain arrived, creating dark circles on the dry ground.

Edmund rose and began to move to a more sheltered position when he saw William heading in his direction; he was carrying a small bamboo box.

'We need to hurry,' William said. 'I want to make sure Yong has been able to obtain the carts for our journey northwards.'

'Shouldn't we wait until the rain has eased? We'll get soaked and so will your package.'

William covered the container within the folds of his jacket and gestured for Edmund to follow him. He strode away from the temple, across the bridge, and quickly moved along the meandering path that led to the exit of the garden. Edmund had to hurry to keep up with him; there was no chance to ask more questions, let alone stay to examine the architecture more closely.

The pavement was sticky. His hair fell down in front of his eyes and Edmund almost lost his footing in his haste to keep up with William. The rain eased almost as suddenly as it had arrived. The sun beat down on the sodden path and vapour rose in circles around their feet. The people who had disappeared from the streets during the deluge re-emerged, jostling with one another and continuing as before. When they reached the next corner, the shop owner had just finished unfolding the waterproof covers over his display of rattan furniture and basketware. William stopped in his tracks, asked the vendor a question in Cantonese, and disappeared within the dark recesses of the shop. Moments later, he emerged carrying a splendid bamboo birdcage with what looked like a piece of fabric lying inside it. He nodded to Edmund and they hurried back towards the quay.

The boat that had been their home for the last few weeks had gone. In its place, lined up neatly along the jetty, were three heavily laden handcarts. Everything had been packed up during the morning and the rest of the party was ready to depart. William sent Yong and the two bearers to fetch some food from the hawker stalls, and while they were away, he made the pretence of checking the wagons. By the time they started to move, he was no longer clutching his coat close to his body. The small box had disappeared and the birdcage had been safely stowed away.

*****

By the end of the afternoon, they had covered about six miles, and had reached a village to the north of Panyu; they were well along the road that would eventually lead them to Samshan on the banks of the Pearl River. At dusk, they arrived at a small farm, where they were made welcome. When the farmer discovered they were making their way overland to Guangzhou, he insisted they spend the night in one of his empty barns; he told them that he had very few visitors and would be glad of their company. They shared the food they had brought with them and their host produced copious amounts of rice wine.

The farmer spoke only Cantonese, so most of the conversation was conducted with Yong and the bearers; William occasionally joining in. Eventually, he excused himself, saying that he needed to make plans for the following day. He made his way towards the carts, which had been brought into the barn in case of rain. He nodded to Edmund, indicating that he should follow.

'What happened between you and Shi Jingsu? You've been on edge ever since you emerged from the temple. I presume you have something hidden in that bamboo box, but why did you suddenly decide to purchase a birdcage – we don't have any birds!'

'Keep your voice low,' William said. 'What I have to tell you must remain with as few people as possible.'

'Not even my brother – or Dick? We said we'd tell each other everything after that occasion when Dick met the Frenchman. Is that it? Has this got something to do with the Frenchman?'

William walked around to the far side of the handcarts, seeming to check the straps that held everything together. When he reached the cart that he'd spent most of the afternoon pushing himself, he loosened one of the ties and pulled out the bamboo box. Edmund edged closer. The light was poor, but William didn't want to attract attention by fetching one of the lamps. He slowly lifted the lid of the box and both men peered inside.

'What am I looking at?' Edmund said. All he could distinguish was a few slender, arching leaves clustering around a central stem. 'And what is that delicate perfume?'

'It's that fragrance we need to be most careful about,' William said. 'It will be scarcely noticeable in the morning, but its intensity increases throughout the day and as you have noticed it is now at its most pervasive.'

'You still haven't told me what it is and why all the secrecy.'

'It is a very rare orchid. Shi Jingsu found several of these plants in the wild many years ago. He has been tending them and propagating them in his garden ever since, but a few months ago they were attacked by some form of pest and only two remain. Shi Jingsu is old and his health is not good. When he discovered I'd arrived in Panyu, he decided to send for me. He asked me to take one of the remaining plants to ensure its survival. I made a promise that I would do so.'

'I see, but surely keeping it inside a box will do it no good?'

'That is why I purchased the birdcage; there is a cover which is used to encourage birds to sleep. Anyone who sees the cage will assume we have a feathered companion who is taking a snooze, but the orchid will at least have some air circulating around it and hopefully we'll be back in Guangzhou within the week.'

'And until we reach your home, you would prefer I didn't mention this to either James or Dick?'

'Actually, no. You can share the information with your brother when you are walking together tomorrow, but be sure to explain the need for secrecy. This is exactly the sort of specimen the Frenchman would be interested in, and I don't want the bearers to know anything about it. However, I would like you to wake Dick as soon as it is light in the morning. The plant has one remaining flower and whilst I'm confident the plant will survive the next few days; it's possible that being bumped along country roads will not suit such a delicate bloom. I would like Dick to draw it as soon as possible.'

*****

Just after dawn, Edmund scrambled into his breeches and searched around for the shirt he'd abandoned the previous evening. He gave it a good shake to make sure no insects or field mice had taken up residence during the night, and then pulled it over his head. Dick was curled up on a pile of straw next to the wall of the barn and was still fast asleep. Edmund gave him a gentle nudge, but he simply turned over and carried on with whatever dream he was having. Edmund knelt down beside him, anxious not to disturb James or any of the others. He shook Dick more forcefully this time, but had his hand ready to cover his friend's mouth should he cry out in alarm.

Dick turned back again and opened his eyes. 'What time is it? Have I overslept?' he asked when he saw Edmund kneeling at his side.

'Get your clothes on and follow me,' Edmund whispered.

'William has something he needs you to draw, but it's a secret. Try not to make any noise, the others are still sleeping and we don't want to disturb them.'

Dick stepped out of his sarong and donned his everyday clothes as if he was a clockwork toy. When he was dressed, Edmund said, 'Don't forget your sketch pad and pencils.'

By now, Dick's curiosity had been aroused. He followed Edmund to the other end of the barn; he felt both hesitant and curious all at the same time. What could William possibly want him to draw at this early hour – and why all the mystery?

They found William gently snoring, with his back propped against the wheel of one of the wagons; he had evidently been there all night. As Edmund bent down to rouse him, William woke with a start. Once his eyes had become accustomed to the light, he rose to his feet and began to tell Dick everything that he'd told Edmund the night before. William then explained what he wanted done, and Dick nodded in agreement.

Shafts of sunlight had already begun to enter that end of the barn when the orchid was carefully lifted from the bamboo box and placed in a position from which Dick could capture every detail. Its one remaining flower was small and white. It had five long, slender petals surrounding a sixth one, which resembled a small measuring spoon with a pointed tip. He examined it carefully before making the first mark on the paper. He began to outline the shapes. Slowly, the lines changed from mere strokes on the page to a perfect replica of the plant – even the distinctive band of spots on the lip disc was clear. Behind the flower, he etched in the stems and the leaves; added more shading and the sketch was complete. He made a note of the colours at each part of the plant – maroon spots on the lip, ochre tones for the stamens and different shades of green for the leaves and stem. All those details could be added later.

'Marvellous,' William said, 'simply marvellous.'

Edmund and Dick helped William prepare the bamboo cage, making a deep bed of moss on the base. The orchid was lifted into its new home and surrounded with more moss to keep it secure. Finally, William added some stones before covering the cage with a fabric hood – the material that Edmund had observed inside the birdcage when it was purchased.

'Why the stones?' Dick asked in a hushed tone.

'The weight will make it more stable as we travel,' William said, 'and if anyone else picks it up they might even be led to believe there is a bird inside.'

Edmund smiled to himself. He thought such a notion was highly unlikely but was happy to go along with the idea in order to humour their friend.

CHAPTER 12
China, December 1825

During the course of the next two days, William's party crossed numerous small rivers and meandering streams; each stretch of water would eventually join together and form part of the mighty Pearl River delta. The route they had chosen to take was hard work, but it was much shorter than continuing along a waterway that would eventually join the delta further downstream; it took them across uneven countryside, along rough tracks and across rickety bridges. All seven men took it in turn to push the handcarts, but William was never far away from the one that carried the birdcage. Each evening, when he was sure no-one was looking, he removed the cover to check on the precious plant and give it a chance to enjoy the last hours of daylight.

The rice paddies were much the same as those they had seen at the beginning of their journey, but now they had become commonplace and no longer held any fascination for the brothers.

Tired and footsore, the party at last reached Samshan, from where they could take a ferry across the river. William paid the two bearers, who were keen to return to their village, and Yong went to negotiate a passage with one of the ferry-boat owners. It took a while for him to find someone who was willing to take three heavily laden carts plus five men, but at last he found someone who was happy to accommodate them.

It was a man who had brought several passengers over from Guangzhou earlier in the day and was only too pleased to find someone willing to pay him for the return crossing.

Dick felt exhilarated by the many different types of craft that filled the waterway; it reminded him of the vast array of vessels he often watched coming and going back home in Singapore. For a moment, he felt lonely amongst all this activity; his stomach fluttered and his throat was dry. Homesickness was something he'd never experienced before. Edmund and his brother watched the spectacle that surrounded them, feeling exhausted by all the activity. Fatigue outweighed their usual enthusiasm; all they wanted to do was reach the opposite shore.

*****

It was only a short journey from the quay to William's house, but they met several people along the way who wanted to engage them in conversation. William had been away for well over six weeks and he had been missed. He introduced his companions and gave his friends a brief outline of the journey they had undertaken together, then excused himself so that they could reach the house before it grew dark.

Chi Yu, who took care of the house when William was away on his travels and attended to him when he was at home, shuffled forward at great speed. He kept his hands clasped beneath the ample sleeves of his plain blue jacket as he bowed to each of them in turn. His hair was pulled back into the usual *queue*, allowing the soft, yellow light from the lamp he now held aloft to produce a halo around his broad forehead.

'Rel-cum, rel-cum,' he said. He fetched additional lamps to provide enough light to unload the carts, then he scurried away to make ready accommodation for the visitors. Everyone was too tired to care much about eating, but Chi Yu insisted they tasted a bowl of his special soup. He told them he always had some stock prepared so that he could quickly produce such a delicacy; his family had brought him up to believe it was important always to make every visitor feel welcome.

*****

The following morning, William rose early to bid farewell to Yong who was anxious to get back to his family. Then, he went with Chi Yu to the market to stock up on food supplies; tomorrow they would celebrate the Christmas festival quietly, but nevertheless, he purchased additional items, including several bottles of rice wine and a locally made version of brandy. When they returned to the house, the others had emerged from their slumbers, washed, put on fresh clothes, and were ready for breakfast.

They spent the rest of that day sorting out everything they had unpacked the previous evening. The plants had to be properly labelled and categorised. Edmund and James visited the harbour master to ascertain the best method of getting them back to England safely. The captain of the ship they chose needed to be trustworthy as well as have a good reputation in seamanship. He would, after all, be in sole charge of the precious specimens until they reached the English port. They were advised to return in three days, when the harbour master should be able to provide them with two or three alternatives to meet their needs.

Meanwhile, Dick sorted out the numerous sketches he'd made, ensuring that each one was labelled correctly, and William found a new home for Shi Jingsu's precious orchid.

There was no longer any significant Christian congregation in Guangzhou, so Christmas came and went without any fuss. As sons of a clergyman, James and Edmund found this slightly strange, but Dick had never lived anywhere that offered any form of regular worship so had no particular expectations. However, this was the time of year when he missed Raffles the most, remembering some of the visitors who had arrived around this season and the meals they had all shared. This year, it was his turn to be the visitor, along with Edmund and James. The last few weeks had been exhausting, so once the pangs of nostalgia had subsided, he was content to spend the day quietly with his new friends.

*****

On the evening of December 27th, William rose from the dinner table to announce that he would be taking them all on a visit to the famous Fa-tee Nursery the following day. They would need to make an early start. It was something that Edmund had been looking forward to enormously, but he knew William had reservations about the place because it attracted dubious traders whose business conduct was often suspect.

The four men left the house just after first light. William gave clear instructions to Chi Yu, telling him not to admit anyone into the courtyard whilst he was away from the house. They walked in silence, with only the regular click of their boots on cobblestones for company.

At the end of Old China Street, they turned the corner to find themselves amongst coolies trotting along, balancing pots of water on their shoulders and market traders already occupied with the business of the day. Soon, many of the stall-holders would be calling out to announce what delicacies they had to offer. Already, mouth-watering aromas wafted towards William and his friends, filling their nostrils and making their stomachs rumble. When they reached the quay, groups of fishermen and the men who would later on compete with each other for customers to hire their boats had already been served. But for the moment, their interest was concentrated solely upon steaming bowls of *congee*, noodle dishes, soups and dumplings. Dick and the two brothers looked at William longingly; he smiled and nodded his assent.

'You didn't think I'd overlook breakfast, did you?' he said. 'Come, the old woman in the floral blouse at the stall over there serves particularly good *congee*.'

During their time together, none of them had completely adjusted to the Chinese eating pattern – a light breakfast, with the main meals at lunchtime and in the evening. Dick, Edmund and James – even William – all felt the need for something substantial to start the day, but then they often ate very little until they'd returned to their base in the evening. Meanwhile, Yong and the two bearers always tucked into various snacks and the sizeable portions of food they carried with them, folded into banana leaves and the like.

Today, however, there was no need for increased energy, so Dick, James and Edmund enjoyed tasting the local rice porridge for the first time.

'It's quite different from what I was expecting,' Edmund said. 'I thought it might be a soupy version of chicken rice, but I can definitely taste ginger and garlic.'

'There are mushrooms too,' James added. 'I really like it.'

'It can be very bland,' Dick added. 'Some of the bowls I've tasted in Singapore are made with water and the result isn't very exciting, but when it's made with stock – it can be meat or vegetables – that's when it becomes tasty. The rice soaks up the flavours, you see, and then you can add other toppings, anything you like really.'

When they had almost finished, William handed each of them a piece of fried dough about the size of a fat English sausage. 'It's called *youtiao*,' he said. 'You use it to mop up the last juices.'

While the three of them wiped their bowls clean, William

strolled further along the quay to find a boat that would take them to the famous garden.

*****

It was a three-mile journey up river to the Fa-tee nursery. The waterway was busy with all kinds of vessels; some carrying passengers across to the island, some taking goods and passengers to Whampoa. That was the place where they would be transferred to the larger, ocean-going vessels whose size prevented them from coming further upstream. Harsh voices of people in a hurry competed with the noise of oars squeaking in their rowlocks and waves crashing against wood on vessels when they suddenly changed direction. Gradually, the familiar stench – a mixture of seaweed and detritus – replaced the comforting aromas of food as they moved further and further away from the wharf.

William pointed out some of the well-known landmarks. He told them about the people who lived all their lives on the boats that clustered, in an unremarkable smudge, along the riverbank. Dick took advantage of this time to sketch the scene before him. He had it in mind to make several drawings whilst he was here; he wanted to create a souvenir that he could present to Chin Ming and Wing Yee when he returned to Singapore. James and Edmund bombarded William with questions about the old city, its many gates and the graves they could see on the otherwise bare northern hills.

When they reached their destination, Dick was still sketching furiously, trying to capture the key features of the vast panorama. He was pleased with the outline, but he still needed to fill in the detail. He committed to memory images of colourful dragons and mystical beasts that adorned some of the buildings, fishermen mending their nets and small children playing along the shoreline, so that he could come back to the drawing and finish it later. He hung back once the boat was tied up, letting Edmund and James leap ahead, allowing him to continue scribbling notes to himself in the margin.

'So many Europeans,' James said. 'They look so out of place, pacing about in their long, black jackets, stiff collars and tight waistcoats.'

'Maybe we look strange to the locals too,' Edmund said.

'The only thing you have in common with these people,' William replied, 'is your height and the colour of your skin. Look at the way they strut around, shouting in English, French or Dutch to make themselves understood. They compete to outbid each other in order to obtain the most exotic plants, and think the louder they bellow and the more commotion they make, the more successful they will be.'

'I had no idea we would see so many of them here,' James continued.

'I'm afraid the fame of these gardens has grown, and it's become customary for western traders and officers of the East India Company to visit the nursery whilst they're in Guangzhou,' William said. 'Most of the sea captains like to buy plants from one of the many nurseries in Guangzhou before they return to England. Some take a boat across to Honam Island in the estuary to buy anything considered to be exotic, and some are invited by one of the wealthy Hong merchants to places on the outskirts of town, but those people are interested only in making a huge profit from the animals and plants they gather together. Their samples are rarely packed well enough to endure the long haul back to England and many have no chance of surviving the journey.'

'I suppose that's why the specimens that do make it back to England are sold at such exorbitant prices,' James said. 'I've heard of wealthy landowners who like to boast of their exotic collections. Unfortunately, it's becoming something of a status symbol.'

'Well, rest assured,' Edmund said, looking straight at William, 'I've never been interested in getting involved in anything like that. As you know, I simply want a few samples so that they can be propagated and studied.'

William slapped Edmund gently on his shoulders. 'I know, I know,' he said, 'and that's why I've been glad to be of assistance.'

'Fa-tee's reputation is certainly widespread,' Edmund said. 'I'd even heard about the nursery before we left England. When I visited Kew, everyone I met seemed to be talking about this place. I had no appreciation of its size, of course, let alone the vast array of flowers we would see here.'

'Is it always like this?' Dick asked.

'The lunar new year will be celebrated in just over a month's time; there are always more flowers available during the period leading up to the festivities, but as you've already realised, this place is popular and therefore it is permanently well-stocked.'

William went on to tell them that Fa-tee delivered cut flowers, rented out potted flowers for celebrations and sold seeds and plants of various kinds. They spent the morning wandering through displays of chrysanthemums, orchids, tree peonies, dwarf trees, citrus and other fruit trees. They saw camellias, azaleas, and numerous ornamental potted plants that they didn't recognise. They watched as some of the other European visitors handed over vast sums for plants such as the ink orchid, which William assured them was not at all uncommon.

'All they can think about is the profit they'll make when they sell those plants back in England,' he told Edmund. 'But if any of the items you've seen purchased today is to stand a chance of surviving the journey, packing them correctly is absolutely essential. That is why we must be very thorough and pack your collection carefully. Then we need to choose a ship's captain who can be trusted.'

By the end of the morning, Edmund had purchased a small selection of seeds, but he believed the plants they had selected with such care during their travels would offer a far better opportunity for study than the cultivated varieties available here, and that was all he cared about.

As they prepared to leave, Dick turned to a fresh page of his sketchbook, hastily trying to capture some details from the garden to add to his earlier drawings of the riverbank. His eye fell upon some peonies and he remembered seeing embroidered versions of these flowers on dresses often worn by Chin Ming and Wing Yee. Maybe he could include one or two of these images in the painting he intended to produce for them.

William and the two brothers had already headed off towards the wharf when Dick froze in his tracks; once again he was being observed. He recognised the man standing straight across from where he stood, but it seemed like an eternity for his brain to catch up with his vision. His throat became parched and he was unable to utter even the smallest of sounds. He flipped the sketchpad closed, thrust his pencils into his pocket and hurried after the others. When he reached them, they had already boarded the ferry that would take them back to the centre of town.

'Whatever's the matter?' James asked. 'You look as if you've seen a ghost.'

'The Frenchman,' Dick said. 'I've just seen the Frenchman; he was looking straight at me. I don't know how long he'd been there. He didn't say anything, but he wore a very strange expression and made no attempt to duck out of sight.'

'It was inevitable that he would turn up again,' William said. 'It wouldn't at all surprise me if he didn't come straight back to Guangzhou once he realised we had changed our plans.'

The vessel they had chosen for their return journey was

already moving into the river, but nevertheless, William now lowered his voice. 'The Frenchman has no knowledge of the gift we received from Shi Jingsu,' he said, 'and I see no way of his finding out about it. If he chances to engage any of us in conversation at a future date, we just need to make sure we reveal nothing about the meeting at the Temple of Lord Bao, nor the gift I received. This evening, we should agree what to tell him about our journey from Shunde to Panyu and from Panyu to Guangzhou, should such an occasion ever arise.'

CHAPTER 13
December 1825

Dick had almost forgotten about the young Chinese artist George Chinnery had suggested he met once they reached Guangzhou. He came across the address, scribbled on the back of a drawing, when he decided to look back at the early sketches he'd made in Macao. He handed it to William, asking him for directions to the studio.

'I'd be glad to show you the way,' William said. 'You might need someone to translate for you. I'm not sure whether Lam Qua speaks English.'

So, it was agreed that William would accompany Dick, whilst Edmund and James made their way to the harbour master's office the following morning to enquire about any ships due to depart for England within the next week or two.

*****

It was useful to have William make the introductions. Lam Qua had a partial English vocabulary, but Dick knew even less Cantonese. Initially, it was the mention of George Chinnery's name that made it possible for the two young men to invest in each other's time. Dick pulled one of his sketchbooks from his bag and slowly turned the pages to reveal the full extent of his talent. It provided the perfect catalyst for Lam Qua's admiration. Neither of them noticed when William quietly withdrew from the studio, leaving them to their own devices.

'You paint portrait in Nanyang?'

Dick remembered this word, often used to describe Singapore by people who had migrated there from China, but he hadn't come across it for some time. 'Yes,' he said. 'Nanyang – the southern seas; now, we call our island Singapore.'

'Sin-ga-pore,' Lam Qua repeated slowly.

Dick smiled. 'I use pen and ink; most of my paintings are watercolours.' He looked around to find some object that might help with his explanation. A large jug of water was all he could find, but as soon as he pointed to its contents, Lam Qua understood.

'You no use oil paint?'

'Not yet, but I would like to learn. Mr Chinnery showed me his paintings. He spoke about you. He said you might teach me.'

'Come, come,' Lam Qua said.

It seemed that no more negotiation was necessary. Lam Qua led the way into the adjoining room, where he asked Dick to sit at a large table stained with a miscellany of different hues, all reminders of previous work.

Dick's eyes lit up. It felt as if he'd been plunged into the middle of Aladdin's cave. He was surrounded by a treasure trove of different colours, shapes and subject matter. Lam Qua handed him a brush and led him to another table, back in the main studio. He placed a small frame in front of Dick and dropped a small quantity of each colour – red, blue and yellow onto the canvas. 'You play with paint,' he said. 'See what colour you make.'

Dick was accustomed to the magic of mixing watercolours together, but the way oils interacted with each other was entirely different. Initially, he found the heady new aromas that filled the studio overwhelming and was glad the place was well ventilated, but by the end of the day he hardly noticed it.

He experimented with new techniques; making the colours warm or cool, building up from only one colour and discovering its many shades by adding black, or creating various tints by adding white. With each new discovery, he became more and more delighted.

Lam Qua beamed. It gave him great pleasure to work with someone as enthusiastic as Dick. 'You come back tomorrow, me show you new things,' he said.

*****

It took two more visits to the docks during the course of that day for Edmund and his brother to track down the harbour master. He told them about two possibilities; one involved a Company vessel anchored at Whampoa and the other meant waiting another week or so for the next ship to arrive.

Witnessing the cavalier attitude shown by many of the merchants making their purchases at the Fa-tee nursery had caused Edmund to feel nervous. How could he ever be sure that a ship's captain would guard his precious plants well enough and give them the best possible chance of surviving the long journey back to England? When he shared his concern with his brother, James suggested they abandon their plans to visit Sumatra and travel back to England with the specimens themselves. They continued to struggle with this dilemma until William returned to the house.

'Where's Dick?' Edmund asked. He was worried about telling their young friend they might not be venturing as far as Sumatra after all. He felt sure the thought of revisiting the place had been an important factor in persuading him to join their expedition. Now, they might have to break their promise.

'I left him with the Chinese painter,' William said. 'They seem to be able to understand each other with a mixture of broken English, many hand gestures and much pointing. He was having his first instruction in the use of oils when I left and I think he may be there for some time.'

Edmund began to voice his concerns about the safety of his collection and the possibility of changing their plans.

'It would be a great pity to miss the opportunity of visiting Sumatra,' William said, 'and I might be able to help with your predicament.'

'What do you have in mind?'

'When I left Dick, I wandered down to the quay, thinking you might still be there. I bumped into an old friend of mine, a fellow who has been working in Fujian. He is due to return to England on leave, but none of the ships departing from his base in Amoy are going further than Calcutta; he came here hoping to find a passage on one of the Indiamen.'

Edmund's shoulders dropped. He rubbed the back of his neck and closed his eyes. He still had no idea what William had in mind.

'My friend has secured a berth on the *Repulse*, which leaves in two days. If we can arrange with the captain to take your collection on board, I'm sure my friend would be happy to keep an eye on them for you. He'll be arriving here shortly – I've offered him a bed for the next two nights – so you'll be able to make up your own mind about him. His name is Charles Sumner.'

Mr Sumner arrived at dusk. In the fading light, he reminded Edmund of the poet, William Wordsworth. They had met when he'd returned home from Oxford to find his father entertaining a whole group of literary figures, including Mr Wordsworth. Charles Sumner stood with his arms folded, listening to something James was saying and nodding in agreement now and again. He wore a long, dark coat over an even darker waistcoat and his cravat was neatly tied. The white curls which cascaded down over his collar, like an Elizabethan ruff, more than made up for the lack of hair on top of his head.

During the course of the evening, Edmund warmed to the older man. He too had taken an interest in the local flora during the years he had spent in this part of China. He was extremely knowledgeable and understood the challenge he would be undertaking, but it was one he was more than happy to accept.

'As long as there is space available on the *Repulse* and the captain has no concerns, I would be delighted to care for your plants during the voyage back to England,' Sumner said.

Just then, Dick came hurrying through the door. His cheeks were flushed and his eyes shone like black sapphires. Everyone turned round to gaze at him.

'I thought you'd got lost,' William said. 'I was just about to send out a search party.'

Dick's toes curled up in his sandals and he thrust his hands into his pockets. 'I'm sor...,' he gulped. He continued to stutter in his desire to communicate quickly and overcome his awkwardness about being late.

'There's no problem,' William said, 'just as long as you are safe. Come, let me introduce you to my friend Charles; he'll be staying with us until his ship leaves in a couple of days' time.'

The remainder of the evening was spent exchanging news, ideas, and plans for the future. Dick was brought up to date about the possibility of Charles Sumner taking charge of Edmund's precious collection and Dick told them all about Lam Qua, his abilities as an artist and how he'd invited Dick back to his studio so that he could continue teaching him the techniques of oil painting.

*****

Charles took Edmund and James to the quay as soon as breakfast was over. If the ship's captain agreed to take the plants, there would only be a short time in which to pack the collection securely and then transfer the various containers to the ship. The three men jumped into the first available lighter and held tight as the small craft threaded its way between the frenzied confusion of river traffic that swarmed all around the quay. The familiar pungent tang of seaweed and the usual odour of decay swirled all around them.

Eventually, a tapestry of masts came into sight. Charles pointed to a ship that was anchored slightly apart from the others.

'What a beauty,' James said as the lighter turned towards it.

'These ships were built to carry as much cargo as possible, rather than for speed,' Charles said. 'Every trading nation in Europe uses them,' he continued, 'but as you know, they now take passengers as well as goods; some have more space than others.'

The lighter pulled alongside the vessel and Charles asked permission to come aboard. An hour later, they had enjoyed a tour of the ship, inspected the best places to lash down the barrels in which the plants would travel, and had agreed on a transportation fee with the captain. Before they knew it, they were on their way back to the quay, eager to spend the rest of the day making the collection ready for the voyage.

*****

Dick left William's house at the same time as his friends, but turned in the opposite direction when they reached Old China Street. He ran the last few yards and arrived at the studio almost out of breath. Lam Qua looked up and beamed. He pointed to two canvases, each stretched across a small frame.

'This ready for you,' he said pointing to the one on the left. 'This one, you make ready.'

'What do you want me to do?' Dick said.

Lam Qua picked up a pot containing rabbit skin glue and

a large, flat brush. He demonstrated the technique required, applying the paste in a thin layer across the top of the canvas, then handed it to Dick. 'Seal canvas,' he said, 'pro-tect; make ready for paint.'

Once Dick had finished with the rabbit glue, Lam Qua handed him the other canvas and led him to a table which held pots of paint and a bamboo container displaying brushes of various sizes, shapes, and textures. The glue had an odour which reminded him of meat bones being slowly heated to make soup, but the pungent tang given off from the paints almost took his breath away. He began, once again, by mixing different combinations of colours together; then he became more ambitious and set off on a journey of discovery, using each of the techniques Lam Qua showed him and enhancing them with his own ideas.

He returned to William's house at the end of the day exhausted, but bursting with the excitement of his new abilities. He learned other skills during the next few days and he experimented with a still life in monochrome. It was not until he embarked upon a small painting of the flowers in Lam Qua's garden, however, that he realised if he was to improve, he would need to spend more time in Guangzhou.

*****

On the last day of 1825, the two Beaumont brothers returned to the quay. The lighterman who had rowed them out to the *Repulse* the previous day hailed them as soon as they arrived. They spent the best part of the day – and several journeys back and forth – transferring the barrels, which now held the specimens they had carefully collected from the banks of the rivers and the mountain ranges between Macao and Guangzhou. The sun was already losing its heat when everything was safely on board and they travelled to the ship for one last time. They had insisted on helping Charles with his luggage and he was glad enough of their company. The *Repulse* was due to sail on the next tide.

When they returned to the quay, the harbour master was waiting for them. He was aware that the plant collection had been dealt with and he had news of a boat to take them to Sumatra. 'There's a local trader who arrived here from Palembang this morning. We don't get many at this time of year. They usually arrive around October and don't come back again until the end of April. He's returning in three days' time. I could introduce you to him if you don't mind roughing it.'

'Would there be room for three of us?' Edmund asked.

'I don't see why not, it's a fair-sized *lancha*. Come back and see me tomorrow if you're interested and I'll make the introductions.'

Neither James nor Edmund had heard the word lancha before, but they imagined it was a vessel similar to the dhows used by the traders who came to Asia from Arabia. They told the harbour master they would discuss his offer and return to let him know their decision in the morning.

*****

Lam Qua had been delighted to discover that Dick's interest in learning the skills of painting in oils was not a passing fancy. He enjoyed handing on some of the skills he had been taught by George Chinnery and he made it clear that he hoped Dick would indeed be able to stay a little longer in China.

Dick hummed to himself all the way back to William's house that afternoon. By the time he crossed the courtyard, he was grinning from ear to ear. He bounced from one foot to the other, leaping across the flagstones, avoiding the lines made by their outer edges so as to hold on to his good fortune. It was only when he realised William was observing him that he came down to earth. He needed to ask the older man a favour.

'You've obviously had a good day,' William said.

'I'm learning so much. I never realised how exciting working in oils would be; even mixing the colours and making new ones is so different to using watercolours. I've just started my first piece, in different shades of green. I've already sketched in some of the flowers in Lam Qua's garden, so they can be painted later.'

'Later?' William said. 'You know Edmund and James are planning to leave here soon? Now their collection is on its way to England. I think they'll be anxious to continue with their plan to travel to Sumatra.'

Dick stood very still. He took a deep breath. The sparkle had gone from his eyes and he looked at William longingly. 'How would you feel ...' He bit his lip and cleared his throat before continuing. 'Would I ... could I, possibly? I was wondering if ... ?'

'You'd like to stay a little longer in Guangzhou to continue your painting lessons and want to know if you can stay on in my house,' William said in a matter-of-fact manner.

Dick slowly raised his eyes, hoping that William would agree. He nodded his head.

'Of course you can stay,' William said. 'Stay as long as you like. I'll be glad of your company. I'm not sure what young Edmund will say, of course. You'd better think of what you are going to tell him.'

*****

'But I don't understand,' Edmund said, collapsing into the nearest chair. 'I thought it was the idea of going to Sumatra that persuaded you to join us in the first place.'

Dick paced up and down; he took a deep breath and swallowed hard. What Edmund said was correct. 'It's just that ...'

He could feel his face warming as he struggled to find the right words.

Edmund looked away. He'd been so sure that Dick had enjoyed their time together. Whenever he'd watched him sketching, looking at the new landscapes, the brilliant colours, the shapes of the mountains, he'd been convinced that his new friend had been as enthralled with their adventure as he was himself.

Dick continued to pace up and down in front of him. 'I don't want to let you down,' he managed to say, 'but this is something I need to do.'

He could tell from the expression on Edmund's face that the Englishman hadn't the slightest idea what he was talking about. 'It's similar to the feeling I had when Raffles thought I would be returning to England with him.'

Edmund frowned. He didn't see the connection. He waited for Dick to continue.

'I've been able to establish myself as an artist in Singapore, but I've only been able to use watercolours. As the Settlement grows and the merchant's wealth increases, they are likely to want something new. Lam Qua is not much older than me, but he's been painting in oils for ages; Mr Chinnery taught him – and now Lam Qua wants to teach me. But if I'm going to be any good at it, I need to practise and the only way that can happen is to stay here a while longer. I want to develop as many skills as possible.'

Edmund sighed. 'I see,' he said.

'We've become good friends, Edmund, but you will be returning to England. My life is in Singapore and I need to be the best artist I possibly can; Raffles would want that for me, too.'

Edmund remained silent; it was all too much to take in. When he raised his head, the first thing he saw was the look of anticipation on Dick's face. 'Selfishly, I'd much prefer it if you came with us,' he said, 'but of course you must take this opportunity. You are an extremely talented artist, Dick. I can only wish you well.'

And so it was agreed. Dick would stay in Guangzhou and the brothers would proceed to Sumatra. They would meet up again in Singapore in two months' time.

CHAPTER 14
Guangzhou, 3rd January 1826

Dick could still feel the imprint of Edmund's firm handshake against his palm, but the lighter transporting the two brothers was already fading into the golden glow of late afternoon. He continued to stare after the small craft until William gently squeezed his shoulder and indicated that they should make a move. He sighed. He'd only known the brothers for a few months and yet their departure made him feel forlorn. It was his own decision to remain in Guangzhou for a while, to forgo the adventure that a return visit to Sumatra might hold. It was he alone who had decided the opportunity to improve his artistic skills was more important than continuing on the journey he could have shared with his new friends. And yet ...?

As if he knew what was going on in the young man's head, William remained quiet as they began to make their way. Their progress was slow at first, weaving between the coils of rope and overflowing baskets of produce that filled the quay, but when they reached Old China Street, they found it quite empty apart from the tiny coffee shop on the corner.

'Let me buy us a drink – and a couple of those banana fritters that you like so much,' William said.

They sat across from each other, on a couple of cane chairs that had seen better days, at the round, marble-topped table. William stretched his long legs to one side of the decorative wrought iron base, hoping that no-one would trip over him.

Dick sat clutching his knees, with his eyes firmly fixed on the black, irregular marks that made such interesting shapes within the marble. An old man in the familiar singlet and shorts shuffled towards them, placing thick, white cups decorated with dark green foliage in front of them. Some of the steaming hot liquid had spilled, and the grease from the banana fritters moved in glistening contours around the large, matching saucers.Dick looked up. He welcomed the diversion. He appreciated the fact that William was happy for him to stay in his house for the remainder of his time in the city. 'I've just realised,' he said, 'this is only the second time in my whole life that I've made a major decision about my own destiny.'

'No wonder you're feeling a bit overwhelmed,' William said. 'When was the first time? Did you feel the same way then?'

'It was a few months before Raffles left Singapore. He asked me what I'd miss most about the place and I had to tell him that I wanted to stay there rather than accompany him back to England.'

'That must have taken quite a lot of courage.'

'He made it easy. He was always a good listener – and although I knew he was disappointed, he genuinely wanted me to be happy; he never demanded anything from me. That's when I started to call him Raffles, as everyone else does, rather than Uncle, which suddenly seemed childish.'

'And how did you feel once you'd made that decision?'

Dick thought carefully before giving an answer. 'For a while, I felt guilty; I thought I was letting him down. He'd always been good to me and I still think he was hoping I would change my mind, but he never said anything. In fact, it was Raffles who suggested I might move into Mr Johnston's house after he and Sophia left.'

The expression on William's face, as he looked at Dick, was one of amusement.

'What's the matter? What is so funny?'

'It seems to me,' William said, 'there is a great deal of similarity between that occasion and the one you now find yourself in. You are feeling uneasy about staying here instead of continuing your travels with Edmund, because you feel you're letting him down.'

'Had the two of you not met in Singapore, or had you not got on well together, he would have come here as originally planned and maybe found a local artist to sketch some of the plants we came across. He would then have continued to Sumatra – as intended, with only his brother. He's been lucky to have someone with your talents for the major part of his expedition. It's good that you've become friends, of course, but don't let that get in the way of you forging your own path. Eventually, the brothers will return to England and you will stay in Singapore.'

'That's how I tried to explain it to him – I think he understands – and having this opportunity is important to me. Lam Qua is a good teacher. I know I'm lucky to have found him.'

*****

For the next few weeks, Dick spent his time perfecting the techniques involved in oil painting. He built upon the skills he already possessed and marvelled at the different effects he could conjure up with these new materials. He felt more in control than when he painted in watercolours; he got to love the smell of the paint, the textures he could build and the range of colours that were so much richer than the delicate palette he was used to. Above all, he enjoyed the fact that he could so easily change his mind if he wanted to and paint over any idea that proved to be unsatisfactory.

*****

At the beginning of February, Lam Qua told Dick that he would be travelling to Macau to spend the Lunar New Year with family. By this time, Dick had produced several small pieces, and his increased confidence had inspired him to embark upon a landscape of Guangzhou. He told Lam Qua that it was something he wanted to take back home to his friends – a memento of the city in which they had both lived before coming to Singapore.

'You make many sketch of town,' Lam Qua told him, 'You use now for special picture. Can do while Lam Qua in Macau.' He gave Dick a key to the studio and told him that he was happy for him to continue to use the space whilst he was away.

By the eve of the festival, when everyone in the city was busy cleaning, cooking and decorating their homes, Dick had completed a painting of Guangzhou from the waterfront – showing the Flower Pagoda and the walls of the old town. He stood back, scrutinising his effort. The perspective was good. The colours perfectly matched the stone, the foliage and the water that lapped against the side of the quay – and yet he felt that something was missing.

He took a couple of paces away from his easel and looked intently at the landscape he'd created. His concentration was so focused that he failed to hear the click of the door and the approach of William's soft footsteps as he entered the studio.

'That really is remarkable,' William said 'You've excelled yourself.'

Dick swung round quickly and almost lost his balance. Once he'd regained his composure, he shrugged his shoulders and sighed heavily. 'There's something missing,' he said. 'I look at it and I know it's an accurate reflection, but I want it to be more than that. I want Wing Yee and Chin Ming to be able to breathe the air, feel the movement of the waves, hear the birdsong and smell the smoke rising from the charcoal burners along the quay.'

William remained silent. He loved the passion that Dick displayed, his enthusiasm, his commitment. He thought the two young women in Singapore must be very special – they were certainly very lucky to have such a devoted friend. He studied the painting again and considered what Dick had said. 'If that's how you feel,' he said, 'why don't you put your friends in the painting?'

'What do you mean, put them in the painting?'

'You told me the other evening that one of the things you most enjoyed about using oils was the fact that you can paint over whatever you've already done before. You have the landscape and it's wonderful; why don't you now place your friends somewhere within the scene – make them a part of it?'

Dick turned back to the picture. He tried to imagine what it would look like with two figures added. Should they be together or apart? Where he would put them? What would they wear?

'It's only a suggestion,' William said. 'You're used to painting portraits and I'm sure you remember what your friends look like. You could always try out the idea on a separate canvas first if you're unsure that it would work. You could think about it while we join in the festivities tomorrow, then decide what to do when you return here in a few days' time.'

*****

The following morning, pale sunshine crept across the room in which Dick was sleeping and bathed his face in its golden glow. A spider lowered itself from the ceiling to enjoy the warmth, narrowly escaping Dick's arm as he left his dreams behind, became aware of the bright light and tried to shade his eyes. He thought he could hear William moving around somewhere below. Chi Yu, like many other houseboys, had been given a few days off to visit family, so he knew it could only be William. I'd better get up to help prepare breakfast, he thought, scrambling out of bed and tying a sarong around his middle. He clattered down the stairs, bursting into the kitchen just in time to see the door to the courtyard closing and the sound of boots running away at speed.

Dick dodged between the furniture and hurried outside; the courtyard was empty. He ran straight to the door that opened out onto the street, but when he looked up and down, there was no-one to be seen, no sign of any activity, and only silence to be heard. Had he imagined the sound of someone moving around the house? Had he invented the figure disappearing through the kitchen door?

'What on earth are you doing out there in the chilly morning air, wearing only a sarong?' William said as he returned to the warmth of the kitchen.

'I thought I heard you moving about,' Dick said. 'I came down here to help, but there was no sign of you. But then I heard the sound of someone hurrying away. The door was open, so I went outside. I imagined you'd gone into the courtyard to check on something, but there was no-one to be seen. I ran across to the outer door, but when I looked up and down the lane, it was completely empty.'

William turned pale. 'Come with me,' he said. He took Dick's arm and ushered him back outside. He looked around quickly and when he was sure there was no-one in sight, he indicated for Dick to follow. They moved swiftly to the side of the house, down a small flight of steps and into a smaller courtyard not visible from the main approach. The far wall was taken up with a long, wooden building which looked ordinary enough from a distance. On closer inspection, Dick realised that it was a construction given over entirely to the cultivation of plants. William took Dick's arm again and pushed open the door; immediately the air was heady with a potpourri of different perfumes – roses, gardenias, camellias.

He was glad of the warmth the plant-house had to offer.

William hurried to the far end of the building, he pulled back the many resplendent fronds of a red bamboo and heaved a sigh of relief; the orchid was where he'd hidden it when they arrived back home on Christmas Eve. It was progressing well, with a couple of healthy new shoots.

Over breakfast, they discussed what had happened earlier. Dick couldn't be absolutely certain he'd heard anyone moving around inside the house. Could an intruder have been loitering in the kitchen, but if not, why was the door slightly ajar? Had someone actually run across the courtyard, escaped through the gate and then simply disappeared? There was no way of telling, but with Chi Yu away for the festival, William decided to take a few precautions before he and Dick left to see the celebrations down at the quay. When they had finished eating, he returned to the plant-house with a basket. Then, he wrapped the orchid in a swathe of yellow silk, placed it in the basket and cut some camellias to lay on top. He held one of the large, red flowers to his nose, taking in the subtle aroma as he crossed back to the house. If anyone was watching, he hoped they would think he was simply cutting some blooms to decorate the house for the spring festival. After all, his Chinese friends constantly reminded him about the significance of the colour red – the symbol of life – especially at this time of year. He took the basket to his bedroom and placed it behind the washstand. The camellias were displayed in a white ceramic bowl and given pride of place on a windowsill in the main part of the house.

When they left, a short time later, William locked all the doors and put a padlock on the outer gate. A few people hurried along the street in front of them, all being anxious to get to the quay in time to see the parade. As soon as they turned the corner, the air was filled with the dark, explosive sound of cymbals being clashed together; the closer they got to the quay, the louder it became. A large crowd was already assembled, but they managed to find a space near to one of the jetties which provided a good vantage point. Dick could see flashes of yellow and white disappearing into the distance, but when William nudged his arm and pointed in the other direction, he saw a huge, red creature dancing around in front of him.

Dick was immediately reminded of the story Chin Ming had told him, about the day she had come here with her father, the day they had become separated, and she lost sight of him forever. Instinctively, he began to search the faces in the crowd. He didn't know who he was looking for, but it was possible that the Frenchman might be lurking somewhere nearby.

Apart from Yong, who had now returned to Macau, Dick was the only person to have encountered the mysterious Frenchman. When they'd spoken at the gardens in Shunde, Dick had assumed the man was merely making casual conversation to pass the time of day. It was only later that he'd learned about the rumours surrounding the man and his reputation. It was clear that William thought this morning's intruder could have been the same person. Had he somehow heard about the orchid they'd been given? Did he know that Chi Yu was away for the festivities? Had he taken a chance and managed to enter the house before anyone was awake? If that was true, Dick felt sure the man would return, that he was probably looking for an opportunity right now, watching them and deciding what his next move might be.

*****

Dick spent the next few days at the studio; each evening he worried about being followed back to the house. Once safely inside, he relaxed and enjoyed talking to William about the

155

different parts of Guangzhou they'd visited together. It reminded him of the many evenings he'd shared with Raffles, discussing anything and everything from who was due to arrive on the next ship, to problems with the more difficult European merchants, and the small successes they each enjoyed.

Each morning, he returned to the dilemma of what to do with his landscape. His original thought was merely to create a pleasant reminder of Guangzhou for Chin Ming and Wing Yee, but the more he thought about William's suggestion, the more the idea began to grow on him. Once he'd made the decision to include them in the painting, he thought it was logical to have them in the foreground, looking in at the scene. Three days after the spring festival began, he lifted his brush and made an outline for each of the women. They stood side by side, close enough to show that they were not strangers. Wing Yee was taller than Chin Ming, her hair shorter, hanging only as far as her shoulders. Chin Ming's hair hung in a shiny swathe of black silk almost down to her waist. Both women were slim, and Dick dressed them in the garments that Raffles and Sophia had given them two years earlier. They had worn those same garments the evening before they had all departed from Singapore; he could remember every detail. Dick felt his throat constrict as memories of Raffles, Singapore, and his friends flooded his consciousness. This was the second time he'd experienced this strange, empty feeling; was it homesickness – or was it something else? He would have to finish the fine detail of the women's garments once the initial layer of paint was dry, but as soon as that was done, he would tell William it was time for him to return home.

CHAPTER 15
Guangzhou, February 1826

Dick decided to keep his thoughts to himself that evening, but on his way to the studio the following morning he became aware that he was walking with a sense of urgency; he wanted to get on with the painting.

As he approached, he recognised the figure leaning casually against the door; it was Lam Qua. He waved and, when he stepped into the road, nearly collided with a coolie weighed down with overstuffed baskets. He put his hands together and bowed slightly, by way of apology, and hurried on to join Lam Qua. 'I hadn't realised you'd be back so soon,' he said.

'I eat too much food, drink too much wine; if stay longer, I get fat.' He laughed as he rubbed his stomach, but the smile disappeared as soon as he took Dick to one side. 'You have visitor,' he said in a conspiratorial manner.

'Visitor for me? I don't know anyone in Guangzhou – apart from you and William.'

'Not nice man,' Lam Qua said. 'Me, not trust. He want portrait.'

Dick couldn't imagine who would be asking for him, who in this part of the world would even know that he painted portraits. Maybe it was someone from Singapore who'd heard that he was here. He shrugged his shoulders and shook his head. Lam Qua had no more to add. They ascended the stairs, one behind the other. As Dick pushed open the door to the studio, his heart sank.

'*Bonjour, mon ami,*' the man said.

A casual greeting, similar to the one he'd used when they parted at the Qinghui Gardens; the scar over his left eye was as menacing as ever. He rose from the couch he'd been sprawled upon and strode to shake Dick's hand as if they were old friends.

'Those sketches I saw you working on in Shunde were good, I think I said so at the time? I was telling someone I know – a man who spent some time in Singapore – that I'd met a young artist from there. He recognised you from my description; he told me you're the adopted son of Stamford Raffles. He also said, rather than return to England with him, you decided to stay in Singapore and you now make a living painting portraits.'

Dick cleared his throat; he swallowed hard but no words would come. He was angry with himself for his sudden immobility and tried to calm himself down, to relax. The walls of the studio felt as if they were closing in on him and he wanted to hurry back to the street.

'Perhaps you could paint my portrait?'

Dick registered what was being said, but couldn't quite believe the actual words.

He stood looking at the visitor for what seemed an eternity, then he said, 'But I don't even know your name; how can I paint the portrait of someone whose name I don't know?'

'My name is Pierre Volande,' he said, narrowing his eyes as he stared at Dick. His gaze became more intense, as if challenging the young man to ask any further questions.

'Well, Mr Volande,' Dick said, 'I'm sure my friend Lam Qua would do a much better job, he is a far more experienced artist, and he lives right here in Guangzhou.'

'Is it not your intention to stay here for long then?' the Frenchman said,

No-one yet knew of Dick's plan to return to Singapore as quickly as possible, not even William. He certainly was not about to reveal his intentions to a stranger, a man who no-one seemed to like very much. 'I still have a lot to learn,' he said. 'Lam Qua is teaching me to paint in oils, that's why I said it would be better if you asked him to paint your portrait.'

'I not paint people,' Lam Qua said. 'I paint landscape.'

Dick wished his friend had not uttered this unhelpful comment, but there was nothing he could do now. 'I'll have to think about it,' he said. 'Why don't you come back tomorrow, when I've had a chance to discuss it with Lam Qua?'

'Fair enough,' Volande said, but made no effort to move.

While Dick and Lam Qua moved around the studio, rearranging the space that Dick had occupied for the past ten days, the Frenchman remained seated on the one comfortable chair. It was obvious that he had no intention of leaving yet awhile. Dick looked at Lam Qua with a pleading expression on his face; he had nothing more to say to the unexpected visitor.

'You didn't visit Foshan after all?' Volande said, breaking the silence that filled the room.

Dick swallowed hard. He didn't want the man to interpret anything he said as unusual, but he needed to steady himself. 'That's correct.' He took another deep breath. 'It was a last-minute decision, but William – Mr Lawrence – thought it might be more interesting to take the overland route back to Guangzhou.'

'That was after you met the monk at the temple in Panyu, I presume?' Volande said through a lopsided grin.

Dick remained silent. Their alternative route hadn't begun as an overland journey; they had continued by boat as far as Panyu and then exchanged it for the handcarts. How had the Frenchman found out? He could feel his heart rate quickening, but tried his best to keep calm. Was it another trick? Did the Frenchman know about the meeting with Shi Jingsu? If he told a lie and Volande did know something, would that make the situation worse?

'I met a villager who turned up in Macau at the end of December,' Volande said. 'The man was eager to spend his earnings. Said he'd been travelling with a party of European plant collectors. He told lots of stories about his journey along the Xi River and the strange habits of his compatriots. He was throwing his money around, inviting everyone to drink with him. His tongue had already been loosened by a surfeit of rice spirit, but it was when he described you amongst the party that I realised who he'd been talking about.'

Dick said nothing.

'He was one of your bearers; said you'd taken one of the tributaries to Shunde instead of continuing north. He grumbled a great deal because you exchanged the boat for handcarts when you reached Panyu; he complained bitterly about the callouses on his hands.'

Dick's heart was now beating fast. Would the Frenchman mention the temple in Zini village? He was sure that the bearers had no knowledge of where William went that last morning or who he met. He continued to stare at the Frenchman, telling himself he mustn't panic, he must reveal nothing about the visit to the Buddhist monk.

'The man was clearly unhappy about the change of plan. Might have been the alcohol talking, of course, but he was clearly annoyed about the delay in Panyu. A whole morning wasted, according to him, while your Mr Lawrence went off to visit a temple. Said, when he returned to the quay a few hours later, he was carrying some sort of exotic bird.'

Dick blinked, his mind galloping ahead. He'd overlooked the fact that everyone was waiting to move off when William and Edmund returned; of course, they would have noticed the birdcage. No-one had ever asked what was inside it, however, let alone viewed its contents – he was sure of that. William always kept it covered whilst they travelled from one village to another and had kept it close to him each night. He had never actually said what was inside the cage, but it was fair to assume it was a bird or some other small animal. What a clever move that had been. Nevertheless, the Frenchman seemed to know instinctively that William had obtained something of value, something he wanted to keep hidden. Was this what the intruder – most likely the Frenchman – had been searching for when Dick had disturbed him, the morning of the lunar new year?

Lam Qua, who had removed himself to a quiet corner of the studio, stood up and started to sort through a pile of canvases; he refused to look at the visitor. Dick strode towards him, not wanting to continue any sort of conversation with the Frenchman, who still made no sign of leaving. He wished he knew what Lam Qua was thinking. He also wished he knew what William was doing right now.

When they could find nothing else to tidy or rearrange, Lam Qua prepared to ask the visitor to leave. As he turned to face him, Pierre Volande was already on his feet, towering over the two artists and far too close for comfort. Dick took a step backwards, he was trying to think what to say about the proposed portrait, but before he had time to compose himself, Volande moved away. His face contorted into a lopsided smile, he opened the door and raised his arm in an exaggerated farewell gesture.

'Tell Mr Lawrence, if he ever wants to sell his feathered friend, I can always find a customer willing to pay a princely sum for anything exotic.' He stared at Dick for another moment only. '*Au revoir*,' he said, stepping onto the top stair; then the clatter of his boots descending to the street was all that was left of the encounter.

Dick stood still, unable to move at first; his mouth fell open, then he grabbed onto Lam Qua's arm. His friend looked annoyed.

'I say, this man, he no good.'

'How do you know that?'

'He have bad reputation. He big cheat.'

'I ought to warn William,' Dick said.

'You not go yet. Maybe he wait to follow.'

'He's trying to check whether his suspicions are right, isn't he?'

Lam Qua nodded.

'Maybe I ought to paint his portrait. I can discuss everything with William tonight and we can work out what I should ask him when he returns in the morning.'

'He not come back. He not have portrait.'

'What makes you so sure?' Dick said.

'Portrait show people what bad man looks like. He not take such risk.'

'Of course, how stupid of me. I should have agreed to do it, to do a rough sketch at least while he was here today.'

A grin spread across Lam Qua's face, then he padded over to the far corner of the studio. From behind the pile of canvases he had seemingly been sorting out, he pulled out a sketchpad. Dick raised an eyebrow as he walked over to join him. With a flourish, Lam Qua flicked over the pages until he reached the section he was looking for, then he held it up in front of his friend.

'I thought you said you didn't do portraits!' Dick said.

*****

Dick waited another couple of hours before returning to William's house. He took his time to walk the entire length of Old China Street and made a point of calling in to chat at one or two of the shophouses along the way. This gave him the opportunity to glance around casually to check whether or not he was being followed. He was safe in thinking Chi Yu would not admit any visitors unless William told him to do so, and particularly if no-one else was at home.

When he opened the gate and crossed the courtyard, he found William engrossed with a pile of papers. He pulled a chair away from the table and sat opposite him, quietly waiting for an opportunity to share the news.

When Dick was finished, William shook his head from side to side, drawing his mouth into a straight line and biting his lip. Then, he pushed his own chair away from the table, glanced around to quickly check that the gate was firmly closed and stood, looking across at Dick and frowning a good deal. He gave an impatient huff, then said, 'I need to have a word with Chi Yu. We'll talk again over supper.'

*****

Two hours later, the two men sat facing each other once again. Chi Yu carried a tray from the kitchen, containing a platter of chicken with mixed vegetables and a number of small side dishes. Then he placed a bowl of rice in front of each of them and retreated into the shadows.

'When you leave for Lam Qua's studio in the morning, I will accompany you,' William said. 'If the Frenchman does come back, he can talk to me directly.'

Dick's lips fell apart. 'Do you think he will actually do that?' Dick said, 'Lam Qua is convinced that he wasn't at all serious about having his portrait painted and it was just a ploy to find out whether the rumour he'd heard about the so-called exotic bird was true.'

'You said the Frenchman wasn't aware that Lam Qua was making a likeness of him whilst you talked?'

'I'm sure he would have said something. He struck me as someone who is quite vain, he wouldn't have been able to resist asking to see it if he'd known what was happening.'

'That's the reason he might return, of course. I imagine he has no idea that we know of his reputation; I believe he's the type of person who is conceited and arrogant enough to flaunt his presence without feeling at all at risk.'

'So, if he does return, what do you want me to do?' Dick said.

'I want you to agree to paint his portrait. It should take at least five days, preferably a whole week. During that time, I suggest you bring a few of the belongings you've left at the studio back here each evening.'

Dick sat very still, his mind racing. He wanted so much to tell William about his desire to return home after completing the painting for Chin Ming and Wing Yee, but he knew how important it was to help William protect the orchid – not that he had any idea of what William intended to do. He paused briefly, with a piece of chicken carefully balanced on his chopsticks. 'Can you tell me what you have in mind?' he said.

'Of course, my apologies.'

Dick straightened his back, put down his chopsticks and gave William his full attention.

'When you went to your room to wash, I checked that the orchid was still safe. Then I had a word with Chi Yu. He is a trusted member of this household and I've told him every-thing; how I came to acquire the orchid and what I propose to do to protect it. Then, I sent him shopping.'

Dick raised both eyebrows and tilted his head to one side.

'Bear with me,' William said. 'I simply sent him shopping for extra vegetables. It just so happens that Chi Yu's cousin sells the best wood ear mushrooms in Guangzhou.' He lowered his voice before continuing. 'He also has an interesting collection of parakeets – one with a pink-coloured head and others that he's purchased from sailors who regularly travel between here and India. The bird which he treasures the most is, I believe, a blue-rumped parrot that came from Burma.'

Dick's face relaxed as a broad smile spread from ear to ear. 'You're not going to ...?'

'Chi Yu has asked whether we might borrow the pink-headed parakeet. I wouldn't want to risk the blue parrot in case anything goes wrong with my plan.'

'Which is?' Dick said, still smiling.

'In a couple of days, Chi Yu will go shopping in the morning, as usual. He'll take the small handcart because he'll need to buy a sack of rice as well as our usual provisions. Under the sacking which we use to protect the provisions from the elements, I will hide the birdcage that I purchased in Zini village. He will go to his cousin's shop as usual and the things we need will be waiting for him. He will load the cart and return here straight away.'

'Why not do all that tomorrow?'

'We must be sure that we are not being watched. If we behave as normally as possible for a couple of days, I'm hoping the Frenchman will conclude, either that we have nothing to hide, or that you have not told me about his visit to the studio.'

'But you said you intend to come with me tomorrow?'

'It's not unusual for me to visit the studio and besides, I want to see Lam Qua's sketch. If your Monsieur Volande turns up, we will have a discussion about how much to charge for his portrait, if not, we'll discuss the best way to get you back to Singapore safely.'

'How? When did you ...?'

'Lam Qua told me he thought you might be getting home-sick. Besides, it all fits in with my plan nicely; the only problem is that there is no ship leaving for at least another week.'

'There's another part to your plan? Does it involve telling Volande anything about purchasing an exotic bird?'

'I might pretend to be interested in selling,' William said. 'I thought I might say that I intend to go away again soon and can't look after it properly. I'll ask him what price he's thinking of.'

Dick looked horrified. If the Frenchman was as much of a rogue as his reputation would have you believe, this idea was too risky.

'Don't look so worried,' William said. 'I have something else in mind, but the less you know about it, right now, the easier it will be for you to feign ignorance should Monsieur Volande decide to interrogate you.'

Dick's eyes widened and he slowly shook his head. 'You're quite devious,' he said, 'for a missionary, I mean.'

They both laughed.

'There is something else,' William said, suddenly becoming serious.

The day was becoming more and more bizarre by the minute, but Dick was completely taken aback by what William had to say next.

'As long as the orchid remains with me, it will never be safe. I want you to take it back to Singapore and ask Edmund to take it to England. He can choose whether he gives it to the Physic Garden in Oxford or to one of the experts at Kew.'

Dick and William continued to talk, exploring all the possibilities they could think of that would ensure the safe passage of the precious flower. It was only when they noticed the oil lamp had burned low and the insects had flown elsewhere that they decided it was time for them to retire.

CHAPTER 16
Guangzhou, February 1826

Before they left for the studio the following day, William checked once more that the orchid was safe; he tested the lock on the outer door and reminded Chi Yu not to admit anyone at all whilst he was away.

'We should engage in conversation,' William said to a nervous-looking Dick as soon as they left the confines of the house behind. 'It's important to behave as naturally as possible and what could be more normal than two people talking to each other? Besides, if we're chatting, it will also prevent either of us being tempted to turn around and give any indication that we are expecting to be followed.'

'What do you suggest we talk about?'

'You've never told me much about your life with Raffles, but it's obvious that you're very fond of him. You could tell me how you felt when he decided to adopt you? Or, what about the sort of things you did together when you first arrived in Singapore?'

Dick wrinkled his brow; he wasn't convinced this was a good idea. He put on a fake smile, but avoided direct eye contact with William.

'Don't worry, if the Frenchman is watching, I'm sure he won't do anything untoward in broad daylight. It will be good to give him the impression that we are oblivious to his attentions.'

At the end of the street, Dick's focus was drawn to the fabric shop, with row upon row of brightly coloured silks glinting in the pale sunshine. Yet again, his memory flew back to the first day he'd entered Baba Tan's emporium in Singapore and the magical feeling it had created. Instead of talking about Raffles, whom he still missed too much to talk of for long, he told William all about the Peranakan merchant who had become such a significant figure in all of their lives. By the time they reached the studio, William knew a great deal about the man who had come to Singapore from Malacca and built a successful business from humble beginnings.

*****

Lam Qua nodded as William entered the studio alongside Dick. He was used to seeing the man with whom his new pupil was lodging, but his curiosity rose when he saw Dick glance back down the stairs and close the door tight shut. William took Lam Qua into the corner and spoke to him in Cantonese. He told him about acquiring the orchid and his concern for its safety, knowing there would always be unscrupulous people, such as the Frenchman, looking for an opportunity to make money illegally. He explained his plans for Dick and the precious plant in hushed tones and asked for Lam's Qua's help.

'I show you bad man picture,' he told William, then he turned to Dick. 'You keep lookout.'

William examined the sketch closely before saying anything further. He was trying to make a mental note of the rogue for future reference.

'I'm sure Lam Qua would let you take it,' Dick said as he appeared beside William. 'It might be better if the Frenchman doesn't know of its existence and there are not many places here to keep it safely hidden.'

Lam Qua needed no translation or explanation of Dick's

idea. He eased the page out of his sketchbook and handed it to William. 'You take, you take,' he said.

*****

Once William had departed, the two young artists spent a couple of hours sorting through the various pieces that Dick had worked upon during the few weeks he had been working in oils. Both of them were so intent upon their task that they failed to notice the muffled sound of an outside door creaking open and the hint of movement on the stairs; it was only when the latch on the door into the studio made a loud click that they looked up. Immediately, a heady perfume of musk and scented oils pervaded the air; the Frenchman filled the door-frame and stood gazing across the room.

'You look surprised to see me, *mon ami*,' Volande said.

'Well, yes,' Dick said, clearing his throat. 'I wasn't sure you were serious yesterday. When you spoke of having your portrait painted, I thought it might just be a passing whim.' He hoped he sounded much calmer than he was feeling inside.

'Was that why you gave the impression of not being interested – how quaint. However, you promised me to think about it and I agreed to return this morning to hear your decision. I am a man of my word, so here I am.'

Dick couldn't believe his ears, the sheer audacity of the man – a man of his word indeed. He turned away to hide the raging tiger that was beginning to envelop him. It looked very much as if William's suspicions had been correct; the man was both vain and full of his own self-importance. It had not occurred to him, it seemed, that they might have heard the rumours of his evil reputation or perhaps he simply didn't care. Lam Qua came quickly to Dick's rescue, before their visitor had a chance to say anything further.

'He can do picture. You want start soon? How much you pay?'

The ensuing conversation followed the usual pattern of haggling, with Lam Qua taking the lead, but he shook his head a great deal whenever he became frustrated. They began all over again once he discovered Volande could speak Cantonese. They discussed the size of the canvas that might be used, the amount of time required to complete the task, the skill of the artist and how the portrait was to be framed. Volande tried to bring the price down, saying what was accepted as the usual fee should be reduced because of Dick's inexperience with oils. Lam Qua defended his pupil, reminding the Frenchman that Dick had gained an impressive reputation for his work in Singapore and that he had been expertly coached in using the new medium. Dick was relieved when they eventually stopped quibbling and agreed upon a sum that was acceptable to everyone. If he was to do this portrait, the sooner he made a start the sooner it would be over. He looked expectantly at his mentor for guidance.

'We make ready canvas today,' Lam Qua said, 'You come tomorrow morning, then he make start.'

The Frenchman cast his eye around the studio. 'That's the size I want,' he said, pointing to the Guangzhou landscape that Dick had now completed.

Was it coincidence that Volande had chosen this particular painting; it was larger than the size first discussed? How much did he know about Dick's life in Singapore? Was he aware the silhouettes represented his two closest friends? His chest tightened and his blood ran cold. The Frenchman's expression gave nothing away and Dick decided he was letting his imagination run away with him. It was more likely that the dimensions Volande had chosen related more to the size of his ego.

*****

The Frenchman arrived early the following day and Dick spent the whole morning drawing an outline of him before focusing on the finer detail, but he was not an easy subject. He fidgeted a good deal and constantly tried to start a conversation.

'I thought I saw your Mr Lawrence leaving here as I approached this morning, but he was in too much of a hurry for me to introduce myself.'

Dick's grip on the brush he was using tightened and the line of Volande's jaw skidded across the canvas. He quickly covered the blunder, wiping it with an oily rag.

'Does he have any plans to go travelling again soon?' The Frenchman was gazing out of the window with a faraway look on his face.

'Mr Volande,' Dick said, 'I must ask you to keep still, absolutely still, while I try to capture the main features of your face.'

'Not just my face, I hope,' Volande replied 'I've worn my best coat and breeches especially for the occasion, I'm expecting you to make me look like the emperor himself, sitting on his throne!'

Lam Qua snorted and made no pretence of his dislike for the man. Dick stifled his annoyance; Volande was displaying all the signs of vanity that he and William had anticipated. 'Of course,' he said. 'I will do my best, but you must STOP talking.'

Dick continued to work for another hour, but each time he needed to look at his subject, he saw the Frenchman scrutinising him. He may have curtailed the questions for now, but he knew they would be posed again, sooner or later. Once he was satisfied with the composition of the portrait, he began to make some notes; the colours of the garments, how they fell and where the shadows created by the winter sunshine highlighted the Frenchman's features.

'Surely you've got enough detail to be getting on with by now?' Volande said, leaping up from his chair. 'By God, I've not been so idle in many a year. I presume you don't need me to be here for every single detail, I'll come back in a couple of days to check on progress.'

'But ...' Dick said.

'But nothing. I've had enough for one day of remaining still and keeping my mouth shut. Besides, I have a luncheon date with a very pretty lady. *Au revoir, mon ami.*'

He opened the door, but before he disappeared down the stairs to the street, he paused; he narrowed his eyes and pointed a finger towards Dick. 'Don't forget to ask your Mr Lawrence about the bird,' he said.

The door closed behind him. A wave of nausea consumed Dick; he wanted to scream, but the back of his throat was dry and it felt as if a leather strap was beginning to tighten around his head. He laid his brushes on the table beside him and sat with his head in his hands rubbing his temples to ease the discomfort.

*****

William returned to the studio later in the day with the intention of helping Dick convey some of his paintings back to the house. The first thing he noticed on entering the studio was the image of an arrogant-looking man beginning to take shape; it stared out from a large canvas with a defiant expression, daring anyone who looked in his direction to pick a fight. The detail had yet to be completed, but already the image matched the one that Lam Qua had given him earlier in the day.

'I was right in thinking he wouldn't be able to resist coming back then,' William said.

Dick turned, wrinkling his nose as he did so. His eyes had lost all of their warmth and he muttered to himself as he shook his head slowly from side to side.

'I understand that you are not enjoying this,' William said, 'and I'm sorry I've asked you to do it, but it gives me time to put everything in place for your journey back to Singapore. Whilst the Frenchman was here, wallowing in his own self-importance, I've designed a crate that will not only convey your paintings safely, but will also conceal the orchid without anyone having the slightest idea that you have it with you. I've also spoken to the harbour master and worked out how to get you on board without much fuss. It's best that I don't tell you what I've got in mind until nearer the time; the less you have to worry about, the better. Just trust me.'

'Oh, I do,' Dick said. He knew William only had his best interests at heart and for the moment, at least, he was happy to remain ignorant.

'Did he ask anything about the bird?'

'He kept trying to start a conversation, but I fended him off most of the time. Every time he began to speak, I insisted he needed to keep perfectly still if the portrait was to be any good. Eventually, he gave up asking questions but then he grew bored and decided to leave. He said he'd be back in a couple of days. I was just about to relax when, as a parting shot, he reminded me to ask you about the bird.'

'Well done!' William said. 'If you can stall him for another few days all the better and you'll be able to leave around the beginning of next week.'

'What if Volande asks about the bird next time? I can't keep avoiding his questions.'

'By then, I should have a feathered guest installed at home and I'll have an answer you can give him, but don't worry about that now, you look exhausted. Let's take just a few of your paintings tonight, the rest can wait until tomorrow.'

*****

Lam Qua helped Dick with the portrait during the next two days, to the point where it was almost finished, then they put it on one side. Dick was worried that when Volande did put in an appearance, he would notice the stack of paintings, which had previously taken up much of the studio space, was now depleted. What sort of explanation could he give for their removal, and might it make the Frenchman suspicious? This time it was Lam Qua who came up with an idea.

*****

They both stood slightly back from the window, but positioned themselves where they had a good view of the street below. As soon as they saw Volande come into view, they returned to stand beside the remaining canvases. They listened hard for the click of the door below and when the sound of his boots rose from the first stair, they began a heated discussion.

'No, all must go now,' Lam Qua said in a very loud voice. 'I need space for new delivery.'

'Could I not leave them here for a few more days?' Dick said, trying to sound anxious.

'Too many, all must go tomorrow, no more time,' Lam Qua added. 'Many new material come from Shanghai. Need space, no more room.'

'Ahem, excuse me, gentlemen,' Volande said. He looked genuinely surprised to witness what he'd interpreted as a dispute between the two young artists. 'What's the problem?'

'Oh, nothing really,' Dick said. 'Lam Qua needs me to clear this area that's all. I've taken some of my paintings back to Will ..., Mr Lawrence's house and I thought it was enough. It's no problem, we'll sort it out.'

'I wrap for you, you show portrait,' Lam Qua said, traipsing off to the other end of the room.

Volande shrugged his shoulders. 'Well, that's what I've come for; when will it be ready for me to collect?'

'Can collect when bring money!' Lam Qua could be heard

shouting from the adjacent room.

'If you approve,' Dick said, 'then I can add the final details this afternoon. It will need to thoroughly dry before it can be framed of course, but I imagine you will be able to take it at the beginning of next week.'

Volande stood in front of his own image and beamed; he obviously liked what he saw. He moved closer and gazed into his own eyes, he took a step backwards and nodded his approval. 'You are indeed extremely talented,' he said, 'but I think you've made too much of the scar. We don't want to frighten the ladies, do we? Can you just get rid of it altogether?'

'If that's what you want,' said Dick, gritting his teeth. 'Could you sit in the chair over there, whilst I make a few adjustments? I want to ensure the folds of your coat look realistic and the tone of your complexion is as flattering as possible.'

Volande lowered himself into the chair, lay back against the cushions and sat with his nose pressed up against the knuckles of his right hand as if he was deep in thought.

'Could you lower your arm for me please,' Dick said. 'The other day you had your hands on the arms of the chair, that's how I've portrayed you. I could paint over that, of course, but then it will take longer to complete.'

The Frenchman gripped the arms of the chair and sat upright, looking straight into Dick's eyes. 'No, no,' he said, 'let's get it finished.'

Dick heaved a sigh of relief, he too wanted to get the painting over and done with. He added some black to accentuate the folds of the coat and made some notes that would remind him to remove the scar. 'I think that's all I need for now,' he said. 'Your painting will be ready to collect on Monday morning.'

'And the bird, did you remember to ask your friend whether he might be interested in selling the bird?'

Dick swallowed hard, frantically trying to think how he might respond. William had promised to come to the studio today; he'd said he would have an answer to give to the Frenchman, what could be holding him up? How much longer could he evade Volande's questions? 'I did remember,' he said, 'I asked him only last night, I think …'

Just then, the latch of the door to the studio clicked open. The dilapidated wooden panel swung ajar to reveal William's tall, upright figure. He strode straight towards the Frenchman with his hand outstretched, 'You must be Monsieur Volande,' he said.

Pierre Volande took a step sideways. He gulped in air and touched his throat. His voice was noticeably higher when he managed to say, 'I am.' He took another breath before regaining his composure and adding, 'And you must be William Lawrence.'

'Dick tells me you've been asking about the bird I have in my care?'

'So, the rumour is correct, you do have an exotic companion.'

'I'm not sure about exotic, he's certainly extremely handsome, but I'm afraid he's not for sale.'

'May I at least come to see it,' Volande said. 'It's not often that I have such an opportunity.'

'Well, I see no reason why not,' William replied, 'as long as you understand that I have no intention of selling.'

By this point, Dick was beginning to feel lightheaded. He had no idea what game William was playing, but he knew instinctively he needed to remain calm; he mustn't do anything that would make the Frenchman suspicious.

'It would be best if you left it for two or three days,' William said. 'The bird is in the middle of moulting at the moment and doesn't look his best right now. It would be far better to wait until you can see the full delight of his rich plumage. You'll be able to appreciate his magnificent colours much better by then. Shall we say – next Monday?

CHAPTER 17
Guangzhou, Monday 20th February 1826

All except three of Dick's paintings had been carefully wrapped and placed in the crate the previous evening. Dick had watched William lower the orchid, carefully swathed in dampened moss, into the centre of the container, then pack it tight with small pieces of bark and coconut fibre. He'd made a canopy out of chicken wire to sit above the plant. 'That will allow air to circulate above it and protect it from those smaller canvases I intend to lay on top of the frame,' William had explained. 'We'll nail down the lid in the morning, but you'll need to remove it once you get safely out to sea, to allow the air to circulate. It should be able to thrive as long as you lift it out occasionally, dampen its leaves and make sure the moss is kept moist for the entire journey.'

*****

It was early and Dick had been able to eat very little of the breakfast William had prepared. He had an empty feeling in the pit of his stomach, his mouth felt dry and he was beginning to get a headache.

'Not much longer,' William said, 'It's a pity you'll miss the Lantern Festival this evening. I always look forward to seeing all the different-coloured lights being paraded around the town. Some of the lanterns are quite breathtaking and it's a delightful way of bringing the spring festival to its conclusion. Never mind, this year I'm afraid getting you back to Singapore has to take priority. Lam Qua will be here soon to help with the handcart, but when you leave, I'll stay here to welcome Monsieur Volande and keep him entertained.'

'What if he arrives before Lam Qua gets here?' Dick said. 'How will we explain me going away before he's collected his portrait?'

'If I was a gambling man, I would lay a bet that the Frenchman will arrive at a more gentile hour – around the middle of the morning. He may be a rogue, but he will not want to appear too anxious to view the bird – that would give his game away. I'll give your excuses and tell him you were feeling homesick. I'll say we heard of a ship in the harbour about to leave for Singapore and fortunately, there was space available for a passenger.'

Dick gulped. A shiver ran down his spine and the hairs on the back of his neck stood to attention. He wouldn't be able to settle until he was safely on board the junk that was waiting for him in the harbour and its anchor had been lifted.

Chi Yu, who had been waiting beside the gate to the courtyard, now appeared, accompanied by Lam Qua. William pointed to the crate and asked Lam Qua to help him lift it onto the handcart. Another small bag containing the remainder of Dick's belongings was placed beside it. Lam Qua put his hands together and kowtowed towards William; no words were exchanged. William took Dick by the shoulders and pulled him into a bear-like embrace. He observed the young man's downcast expression and said, 'Try not to worry. You've been brave in the past, you can be brave again. Take care of yourself – and your paintings. Give my regards to Edmund and James when you all meet up again.' He nodded to Chi Yu to open the gate and Lam Qua began to push the cart. Dick took one last look at William and his house, then hurried to help Lam Qua negotiate the passage through the gate into the street.

When they reached the square, they threaded their way between the hawkers already set up to start the business of the day. At one point, the space between the stalls was so tight that they had to retreat and find an alternative route. They narrowly missed bumping into a figure who lunged across the road ahead of them. The man had his collar turned up and a hat pulled down over his face. He was dressed oddly and Dick had to work hard to convince himself it was not the Frenchman. He felt queasy, but Lam Qua had already continued on his way apparently unperturbed. Dick hurried after him. Now was not the time to share his concerns; they had, at last, reached the quay. They found two coolies to help them carry the crate on board the junk. The captain was anxious to catch the tide and was ready to sail. Dick kowtowed to Lam Qua and thanked him for his help. The two of them had formed a bond during the time they'd spent together – and not merely because of their shared interest in painting; it was hard to say goodbye. There was a half-hearted attempt at a handshake and then Dick hurried up the gangplank. It is only then that he noticed the name of the ship; it was the *Golden Phoenix*.

*****

The anchor was already being raised and Lam Qua had been reduced to the size of a wooden toy when the two friends waved a final farewell to each other. Dick heard the sails flapping in the wind and waves splashing against the side of the vessel. He was relieved to have missed colliding with the Frenchman and he knew he should now be able to relax a little. However, all he could think about was the name he'd seen on the side of the ship; he was on board the same junk that had brought Chin Ming and Wing Yee to Singapore three and a half years ago.

*****

The vessel started to shift away from the quay. It was skilfully manoeuvred between the smaller vessels bobbing about in the harbour and made its way out into the swirling waters of the delta. Dick found himself surrounded by a hive of activity: the ship's crew, busy with their everyday tasks. A light breeze began to play with the hem of his coat and it brought with it the ever-fading aromas of the port – fish, spices and oyster sauce; seaweed, sweat and decay. He'd seen the crate safely stowed before the gangplank was lifted and was glad that he had a cabin all to himself, but for the time being he wanted to stay on deck. He gazed on Guangzhou for one last time, trying to embed the image in his heart. He was pleased that the weather was set fair for their journey

The landmarks with which he had become familiar were still obvious, and beyond the town he contemplated the range of bare, weathered hills against a background of clear blue sky. Instinctively, he cast his eye in the direction of Lam Qua's studio, wondering if his friend had yet returned there after reporting news of his safe departure to William. He puzzled about the intensity of a strange light radiating from that part of the town, then told himself the extravaganza of the lantern lighting might already be on the way; either that or it was simply the early-morning glare bouncing off the water. A hand tapped his shoulder and he turned to see an imposing figure, commanding and self-confident. The man's voice was calm and his use of English precise. 'My name is Lim Chan Seng,' he said, 'I am captain of the *Golden Phoenix*; welcome.'

Dick extended his hand. 'Thank you for having me on board,' he said. There hadn't been time for William to tell him how much Captain Lim had been told about his need to get away from Guangzhou quickly, but he presumed some sort of understanding had been reached between the two men. He decided to say nothing for the time being, either about the orchid or his knowledge of Lim's part in bringing Wing Yee and Chin Ming to Singapore.

Both Dick and Captain Lim took a final glance towards the shore. The bright glare that Dick had seen previously was still evident and now it looked as if it had acquired an orange glow. He was sure William had told him the lantern parade happened in the evening, once it got dark, so what was this strange phenomenon, he wondered.

*****

William invited Lam Qua to sit down. He had hurried away from the quay the moment the *Golden Phoenix* began to move into the estuary and now he was looking flushed. He was pleased to report that everything had gone to plan. The two men exchanged pleasantries, sharing the delight they had each experienced during the weeks they had enjoyed Dick's company. Chi Yu had brought tea and was in the process of placing small, porcelain cups on the table in front of them when they heard someone knocking at the outside gate. Lam Qua looked at William; the knocking intensified in volume and Chi Yu was asked to admit the visitor.

Seconds later, Pierre Volande was standing before them. His eyes narrowed when he noticed Lam Qua sitting beside William; he slipped his hands into his pockets and hastily glanced at William's clock. He ran his fingers through his long, unkempt hair and as he did so, William noticed a dark smudge along one side of his brow; there was another one under his chin.

'*Bonjour,*' he said, producing a quick, false smile. 'This is the day I was promised an introduction to your feathered companion, I believe.'

'That is correct,' William said. 'But first, let me offer you some tea, it is freshly made.'

Volande looked annoyed, but he knew better than to voice his displeasure. If his host wanted to keep him on tenterhooks and go along with traditional Chinese hospitality, then he must bide his time. He nodded in acceptance and flopped down in the chair opposite Lam Qua, causing it to move sideways from the force of his descent.

His tea was poured and as William handed it to Volande he said, 'Lam Qua has just returned from the harbour; he kindly agreed to help Dick transport his paintings.' He casually glossed over Dick's homesickness and the coincidence of a junk leaving for Singapore. 'It seemed too good an opportunity to miss,' he added. 'His ship left just over an hour ago; the house will seem very empty without him.'

Volande gasped and a sullen expression drenched his whole face. His eyes became immobile, tightened into an incredulous stare, holding onto infinity. For once in his life, he was lost for words.

'Not worry about portrait,' Lam Qua said. 'I give you. I take money now?'

All the colour drained from Volande's face, emphasising the dark smear of something that looked remarkably like soot on his forehead.

'That's a good idea,' William said, 'I meant to tell you, Dick was most insistent that Lam Qua should have his fee, in exchange for the tuition he's enjoyed from our friend here.'

Volande slid down further into the chair. 'I don't have the full amount on my person,' he managed to say.

William and Lam Qua gazed at him, but said nothing. He stood up and thrust his hand into his pocket, bringing out a handful of silver coins 'Here,' he said, placing them on the table in front of Lam Qua, 'that's all I have – take it.'

'Bring balance when collect painting,' Lam Qua said.

'Of course,' Volande replied with a dismissive nod. He

sighed noisily before turning to William, raising his voice as he asked once again if he might see the bird. This time, William agreed.

Lam Qua made his excuses, saying that he wanted to prepare his lantern for the parade later in the day. He told them he had in mind a design that would remind them of Dick. Chi Yu accompanied him to the gate and watched until he disappeared around the corner into the next street.

'You'll need to follow me,' William said to the Frenchman, opening the door into the courtyard.

Volande, who stood waiting, frowned. The old wall clock struck the hour; he jumped and looked horrified as he stared at the pendulum swinging back and forth. Once again, he ran his hands swiftly through his hair and started to fidget.

'Come,' said William, 'I thought you were keen to see our feathered friend.'

William led the way to the smaller courtyard. It was completely invisible from the front of the house and it was only when they reached the small flight of steps leading downwards that Volande had the slightest idea about the existence of this sunken addition to the property. He was instructed to wait just inside the door of a long wooden building that appeared to be full of plants. William made his way between the richly abundant vegetation – bamboo, juniper, and a dwarf plum tree. The air was heady with the scent of gardenias. Volande was mesmerised as he cast his eyes around, initially seeing what he thought might be a scarlet-coloured camelia, then several different varieties of begonia; finally, his eyes fell upon a shrub that he didn't recognise. It was just coming into blossom, with only a few buds fully open. Each of these large, goblet-shaped flowers was an unusual shade of cream with a flash of magenta rising from the base of each bloom. Volande was already thinking of the many people to whom he might sell such a plant.

There was a rustle amongst the foliage and William appeared. He was carrying the birdcage, covered in a loosely fitting hood made out of deep blue fabric. He placed it down gently on the ground, a few paces away from the Frenchman.

Volande took a step forward and as he did so, William noticed the sheen of sweat on his brow. He edged even closer, letting out a long breath and smiling at William.

'I think he'll be settled now,' William said, 'but I'll lift the cover very slowly, I don't want to frighten him.'

Volande moved even closer to where William was positioned. He rubbed his sweaty palms along the sleeves of his coat. His eyes shone brightly as he focused his attention on the blue cotton cover; William slowly revealed the birdcage and its occupant.

The bird blinked in the sudden bright light, then it issued a high-pitched, indignant screech as Volande stepped even closer. Its body was pale green, with darker hues on the tail and wings. The head was pink, changing to pale blue at the crown; it wore a narrow black neck collar with a matching stripe on its chin.

'It's a pink-headed parakeet,' William said, ignoring the pained expression on the Frenchman's face. 'I'm taking care of it while its owner extends his aviary. I'll be returning it at the end of the week.'

'I know very well what it is! Do you take me for a fool?' Volande shouted. 'Young boys bring them to me all the time; they catch them in the forest. Coming here was a mistake.'

'I'm sorry to disappoint you, Monsieur Volande,' William said. 'I'm not an expert, but I thought he was rather handsome, despite the noise he tends to make.'

Volande's eyes narrowed; he clenched his fists, trying to keep his temper under control. This specimen couldn't possibly be the subject of the conversation he'd overheard in Macau; there must be something else. He decided to change tack.

'Your plant collection is quite impressive. Tell, me what is this beauty called?'

'Some people call it a tulip tree,' William said, 'most probably because of the shape of the flowers. It's actually a member of the magnolia family. You should see it when it's in full flower, each bloom looks like the rising sun just after dawn.'

'And may I ask where you obtained this particular specimen?'

'This is a variety particularly favoured by Buddhist priests; they like to cultivate them in and around their temples. I have a friend, who is the spiritual master at a temple near Panyu; he gave this plant to me as a sapling many years ago, and before you ask, it is most definitely not for sale.'

Was Lawrence telling the truth? Volande wondered. Had he really been given this plant years ago, or was it a rare specimen that he and his friends had recently brought back to Guangzhou? They could easily have hidden it in one of the handcarts. He knew he could make a great deal of money from selling this shrub. It was all extremely irritating and time was now running out.

'Maybe, one day you'll change your mind, Mr Lawrence, but in the meantime, I don't have time for your games. I have an urgent appointment in Macau and I must leave straight away.'

'Of course,' William said. 'I'll just return the bird to its shady corner; it will be more comfortable there, then I will show you out.'

Pierre Volande nodded, but remained silent.

As soon as William was out of sight, he grabbed the tulip tree and made for the door. The plant was cumbersome, but he still managed the steps two at a time. He dashed straight across the courtyard and then ran as fast as his legs would carry him, down the street and out of sight.

*****

An hour later, William sat on the veranda, regretting the folly of leaving the Frenchman alone, when he heard someone knocking furiously on the outer door. Chi Yu had long ago given up waiting to prepare lunch and had disappeared to his own small garden at the back of the house. William hurried across the courtyard as the knocking became more urgent and the agitation in the visitor's voice increased in volume.

'Mr Will'am, Mr Will'am, come quick.' It was the voice of Lam Qua.

William drew back the gate to find the young artist bent double; he was coughing loudly and gasping for breath. When he looked up, William saw that his blackened face was streaked with tears, that his *queue* was singed and his tunic was torn. He carried the remains of a large painting; the frame was still intact and the canvas charred, but what remained of the image had not altogether disappeared.

William took the frame away from Lam Qua; it was still hot. He looked up and down the empty lane, then pulled Lam Qua into the courtyard. 'What happened?' he asked.

Lam Qua was unable to speak for several minutes; when he did, it was in Cantonese. He told William that before he even reached his studio, some of his neighbours met him at the corner of Old China Street. They had discovered a fire in his studio when they opened up for business. They had intended to break down the door, not knowing whether or not their friend was still inside, but had discovered the door was already open. All his neighbours had joined together, handing buckets of water, one to another, in a long chain. They had done their best to extinguish the fire, but oil paint and the materials used for cleaning had acted as tinder. Most of the paintings and the materials recently delivered from Shanghai had been destroyed. Once the smoke had been subdued, Lam

Qua had insisted on entering the building. He'd found Dick's painting of the Frenchman in the room adjoining the main studio. It had been placed there ready for collection. The smoke had caused it to be considerably damaged, and being able to recognise the sitter was questionable.

'Damn the wretched Frenchman, he's gone too far this time,' William exclaimed at the top of his voice. 'But remember Lam Qua, I still have the sketch you made of the fellow, I shall make sure the authorities have sight of it. Even if the painting is destroyed, Monsieur Volande can still be identified – and mark my words, he will pay for this!'

CHAPTER 18
Singapore, Friday 17th March 1826

The weather had remained fair throughout the whole voyage and unlike the journey undertaken by Chin Ming and Wing Yee in 1822, the *Golden Phoenix* arrived ahead of schedule. Captain Lim had no idea of Dick's connection with Wing Yee and Chin Ming and Dick had chosen not to bring it to his attention. Instead, he'd kept himself to himself during the whole three and a half weeks at sea, sketching the activities of the crew and enjoying a book William had given him about Chinese painting. He'd delighted in perusing its contents from cover to cover, learning about different techniques and admiring the skill of the artists. Occasionally, he'd checked on his crate, giving the excuse that he needed to make sure his paintings were still well protected from the sea air, and when no-one was looking, he'd checked on the orchid and cared for it as William had instructed.

He heard the sound of chains clanging against each other in a regular rhythm as the anchor descended towards the sea bed. It was a fine day and the view of the expanding town made his heart miss a beat. Dick hurried to his cabin to retrieve his sketchbook, for even during the few short months he'd been away, the panorama had changed considerably. He noted three new houses at the far end of Beach Road; their red tiles matching those of the other houses in the area and their gleaming white walls announcing their status as the home of a successful merchant. This being the season of the northeast monsoon, the harbour was filled with numerous junks from China, Cochin and Siam, bringing tea, raw silk, camphor and earthenware to the ever-expanding port. As he was finishing his sketch, several small riverboats and sampans had already begun to make their way towards the *Golden Phoenix* and soon it would be time to go ashore.

'I instruct some of the crew to help you disembark,' Captain Lim said as he approached Dick. 'There is room for you in number three boat.'

Dick thanked him. 'It was good of you to have me on board, and especially at such short notice,' he said. 'I've enjoyed the last few weeks.'

'You make many drawings every day. Sometime parts of ship, but mostly it is men doing work.'

'Have I upset someone?' Dick said. 'Should I have asked their permission – or maybe I should have gained your consent first?'

'No need to ask. Men are flattered, but maybe I ask you for one drawing for – what is English – for remembering.'

'A souvenir, a keepsake, a reminder of the time we spent together,' Dick said. 'Of course, I will happily give you one of the drawings – here, take my sketchbook and choose which one you'd like.' He offered the pad to Captain Lim; Lim turned the pages slowly and finally chose a view looking back on the coast of Cho Lan, the place where they had taken on fresh water.

*****

As usual on Fridays, school had finished around noon. Abdullah had left to attend the mosque and Chin Ming had taken her time to pack up her books and tidy the classroom. Knowing she had the afternoon to herself she made her way towards the quay; she was hungry and hoped her favourite hawker stall would still have some *mee soup* available. She threaded her way between the other stalls and found Ah Pin busily cleaning a large wok. Like Baba Tan, Ah Pin was of Peranakan descent. He made his own noodles and his food was delicious.

'You want soup, missy?' he said.

'Yes please,' Chin Ming said. 'I've had a busy morning and I've been looking forward to this all the way from the school-house.'

'Sit, sit, I make for you.' Ah Pin gathered together a selection of vegetables, plunged them into his special broth and added a handful of noodles. He stirred the whole concoction together, scooping the contents into the air several times and returning them to the steaming liquid. Then, he poured the soup into a blue and white bowl, topped it with fresh-cut chilli and coriander and placed it in front of Chin Ming. She savoured the aroma for only a moment before dipping her spoon into the broth; she enjoyed every mouthful.

'New ship arrive this morning,' Ah Pin said as she returned her bowl, spoon and chopsticks.

'Where is it from?' she said. Both she and Wing Yee believed Dick and the two brothers would be away for about fifteen weeks, but it was now almost six months since they had left. Surely, they must return to Singapore soon.

'Not sure,' Ah Pin said, 'but some say it come from Guang-zhou.'

Her heart missed a beat. Even now, all this time later, Chin Ming could not hear the name of that town without thinking of her father. Once again, she was reminded of the date she had lost sight of him and of the day, several months later, when she stole aboard a junk thinking that she might find him here in Singapore.

She said goodbye to Ah Pin and with his news in her ears, she was drawn towards the place where the bumboats, bringing cargo from newly arrived ships, tied up.

*****

As the lighter approached the quay, Dick hoped there would be enough coolies around to help transport his crate from the harbour to the house he shared with Alexander Johnston. He shielded his eyes from the bright sunlight, but even then it was too intense to see anything clearly; he would just have to wait. The boat bumped against the wall of the quay and he grabbed at the crate to prevent it from sliding away from him. Two members of the ship's crew, who had accompanied him to shore, grinned at him. They stood confidently, despite the swell of water as it slapped against the side of the small vessel, causing it to move up and down in a regular rhythm. The men indicated that they would help Dick haul his baggage safely onto land.

They lifted the crate as easily as if it were empty, the tight muscles on their upper arms being the only indication that this was far from the truth. The first man stepped onto the sodden steps that led from the water up to the quay, taking all the weight of the box until his companion was able to follow suit; they moved swiftly and minutes later, the precious package was back on dry land.

Dick followed quickly behind the pair, but before he could properly thank them, they had disappeared amongst the hawker stalls. He sat on top of the crate, wondering what to do next. When he looked up, he saw Chin Ming walking towards him. He couldn't believe his eyes at first and blinked several times to make sure he wasn't dreaming. He was afraid she hadn't seen him; he leapt up, waving frantically and laughing as he did so.

'Dick, is it really you?' she said. 'You've been away so long. Where are the others?'

Without thinking, Dick took her by the shoulders and held her in his gaze. 'I'm so pleased to see you,' he said.

She gasped. She was pleased to see him too, but such close proximity, in public, made her feel uncomfortable.

'But where are the two brothers?' she repeated, releasing herself from his grasp.

Still grinning and seeming not to notice her unease, Dick went on to outline the bare bones of their revised plans. 'Edmund and James left for Sumatra at the beginning of January; I decided to stay in Guangzhou for a while. I've been learning to paint in oils; those are my paintings in this chest, I can't wait to show you.'

'I look forward to that,' she said, 'but we need to move away from the wharf. Why don't I stay here with your baggage while you go to find some people to take it all back to Mr Johnston's house?'

*****

The following day, Dick spent the entire morning carefully unpacking the crate and transferring most of the paintings to his room. The landscape of Guangzhou was left in the dining room, ready to present to Chin Ming and Wing Yee when they arrived that evening for a celebratory dinner.

He'd removed the orchid from its hiding place as soon as the coolies had helped offload the crate from their cart the previous afternoon. By the time Alexander Johnston returned from his warehouse, Dick had refreshed the bark and moss surrounding its roots and gently wiped its leaves with a cloth soaked in tepid water. He'd followed William's instructions to the letter and the precious plant looked healthy enough, but he secretly hoped Wing Yee would now take charge and look after it until Edmund returned.

*****

Baba Tan arrived with his three female charges at exactly seven o'clock. His wife pointed out the first stars winking at them and Wing Yee took a deep breath. She always enjoyed the aromatic perfume that pervaded Mr Johnston's garden and was glad to be back here again. The heat of the day had dissipated; tomorrow there was no school for Chin Ming and no business for Baba Tan and Wing Yee to conduct, so they were all looking forward to a relaxing evening, exchanging their news over a leisurely meal.

Dick stood on the threshold, with a broad grin across his face. He greeted each of the guests in turn, but could not contain his excitement for a moment longer than was necessary. He led them onto the veranda and invited them to sit down. Alexander Johnston joined them and added his own welcome.

Dick moved inside the door for just a moment, then reappeared carrying a rectangular shape, draped in a piece of hessian. Johnston helped him to carry it and place it against a chair, directly in front of Wing Yee and Chin Ming.

'What might that be?' Baba Tan asked.

'It's a present, it's for both of you,' Dick said, beaming at his friends. 'Something I painted while I was working with Lam Qua.'

Chin Ming and Wing Yee exchanged glances, then they waited for Dick to reveal whatever was under the sacking.

As soon as he began to loosen the rope that held the whole thing together, Dick's excitement turned to apprehension. What if they didn't like it? What if it brought back unhappy memories instead of the pleasant recollections he'd imagined when he embarked upon the project?

He needn't have worried; as soon as the hessian fell to the floor, both women gasped. It was just like looking through a window onto the panorama that had dominated such a significant part of their lives. They rose from their chairs together and stepped closer to the painting. Wing Yee ran her finger along the outline of the figure who she recognised as herself; Chin Ming took a deep breath, remembering the last time she had looked upon this scene. Both women turned towards Dick, 'Thank you, thank you so much,' they said almost at the same time. Then Chin Ming added, 'You couldn't have given us a better present, we will treasure it always.'

'I'm glad you like it,' Dick said, much relieved.

'Tonight, like evening before you go away,' Wing Yee said. 'All friends together to share meal and tell stories.'

'Not quite the same,' Chin Ming said, her eyes brightening as she recalled the occasion. 'That night, we had the Beaumont brothers with us too.'

'Ah yes,' Baba Tan replied, turning to Dick, 'the two young men who persuaded you to leave us. When did you say they might return?'

'I don't think I mentioned an exact date,' Dick said. He raised his eyebrows as he looked at Chin Ming. Was he imagining it, or did she look flustered? 'When they left Guangzhou in January, we agreed to meet back here in a couple of months. I thought they might even be here ahead of me.'

'I think that was a little optimistic,' Johnston said. 'You said they travelled in a local trading vessel?'

'That's right,' Dick said. 'It was a *lancha* from Palembang, but a fair-sized one and well-used to that particular route. You don't think anything has happened to them, do you?'

'Not at all, but at that time of year the seas would be rough, especially once they reached the Sundra Strait. I would imagine it took them all of six weeks to reach Palembang. If they intended to travel around the coast to Bencoolen as you said,' Johnston added, 'I wouldn't expect them to return back here for quite a while yet.'

For the rest of the evening, the focus remained on Dick; everyone had questions to ask. He began by telling them about the different types of food he'd enjoyed, then described the wonder of the mountains; the plants they'd collected along the way and the industry he'd witnessed amongst the people working in the padi fields. However, his greatest pleasure came from telling them about Lam Qua and the newly acquired skills he'd learned.

'Do you think you'll continue to work in oils? Or will you go back to watercolours?' Chin Ming said.

'Both, I hope,' Dick said. 'It's much easier to acquire watercolours here, of course, but I did bring some oil paints back with me and I can always ask Lam Qua to send me more.'

There was a brief silence. 'You haven't said very much about William Lawrence,' Johnston said, 'or why he wanted Edmund and his brother to disembark in Macao instead of Guangzhou. Come to think of it, you haven't said a great deal about your actual journey, did something go wrong? What is it that you're not telling us?'

Dick looked pensive. He'd been wondering about this part of the story all day. There was no reason at all why he shouldn't tell them about the Frenchman, but he didn't want to upset Chin Ming and Wing Yee. It was now three years since Pieter Steffens, the Dutchman who had treated them so badly, had been arrested and taken off to Calcutta, but he knew anything that reminded them of that time often brought back unpleasant memories. Volande was yet another European; a man like Steffens who was arrogant, someone who flouted the law and would go to any lengths to get his own way. How much should he tell them without causing undue distress?

'It was more of a nuisance than a problem,' he said having considered his words carefully.

Five pairs of eyes stared straight at him. No-one spoke, but it was clear that they were all expecting him to continue.

He gulped down a glass of coconut water while he considered how to continue. He concluded that his encounter with the Frenchman was entirely different to the suffering inflicted upon his friends by the Dutchman; Volande was a rogue but he'd never stooped to violence, and anyway he was now miles away and there was nothing to worry about. Besides, Dick thought, I've arrived home safely and the orchid is thriving.

'There was a Frenchman – he had a bad reputation ...'

'What sort of bad reputation?' Baba Tan asked.

'He obtains things that people will pay a lot of money for and isn't too fussy about how he acquires them.'

Everyone looked at him as if he was speaking a language which none of them quite understood. Johnston broke the silence. 'What has this man got to do with William Lawrence's change of plan?'

'William knew all about a Frenchman; he'd been warned that he might try to disrupt the expedition – that's why he met us in Macao. We spent two days there and then began our journey along the Xi River. We spent the first night with one of William's friends – but the next morning, we discovered that a European with a strange accent had been asking all sorts of questions about our route. William suspected it was the man he'd been warned about and was shocked to find he'd moved to Macau.'

Dick continued, briefly mentioning the precautions they'd taken during the weeks following that first incident. Neither Chin Ming nor Wing Yee seemed unduly perturbed by the tale and so, he was able to relax.

'Did you see this man again, and why did you think he was French?' Chin Ming said.

'The man William had been told about was supposed to be French – and when we reached Shunde, a European approached me when I was on my own; he used that phrase that you sometimes use, you know, the one that means farewell.'

Chin Ming's eyes grew large. Everyone moved to the edge of their chairs, listening intently. Wing Yee absentmindedly helped herself to a rambutan from the fruit bowl; she peeled back the red, hairy flesh and sucked the soft, translucent flesh, totally enthralled with Dick's tale.

He slowly and carefully recounted the rest of the story, including the gift of the rare orchid and the trouble William had taken to conceal it. Then, he told them about the Frenchman turning up at Lam Qua's studio, wanting to have his portrait painted and the constant round of questions he'd asked.

'That was when William decided the orchid would never be safe as long as it remained in Guangzhou,' Dick said. He took a deep breath before continuing: 'William asked me to bring it to Singapore; he wants Edmund to take it back to England.'

CHAPTER 19
Palembang, Sumatra, 31st March 1826

When Raffles met with James and Edmund in London and told them about his life in Bencoolen, it had been the East India Company's farthest-flung trading post. Edmund was particularly looking forward to travelling there. However, when he and James reached Palembang in the middle of February, they discovered it would take far too long to sail around to the other side of the island. The Dutch administration, which had abolished the Palembang Sultanate only last year, had also not been helpful.

Instead, the brothers had spent the last six weeks travelling from Palembang along the Musi River; one of its main tributaries took them further inland to a place from which they could begin their climb into the Bukit Barisan mountains.

The weather was not as kind to them here as it had been in China; they'd experienced heavy downfalls, numerous mudslides and frequent soakings. It was on their return from this expedition that James had missed his footing, slithered down a ravine and badly sprained his ankle. Their only reward was the acquisition of several more plants along the way, together with a small collection of pressed leaves and flowers that would be handed over to Dick when they returned to Singapore; the sketches of this new collection would be added to his other drawings.

During the days that James had been resting, Edmund had

explored Palembang on his own. He brought back tales of the time when the town had been the capital of the Srivijaya kingdom and the most important trading centre in this part of Asia. He had begun, at last, to understand why Raffles had developed a fascination with the history of this part of the world. Tonight, however, he had a different story to tell.

As he sat on the veranda of their lodging house looking at the darkening sky, the first star winked at him and he smiled to himself. The warmth of the evening engulfed him like a familiar blanket; he closed his eyes and took a deep breath. The sweet smell of frangipani filled his nostrils, and he was immediately transported back to their last night in Singapore. It was the same fragrance he'd noticed when Dick had introduced him to Chin Ming; she was wearing a spray of frangipani flowers in her hair. There had only been time for the briefest of introductions before they'd been invited to sit down to dinner. He remembered being pleased to find her sitting directly opposite him – a beautiful young woman. He'd been surprised by the way she'd talked about her work in the fledgling school, a mixture of passion and delight. Her eyes, full of curiosity, had sparkled in the soft light of the oil lamps. It was the memory of those eyes that came into his mind when he'd seen the stranger at the quay this afternoon.

'Daydreaming again?' James said as he hobbled towards his brother.

'I was enjoying the balmy evening and remembering those first few days in the tropics. Do you realise that it's been ten months since we left England, and almost six months since we left Singapore?'

'Which place are you missing the most, little brother?'

'What does that mean?'

'I think you might be quite interested in re-acquainting yourself with a certain young woman; what was her name?' James paused, knowing his banter was making Edmund feel uncomfortable. 'Ah yes, it was Chin Ming, I believe.'

'It would be a pleasure to get to know both of the young ladies we met there.' Edmund spoke quickly, hoping that the warm glow he was feeling on his cheeks was not obvious to his brother. 'Both Wing Yee and Chin Ming had interesting things to say, I seem to remember.'

James remembered the look of disappointment he'd seen in his brother's eyes when only Wing Yee and Baba Tan arrived at the quay to see them off the following day. He hadn't realised until now that Edmund was still thinking of her fondly; maybe it was time for him to stop teasing his brother.

'Well, now my ankle has mended we can begin to think of our return journey,' James said. 'We can have a word with the harbour master tomorrow if you like?'

'I'm not sure you should be travelling yet awhile,' Edmund said. 'It was a very nasty sprain, after all.'

'Maybe, but I can put my weight on it for a little while longer each day – and we can't stay here forever, our funds are getting low.'

Edmund knew James was right, they did need to be careful. However, what he thought he'd witnessed this afternoon might be of even greater concern; he was yet to share this information with his brother.

*****

James studied the expression on Edmund's face and tried to work out what was different about him this evening. It was the first time in over a week that he hadn't rushed back to disclose what he'd discovered on that particular day and James had become accustomed to hearing about his brother's adventures at places such as the Kuto Besak Fortress and the Great Mosque. Edmund had the knack of making even the most mundane stories – about the people he'd met, the strange aromas that filled his nostrils, the sounds and sights he'd come across in the local market – sound exciting.

'You're looking somewhat pensive this evening, little brother. Is there anything you'd like to share with me?' James said.

'When I told you earlier that I was thinking about Singapore, it was because of something that happened today, not just the balminess of the evening.'

'I knew it; you do want to get to know Chin Ming better.'

'Will you stop that, James? This is something quite different. Yes, it's about, or rather it might be connected with Chin Ming – at least I think it is – but it's nothing to do with any feelings I might or might not have for her.'

'But you do find her attractive?' James said, pleased with himself that he hadn't misread the expression he'd seen on his brother's face.

Edmund let out a deep, frustrated breath and waited for his brother to stop asking awkward questions. He shook his head slowly from side to side, then stared at the wooden boards of the veranda until James eventually ran out of steam.

'Sorry,' James said, 'I was only thinking it would be good for you ... here I go again. My apologies, Edmund, there is obviously something on your mind. I promise not to interrupt again; please continue.'

There was a silence. Edmund covered his mouth with his hand whilst he thought of where to start. He pursed his lips and put his head on one side, then he began.

'I took one of the *kajang* boats across the river to the Chinese kampong today.'

James wondered why Edmund had seemed reluctant to begin; it sounded as if today's story was similar to all the others he'd heard over the last few days – descriptions of temples similar to those they'd seen in and around Guangzhou, buildings like the ones in Singapore or the mixture of different dishes being offered by the hawkers. He decided to wait patiently; soon he realised his brother had yet to move on to what might be the most significant part of the story.

'When I returned to the wharf,' Edmund said, 'a crowd was beginning to form, and I wondered what was happening. I couldn't see what the commotion was all about for a long time, but then the crowd parted and two men were helped from one of the local trading boats onto the quay.'

'Two men?' James said. 'For a moment, I thought you were going to tell me you'd seen the Frenchman who pursued us in China. So, what was so special about the men you saw and why did they attract such a large gathering?'

'I was told that they'd just arrived from one of the islands, Bangka or Belitung, I can't remember which one.'

'You still haven't answered my question. Did you manage to find out anything else about them?' James asked.

Edmund looked directly into his brother's eyes. Should he continue and share his suspicions with James; after all, he had no actual evidence? The thoughts that had been doing somersaults inside his head for the last couple of hours were all based on speculation.

'One of them was wearing the robes of a Franciscan monk,' Edmund said, 'and the other man – who looked very frail – was Chinese. He was very thin and his hair was completely white, the light had gone out of his eyes, but there was something about him that reminded me of Chin Ming. I've been thinking about it ever since.'

James gasped. 'You don't think it might be ... you do, don't you?'

'Yes,' Edmund said. 'I think it might be Chin Ming's father.'

*****

The two brothers sat in silence. James struggled with the possibility of what Edmund had just whispered; how could it possibly be true after all this time? Could it be that his brother's head was so full of thoughts of Chin Ming when he had seen the two figures on the quay that he'd simply jumped to the wrong conclusion? How likely was it that the white-haired man could be her father? Everything Dick had told them about his disappearance indicated that he would not have survived his abduction. The man was an intellectual, not used to the rough ways that would be commonplace for his captors; if he'd tried to reason with them, it was far more likely that they would have increased their brutality rather than responded to his persuasiveness.

*****

Edmund studied his brother's face. He could tell that he was reflecting on what had just been said, but he had no idea what was going on in his head and where his thoughts were leading him. Was it possible that James believed he had imagined the scene at the quay? He had no proof, of course, he didn't even know what Chin Ming's father actually looked like, but the fact that this man had been accompanied by a Franciscan surely gave the coincidence some sort of credibility.

'You think I'm imagining things, don't you?' he said at last.

'It's not that,' James replied, 'but I was wondering about the likelihood of it being true. It's how long since he went missing? Where has he been in the meantime? How did he get here? And more importantly, why hasn't he tried to contact his daughter?'

'I can't answer any of those questions,' Edmund said. 'But surely the fact that the man I saw was accompanied by a Franciscan monk must have some significance? Dick told us that Chin Ming had been looked after by a Franciscan, a priest who had been a close friend of her father.'

'The only way to establish the truth is to locate the two

men you saw today. We can then try to find out who they are and what they are doing here,' James said. 'We can make a start first thing tomorrow morning; it will do me good to get out and about again.'

*****

The two brothers made slow progress to the quay; James was anxious to accompany Edmund, but he could only walk slowly. Edmund, on the other hand, was keen to find someone to ask about the men he'd seen the previous day and each time he realised James was lagging behind, part of him wished that he was doing this on his own.

The pain in James' ankle was beginning to return; he was doing his best to keep up with Edmund, but it was no use; he still wasn't strong enough to walk very far. When he finally reached the place where Edmund was waiting for him, he made an effort to lighten the mood. 'It's as well you witnessed the visitors' arrival yesterday, rather than today,' he said.

'What do you mean?'

'Today is April 1st – All Fools' Day,' James said, 'I might have said you were playing a trick on me if you'd come back with your story today.'

'We might be made fools of anyway,' Edmund said. After a night's sleep, even he was beginning to wonder whether his eyes had been playing tricks on him after all.

It didn't take them long to establish that two men had arrived at the quay from Belitung the previous afternoon. It was more difficult, however, to establish what had then happened to them. Their knowledge of the local language was almost non-existent and now that Palembang was under Dutch administration it was not easy to find anyone willing to speak in English. At the end of the morning, they were no further forward.

'I need to rest my ankle,' James told his brother. 'Why don't I stay here for a while? It will enable you to cover more ground and I can always watch out for anyone who might be able to help.'

Trying his best to keep his feeling of relief to himself, Edmund agreed. He went off in the direction of the Catholic church, with the intention of asking about any visitors who had sought their help recently. He left James sitting outside a local coffee shop, ready to order. There, he would be able to watch passers-by while relaxing and recovering his strength.

James was nodding in the sultry afternoon heat when something tickled his arm. He slapped at it, thinking it was some uninvited insect, but when he looked up, he was holding onto the garment of a Franciscan monk. He let go of the sleeve immediately and struggled to his feet. He apologised. The man accepted his explanation; he even seemed amused.

'It's not the first time my habit has caused a problem,' he said. 'These wide sleeves are useful for keeping me cool, but they do tend to flap about when I walk faster than normal.'

James introduced himself. 'Did you by any chance arrive here yesterday afternoon?' he said. He then felt rather foolish; the man had probably lived in Palembang for years.

'We landed just before sunset,' the priest said. 'The sea was very rough and there was a time when I thought we would be joining the fish. I've been looking for a passage on one of the local vessels for over a week, but the one that brought us here was old and very slow.'

James wondered what had happened to Edmund. It should be his brother asking the questions, but he decided to do his best by engaging this man in conversation and trying to find out what he could. 'You came with a companion?'

'Yes, I brought a friend over from the island; he has not been at all well, but now we are ready to travel again. Once we have recovered from the trauma of yesterday's journey, I'll be looking for a vessel to take us to Singapore.'

'Excuse me, Father,' James said, 'you must think I'm very impertinent asking so many questions, but may I ask just one more?'

The priest looked at him quizzically, paused for the briefest of moments, then nodded.

'I was wondering whether you and your companion travelled to Belitung from Guangzhou – and if so, how long have you been there?'

Before the priest could answer, Edmund came rushing up to join them. He was flushed and had clearly been running. He bent double to regain control of his breathing. When he stood upright, there were two pairs of eyes looking anxious; he beamed. 'I believe you might be the priest we've heard so much about from a young lady called Chin Ming,' he said. 'Am I right in thinking you are Father John?'

The man in the brown habit sat down on the chair opposite James. 'I was just about to introduce myself to your friend here,' he said. 'Yes, I am Father John and I arrived in Belitung from Guangzhou a few months ago, but now I have to ask you some questions. When and where did you meet Chin Ming? Tell me please, who are you – and how do you know the young lady in question?'

The brothers introduced themselves and told the priest about meeting Raffles in London, about being introduced to Chin Ming and her friend Wing Yee in Singapore, their subsequent travels in China and taking a detour to Sumatra before returning to Singapore again. All three men continued to ask questions of each other for the next hour and eventually, Father John told them his story.

*****

'Three years ago, I received a letter from Stamford Raffles telling me of Chin Ming's arrival in Singapore and some of the terrible things that she'd endured. He told me that she was now safe, but continued to be troubled about her father. It was obvious to me at the time that my suspicions had been correct and my dear friend, Li Soong Heng, was dead.'

Edmund opened his mouth to ask a question, but James gestured to him to wait a while longer. 'In July last year, I received a directive expelling all Franciscans from China. I spent a few weeks arranging passages for the other monks to travel to India, where they would join the order there. My plan was to follow them a few weeks later. At the beginning of August, I was on my way to the docks to make the final arrangements, but I was forced to take refuge in the doorway of a warehouse when a sudden storm charged through the streets, sweeping everything out of its path. The wall of the building was thin, and I heard two men arguing furiously just beyond the place where I was sheltering.'

Edmund did his best to contain all the questions that were piling up in his head, but when he began to fidget on his chair Father John decided he needed to get to the point of the story.

'In between the cacophony of noise, I recognised various words that made me listen more intently. Amongst them were *Dutchman, Amoy, opium* and finally the name of my dear friend. I pressed my ear to the wall and over the next half-hour I was able to ascertain that after his abduction, Soon Heng had been taken to Amoy and then put on a ship called the *Tek Sing*, bound for Batavia. I had heard about that ship being wrecked on a reef in the South China Sea. At the time, it was rumoured that an Indiaman had passed through the area shortly afterwards and managed to rescue some of the survivors. Another story said that a small Chinese junk had also been in those parts and perhaps they too had picked up survivors.'

Edmund moved to the edge of his seat, anxious now not to miss a word. James, too, gave all of his attention to Father John.

'I realised the argument was something to do with them losing what they referred to as their prize; each was blaming the other. It became apparent that the prize they referred to was Soong Heng. No-one knew whether he had survived the shipwreck or not. It was at that moment that I decided I needed to find out for myself.'

'Instead of travelling to Calcutta, I booked a passage to Palembang. It was the port nearest to where the ship had gone down. I arrived here last October. At first, I thought my journey had been wasted, but then I heard about a so-called hermit living on Belitung. The more I heard about the man, the more familiar he seemed, so I arranged to be taken across to the island.'

'And you found your friend?' James said.

'I found a shadow of the man I'd known in Guangzhou. He was living in a cave, living on fish and wild berries, washing in the nearby stream. A young boy, who had also survived the wreck, was taking care of him as best he could.'

'But that was six months ago,' Edmund said.

'Indeed, it was,' Father John said. 'I'm afraid my friend had lost his memory; he had no idea who I was at that time. I've been working with him over the past months, helping him to remember bits and pieces from his former life, helping him to regain his interest in life. He isn't there yet, but I decided if we could get to Singapore and find his daughter, then the missing parts of the puzzle might begin to fall into place.'

CHAPTER 20
Palembang, Sumatra, April 1826

The day after his conversation with Father John – and the many surprises it had revealed – Edmund went to the harbour to make enquiries about any vessels due to leave for Singapore. He was fulfilling the promise he'd made to James, but he also intended to pass on any useful information to the priest. It didn't take him long to discover there was a problem.

In five days' time, the fasting month of Ramadan would begin and after that, none of the local *latchas* would be available for at least two weeks. He was about to give up on the task when he recognised Arif, the man who had brought them to Palembang over six weeks ago. Edmund waved frantically and ran along the quay to where Arif's *latcha* was tied up.

Arif was pleased to see him, but explained that he couldn't help for the exact same reasons that Edmund had discovered earlier. None of the local traders would be prepared to embark upon a journey that resulted in them being away from home during the fasting month.

'You need Chinese ship,' Arif said. 'None here for some time.'

'Do you know if any are expected within the next couple of weeks?'

Arif shouted across to the men in the other boats that butted against each other along that part of the quay. Edmund had no idea what was being said; he'd picked up the odd word of Malay from Dick and while the language spoken here was similar, he remained at a loss. Questions and answers bounced backwards and forwards between the various vessels; some of the men just shrugged their shoulders, some smiled benignly then carried on with whatever task they had embarked upon. Arif cupped his hands over his mouth and shouted to a *latcha* that was moored a little further out. The response was inaudible at first and Arif responded by shouting even louder in that direction. Edmund heard the word *tiga*, which he knew meant three, but he would have to wait for Arif to translate the remainder of the conversation.

*****

There was no sign of Father John when Edmund returned to the coffee shop the following day. No-one knew whether or not to expect him, so Edmund decided to make it his business to locate the small rest house where the priest had told him he was staying. He headed back towards the Catholic church, but just short of the attap building which displayed a cross above its main door, he bumped into the man he'd spoken to only two days ago. The man was a French missionary who had previously worked in Java. He pointed to a small, cobbled lane beside the church where he told Edmund he would find the rest house.

He discovered the place easily enough. It was built of the same materials as the church, but the floor was raised on stilts with low walls and many windows. The high, sloping roof cascaded down over the veranda and standing there in full view, Edmund recognised Father John; he appeared to be talking to someone seated on a low-slung rattan chair. The other man had his back towards Edmund.

The steps leading up to the balcony were loose and squeaked whenever any pressure was put upon them. When

Edmund reached the second step, Father John turned to face him.

'I'm afraid Soong Heng has just fallen asleep,' he said. 'He tires very easily these days, but I'm sure it will only be a short nap and then I can introduce you.'

Edmund glanced at the figure reclining in the chair. His hair was completely white and despite his sallow complexion, he looked comfortable and relaxed.

'I've discovered a small Chinese junk is expected to arrive here in two or three days. It will be off-loading some of its cargo and then it's due to sail for Singapore; it's possible that the captain might be willing to take on passengers. If the two of you are interested and able to travel, then I could ask the harbour master to negotiate on our behalf.'

'That's excellent news!' Father John said, 'but there will be three of us. The young boy who has been looking after Soong Heng since the accident came with us from Belitung. I think my friend will benefit greatly from such a journey, but Chang will need to come too; they have come to rely upon one another.'

Edmund and the priest continued to talk for nearly an hour, exchanging ideas and sharing their concerns about the devastating effect of the opium trade in China. Finally, Edmund pushed back his chair and made ready to leave; he was about to say goodbye when he realised, he was being observed. Soong Heng had his head turned on one side and his pale, hazel eyes scrutinised Edmund from top to toe.

'Have I met this young man before?' Soong Heng said in Cantonese, looking to the priest for an explanation. Despite being a great linguist since he was a young man himself, Soong Heng spoke only one language these days. It was Chang's tongue and the one that they'd shared during the years spent together after the shipwreck.

'No, you've not met before today,' said Father John,

replying in Cantonese. 'This is Edmund Beaumont, he is from England, but has been travelling in China for several months. I met Edmund and his brother in town the other day. They too are looking for passage back to Singapore.'

Edmund stood quietly, not understanding any Cantonese, but from the way the priest glanced from Soong Heng to himself and back again, he gathered some sort of introduction was being made.

Soong Heng looked confused. There was something about this Englishman – something reassuring that made him feel he wanted to get to know him better. He saw a kind face and intelligent eyes; had they really never met before today? – if only he could remember the time before the shipwreck. He turned his gaze to Father John, seeking reassurance. There was so much of the past that he could no longer recollect; the only thing he was certain of was a sense of grief, maybe even a fleeting memory involving torture, but he couldn't believe this young man had played any part in that.

Father John knelt down beside his friend and took his hand. He stroked the long, slender fingers until they stopped shaking. 'Edmund is a plant collector. He and his brother have been travelling around Guangdong Province with my friend William Lawrence,' he said, struggling to make sure his intonation was correct.

'Will – am...' Soong Heng said, 'Law – lence, you say ...' He rubbed his forehead with his left hand and screwed up his eyes. He tightened his lips and looked at Father John, shaking his head from side to side. 'I'm sorry,' he said, 'I cannot remember anyone of that name.'

'Not to worry,' Father John said. 'I'm not sure you actually met him, but you might have heard me talk about him occasionally. He used to visit the mission, when he returned from his travels to tell me all about the plants that he'd seen and the monasteries he'd visited along the way.'

Edmund took a step closer to Soong Heng. 'Can you translate for me please?' he said, looking at Father John. He knelt down, so that his eyes gazed directly into those of Soong Heng.

'My name is Edmund Beaumont, sir. My brother is called James. He hurt his ankle a little while ago and is resting it now, but I know he would very much like to meet you too.'

Father John translated those parts of Edmund's speech that hadn't already been disclosed, then he went on to say, 'Edmund tells me there is a possibility of obtaining a passage to Singapore at the end of this week.'

Soong Heng's eyes brightened; he smiled as he turned towards Edmund, 'Stam-ford Raffles,' he said. These were the first words Soong Heng had spoken in English for a long, long time.

Edmund's chest tightened; that smile was so familiar. It was the mental image he'd been carrying around with him for the past six months. There was no doubt that this was Chin Ming's father.

*****

On Thursday morning, news of the arrival of the Chinese junk spread quickly. James persuaded his brother that he was now fit enough to accompany him to the quay. They went straight there and found the harbour master seated at his desk inside his house. On the table, Edmund noticed a bottle of *Ould Jenever* and an empty tulip-shaped glass; surely the man had not started drinking so early in the day? The Dutchman pulled himself to his feet, laying the pipe he'd been smoking to one side; the stench of vanilla tobacco filled the room.

Edmund had been told there was a good deal of corruption amongst the Dutch administrators and he was not expecting the negotiation to be straightforward.

Initially, they were told it would be impossible to secure a passage. The junk was small, the journey from Macao had taken longer than usual and there was a sick passenger on board. Edmund was not to be put off, but even his powers of persuasion made little progress with the overbearing Dutch-man.

'One of our party is a priest,' James said, hoping that this might make a difference.

'What sort of priest?' the harbour master asked, his accent heavy and guttural.

'He's a Franciscan. His order was told to leave China and most of them have returned to the main house in Calcutta.'

A sullen expression settled across the face of the harbour master, 'I will see what is to be done,' he said. 'We do not want any more Catholic missionaries – or any of their friends – staying here too long; the authorities would not like that at all. Come back this afternoon – and bring the priest fellow with you.'

*****

By the time they reached the rest house, the news of the ship's arrival had already reached Father John.

'I've tried to explain everything to Soong Heng, but I'm afraid I haven't made much headway. Every time I mention Singapore, he says Stamford Raffles, in exactly the same way that he did when you were here the other day. He has not once mentioned his daughter, either in English or Cantonese. I do hope I'm doing the right thing, taking him there to meet her.'

Before either Edmund or James could respond, Soong Heng appeared on the veranda. Father John introduced him to both brothers, assuming he would not remember meeting Edmund earlier in the week. Soong Heng bowed politely to James, but as soon as Edmund's name was mentioned, he took his hand and led him to a quiet corner of the veranda. They sat, looking into each other's eyes, both men searching for something, but neither knowing what that something was.

Edmund examined the older man's face for other reminders of Chin Ming. Soong Heng pinched his lips together and tapped his fingertips against the side of his head. He took a deep breath and shook his head from side to side. When he looked up, Edmund noticed that his eyes were filled with tears.

'Forgive,' he said as he wiped his hand over his face as if to wash away all his pent-up emotion. Another English word, dredged from the depths of his memory.

'What does he mean?' Edmund said, looking towards Father John.

The priest joined them, seating himself in a nearby chair. 'He can't remember what happened, but the confusion causes great distress and tears come easily. Such weakness, for him, shows loss of face,' he said.

Soong Heng nodded; the essence of his friend's explanation understood. Then, he lifted his *queue* and pointed to an angry-looking scar at the base of his skull.

'He can't remember what happened,' Father John said. 'I believe he either fell upon something heavy and hit his head or, much more likely, he was deliberately struck by a weighty object. We may never know for sure, of course.'

At the end of the morning, Soong Heng was still sitting quietly beside Edmund; it was as if he was finding some sort of comfort in his very presence. Chang served a light lunch and then James suggested they ought to make their way back to the harbour master before he changed his mind about helping them.

'I'm sure there's no need for all of us to go,' Edmund said. 'Why don't you go with Father John and I'll stay here to keep Soong Heng company?'

James blinked; he raised his eyebrows, not quite believing the words his brother had just uttered. Edmund had always been the one who wanted to take the lead; why should he now choose to stay with Soong Heng, especially as they had virtually no language in common?

'It will be fine,' Edmund said, sensing the huge question that was hanging in the air above his brother's head.

'It will be good for Soong Heng to have the company of someone other than me,' Father John said, 'and besides, Chang is here if you have any problems.'

*****

After they left, Edmund moved his chair so that the bright, afternoon light was not in his eyes. Soong Heng leant against the back of his own chair; he took a deep breath and when he exhaled, he looked up into Edmund's face, as if he was still searching for an answer.

Edmund wondered whether he should remain quiet – maybe Soong Heng would like to sleep for a while – or he should talk, hoping that his voice soothed the older man. After a while, he decided on the latter course of action. He began by talking about Raffles – his return to England and how they had met in London. Whenever Soong Heng heard the name Raffles mentioned he closed his eyes, squeezed his lips together and tapped the index finger of his right hand on his leg.

Edmund filled the next couple of hours with the story of his journey out to Singapore, the few days he and James had enjoyed there and the months they'd spent in China. He did not refer to Chin Ming by name, partly because he didn't want to cause any upset and partly because he wasn't sure he would be able to talk about her in a dispassionate way. He wasn't expecting Soong Heng to remain awake for the length of his discourse, but if anything, his companion looked more alert now than at the beginning of the tale.

'Sin-ga-pore?' Soong Heng said.

This time, Edmund told him what he knew of the history of the island. Raffles had spoken with such great passion about the fourteenth-century kingdom and during the days he'd spent there, Dick had taken both brothers to the *Keramat* – the tomb of the last Singapore king. Wing Yee had joined them and led them to the Spice Garden on the lower slopes of Bukit Larangan; there, she'd introduced them to the various plants she was cultivating. Edmund's enthusiasm increased as he warmed to his subject. Soon, he was telling his companion about the dinner party, held the night before they departed for Macao; the evening he'd met Chin Ming for the first time.

Despite the fact he'd managed not to mention her by name, the light in his eyes gave away his secret. When he looked up, Soong Heng was nodding his head; the mask of sorrow was beginning to lift, some of his pain diffused in the tears wetting his cheeks.

'I – have – daughter,' he said. Soong Heng's use of English was beginning to return. It had taken over four years.

CHAPTER 21
Sumatra, April 1826

For the remainder of the week, the brothers saw very little of each other. As soon as breakfast was over, Edmund made his way to the rest house. Soong Heng was, as always, sitting on the balcony awaiting his arrival. It was a puzzle to everyone that this young Englishman had captivated Soong Heng's attention and even more of a mystery that their relationship had seemingly triggered his ability to speak in a language other than Cantonese. They all hoped it was an indication that other imprisoned memories could be released, and it made Father John more confident about reuniting father and daughter in Singapore.

*****

Saturday 8th April 1826
It was towards the end of the afternoon by the time the small ship was ready to leave Palembang behind. More than twenty local boats, tied up and left to rest whilst their owners made their preparations for the beginning of Ramadan, rubbed against each other along the entire length of the quay. The enticing aromas from the hawker stalls that normally pervaded the air were missing today, making the stench of decay – rotting seaweed, animal remains and open latrines – all the more potent.

The five new passengers had been allocated three small cabins to share between them; Soong Heng shared his with Chang, Edmund was with James and Father John took the one that was not much bigger than a cupboard. They learned that somewhere towards the stern, another passenger was taking refuge. Nothing was known about the person concerned; all they had been told was that he had joined the ship in Macao and the state of his health meant that he was likely to keep to his quarters throughout the entire journey

When the sun dropped over the horizon, Sumatra was well behind them. Now, all that was left was a faint orange glow that slowly gave way to a sky the colour of a well-ripened aubergine. James and Edmund stood, side by side, completely enthralled by the vastness of the ocean. They didn't hear the soft tread of Father John's sandals until he was almost parallel with them. He pointed to a place in the western sky, not far from the point where the sun had disappeared; there, they could now see the finest crescent of white light. It was as if someone had drawn a large white arc with a phantom compass, leaving a mantle of chalk dust in its wake.

'They will be pleased to see that in Palembang,' he said. 'It means that Ramadan can now officially begin.'

*****

For the next six weeks, the two brothers, the priest, the boy and Soong Heng consolidated their friendship. Chang learned an eclectic mix of English words during the voyage, and liked to practice whenever he came across either of the Beaumont brothers.

James spent many hours with Father John, telling him about the death of his wife and the child he had left behind with her grandparents. Since leaving England the pain of loss had lessened with time, but he very rarely spoke about Margaret. Father John was a good listener, and he began to feel that returning to life in the Wiltshire countryside would not be so bad after all.

Edmund spent nearly every waking hour with Soong Heng, sharing his interests, his passions and his hopes, but carefully omitting any mention of Chin Ming. Occasionally, the gossamer threads of memory began to unravel and Soong Heng's vocabulary, along with his confidence, increased, but the convoluted rope containing the long-forgotten details of his story remained tightly knotted; he continued to tire easily and spent most afternoons asleep in his cabin.

A few days into the seventh week, one of the crew sighted their destination at the point where the sky met the sea; it was announced that they would drop anchor in Singapore the following day.

*****

Since returning from China, Dick had started to address Alexander Johnston by his first name. Until then, he'd never been comfortable with the familiarity of it, but just as he had come to address Raffles by the name that everyone else used, rather than 'uncle', he had now reached a point where he was ready to move on in his relationship with his new guardian.

'I know Alexander said I shouldn't worry about the Beaumont brothers,' Dick said when he visited Baba Tan's house one evening, 'but surely they ought to be back here soon?'

Chin Ming stabbed her finger with the needle she was using to mend a tear in her tunic. She sucked the bright-red pinpoint of blood that mocked her, but was glad to have a distraction away from Dick's direct gaze. She too was concerned that James and Edmund had been away so long, but she was afraid her closest friends might think it strange if she showed any particular alarm – especially about a man she had only met briefly.

'Now that Ramadan is over, there will be more traffic from the islands,' Baba Tan said. 'I am expecting a consignment of cloves and nutmegs any day now.'

'Our nutmeg trees growing well,' Wing Yee said. 'We have own fruit soon.'

'I'm not sure the soil on Bukit Larangan will ever produce sufficient for exporting to Europe, but we will do well just to have enough freshly harvested fruits for our own use,' Baba Tan said.

Wing Yee looked disappointed; she had great hopes for the immature Spice Garden.

'It is possible, of course,' Baba Tan said, returning to the subject, 'that your friends might return here on one of the small, local vessels. They could take advantage of any of the boats that call into Sumatra. I heard a rumour only last week that a small ship from Macao, which took on new cargo in Palembang, is due to arrive here any day.'

*****

Wednesday 24th May 1826

Wing Yee had finished her latest batch of medicinal potions the previous evening; now she was waiting for more dried herbs to be delivered. She decided to find Dick and suggest they walk down to the quay together to see if there was any news of the junk Baba Tan had mentioned last night.

As always, Dick needed no persuading. The painting he'd finished the previous day would not be ready to frame until the end of the week and the merchant who had commissioned it was in no hurry. He loved spending time with Wing Yee; they had many common interests, and he'd missed their conversations during the months he'd been away; now he seized any opportunity to share his ideas with her.

When they arrived at the river, it looked the same as it

always did. The warehouses and jetties along Boat Quay were already a hive of activity – gangs of coolies busy loading and unloading goods. Their vantage point, at the mouth of the river, provided an excellent view of the harbour, crammed with ketches, sloops, frigates and junks as well as the local Malay boats. Dick put both hands over his eyes to shield them from the strong sunlight, but it was impossible to decide whether the number of vessels present today was any different to those that had been there the previous evening.

Wing Yee tugged at his sleeve and pointed to the flagstaff on top of the hill. A flag was flying, indicating the arrival of a ship new into port.

'Let's ask if anyone knows what type of vessel it is and where it's from,' Dick said. They began to make their way along the path which led to the edge of the quay. This was where all the bumboats congregated, but everyone they spoke to was too busy to engage in conversation. Dick stared out into the harbour once again, trying to make out whether he could distinguish anything new. The strength of the light made it difficult to see anything clearly, but then the water began to push and pull all the small craft taking shelter against the harbour wall. A contingent of six bumboats had turned into the mouth of the river; each was being rowed at a strong and steady pace by an oarsman anxious to offload one consignment as quickly as possible, so that he could return for the next. Together, the craft forced the waters to part in front of them and cause large waves to toss everything about and discharge the familiar tang of seaweed into the air.

As usual, the first boats contained cargo; they always had priority so that the goods they carried could be divested and sent to the appropriate go-downs. Wing Yee wondered if the spices Baba Tan was expecting would be amongst this load. The last two boats waited further downstream until the freight had been dealt with; then, they nudged their way towards the quay.

'I think those European men,' Wing Yee said .'They have pale skin and ...'

'What is it?' Dick said. 'What have you seen?' He was well aware that her eyesight was far keener than his own, despite being his senior by several years.

'Four men and one boy,' she said. 'Two men wear European clothes, one man in long, brown dress. Other man cannot see; the boy, he Chinese.'

'Can you see what is in the last boat?' Dick said.

'Sun too bright,' Wing Yee said. 'Look, they start to come near.'

*****

During the journey from the junk to the mouth of the river, James had pointed out various landmarks to Father John, but the one that interested the priest most was the house on top of Bukit Larangan. It had been built by Raffles and was now occupied by the current Resident, John Crawfurd. Chang huddled close to Soong Heng, suddenly uncertain what his future here might hold. Meanwhile, Soong Heng appeared to be in a trance as he gazed along the entire length of the Esplanade and the merchant houses on Beach Road. Neither did he comment as he viewed the burgeoning town that was spreading from the river to the rounded foothills in one direction and the untamed jungle in the other.

The boat bumped against the wall of the quay and Edmund took Soong Heng's arm. James and Father John led the way up the dank and sticky steps, followed closely by Chang. Edmund was happy to bide his time, waiting for the moment when Soong Heng was ready to make a move.

*****

Dick had managed to get closer to the steps only seconds before he saw James, tossing back his mop of sandy-coloured hair as he stepped onto the quay. Then, he looked down to see Edmund, still in the bumboat, helping another passenger. Dick turned to Wing Yee and guided her to a place where they could welcome the brothers properly. 'What a pity Chin Ming is busy teaching today,' he said.

*****

Soong Heng turned to Edmund, as if he was seeking reassurance. Father John had tried to explain about coming here, but he'd told the brothers that in Soong Heng's mind it probably made no more sense than their move from Belitung to Palembang

'It will be alright,' Edmund said. He could see that their oarsman was impatient to move on to his next ferrying job. 'Take my arm,' Edmund said, 'the steps are wet and may be slippery, but I will hold you steady.'

They made slow progress, but when they reached the last step Father John and James both held out their arms to support Soong Heng over the final hurdle. As they did so, they could hear a familiar voice calling out.

'James, Edmund, over here!'

*****

Neither James nor Edmund could believe the probability of Dick being on the quay to greet them. Wing Yee hung back until Dick encouraged her to join them.

'Look who else is here,' he said.

For the briefest of seconds, Edmund took his eyes off his charge to search the faces of the people standing nearby.

James recognised Wing Yee immediately. 'It seems such a

ong time since you were here to see us off,' he said. 'Your notes on medicinal plants proved so useful, even our friend William Lawrence had not come across some of that information.'

'Many month,' Wing Yee said. 'You away many month.'

James nodded, then said, 'Forgive my bad manners; let me introduce you to our companions.' He began to explain about their travels in Sumatra and their meeting with the priest when they returned to Palembang, but before he could introduce the two men by name, the one leaning on Edmund's arm slumped to the ground.

'I'm afraid my friend is exhausted,' Father John explained. He and Edmund bent down beside the prone figure to check that no bones had been broken. When Soong Heng regained consciousness, they helped him to sit up and encouraged him to take deep breaths.

Dick dragged an old wooden crate to the place where the newcomer was sitting and helped Edmund raise him onto it. Edmund put his arm around Soong Heng's shoulders and tried to reassure him.

Once he was satisfied calm had been restored, Father John introduced himself to Dick. He told him what he'd found out about the wreck of the *Tek Sing* and the rumour he'd heard about some of the ship's survivors, then he explained how he'd made the decision to find out for himself what had really happened. Finally, he introduced Dick and Wing Yee to his friend.

'This is Li Soong Heng,' he said. 'He has suffered a great deal during the past four years, but he remembers nothing of what happened to him, nothing about the men who captured him and forced him onto that fateful ship. I've brought him here to meet his daughter, hoping it will help restore his memory.'

Neither Dick nor Wing Yee could believe what was being

said. It was the name they'd heard Chin Ming mention so often; this must be her lost father, the man she had originally come to Singapore to find. It was the man she'd risked her life for, had agonised over, had worried about and whom she had never given up on. It was the letter her father had written to Stamford Raffles that proved vital in bringing Pieter Steffens to justice, and Chin Ming had always held on to the belief that one day her father might come here to look for her.

'It's a marvel,' Dick said. 'I must go and find her.'

'Wait a minute,' James said. 'Surely this will be a great shock. We don't want someone else fainting on the quay – and besides, I think father and daughter deserve some privacy. Should we not take Soong Heng and Father John either to Baba Tan's house – or maybe Mr Johnston's – a secluded place where Chin Ming could come to meet him, a place where she can learn about everything that has happened?'

*****

It was agreed that Johnston's house would be the better option. It had the advantage of being able to offer accommodation to guests and Dick was sure that Alexander would want to help.

'You go see about house,' Wing Yee said to Dick. Having remained quiet during all the male conversation, it was now time for her to intervene. 'You find coolies to help with luggage,' she said to James, and to Edmund, 'You take care of Chin Ming's papa. When all arranged, I go to school and bring Chin Ming to house.'

No-one questioned Wing Yee's quiet authority, and they all set about their assigned tasks. James managed to find a couple of people willing to help with the luggage, but as soon as they saw how much was involved, they shook their heads and wandered back in the direction of the hawker stalls. Dick had already disappeared in the direction of Johnston's warehouse so there was nothing for it but to sit with the various bags, crates and cases until he returned. Edmund and Father John had led Soong Heng away from the crowd to a sheltered spot where they could drink tea. Between them they tried to explain what was about to happen.

*****

Whilst all the negotiations had been going on, no-one had noticed the passenger from the last bumboat being brought ashore. He hadn't been seen during the voyage and because of the state of his health he had been the last person to reach the quay. The man himself remained delirious and was completely unaware of being carried past Edmund, James and Dick by members of the crew who had been given the task of carrying his makeshift cot to the house of an Indian merchant.

Edmund and James had long forgotten the troublesome passenger who had arrived with them on their first visit to Singapore, so even if they hadn't been distracted by listening to Wing Yee's instructions it would not have occurred to them that this could be the same man.

Dick was so intent on offering Johnston's house as a place to welcome Soong Heng that he was completely unaware of the cot passing him by, of the man lying motionless in his torn shirt and dark blue breeches that had seen better days, of the long unkempt hair and the sunken eyes; neither had he been in a position to observe the scar on the man's feverish brow.

CHAPTER 22
Singapore, 24th May 1826

Wing Yee arrived at the school at the exact moment Chin Ming turned the key to lock the outer door.

'I didn't realise you planned to meet me today,' she said, 'I assume the herbs you were expecting to be delivered haven't arrived?'

'Not yet,' Wing Yee said. They spoke mainly in Cantonese when they were alone, though sometimes Wing Yee insisted on English because she said she needed to practice. Today, however, because she had wanted to fetch Chin Ming herself, but now had no idea how she was going to break the news, she continued in Cantonese.

'I have a surprise for you,' Wing Yee said.

Chin Ming frowned. 'Will I like it?' she said. She was one of those people who was constantly saying that she liked surprises, but often felt awkward or confused if something happened that she hadn't anticipated.

'I think you will,' said Wing Yee, trying to keep calm. Now she was here, she regretted volunteering to meet her friend; she had no idea where to begin, no idea how to share such an important piece of information – either in English or Cantonese. As they walked along the road together, she became more and more uncomfortable, but having heard the word 'surprise', Chin Ming was waiting for her to continue. She decided to begin by telling her friend about the arrival of the ship and the return of the two brothers; she would save the most important part until they reached Mr Johnston's house.

'Are you going to tell me anything further?' Chin Ming asked, as if she had read Wing Yee's thoughts, 'or do I have to keep guessing?'

'Actually, it's not really my surprise.'

'I don't understand. when you arrived at the schoolhouse, I distinctly heard you say that YOU had a surprise for me.'

'Well yes, but the main news is about Edmund and what he has brought back from Sumatra for you!'

'Edmund,' Chin Ming repeated. A pink glow spread across her cheeks, making her look as if she had been standing in the sun for several hours. 'Edmund Beaumont has returned to Singapore?'

'He arrived early today,' said Wing Yee. She was annoyed with herself for blurting out this information so quickly, but pleased that Chin Ming was obviously happy to hear this news. She stopped herself from making any sort of comment. 'He and his brother travelled on a junk which came from Palembang, just as Baba Tan said they might.'

'But how do you know? Have you actually seen them? Did they visit Baba Tan?'

'No, not yet. I had no urgent work today, so when I left the house this morning, I went to see if Dick was interested in going to the harbour. We asked some coolies if any boats might be expected soon. Then, I noticed the flag flying out on top of the hill so we realised a new boat had already arrived. We waited to see who came ashore. We stayed a long time; the first boats had only cargo, so we continued to wait. We wanted to see if there was anything, or anyone, else on the last two boats.'

She very carefully avoided mentioning anything about the other three passengers and Chin Ming was too excited to ask any questions other than those that related to the brothers.

'Where are they? Is Dick still with them? Will we be having dinner with them soon?'

'I'm sure Mr Johnston will arrange some form of celebration to welcome them back; I think he and Dick like having parties,' Wing Yee said. 'But you will meet them very soon. Dick has taken them to Mr Johnston's house; I've been sent to meet you from school. I told them I would bring you to join the others.'

'What,' Chin Ming said, 'I can't possibly do that. Look at me, I'm covered in chalk dust and my hair needs to be tidied. What will they think?'

'They'll think you've been working hard, helping small children to learn their letters. You told Edmund yourself about working at the school and he wanted to know more. The day they left, Baba Tan and I went to wave goodbye. I remember he looked very disappointed when he realised you weren't with us. I told him you were at the schoolhouse. I said that is where he would find you when he returned from Guangzhou.'

'So why didn't he come to find me himself?'

'Because he needed to take care of the surprise he has brought for you. Look, we have almost reached the house. Take my hand, we'll go in to meet him together.'

*****

As soon as they stepped off the path at the side of the house, Alexander Johnston strode away from the veranda to greet them. He could tell from the way Wing Yee kept clearing her throat and fidgeting that she had not disclosed the true reason to call in at this time in the afternoon. He led both women past one of the slender, white pillars that supported the sloping roof of the veranda and into the shade. There, waiting for them, sat Edmund Beaumont. When the formal introductions had been made, Johnston reminded each of the young people of their previous meeting. This made them both feel extremely self-conscious, but no-one else appeared to notice. Then, Johnston moved to a position immediately behind Chin Ming, moving his head slowly from side to side, to indicate that she was unaware of the news. Now, it was up to Edmund.

Before anything further could be said, Johnston excused himself and returned to join Dick and the other guests in the drawing room. Wing Yee seated herself on one of the sofas a little way apart from Chin Ming, but close enough to observe her friend's reaction to the news; she would be able to come to the rescue if needed.

There was an uneasiness between Edmund and Chin Ming for several minutes, both of them tongue-tied and unsure what to say to the other.

Edmund wondered if he ought to have asked Dick to break the news – or maybe he should ask Father John to join him. Now that she was here, sitting in front of him, looking every bit as attractive as he remembered, he had no idea what he was going to say.

Chin Ming sat with her hands in her lap, wishing Edmund would begin to declare whatever was on his mind. What was this surprise that Wing Yee had spoken of? Why was everyone behaving so mysteriously? Finally, she broke the silence hanging between them.

'You have been away many months; I hope that it has been a successful expedition.'

'I'm sure Dick has already told you about our adventures in China,' Edmund said. 'It was so good to have him with us; he is such an accomplished artist.'

'He is indeed. He brought back one of his paintings as a present for us – Wing Yee and me – it is a wonderful painting in oils, it is to remind us of Guangzhou.'

'I didn't know that. Maybe you could show it to me sometime? It must have been done after we left for Sumatra.'

'That is where you have just come from?'

Their conversation remained stilted, polite and cautious for the next few minutes. Edmund could see Father John hovering in the doorway that led inside the house; perhaps he was waiting for an opportune moment to join them? When he looked back towards Chin Ming, her head was tilted to one side and a smile was slowly creeping across her face.

'I tell her you have surprise,' Wing Yee said, unable to keep quiet any longer.

Edmund decided there was nothing for it but to deal with the situation head-on.

'We spent almost two months in Sumatra,' he said. 'It was longer than originally intended, but I'm glad it worked out the way it did.'

Wing Yee shuffled her feet, urging him to get on with the story. Chin Ming waited patiently, enjoying this opportunity to study his eyes.

'When we returned to Palembang, I met a group of people who had only just arrived there themselves.'

Chin Ming started to wonder where this story was going, and if, as Wing Yee had suggested, he had something special to tell her, when he was going to get around to it.

Edmund cleared his throat. 'Dick told me you asked him if he'd seen Father John when we were in Guangzhou,' he said, 'and he told you we discovered the mission had closed and everyone had moved to Calcutta.'

Chin Ming nodded.

'Well, that isn't quite correct. You see, Father John was one of the people I met in Palembang.'

'Father John, the priest I stayed with at the mission, are you sure? What was he doing there? Has he started a new mission? Is he well?'

'I'm very well, my child,' Father John said, stepping out of the shadows of the house onto the veranda. He had been listening to the conversation for a little while and decided Edmund might need some help.

She stared at him, not quite believing what she was seeing. She turned her head slightly to one side and frowned; she felt extremely confused.

'I don't understand,' she said. 'Why aren't you in Calcutta with the rest of your order? Why did you go to Sumatra – was your ship blown off course? And what are you doing in Singapore?' As soon as she'd finished speaking, she realised how rude the last phrase sounded. 'I'm sorry,' she said, 'it is good to see you again, very good indeed, but nothing is making any sense.'

'Why don't you move over here,' Edmund said, patting the cushion next to him.

Father John took her right hand and led her to the rattan sofa where Edmund was seated. He lowered himself slowly into the chair immediately opposite, so that he could look into her eyes; he continued to hold her hand. When he began to speak, Edmund moved closer to her and took the other hand without thinking; he stroked it gently whilst the priest told her about her father's abduction from Guangzhou and related as much as he knew of Soong Heng's life during the last four years. She sat, in a daze, letting them hold her hands, quite forgetting the fuss she'd made when Dick had thrown his arms around her at the quay. This was a different feeling; this was comforting. Edmund could see the colour draining from her face as more and more of the story was revealed.

'But,' she began, then her voice died and her body stiffened. She stared, first at Edmund then at Father John. 'How … after all this time? Are you sure, why has he not tried to find me?' Her voice was high-pitched and her breathing rapid. 'It's over four years, why?'

Whenever Chin Ming became distressed, Edmund could feel his hand being squeezed. Occasionally, her eyes filled with tears, but she would not allow herself any hint of what she would consider to be a sign of weakness. Father John paused for a while whenever this happened and waited for her to regain her self-control. He begged her forgiveness for not listening to her concerns about her father's disappearance when she was staying at the mission.

'What made you change your mind?' she said. 'What made you decide to look for him – and why Sumatra?'

They took it in turns to tell her about Soong Heng being forced onto the *Tek Sing* in Amoy and the subsequent sinking of the ship when it hit rocks in the Banda Strait. Father John told her about overhearing a conversation whilst he was sheltering from the storm at the docks and his subsequent decision to discover whether or not anyone had survived the shipwreck. He said he still knew nothing of how her father had survived the shipwreck, because his friend could remember none of those details.

The priest went on to tell her about the young boy who had found Soong Heng wandering along the shore of the island and how they had discovered the cave which became their home. 'Chang has said very little about those years and I'm not sure he is ready to recall any particulars, even now,' he said.

When she discovered that her father had no recollection of the brutality that he'd suffered she was relieved, but when she learned that he also had no memories of life before that fateful visit to the spring festival four years ago, she began to sob. The tears that she'd been holding back blurred her vision and fell onto her tunic; she no longer tried to stop them and moaned quietly to herself. She pulled away from Edmund and the priest and folded her hands across her chest, each clutching the opposite arm. Edmund looked down at the floor and saw the toes on both her feet curl upwards. He wasn't sure what to do and looked across at Father John for guidance. The priest remained silent.

'I'm sure your father's loss of memory has come as a great shock – along with suddenly being told that he's alive, of course,' Edmund said, 'but we think some of his memories are beginning to return.'

'He's here, he's alive,' she whispered softly, as if trying to convince herself what she'd been told was really true. She looked up, letting her hands fall back into her lap. She gazed at him, holding herself completely still, seeking more information.

He wished he knew how to reassure her and give her something to look forward to.

'Before I met him, he was only speaking Cantonese – Father John thought this was because he'd only had Chang for company for such a long time, and so they continued to speak in Cantonese during the months they spent together in Belitung.'

'Edmund knows a few words and phrases,' said Father John, now joining in the conversation, 'words that he picked up during his travels, but he mainly speaks English. He spent many hours with your father during the week we waited for a ship to bring us here; Soong Heng seemed to really enjoy his company. I think neither of us expected any response, but gradually ...'

'Soong Heng began to converse in English again,' Edmund said, a broad grin spreading across his face.

'Does Papa know why you've brought him to Singapore?'

'I've tried to explain. I told him I knew you had arrived in Singapore,' Father John said. 'And then, of course, Edmund confirmed you were still here. He told me about meeting you – and your friend Wing Yee. He told me about your work at the school, teaching the young children. That's when I decided to take the risk and bring your father to meet you.'

Chin Ming nodded. She let herself be sidetracked for a moment, telling him about Abdullah and his belief that everyone should have an opportunity to learn. 'Before he left here, Raffles laid down plans to establish a school for older pupils; it was to be called the Singapore Institution, but it is still to be built. Abdullah and I hope that one day, Raffles' dream will come true.'

She hasn't changed one little bit, Father John thought. She might have grown into a young lady, but she still had the beliefs and dedication she had shown when she lived at the mission. No wonder she had so much respect for Stamford Raffles; they shared the same ideals, the same hopes and dreams. 'Your father will be very proud of you,' he said. 'I'm not sure he understands, as yet, why we are here, but I'm hoping that seeing his daughter again will stimulate much more of his memory.'

Wing Yee had remained on her sofa throughout the conversations between her friend and the two men; Chin Ming turned towards her now, seeking some form of comfort from her friend. Wing Yee gave an understanding nod before her tight lips expanded into a sympathetic smile.

Chin Ming took a deep breath. 'Please,' she said, 'I need to see him. I need to believe that what you are telling me is true. Will you take me to meet Papa now?'

CHAPTER 23
Singapore, 27th May 1826

Pierre Volande passed in and out of consciousness during the first few days he spent in his uncle's house. His arrival was unexpected and it was only the note, handed over at the same time his cot was unceremoniously deposited on the merchant's doorstep, that prevented him being sent on his way.

Chanda Khan prided himself on his commercial success. He was one of the first merchants to establish a business in Commercial Square. He traded side by side with affluent Europeans and other Asians by day, and lived alongside them at his home on the Rochor Plain at night. This air of respectability made the shock of discovering that his sister's wayward son had been delivered to his doorstep all the more distressing.

Growing up in Punjab, Chanda Khan and his siblings had played with the children at the French garrison all the time. No-one had questioned the hours they spent together, the games they played, the swimming parties, the picnics, but as they moved into adulthood they had, with the exception of his youngest sister, moved on to other interests and different groups of people. Amira was sixteen when she ran away with the young French officer and only seventeen when she gave birth to her son. He'd been given a French name and when Amira died, the child had been registered in his father's name, at a boarding school in France.

Chanda Khan had endeavoured to stay in touch with his sister's child, but all his efforts had been rebuffed. When he'd made it his business to seek news of young Pierre, everything he heard was unpleasant. It seemed the boy was an embarrassment to his French grandparents and when they cut him out of their will, he became bitter and full of resentment. Chanda had heard that Pierre had travelled to India and then moved on to China; he knew also that he'd fallen into bad company. There had been no news of him for several years now, not until three days ago.

The servants had been discreet; they had not questioned the arrival of the young man, nor had they asked why their master had given directions for a bed to be made ready for him. They watched the visitor as he tossed and turned, twisting the sheets into knots and soaking them in sweat; the food that was prepared remained untouched. The air in the room was beginning to smell sour, despite the windows being wide open; it was time to bring the situation to their master's attention.

*****

When Abdullah heard Chin Ming's news, he went round to Baba Tan's house straight away.

'You must take time to be with your father,' he said. 'You must not concern yourself about the school, I will be able to manage on my own.'

She pressed her fingers to her lips as they widened into a smile which lit up her whole face. 'Are you sure,' she said, 'what about ...?'

'Two of our families are on the way to their pilgrimage in Mecca,' he said. 'They will be gone for some time. I can combine both classes – and maybe I will encourage some of the older children to help with the younger ones.'

239

'Thank you,' she said.

'When you are ready, bring your father to meet the children. He might enjoy their company – and you can show him what you've been doing for the last few years.' With that, Abdullah made his excuses to leave and bade her farewell.

*****

Early each morning, Chin Ming walked from Baba Tan's house towards the river. When she reached the far side of Monkey Bridge, Dick was always there and always out of breath. Every day, he woke up with the intention of making an early start so that he would be waiting on Baba Tan's doorstep, but for one reason or another he never made it further than the north side of the bridge.

Today, he waved as soon as he saw her distinctive red tunic emerge from the shimmering haze that clothed this part of the river in the early morning. Together, they walked along High Street and then to Alexander Johnston's home on Beach Road. Before they reached the house, Dick told her about any change in her father's manner since she'd left him the previous evening.

When they strolled around to the back of the house, the very first thing she saw was the now-familiar shape of Edmund, sitting with his back towards her at the far end of the veranda. As fond as she was of Dick, she sometimes wished that it was Edmund who might come to escort her across town. The thought immediately made her feel guilty. As it was Edmund spent all his spare time with her father; he had already helped him to recall his knowledge of English. In the last few days, she'd heard the two of them talking about all sorts of things, but it saddened her that every morning Soong Heng had to be reminded that she was his daughter.

Almost as if he could sense her presence, Edmund leapt

from his seat to face her. 'Look who has arrived,' he said to Soong Heng. 'Your daughter is obviously an early riser, just like her father.'

'Chin Ming,' Soong Heng said.

She tried not to show surprise or give any sign that his using her name without a prompt was in any way out of the ordinary. 'Good morning, Papa,' she said, 'have you slept well?'

Dick made his excuses to retire to the kitchen in search of breakfast, whilst Soong Heng searched for an answer to his daughter's question.

Edmund watched Dick leave. 'I think your papa still dreams a lot,' he whispered so that Soong Heng wouldn't hear. 'I've heard small whimpers in the night, but he is much calmer in his sleep now and the dreams no longer appear to disturb him.' He wished he could wave a magic wand and make everything right again for both Chin Ming and her papa. He wished it was he, and not Dick, who met her each morning, he wished there was an opportunity for them to talk together and for him to say how he felt about her. He longed to tell her about his home in England – but now was not the time for any of that.

'Is something worrying you?' Edmund said. This morning, she had a distracted air about her and she lacked her usual energy.

She avoided looking at him and cleared her throat before attempting to reply. 'I'm glad that Papa has been able to stay here with Mr Johnston,' she said, 'but I should be with him all the time, not merely during the hours of daylight. Each night, when I return to Baba Tan's house, I wish there was somewhere for Papa and me to live together.'

'You're probably right,' Edmund said. 'It's more than likely your father's memory would improve considerably if you shared a house, but you might want to prepare yourself for the fact that some things he may never want to remember.'

She winced. She knew exactly what he was referring to, but she still needed to try, to make up for lost time. 'You probably think I'm being selfish, but we have so much catching up to do. Besides, Father John will be leaving for Calcutta in a few weeks, Chang now spends most of his time helping Wing Yee with her plants and I suppose it won't be long before you will be returning to England?'

Edmund froze. He knew that was what everyone would assume – and indeed, James had already suggested they should find out when the next Indiaman was due to arrive. He wanted to tell her he didn't want to go anywhere without her, but his courage failed him. Instead, he said, 'I heard Alexander talking about an English family who returned home on the last ship. The husband works for Guthrie's and was due for some leave. Their house has been closed up, but I think I understood Alexander to say they'd asked him to find someone to rent it while they're away. Would you like me to make some enquiries?'

*****

Chanda Khan was puzzled. The note he'd received when his nephew arrived had been scribbled in haste by an unknown hand. It said that Pierre had got into bad company, had been attacked by a gang and was fleeing for his life. When the young man arrived in Singapore, no questions had been asked even though his body still showed signs of a significant beating.

This morning, one of the servants had asked him to take a look at their dubious guest. The stench of vomit filled his nostrils as soon as he entered the room, despite the recently replenished incense smouldering in burners at the side of the bed.

There was no hint of his Indian ancestry on the face of the

young man; his pallor was as pale as the tusks of an elephant. He was drenched in sweat and when Chanda lifted the sheet, his horror forced him to cover his mouth with his hands, but nothing could stop the low moan that rose from somewhere deep within him; Pierre Volande's belly was bloated and festooned with tiny red veins.

Once he had regained his composure, Chanda gave orders for Pierre to be bathed from top to toe and for all the bedding to be replaced. Then, he announced that he would be leaving the house immediately; he was going out in search of some form of medical help.

*****

Baba Tan had received the news about Chin Ming moving out of his home with a certain amount of sadness, but he knew it was something she needed to do. Fortunately, Wing Yee would remain within his household. He liked having his business partner close by so that they could discuss their ideas for developing a small clinic. His wife liked having her around too and Wing Yee enjoyed helping to look after their young family.

She was out when Chanda Khan arrived at Baba Tan's warehouse. She was cultivating several different types of herbs alongside the nutmegs and cloves which had been plant-ed when the Spice Garden was first established, and they all needed constant attention. Some days, when he wanted to do some sketching, Dick accompanied her, but today he had other things to do and when she met James Beaumont at the start of the path leading to the top of the hill, she was pleased that he'd asked to join her.

'What news of the orchid?' he said, after their initial greet-ing. Wing Yee had been given charge of the tender plant shortly after Dick returned to Singapore and she'd promised to look after it until James and Edmund were ready to return to England.

'Orchid very clever plant,' she said. 'They grow in China for many thousand years; this one very strong.'

'It's been through some tough times getting here, but that's good to know. I think having you caring for it before it has to embark upon yet another long journey will set it in good stead,' James said.

'Good STEAD,' she said, 'what is STEAD, not understand.'

'I'm sorry, we English use some strange phrases, don't we? It means giving something some sort of advantage. What I meant to say, was that the longer the orchid spends with you, the better chance it has of surviving the voyage back to England.'

'You go soon?' she said, lowering her head and swallowing hard.

'It's well over twelve months since we left home – and Edmund needs to deliver a report on his findings. Sorry, he needs to tell his employers about the plants we found on our travels.'

'He send many plant from Guangzhou,' she said. 'Dick tell me when he give me orchid.'

'That's correct. I imagine the plants and seeds we collected will have been delivered to Oxford by now. That's where Edmund is employed – at the Physic Garden – and that's who paid for his expedition. Mind you, he seems somewhat reluctant to make a decision. Whenever I mention returning to England, he changes the subject.'

Wing Yee decided not to share her thoughts on the matter. She had noticed the way the younger Beaumont brother looked at Chin Ming and she was also aware of the way Chin Ming looked at Edmund. It was not worth trying to discuss the matter with James; no good could come of it.

They spent the next two or three hours inspecting the tender young plants. Wing Yee told him about the use of bark and roots and which plants she liked to use in producing herbal remedies. James asked her about the particular medicinal qualities of each one she mentioned and by the end of the morning he had acquired a little knowledge about therapies that went back thousands of years.

* * * * *

When Wing Yee returned to Baba Tan's emporium, she found him seated at a table with a man she had never seen before.

'Come in young lady,' Baba Tan said. 'I would like to introduce you to Chanda Khan; he has business premises in Commercial Square, but today he is here to ask for our help.'

Baba Tan introduced Wing Yee to the tall Indian merchant and sent for more tea. When the formalities were over, Wing Yee looked towards Baba Tan for further information, but nothing was immediately forthcoming.

'Wing Yee is the expert,' Baba Tan said. 'She probably knows more about traditional cures than anyone else in Singapore. I run the commercial side of the business, but it is Wing Yee who develops all the salves and potions. We import herbs from China and the Moluccas, but she is beginning to grow some of them herself now.'

Wing Yee wondered what sort of help Mr Khan was seeking; he looked healthy enough, and it was unusual for members of the Indian community to look beyond their own friends and family for guidance on matters to do with sickness and disease. She sat with her hands in her lap and waited for the visitor to speak.

'Forgive me,' he said at last. 'It is a little embarrassing. I have a young man staying at my house. He is the son of my sister, though he was brought up elsewhere. He has a fever and his belly is swollen; he is delirious and has not been able to tell me what ails him. I am at my wit's end.'

'Chanda Khan would like you to visit his nephew,' Baba

Tan said. 'He would like you to advise him about any possible treatment.'

'You come with me?' Wing Yee said. She knew it was unwise for a woman to enter a stranger's house alone, and that she would be expected to be accompanied by a chaperone.

'Unfortunately, I am needed at the go-down this afternoon, I am expecting a number of important consignments to be delivered from the two ships that arrived in the harbour last night.'

'But ...' Wing Yee said.

'Not to worry,' Baba Tan added, 'I've sent a note to Dick. He's not busy this afternoon and I'm expecting him any minute – he will go with you to Chanda Khan's home.'

*****

Dick remained seated in the corner of the room in which they found the patient; all he could see was the back of Wing Yee as she bent over Chanda Khan's nephew. A light breeze brought with it the sweet fragrance of the mango tree immediately outside the window, but it was not sufficient to obliterate the unpleasant smell that pervaded the whole room. He wasn't sure how Wing Yee could bear to be anywhere near this stranger.

'How long you have fever?' Wing Yee asked, but all she received by way of response was a low moaning sound.

Chanda Khan explained that his nephew had not been lucid since his arrival.

'My servant told me that he has been very restless and there are long periods each day when he is either very hot or very cold.'

'How many times he have fever before?'

'I'm afraid I cannot say. Until a few days ago I had never met my nephew; my sister died and the young man has been brought up in Europe.'

Dick strained his neck to catch a glimpse of the man no-one seemed to know anything about, but the people surrounding the bed blocked his view. He wondered where he'd suddenly come from – and how he knew where to find his uncle.

Wing Yee knelt down and removed several small packages from her basket. She gave one of them to the servant and asked him to steep the ingredients in boiling water; after straining the liquid into a shallow bowl, he was to return as quickly as possible so that the infusion could be consumed while it was still hot. Meanwhile, she pulled out two small glass bottles, each containing some sort of oil. A little of one was poured into the other. She replaced the stopper and turned the flask upside down, swirling the contents until she was satisfied they had formed an emulsion.

'I wipe your skin,' she said, 'make you comfortable.'

Chanda Khan moved away from the bed so that she could move around easily, but the man's head was turned away so Dick could still not catch sight of his face. He observed the gentle manner in which Wing Yee sponged the man's head, then his arms and finally his distended stomach. When the servant arrived with the hot liquid, she took it from him and asked for the patient's head to be held still. It was difficult to get him to take anything at first, but she persevered. It reminded her of the many days she'd spent looking after the young opium addict on their journey from Guangzhou to Singapore. Then, she'd had Chin Ming to help her – making sure the girl was kept hydrated and encouraged to eat, once they had eliminated all signs of the drug from her system.

When the last drop of liquid had passed his lips, the man lay back exhausted and was calmer than when she arrived. He curled his body into a ball and turned away from the light.

'I leave herbs for tea,' she said to Chanda Khan. 'He must drink every two hour. I come back tomorrow.'

'I understand,' Chanda Khan said. He bowed and thanked her using his usual style of English, which was formal and polite.

Dick followed her out of the room, along the corridor and out into the fresh air. He took her basket from her, thinking she looked tired and a little flushed. 'I hope you haven't caught anything from him,' he said.

'What he have is caused by bite,' she said. 'Maybe he get bitten when on boat, but I think not first time this happen.'

'Raffles and Sophia were ill with fever when we lived in Sumatra, maybe it's the same thing,' Dick said.

'Maybe, I see many time before, but not bad like this man. Maybe he get bad because he European.'

'What do you mean, he's Chanda Khan's nephew – his sister's son. He's not European, he's Indian.'

'He not look Indian, he has pale skin.'

'Perhaps that's because he's unwell.' Dick said.

'No,' she said. 'Chanda Khan say his sister die. He say man live with father's family, maybe father not Indian.'

'Can you describe him?' Dick said.

'He have dark hair, very long. Eyes closed most of time, cannot see colour. Shape of face like Mr Johnston, but...' Wing Yee struggled for the correct word.

'But what?' Dick said.

'He has mark; no, he has scar on forehead.'

CHAPTER 24
Singapore, 30th May 1826

Dick was unusually quiet as he and Wing Yee returned to Baba Tan's house. She chatted casually about the *qing guo* plant she had used to help relieve the patient's fever. Dick was only vaguely aware of what she said – something about balancing yin and yang – but all he could think of was the words she'd uttered after leaving Chanda Khan's house.

He kept telling himself that lots of people carried scars – indications of past injuries – some of which might be quite innocent, like falling onto a sharp object as a child. Even Soong Heng had a scar. Admittedly his was not immediately visible, and he'd probably received it through foul play, something that had happened during his abduction, but it was a mark similar to many others Dick had seen all the same.

By the time he said goodbye to Wing Yee, he'd convinced himself that he was being irrational. He hurried away from Market Street towards the river and then made his way towards the offices of Johnston and Company. He thought he might wait for Alexander to finish work for the day, so that they could walk home together. He was only a short distance from the entrance to the building, when the door opened and Alexander Johnston stepped out onto the pavement. Dick broke out into a sprint so that he could catch up with him.

Johnston heard the regular pounding of someone running along behind him and turned to see what could have caused such necessity in the heat of the afternoon. 'Oh, it's you,' he said. 'I thought there must be some sort of emergency.'

Dick smiled briefly before telling him where he had spent the afternoon.

Johnston nodded, but paid no particular interest to the story other than to comment on Wing Yee's knowledge of herbal medicine. 'I decided to come home early because a number of letters have been delivered to my office today; one of them is addressed to you and another one is for Edmund.'

'Do you recognise the handwriting?' Dick said. 'Could mine be from Raffles? I haven't received a letter from him for some while now.'

'It's a hand which is unfamiliar, I'm afraid,' Johnston said. 'But the ship which brought today's mail is on its way to India. I believe a ship is due to arrive from England any day though, maybe that will bring news from Raffles and Sophia.'

*****

Johnston placed Edmund's letter on the small table in the vestibule and handed the other one to Dick. The Malay servant appeared instantly and asked if they would like him to bring some refreshing tea. Johnston nodded, then picked up his copy of the *Singapore Chronicle*; he'd perused the latest edition of the newspaper already but wanted to leave Dick free to read the contents of his letter in peace.

'It's from William,' Dick said, looking up briefly before he settled down to catch up on the news from Guangzhou.

Alexander was reading an article about the ever-increasing number of opium addicts amongst the coolies and men working in the gambier plantations when he heard Dick cry out.

'No!' he shouted. 'Why do that, what has Lam Qua done to deserve it?'

'Whatever's the matter?' Johnston said.

'There's been a fire ... Lam Qua's studio was set ablaze, all his paintings destroyed, I can't believe anyone would be so malicious ...'

'That's a terrible thing to happen,' Johnston said. 'Is there nothing left at all?'

'There's only one painting which isn't completely ruined and even that's badly burnt.' Dick looked at the letter again to recheck William's words '... but William thinks that in itself proves who started the fire.'

'What do you mean?'

'The painting is smoke-damaged, but it's just recognisable. It's the one I left in a room at the rear of the building. It's the portrait I told you about, the one of the Frenchman; he was due to collect it the day I left Guangzhou.'

Johnston understood the significance of the painting, of course. On arrival back in Singapore, Dick had confided in Johnston; he'd told him all about the seemingly random appearances of the mysterious Frenchman and the resulting suspicions his presence had caused. He also knew about the orchid which was now being tended by Wing Yee. It was all too obvious that the person who linked all of these stories together was a man called Pierre Volande, the man whom William now accused of torching Lam Qua's studio.

'Does William say what happened after the fire? Surely, he tried to track the man down if he was so sure of his guilt?'

'He did, but it was too late. Volande arrived at William's house on the day that I left. He looked dishevelled and was in a great hurry. William showed him the parakeet he had in his care, but Volande got angry because it wasn't anything special and left in a bad mood. Shortly afterwards, Lam Qua arrived with the dreadful news.'

'But what makes William so sure that it was Volande who caused the fire?'

'He says the Frenchman had a dark smudge on his face; there was another on his coat. He thought nothing of it at the time, but he thinks it was soot from the fire. Lam Qua was covered in the stuff when he arrived.'

Dick consulted the letter once more before continuing. 'William tried to track him down, but he came to a dead end – and I know why.'

'What do you mean?'

'The person Wing Yee has been treating – she told me he has a scar on his forehead.'

Johnston raised both eyebrows in a manner that required more information.

'Volande has a scar on his forehead,' Dick said. 'I've been trying to persuade myself that I'm imagining things, but now I've read this letter, I can't rid myself of the suspicion; I think the man lying in a state of delirium in Chanda Khan's house is Pierre Volande.'

Johnston's face tightened; he pressed his lips together. 'That's quite an allegation,' he said. 'Even if Wing Yee's patient is the same person as the one who caused all the trouble in Guangzhou, he's in no position to do anything right now. I think the first thing we need to do is find out the name of Chanda Khan's nephew.'

'Baba Tan might know,' Dick said, 'and if not, I'm sure he could easily find out.'

'Find out what?' Edmund said as he and James entered the room.

'Before we go into all that, there's a letter for you from William – from Guangzhou. I think you should read it straight-away,' Johnston said.

*****

Edmund tore open the envelope, scanned the contents quickly, then sat down and read the letter all over again – this time, slowly. He looked up, raised his eyebrows, shook his head in disbelief and passed the letter to his brother.

Like Edmund, James read the contents of the letter twice. 'This is dreadful,' he said, turning to Dick. 'I presume you've received the same news yourself?'

Dick nodded. 'There's something else,' he said. 'I've just remembered. When we met you at the quay last week, there was another boat immediately behind the one that brought you ashore.'

'There was that other passenger; he was already on board when we joined the ship in Palembang. We understood he was sick. We never saw or heard anything of him throughout the entire journey. I didn't give it any thought, but I suppose he must have been brought ashore in that last boat. What with all the excitement of seeing you at the quay I quite forgot about him. What has that to do with William's news?'

'This afternoon, Baba Tan sent for me and asked me to accompany Wing Yee to the house of an Indian merchant called Chanda Khan,' Dick said. 'His nephew is very sick. He'd come to ask for help and Baba Tan explained that it was Wing Yee who knew about herbal medicine. Chanda Khan wanted her to visit his house straightaway, but Baba Tan was unable to chaperone her because he had urgent business to deal with. He asked me to go with her instead.'

Edmund looked from Johnston to James and back to Dick. He wasn't sure what any of this had to do with the news they had just received from William.

'I wasn't able to get a clear view,' Dick said, 'but it was clear that the patient was in a pretty sorry state. They told Wing Yee he'd been feverish since he arrived; she asked him questions, but he didn't answer. It was impossible for me to see him because there was always someone blocking my view. After Wing Yee applied some oils and gave him some of her special tea to drink, he stopped thrashing around so much and became much calmer. On the way back home, I was curious and that's when I asked lots of questions.'

There was a ripple of laughter – Dick was always curious and asking questions.

'She thought the man was European, but I said that was impossible if he's Chanda Khan's nephew. She described the colour of his skin, his hair and eyes; then she told me he'd not been brought up in India.'

'Sorry,' James said, 'what has that got to do with Lam Qua's studio being set alight?'

'The man has a scar on his forehead!'

Edmund took a sharp intake of breath. 'Like the Frenchman – the one who William was anxious to avoid in Guangzhou, the one whose portrait you painted!'

'If I'm right,' Dick said, 'Wing Yee's patient is the same man. I think he could well be Pierre Volande; the person William has accused of setting Lam Qua's studio on fire.'

'How on earth did he reach Singapore?' James said.

'I can't be sure,' Dick said, 'but Chanda Khan told us his nephew arrived here from Macao – and you said the vessel you joined in Palembang began its journey there.'

'So, you think the man who kept to his cabin throughout the voyage, the man they brought ashore after us, is Chanda Khan's nephew?' Edmund said.

'We need to be sure,' James said. 'It could cause a lot of bad feeling if you're wrong.'

'You never saw Volande during our travels, did you?' Dick said. 'Remember, I spent several unpleasant days with him sitting across from me while I painted his portrait. His skin is not as fair as yours and his hair is black. Maybe pretending to be French is all part of the deception game he plays.'

'Has Chanda Khan ever referred to him by name?' Edmund said.

'That's what we were discussing when you arrived,' Alexander said. 'Dick thinks Baba Tan will be able to find that out easily enough.'

'You said Wing Yee has promised to visit him again; will Baba Tan go with her?'

'He is expecting to do so,' Dick said. 'Hopefully, that will give him an opportunity to establish some more facts.'

'You and I need to visit Baba Tan first thing tomorrow morning,' Johnston said, looking at Dick. 'Once he's aware of your suspicions I'm sure he'll be anxious to help, if only to make sure Wing Yee isn't in any sort of danger. Once we know whether your fears have any foundation, we can then decide what to do next.'

*****

Baba Tan arrived at Johnston's house early the following evening; he was accompanied by Wing Yee. When everyone was settled on the veranda with glasses of cooling coconut water, they revealed what they had been able to establish.

'The young man does have a French name,' Baba Tan said. 'It is something like Pee-air Vo-lan; yes, I think that is correct.'

'So why does Chanda Khan say the man is his nephew?' Edmund asked.

'It is a long story. Mr Vo-lan is the son of Chanda Khan's sister who ran away with a French officer. Khan says he's been in and out of trouble all his life. Now I know all this, I believe I may have come across Mr Vo-lan before.'

'What makes you think that?' James said.

'Before you went to China, Dick took both of you to the Spice Garden to meet Wing Yee – do you remember? While you were all there, I was visited by a Frenchman, asking if I was interested in purchasing any rare plants. I became suspicious because he wouldn't tell me anything about himself and

I asked him to leave.'

'But surely if Volande is the same person, you would have recognised him when you accompanied Wing Yee to Chanda Khan's house?' James said,

'I didn't get too close. Wing Yee needed to move around the bed to apply the oils she used. What little I did see of the patient, I have to admit, was nothing like the man who visited me last year; he looked down-at-heel, sweaty and, in fact, quite squalid.'

'Does Volande still have a fever?' Edmund asked, looking at Wing Yee.

'Not so bad,' she said. 'I give him more medicine; in few days he get better again. I go see him Saturday.'

Baba Tan explained that as the patient was now improving, Wing Yee's visits need not be so frequent. 'I think it will be better if Chanda Khan is at home if you intend to confront the Frenchman. Chanda Khan is a very respectable merchant, he is Muslim and we should not risk any sort of upset on the day set aside for Friday prayers; it will be polite to wait until the following day.'

*****

Baba Tan and Wing Yee approached the house on the Rochor Plain around the middle of Saturday morning. Following a short distance behind, and keeping to the shadows, Dick, Edmund and Alexander Johnston made their way slowly to the same destination. Johnston made sure he greeted anyone he recognised along the way so as to avoid any undue curiosity.

Chanda Khan was waiting on the porch. Today, he was dressed casually in a long ochre-coloured tunic over capacious black trousers; he had a broad smile on his face. He told Baba Tan how pleased he was that his nephew was so much improved and thanked Wing Yee for coming to his rescue. She nodded and made her way to his room to check on his progress.

Instead of accompanying her, Baba Tan waited, making polite conversation with Chanda Khan until the others arrived. Johnston and Dick needed no introduction, but Edmund was a stranger; it was necessary to present him according to formal custom.

Their host led them through to a courtyard at the rear of the house, where they were directed towards the circle of the rattan chairs, carefully placed under the shade of an Angsana tree. A servant brought cooling drinks and Indian snacks within seconds of them making themselves comfortable. They settled back against the colourful, plumped-up cushions and exchanged polite conversation until the servant withdrew.

Baba Tan coughed. He didn't know Chanda Khan well and was uncomfortable about sharing their concerns and posing the questions that needed to be asked.

Alexander Johnston intervened. As the senior magistrate in the Settlement, he took it upon himself to take the lead. 'I think you are aware, sir, that your nephew has led a troubled life?' he began. 'My two friends here,' he said, turning to Edmund and Dick to include them in the conversation, 'came across him during their recent visit to Guangdong Province.'

Chanda Khan remained perfectly calm. 'Then you gentlemen might know what happened to him before he decided to come here,' he said. 'It is obvious that he left China in a hurry and I believe he had been attacked – his body is covered in bruises, but he has not spoken of what happened.'

'My brother and I left Guangzhou for Sumatra at the beginning of the year,' Edmund said. 'Dick stayed on to work with a local artist. Before that,' Edmund continued, 'we'd been warned about a Frenchman; a man with a reputation for acquiring rare specimens by underhand means.' He cleared his throat before saying anything further. 'We became suspicious, on a couple of occasions during our travels, that someone was watching us. At Shunde, a stranger appeared in the Qinghui Garden.'

'When I returned there on my own,' Dick said, 'a man followed me around while I was sketching. He bombarded me with questions, but made no attempt to introduce himself and when he left, he spoke in French.'

'We changed our plans after that; we travelled overland to Guangzhou instead of continuing along the river,' Dick said. 'But then the Frenchman turned up at the studio where I was working. He'd heard a rumour; he believed we'd acquired an exotic specimen of some sort, didn't know what, but said he would be interested in acquiring it.'

Chanda Khan picked up his glass and gulped down the remainder of his pineapple juice. He glanced at all of his guests in turn and faced Dick. 'Please go on,' he said. 'Tell me what I need to know.'

'The new route took us via Panyu; our friend William Lawrence visited an elderly Buddhist monk whom he'd known for a number of years.'

'His temple was known for the cultivation of a particular type of orchid, but they'd been attacked by blight and only two had survived,' Edmund added. 'The monk asked William to take one of them, to ensure that the strain continued.'

'Did my nephew try to steal it from you?' Chanda Khan said. 'And you are sure that this Frenchman you speak of is the same man?'

Dick told him about Volande's appearance at the studio, the time he'd spent painting his portrait and all the questions he'd asked. 'I explained that I couldn't paint the portrait of someone when I didn't even know his name – that's when he told me he was Pierre Volande.'

'I see,' said Chanda Khan. He waited for Dick to continue.

'William came up with a plan to fool him. He led him to believe the bird he had in his care was unusual; he invited him to visit – but only after I had taken charge of the orchid and was safely on board a ship bound for Singapore.'

Dick showed Chanda Khan William's letter. He read it with care and when he returned it to Dick, his face had a stony expression. He shook his head from side to side and whispered something inaudible to himself. 'It sounds as if my nephew has upset too many people, in too many places,' Chanda Khan said, taking a long, deep breath. He almost fell into the nearest chair. 'This is far worse than I imagined,' he said. 'My poor, poor sister; I'm glad she is not alive to witness all this.'

* * * * *

When Wing Yee slipped away to attend to her patient, to her surprise, she found him sitting on a small sofa beside the bed. Beside him was a small table displaying the remains of a light meal – a plate, the skin from a slice of papaya and a knife. He was dressed in loose-fitting trousers and a dark green tunic; his sandals, like the rest of his attire, appeared to be a size too large. She assumed Chanda Khan had disposed of the foul-smelling rags the man was wearing when he arrived and had replaced them with some of his own garments. Volande looked up when she entered the room, she looked vaguely familiar, but he couldn't think why.

'You have no fever today?' she said.

'I am completely restored to health,' he said. 'Did my uncle send you?'

The expression on his face was one that she'd seen on the faces of other men, from her long-forgotten days in Guang-zhou. She spoke quickly, before he had time to assume she had been sent simply to entertain him.

'I come many days – give you medicine. I bathe you in

259

special oil and leave tea for you to drink.' She placed her basket containing dried herbs, scented oils and various salves on the floor at the bottom of the bed, but remained standing at a suitable distance from him.

'That foul-tasting liquid? No wonder the fever went, that concoction was enough to frighten anything away; what on earth did you put in it?' He had no appreciation of her skills and the hours she had spent with him, cleansing his skin, mopping his brow, encouraging him to swallow.

'It made from *qinghai*, cannot remember English name. It known in China many years – always use for fever. I have more in basket, but you not need now.'

'I certainly don't, what I need is alcohol – wine, or preferably whisky!'

'You not all better. I know you have fever many time; it come back if you not live better life.'

He ignored her as she bent down to pick up her basket, then he said, 'What's all that noise coming from the courtyard, have you brought all your family with you?'

'My friends come to visit your uncle.'

'Your friends know Chanda Khan, how come? Who are these so-called friends?'

Wing Yee put the basket down again. 'Baba Tan is merchant like your uncle; I think they talk business things. The others are my friends – one I know since I first come Singapore.' She was beginning to feel irritated by this arrogant European; she had come across men like him before and had no time for their stupidity.

'You weren't born here then? So, how did you avoid ending up in the whorehouse? I presume you originally came here from China; did you come alone or did some man bring you here?'

Wing Yee clenched her teeth, trying to put his offensive remarks out of her mind. 'I come with friend,' she said. 'We come from Guangzhou together.' There was no way she was prepared to reveal any more detail to this ignorant man, let alone tell him about the trials she and Chin Ming had encountered.

Pierre Volande frowned; something began to bother him. Then, he remembered the painting he'd seen in Lam Qua's studio – a silhouette of two young Chinese women looking back at a landscape. The artist had told him it was a present for two of his closest friends back in Singapore. Surely this was too much of a coincidence, surely, she couldn't be one of the two women in the picture? But if he was right – and she'd said her friends were waiting in the courtyard – it might mean that the portrait painter was amongst them. He shivered when he realised the one person who could recognise him might be in the house, waiting for this woman to return; he couldn't take that risk

'Is one of your friends a painter, by any chance?' Volande asked, his voice somewhat shaky.

'Yes,' she said, 'Dick is very good painter. You come meet him?'

Once again, she bent down to pick up her basket. When she straightened her back, he was waving the knife she had seen earlier. She dropped the basket, causing some of its contents to spill, then she quickly backed out of the room and ran down the long corridor, into the courtyard, where she crashed straight into Dick.

'Hold on,' he said, 'whatever's the matter? Why are you looking frightened?'

'He know you here,' she shrieked. 'He has knife!'

'I should have come with you,' Dick said, 'I didn't realise he was well enough to ... I should have left the others to speak with Chanda Khan ...'

Johnston and Baba Tan had already risen to their feet

wanting to know why Wing Yee was upset. Edmund was already beside Dick; he held her hands and tried to calm her down.

'Where is he now?' Edmund said.

She pointed in the direction of the room she had just vacated.

'You stay with Wing Yee,' Alexander Johnston said, pointing to Baba Tan and Chanda Khan. 'Dick, Edmund, you come with me.' They hurried along the corridor, but the room Volande had occupied for the last week was now empty. A bunch of herbs from Wing Yee's basket was strewn all over the floor and oil from the shattered bottles had formed a large puddle; the intense noonday light danced on its shiny surface, making rainbows amongst the chaotic disarray. They had amalgamated their individual aromas to fill the air with a mixture of intoxicating scents – citrus, calendula, cloves and others, less easy to identify.

'What's that noise?' Edmund asked.

All three continued along the corridor, arriving in a room that they supposed was Chanda Khan's own bedroom. A few of the drawers and doors were flung open; clothes had been strewn all over the floor, presumably not by the neat and tidy Indian merchant.

'He probably ran here as soon as Wing Yee ran from his room; he must have realised we'd come looking for him,' Edmund said. 'There's no way of telling if he took anything – but I presume he was looking for money.'

'Whatever it was, we're too late,' Dick said. 'Look!' He pointed to the wide-open shutters. They peered outside into the lane, but there was not a soul in sight.

CHAPTER 25
Singapore, 3rd June 1826

Baba Tan escorted Wing Yee back to his home in Market Street and the others made their way back to Beach Road. They all agreed the prospect of finding the Frenchman was pretty bleak, but Dick was still angry about the damage done to Lam Qua and his studio, and Johnston, as a magistrate, felt a need to seek some form of justice. James asked to be excused from the discussion, saying that he and Edmund needed to talk.

*****

As soon as they were alone, James began to voice some of his concerns. 'I'm sure I don't need to remind you again,' he said, 'but we must now give serious thought to returning home. There is a ship due to arrive here at the end of the month. It will depart on 29th June, I believe; Father John has already booked his passage as far as Calcutta.'

Edmund sighed heavily and collapsed into the nearest chair. How could he possibly begin to explain how he felt to his brother? Logically, James was right; their finances had been considerably reduced, and would eventually run out. However, he still needed time to come to terms with his emotions, feelings he had never experienced before.

'There's nothing else you can do here,' James said. 'If anyone can resolve the problems caused by Volande, it is Alexander Johnston – with some help from Dick. If we take the orchid back to England, Wing Yee won't have that to worry about and Baba Tan will take care of her. Chin Ming will be busy looking after her father. Even with Father John gone, she will still have Chang to help – and I think others will be glad to support her when she feels the time is right. You're not needed here any longer – unless of course, there is something you're not telling me?'

Edmund looked up, his gaze clouded over; the fluttering sensation had returned to his stomach and his chest tightened.

'I know that look,' James said.

'Chin Ming ...' Edmund murmured, his words barely audible.

'Are you trying to tell me that your feelings for Chin Ming are serious? Have you thought this through?'

'All I know is that when I'm with her I never want to leave. She looks at me and smiles, she seems to enjoy my company, but I've no idea what she really feels. Is she merely being polite; is her behaviour anything to do with the way she has been brought up? Is it because her father has taught her to be courteous and sophisticated?'

James continued to listen, but made no comment.

'She has known Dick for three years and me not even for so many months. I keep asking myself whether Dick has feelings for her, whether she has feelings for him – I don't know what to do!'

'There is only one thing you can do,' James said. 'You must begin with Dick – find out what he thinks, what his plans are – then can you approach Chin Ming, but only if it is appropriate to do so and if you are absolutely certain about this. Think about it,' he added. 'You will be taking her away from everything she has ever known, her friends, her culture, her role at the school; Dick hated being in England, remember.'

Having put his feelings into words at last, Edmund was much relieved, but James had now introduced a new reason for concern. He was aware of his brother's anxiety to book their passage home and his own procrastination must have been infuriating, but there was still so much to resolve and time was running out. 'I'll speak to Dick in the morning,' he said. 'Thank you, brother.'

*****

When Edmund arrived at the breakfast table, Dick was tucking into a large slice of papaya. He licked his lips to prevent a thin line of golden-coloured juice trickling onto his chin. They joked with each other at first, then reminisced about their travels in China before Edmund eventually got round to embarking upon the delicate question he needed to ask.

'But Chin Ming and I are like brother and sister,' Dick said. 'I've always felt protective towards her, but nothing more than that. Maybe, when she and Wing Yee first came to live with Raffles and Sophia I might have thought otherwise, but during the last couple of years I've realised that having her as one of my closest friends is all I want. We tease each other, we look out for each other; I like to think that we would always confide in each other if we had any worries or troubles – but that's it, neither of us would expect anything more.'

'But she has that locket you gave her; Wing Yee says you made it yourself and she wears it all the time – surely that means something?'

'I gave it to her on her twenty-first birthday. Alexander told me how important it is; he said you English call it coming of age.'

Edmund allowed a smile to surface, but waited for Dick to continue.

'Chin Ming came to Singapore with a letter from her father to Raffles; it was a small scroll, held together with gold thread. She had kept it safe throughout the voyage, but then she lost it. I happened to come across it and when she escaped from the Dutchman, I was able to return it.'

Edmund's eyes grew large. He had no detailed knowledge of the time Chin Ming and Wing Yee had been enslaved; he knew that they had both suffered, of course, but that was all. He continued to listen, not knowing what to expect next.

'The letter contained information which proved the Dutchman had been involved in the opium trade. It was sent, along with all the other evidence used to prove his guilt, to Calcutta. The gold thread which had originally held it together was left behind; when Raffles returned to England, he gave it to me with instructions to pass it on to Chin Ming. That's what is inside the locket. She wears it because, until her father was found, it was all she had left of him.'

Edmund didn't know what to say. Dick had assured him that his feelings towards Chin Ming were purely platonic; he had no romantic intentions. Nevertheless, their friendship was more precious than all the rare orchids in the world. What could he hope to offer her, compared with that?

'You need to tell her how you feel,' Dick said, 'and you need to do it quickly.'

'How do you know how I feel?' Edmund said.

'Why else would you be asking me if I'm in love with her?' Dick said. 'Besides, I only have to look at the two of you ...'

Edmund's body became less tense, his muscles began to unwind and his breathing more regular. He felt relieved and encouraged to hear what Dick had just said, but a small voice inside his head now began to falter, presenting one excuse after another. In reality, there was no reason to avoid telling Chin Ming how he felt and it was something that he needed to do, but the moment he declared his feelings he was risking rejection. Once that happened, there was no rationale he could call upon to delay the return to England; and as soon as that journey began, he would be leaving Singapore behind, together with any possibility of happiness.

'Are you not having any breakfast?' Dick said, breaking the silence.

'I don't really feel like eating,' Edmund replied. 'I'm not hungry.'

'That's the difference between you and me; maybe it's the difference between being in love and friendship. You see, I'm always hungry and I can't imagine anything getting in the way of that!'

*****

The house that Chin Ming had moved into with her father was almost the last one along Beach Road. It was not as spacious as Alexander Johnston's home, but it was plenty large enough for Soong Heng, herself and Chang. Since coming here, Soong Heng had regained much of his strength and significant areas of memory. Father John had been a frequent visitor, as had Edmund Beaumont until a few days ago.

Chang's hearing was finely tuned, and he was the first to be aware of the gentle tap-tap he'd come to associate with the arrival of the young Englishman; he scuttled to the door in response and threw it wide open. He beamed at Edmund and ushered him into the parlour.

Chin Ming looked up from her book. 'I was beginning to think you'd abandoned us,' she said, 'Papa will be so glad to see you again, but I'm afraid he's not up yet. He shows signs of improvement every day, but he still tires easily; some days he rises early, some days much later. Today is one of his later days, but I'm sure he won't be too long.'

'That's good to hear, of course,' Edmund said, 'but it's actually you I wanted to speak to. But will that be acceptable, without a chaperone?'

She took a long look at him. He was constantly moving his hands, tightening them into fists and then loosening them almost immediately. He licked his lips and swallowed hard. She had longed for this moment ever since he'd arrived back in the Settlement; she wasn't going to waste time worrying about what was, and what was not, acceptable right now.

'If you had come to meet me, to escort me from Baba Tan's house to Mr Johnston's when Papa was staying there, instead of Dick, no-one would have raised any objection. It would have been thought most correct.'

'I would have liked to do that,' he almost whispered. 'I thought about it often, but I didn't want to disappoint your father; he seemed to enjoy our conversations a great deal.'

'Are there rules about young ladies being alone with young men in England?'

'That is usually what is expected,' Edmund said.

'Yes, that is certainly so in China, but we are neither in England nor in China.'

Edmund's eyebrow lifted in union with his smile. This was one of the things he loved about her – her spontaneity, her tenacity and her ability to see things from a different angle.

'We are in Singapore,' she continued. 'It is small and is still finding its way, setting its own rules. I have survived many difficulties in the last few years. Before moving into this house with Papa, I was in the school every day with Abdullah and no-one said it was the least bit improper; besides, Chang is in the kitchen and would come running should the need arise.' A smile spread slowly from her lips to her eyes.

Exactly on cue, Chang appeared, carrying a tray with tea and small, colourful rice cakes. He put it down in front of Chin Ming and skipped back to the kitchen. They both started to laugh.

'I hope I will give you no cause for alarm,' Edmund said, 'I simply want to tell you how much I admire you.' He instantly regretted the words he'd chosen; it sounded like the sort of thing he would say to Raffles; he hoped she wasn't laughing at him now. Neither of them said a word; discomfort filled the air. Then, Edmund plucked up his courage and moved closer to her. He picked up her hand and held it in the same way he had when he and Father John had told her about finding her father. She made no effort to remove her hand or to reprimand his action.

He coughed, hoping to do better this time. 'I've come to tell you that from the very first moment I saw you I've been totally captivated. During all those months we spent travelling – in Guangdong and in Sumatra – I couldn't stop thinking about you. Whenever I saw a young woman in the distance, especially if she was wearing a long, red garment, it reminded me of seeing you at Alexander's dinner party. I could recall everything we spoke about that night – and I always ended up feeling lightheaded. I had a similar feeling that day in Palembang, when I met your father for the first time. I saw the resemblance immediately; I was positive he was your father long before Father John introduced me to him.'

Chin Ming kept her head held down, all too aware of the colour flooding her cheeks; her heart was racing.

'I've come to tell you that I've fallen in love with you,' Edmund said, 'and I want to marry you – there, I've said it!'

A bird could be heard singing its heart out, somewhere in the garden. The fragrance of oleander and citronella drifted on warm currents of air. Everything else remained still.

Eventually, Chin Ming looked up. She let her hand remain in his, but tears balanced precariously on the lower lids of her eyes. Slowly, she smiled.

'I would like that very much,' she said, 'but I don't see how it can be possible.'

'What do you mean? I will, of course, ask your father's permission. I think he likes me well enough and I'm sure he would want you to be happy.'

'That's not what I meant,' she said. 'First of all, you need to remember this is Singapore. There are no churches here, there is no-one who can perform a marriage ceremony and besides ...'

Before she could continue, Edmund interrupted. He was like a puppy, full of energy and excitement. 'There are often missionaries passing through the port,' he said, 'and even if there are no missionaries on board the next ship to arrive in the harbour, the captain may be able to help – I'm pretty sure captains of ships are able to perform marriage ceremonies.'

'There is a ship due soon which Father John plans to join. I would rather it was he who married us; I have spoken to him about becoming a Christian, but – dear Edmund – it is impossible. I'm afraid I cannot marry you. You need to return home and I must stay here to take care of Papa. His health is still fragile and I need to be with him.'

'But,' Edmund said, clutching at straws, 'you said he was getting stronger all the time and he hardly ever has to pause to find the correct words now. I even heard him uttering a few words in French the other day.'

'He is making a great effort, it is true, but I believe it will take a long time before he is well enough to enjoy the things he used to – engage in debate, read and write poetry, play chess. He never talks about what happened to him and I think he never will, but we lost more than the four years when we were apart, we have so much catching up to do. I cannot risk losing him again.'

Edmund's heart sank. If she'd said she had no feelings for him, if she'd said he was being foolish, he would still have been heartbroken, but he would have had to accept the fact there was no hope for him. As it was, she'd indicated that she did have feelings for him, that she would like to marry him in any other circumstance. But how could he argue with her reasoning, how could he ask her to abandon the man she most admired in the whole world, who needed her so badly and for whom she had already made so many sacrifices?

'It is you and Father John I have to thank for returning Papa to me,' she said. 'For that, I will always be in your debt.'

He examined her beautiful face as if it was for the last time; a solitary tear escaped and spilled over onto her cheek; it glistened like a diamond in moonlight. He squeezed her hand and slowly let it go.

'I won't give up,' he said. 'I do have to return to England; I have to present a report to my employers. They will need detailed descriptions about the plants and seeds I collected; they will want to ask questions about Dick's drawings. I would like to see Raffles and tell him all about our travels – and to tell him about you. But when I've done all that, I will come back to Singapore; will you wait for me, Chin Ming?'

Now, the tears could be held back no longer, they cascaded down her cheeks and would not stop. She nodded her head up and down, but no words would come. He held her to him, kissed the top of her head and whispered goodbye. The last thing she heard, before the door softly closed was his voice saying, 'Farewell, my love, I will come back to speak to your father within the next few days.'

CHAPTER 26
Singapore, 6th June 1826

Chin Ming hadn't slept well for the last two nights. She was determined not to reveal any of the misery she was feeling to her father. Edmund had said that he would return to Singapore, and she knew he truly intended to do that. But what would happen when he reached England? Would the people in Oxford demand that he continue his work there? Would his friends and family expect him to settle down, resume the life he'd led before he came to the East? Would they persuade him that marrying a woman from a different culture, a different race and living in a far-away country was all too difficult?

She didn't hear the soft tread of Father John's approach. Chang, who was often looking out onto the street, had opened the door to him and pointed to the corner of the garden which she favoured at this time of day; a place where she could sit in the shade and escape into a world of her own.

He watched for a little while before disturbing her reverie. 'I'm sorry to interrupt,' he said. 'You look as if you are deep in thought.'

'Oh, Father John, excuse me. It is good to see you and Papa will be quite delighted. He is already up and waiting for you in the parlour; come, I'll take you through to him.'

She left the two men together and went in search of Chang. When she thought sufficient time had elapsed for the usual exchange of pleasantries to have taken place, she decided to join them. Listening to them talk and joining in their discussion occasionally would help take her mind away from her current worries.

They were talking about a man called Matteo Ricci. It was a name she had never come across before today, but the more she heard, the more enthralled she became.

'But surely, when the emperor gave his permission to erect a tomb for Father Ricci,' Soong Heng said, 'that laid the foundation for the Jesuit mission for ever?'

Chin Ming was delighted to hear her father engaging in this sort of discussion. It was exactly the type of conversation he had revelled in before his abduction. He'd already demonstrated the fact that his extensive English vocabulary had returned; now, it was becoming obvious that his ability to engage in intellectual debate was also beginning to be restored. She pulled her chair closer, so that she could focus on what was being said.

For the remainder of the morning, she was transfixed as her father and the priest exchanged ideas about Father Ricci and his belief that the Confucian classics were not incompatible with Catholicism. Occasionally she asked a question, sometimes she joined in the discussion, but mainly she listened. By the time her father said he needed to rest, she realised she hadn't thought about Edmund for well over an hour. She felt dizzy whenever she returned to the main points of the conversation, but the concept that appealed most of all was the similarity between Confucian and Catholic beliefs. She decided now was the time to talk to Father John and ask for his help.

'I didn't realise before this morning,' she said, 'that it's possible to respect some of the things I learned as a child – things based on Confucian teaching – and to become a Christian.'

'All faiths believe that compassion is the test of true spirituality,' Father John replied. 'It is best described as something known as the Golden Rule.'

Chin Ming frowned; she had not heard the phrase before.

'There are many interpretations,' he said, 'but the easiest way to describe it is, *always treat others as you would wish to be treated yourself.* Confucius was the first person to articulate this idea and most religions have since adopted it in some form or another.'

She smiled; it made perfect sense, though she knew such a notion was not easy. Now she could put aside any remaining qualms and make her decision; she wanted to become a Christian, and it was something she wanted to do whether or not she would be sharing her life with Edmund.

She spent another hour with Father John, discussing some of the issues raised in books she'd read and having answers provided to her many questions. By the time he was ready to leave, he told her that he would be happy to baptise her before he left for Calcutta.

*****

The following day, Chin Ming asked Chang to keep an eye on her father while she paid a brief visit to the school. She hadn't seen Abdullah for several days and she wanted to arrange to take Soong Heng along for a visit.

Around the middle of the morning, Edmund arrived at the house. He had hurried along Beach Road, impatient to see Chin Ming again, but now he was here his stomach began to churn. He had promised to speak to Soong Heng about his proposal and that is what he intended to do, but there was always the possibility that he would be misunderstood. What if Soong Heng was having a bad day? What if he didn't recognise him? What if he was unable to comprehend what Edmund was trying to say?

He needn't have worried. He found Soong Heng in the

garden, collecting the flowers that had fallen from the frangipani tree overnight. 'They still have the most delightful perfume,' he said, extending cupped hands full of slightly bruised and damaged blooms in Edmund's direction. 'I shall ask Chang to float them in a bowl of water so that we might enjoy them for a little while longer.'

Edmund followed him inside and took the seat opposite him when invited to do so.

'I have missed your company,' Soong Heng said.

'I came to see you a few days ago,' Edmund replied, 'but I was too early. Chin Ming told me that some days you need more sleep and that you were still in your room.'

'You spoke to my daughter?'

Edmund instantly regretted his words; he had most likely already caused offence because he'd made Soong Heng aware that he'd spoken to Chin Ming with no chaperone present.

'I am pleased that the two of you had the opportunity to spend some time together,' Soong Heng said. 'I believe you are very fond of each other and it is time that you both unveiled your feelings.'

Edmund liked the word *unveiled*; that was exactly what it felt like – the slow and careful disclosure of pent-up emotion. He quite forgot to be shocked that Soong Heng was being so frank and not at all conventional about him being alone with Chin Ming. He took a deep breath before saying what he had come to say. 'I have asked her to marry me!' he blurted out.

Soong Heng grinned. 'And I hope she agreed to do so?'

Edmund lowered his head onto his chest and bit his lip. 'Not exactly,' he whispered.

'Am I to understand that she said no? Why would she do that, she is obviously in love with you?'

Edmund felt as if he'd been punched in the ribs. Soong Heng was clearly delighted at the suggestion that he and Chin Ming should marry, but she was adamant that her father continued to need her attention, here in Singapore. He was aware that Soong Heng was on good form today, but maybe this was the exception to the rule. He certainly wasn't prepared to reveal Chin Ming's reason for turning him down.

'I have to return to England,' he said. 'I told Chin Ming that I would come to see you – to ask your permission. If you have no objection, then I will return to Singapore as soon as my business in England is finished.'

'Of course, I give my consent, but I can't see why it has to be so complicated. Has she actually said that she has no wish to go to England with you?'

Edmund felt he could not pursue the conversation any further without causing upset. 'I think you should ask Chin Ming to explain,' he said. 'Are you expecting her back soon?'

'She has gone to see the Malay schoolmaster; she wants to arrange for me to visit, to see the place where she works and to meet the children she helps with their learning. I'm afraid I have no idea how long she will be away.'

Edmund changed the subject and spent the next half-hour telling Soong Heng about the ship that was due to arrive at the end of the month. When there was still no sign of Chin Ming, he made his excuses to leave and promised to visit again before too long.

*****

Soong Heng said nothing to his daughter when she returned from the school, other than to ask about her visit. She told him Abdullah would be pleased to see them and had suggested they visit the children on Friday afternoon.

'That will suit me very well,' Soong Heng said. After they had finished their evening meal, he asked her to excuse him and retired to his room. Instead of reading a little and retiring early, however, Soong Heng sat down to write two letters. The

following morning, Chang was instructed to deliver them –
one was addressed to Baba Tan and Wing Yee, the other to
Dick. They were all invited to join Chin Ming and himself at
the school, this coming Friday.

*****

Since Abdullah had been running the school on his own, he
attended Friday prayers before the routine of teaching began.
Running the two classes together was more demanding than
he'd originally thought and he found himself spending additional time making preparations and then staying on after the
children left to clear away their slates and tidy the furniture.

He'd agreed with Chin Ming that the last hour of school on
Friday morning would be a good time to bring her father
along. The children would be tiring by then and glad of a
diversion from their lessons; also, it should not be too taxing
for her father.

*****

Chin Ming and Soong Heng made their way along the path
that led to the door of the schoolhouse. The shutters were wide
open at this time of day, to let in the light and allow any breeze
to circulate. One child, who was either daydreaming or had
lost interest in the lesson, was gazing in their direction. He
leapt up from his bench as soon as he spotted her, let out an
excited squeal, and climbed out of the window.

'Miss Li, Miss Li, you come back!' He ran down the path,
beating aside odd fronds of tronok palm that got in his way.
The other children looked up from their desks and started to
fidget. Abdullah knew there was no point in continuing with
the lesson, but asked them to remain in their places until Miss
Li arrived.

The errant child was Kim Ching, the son of Baba Tan's cousin, who loved his teacher dearly but was not that fond of sitting behind a desk. He held Chin Ming's hand and pulled her into the room.

'Miss Li come visit; our teacher is here.'

All the other children she had taught now came forward. She clapped her hands and asked them to sit. Instead of returning to their seats, they squatted on their haunches around her feet.

Soong Heng had remained in the doorway while all the commotion was going on, but now he made his way into the centre of the room. 'This is my Papa,' she said. 'He has not been well and I have been taking care of him.'

'And what a good job your teacher has done,' Soong Heng said. 'She has made me better so that I may come and visit you today. Now I need to discover how talented she is as a teacher.' He spoke in Cantonese and then in English; some of the children understood straight away, but two spoke only Hokkien and one knew only Malay. Abdullah translated the remarks, and those who had not already demonstrated their approval now joined in to express their enthusiasm. Soong Heng stood tall as a satisfied smile settled across his face.

Chin Ming laughed. It was so good to be surrounded by the children again and share in their delight. All she had ever wanted to do was make her father proud of her, but when she started teaching at the school, she had no idea that a day would dawn when that particular wish would come true.

'Please sit down, Papa,' she said, 'I'm sure the children would like to ask you some questions.'

No-one spoke at first, then one or two looked around to see who would be the first to speak; a brave little voice at the back broke the silence, 'Please sir, what is your name?'

Before he could respond, another voice asked in Cantonese, 'What part of China do you come from?' and a third child asked, 'How old are you?' That was followed quickly by the question, 'What is your favourite food?'

Inquisitive thoughts translated into questions as the children gained more confidence.

On the whole, Soong Heng found it easy to respond and not at all demanding, even when some translation was necessary. Not until Kim Ching asked, 'Why has it taken you so long to visit us?'

Soong Heng's expression changed; his smile disappeared, and he stared at the palms of his hands. He looked forlornly at his daughter; he hadn't got an answer, but how could he explain that to these young children. Chin Ming swallowed hard; she had no idea how to respond either.

Abdullah came to the rescue. 'Li Soong Heng has been travelling. His journey took longer than he thought, but he is with us now and that is all that matters. We are grateful that he has given up his time to come and meet us today; now I want you to show your appreciation and say thank you. You may then pick up your things and return home, I will see you all on Monday morning.'

A rousing chorus of thanks followed, some in Cantonese, some in Hokkien, some in English and one lonely Malay voice that could be heard above all the others, '*Terima kasih*, Mr Li, *terima kasih*, Miss Li.' Nearly all the children bowed politely as they withdrew from the room.

Abdullah and his guests waited until the last child had left the compound before they allowed themselves to laugh, but once they started, they found it difficult to stop. They were still laughing when Dick stepped into the room.

'It's good to see you again,' Soong Heng said, reverting to English.

Chin Ming frowned; she was completely unaware of the letters her father had asked Chang to deliver. She was always pleased to see Dick, but couldn't think what he was doing here.

'Is something wrong?' she said. 'Has something happened to Edmund?' She turned pink immediately. What on earth had caused her to say his name, why hadn't she asked about Wing Yee? 'Or is it Wing Yee,' she added feebly when she realised Baba Tan had followed Dick into the room.

'I asked Baba Tan, Dick and Wing Yee to meet us here today,' Soong Heng said. 'I hope you will be able to stay a little while longer too,' he said, looking at Abdullah.

'I don't understand, Papa, why do you want everyone to meet here, at the school?'

'Because I didn't want to inconvenience anyone. It's quite a long walk to the house where we are living; this place is more central.'

'But you still haven't said what it is you want to talk about.'

'Shall we wait until Wing Yee gets here, then I won't have to repeat myself,' he said.

'There's a hawker stall just along the lane,' Abdullah said. 'Would you like me to get some drinks, or some fruit – something to quench your thirst sir, after all that talking to the children?'

Whilst he was gone, Dick told them about a portrait he was about to embark upon; it was for a Javanese merchant who had only recently arrived in the Settlement. In passing, he mentioned that he'd accompanied Wing Yee to a house on Rochor Plain. Neither he nor Baba Tan chose to disclose any details about the patient she had treated.

Abdullah returned, carrying a tray with an assortment of drinks in vessels made from bamboo – coconut water, pineapple juice and freshly squeezed papaya. Dick helped to distribute the drinks and suggested they make themselves comfortable. Soong Heng and Baba Tan took the teachers' chairs, while Abdullah, Chin Ming and Dick all decided to stand rather than suffer the discomfort of the hard, wooden benches used by the children.

They sipped their drinks slowly, but there was still no sign of Wing Yee.

'Maybe Wing Yee has been held up,' Soong Heng said. 'Perhaps I should begin to tell you why I've asked you to join us.'

Chin Ming rubbed the back of her neck; she had no idea why, but she was beginning to feel tense. She looked anxiously at her father, who had still given her no indication of what he was about to say.

'Two days ago, I received a visit from a delightful young Englishman,' he said.

Chin Ming gasped; she closed her eyes and held her breath, knowing that her face was turning the same shade as the hibiscus nodding its head in the breeze, outside the window.

'Edmund Beaumont came to ask for my blessing; he came to tell me that he wants to marry my daughter.'

'At last!' Dick said

'I trust that means you approve?' Soong Heng said.

'Of course, I approve,' Dick said. Baba Tan and Abdullah both grinned, then nodded their heads to indicate that they too favoured the idea.

'What's the problem?' Dick said.

'Chin Ming is the problem; she has turned him down. She has told him she needs to stay in Singapore to look after me. I wanted her to hear what her friends thought of such a ridiculous notion, such a waste of an opportunity. That's why I asked you to meet with us today – the three of you, and Wing Yee, her closest friends.'

'Wing Yee,' Dick said, suddenly acutely aware of her absence.

'What time did you ask her to arrive?' Chin Ming said looking at her father. 'It is very unusual for her to be late.'

'It's not just unusual,' Dick said, 'she is never late. Something must have happened. I need to check, I need to make sure ... excuse me!' He rushed out of the room, down the gravel path and sped away in the direction of the quay. Baba Tan hurried after him, leaving the others in stunned silence and unsure what to do.

CHAPTER 27
Singapore, 9th June 1826

Dick was well ahead by the time they reached Baba Tan's go-down. The small door, set within the solid entrance gates, was slightly ajar. That in itself was unusual; Baba Tan always made a point of closing it especially when Wing Yee was there alone; sometimes, he even locked it behind him. Her workshop was in a room at the top of a staircase at the far end.

Baba Tan now arrived, slightly out of breath. Dick pointed to the door, then put his index finger to his lips so that neither of them made any sound. Very cautiously, Dick pushed the door open far enough for them both to enter the warehouse. They strained their ears, but there was no noise other than the gentle buzz of coolies shifting cargo further along the quay.

Dick removed his sandals and signalled that he would climb the stairs and that Baba Tan should stay put to keep guard. He moved slowly, keeping to the edge of the building and being careful not to bump against any of the bales of silk jutting out beyond their usual orderly position on the shelves. He reached the steps, scrutinising them as best he could; he had no idea whether there were any loose treads likely to make a noise and give away his presence, but he was pleased that they were flooded with sunlight making it easy for him to examine each step before he placed his foot upon it. In the end, he used all fours, making it easier to move as evenly and quickly as he dared.

He was almost at the top when he heard the commotion. He stayed perfectly still, hoping to catch any significant words and then think about what he should do. The decision was made for him when he heard a high-pitched scream. He took the last two steps in one energetic leap and burst through the door of the workshop. Pierre Volande was bearing down on Wing Yee, yelling abuse in Cantonese and holding a knife which looked very similar to the one she'd described previously at his uncle's house.

'Put that down,' Dick said. 'If you harm her, you'll not only have me to answer to. I'll make sure you're arrested, and with your record there's no way the magistrates are likely to be lenient.'

Volande swung around and glared at Dick. 'You!' he said. 'I might have known you'd try to interfere. She's one of the women in your painting, isn't she? Do you like this one best – or maybe you have more sophisticated tastes? Perhaps I should wait for the other one to join us?'

'You disgust me,' Dick said. 'I've never heard anyone say anything good about you; you're a liar and a cheat, but the worst thing of all was setting fire to Lam Qua's studio. I can never forgive you for that.'

'You can't prove a thing; you weren't even there.'

'I have a letter which tells me about everything that happened.'

Tempers were getting frayed and Wing Yee began to shake; anything might happen. She edged away from the two men.

'When you went to William's house there was soot on your face and on your clothes; you left in a hurry, just before Lam Qua arrived to tell him about the fire damage.'

Wing Yee had reached her workbench; she quickly gathered together several small bottles and began to fill them with the lotion she'd used when she'd visited the Frenchman at his uncle's home. She placed sachets of herbs for making tea in a small pouch.

Volande began to skirt around the edge of the room. He was sweating profusely; the fever had returned and he needed help.

'How do I know what you say is true?' he said. 'You and your friends tricked me once; you led me to believe you'd acquired something rare and valuable on your travels and the only thing Lawrence had to show me was a pink parakeet – a bird of no particular significance.'

'It was you who came looking for us,' Dick yelled. 'You came to the studio, you asked me to paint your portrait. I always thought it strange, but you never intended it to see the light of day, did you? All you wanted was an excuse to bombard me with questions, to ask about some rumour you'd overheard in Macao. More fool you for believing the tale of a man with too much alcohol inside him.'

Wing Yee had not seen Dick so outraged for a long, long time. Horrible images of the man who had assaulted her three years ago came flooding back. Dick had been responsible for rescuing her on that occasion and she had no doubt that he would do so again, but at what cost? She gripped the edge of the table, unable to move. The arrival of the Frenchman had been a shock, but why was he being so unpleasant? Should she blame herself? Had she provoked him by saying she had an appointment and needed to leave? If only she'd made up the lotion straight away, then maybe he would have left her alone and Dick would not have come looking for her.

'He not have place to stay, he not eat well so fever return. I make more medicine,' Wing Yee said quietly, hoping to calm Dick's anger.

'It's not our fault that he's been sleeping rough,' Dick said, still angry. 'He chose to flee from his uncle's house when you told him I was in the courtyard; he's a coward who has always managed to escape from the crimes he's committed – up until now, that is.'

'It's all very well for the likes of you,' Volande said. 'You've been able to do whatever you like, wherever you like. You're not even a blood relation, but because Stamford Raffles chose to adopt you, you have lived a privileged life. My father, on the other hand, rejected me after my grandparents died – no money, no position, nothing!'

'STOP!' Wing Yee shouted. 'Dick not have easy life. You not know; no-one know what trouble other people have.' She picked up the sachets and the bottles full of pale, yellow liquid. 'Take these, make you well,' she said. 'You go now.'

Volande grabbed the package she offered and turned to leave. Dick lunged towards him and managed to knock the knife out of his other hand, but the Frenchman retaliated by punching him in the chest. Dick keeled over and fell to his knees. Volande ran past him and sped down the stairs during the moments it took for him to regain his breath. The Frenchman was fast and more agile than Dick would have thought possible. Having regained his balance, he rushed out of the workshop in pursuit. Volande had reached the bottom of the staircase. Hurrying towards him was Baba Tan, who had heard the commotion. He stood with his arms folded and his legs wide apart, attempting to prevent Volande going any further. However, a man who had been on the run for most of his adult life was well-used to such tactics. He moved to the right, giving the impression that he meant to avoid the person blocking his path, but as soon as Baba Tan took a step in the same direction, Volande ducked down and leapt past on the other side, pushing Baba Tan to the ground as he did so.

Dick stopped briefly to check that Baba Tan wasn't injured, then chased after a blurred impression of a green tunic disappearing through the door.

*****

Edmund followed James out of the harbour master's office with his head hanging down and his shoulders hunched. Their passages had been booked and their tickets paid for. The inevitability of their return to England was finally settled.

'Don't look so glum,' James said. 'She hasn't said she will never marry you; she didn't protest when you said you would come back to Singapore.'

'I don't think she believes me,' Edmund said, shaking his head. He hadn't spoken to Chin Ming on her own for five days now. As soon as he'd told James about the result of their conversation, James had taken it as permission to go ahead with making arrangements for their homeward voyage.

James had done his best to involve Edmund in the decision-making, if only to relieve his brother's obvious misery, but when the plan failed, he took charge of the task alone. He'd managed to get them berths on the same ship that would first of all take Father John to Calcutta. Confirmation had now been received that it was due to arrive in Singapore on 26th June; that gave him a little over two weeks to encourage his brother to be more cheerful.

Halfway along the quay, Edmund stopped walking. He wanted to imprint the image of this part of the Settlement on his heart. It was an image he needed to carry with him for many months. A sour taste filled his mouth as he reminded himself that it might even be a couple of years before he would be able to return. His head began to spin, and it felt as if there was grit behind his eyes; part of him wanted to run to the top of Bukit Larangan and be alone with his sorrow, part of him felt completely devoid of energy and a need to collapse onto the nearest packing case.

'We still have almost three weeks before we sail,' James said. 'Why don't you ask Dick to paint a scene that represents the part of Singapore that you like the most? Maybe he might even have time to complete a quick sketch of Chin Ming – a small part of her to take home with you?'

Edmund brightened almost at once, why hadn't he thought of that? 'What an excellent idea,' he said. 'We should try to find Dick straight away, ask him if it's possible.' He cast his eye along the quay and then let it travel up to the top of the hill. There were so many possibilities, but he thought his preference would be a view of the town and the harbour beyond – the whole panorama from the top of Bukit Larangan, that would be perfect.

When his gaze returned to the river itself, he became aware of the fading light. It was only three o'clock and yet it felt like the last half-hour before the sun faded. There had been no sign of rain since they returned to Singapore, but both he and James were now experienced enough to know that such a sudden change in the weather heralded the onset of a tropical storm. The sky was already full of dark, ominous-looking clouds; below them the last sharp streak of light was losing the battle to fight back. A soft breeze ruffled Edmund's hair, then flipped the hem of his coat up behind him. The gentle ripples that played around the boats tied up along the quay began to swell. The lightermen, knowing what was in store, made sure everything was tied down securely, but already the boats had begun to bump against each other, moving up and down amongst what had now become significant waves.

James felt the first spot of rain; it landed in the middle of his forehead, then several fat droplets bounced off the front of his coat. 'We should take shelter,' he said.

They had almost reached the end of the wharf when they became aware of a figure running towards them. Why should anyone be running in that direction – there was no shelter at the far end of the quay? The man was clutching something to his chest and as he got closer to them, his great haste suggested that he was probably escaping from something or someone. Maybe the package contained something he'd stolen. He was bearing down on them now, heedless of anything in his path.

James wanted to continue on their way but Edmund wasn't sure he agreed. If the runaway turned out to be a rogue who was caught, they might be useful as witnesses. He stepped forward to get a better look at the fugitive; only then did he realise the man was European.

'He's being chased,' James shouted, 'Move, Edmund! Keep out of the way!'

The person in hot pursuit of the runaway was Dick. The rain was coming down more steadily now, occasionally obscuring their vision, but there was no mistake about the person doing the chasing. What on earth was happening?

Before they knew it, the man was almost level with them; neither of them recognised him, but he looked extremely unwell. There were dark shadows under his eyes, pustules on his skin, and his clothes – some sort of green tunic over black, baggy trousers – were torn. He ran past at full pelt along the length of the quay until finally he ran out of options; he'd reached the end of the wharf – and Dick was not far behind.

Edmund ignored the fact that he was now soaked right through and followed after them – the pursued and the pursuer. He wanted to make sure Dick didn't get hurt. He was vaguely aware of James calling after him, but he kept on, quickening his pace as the torrent of water which was now descending made it impossible to see anything beyond a few feet in front.

There was a loud splash followed by a cry of anguish. Edmund began to run; James followed close behind. They both heaved a sigh of relief when they arrived to see Dick scurrying along to the end of the wharf and back again. They caught hold of him and asked what was going on.

'That ...' Dick crossed his hands over his heaving chest, '... was Volande!'

'Chanda Khan's nephew?' Edmund said.

Dick nodded, still trying to stop wheezing. 'He was … he was in Wing Yee's workshop.' He gulped a fresh intake of air. 'He was threatening her … when Baba Tan and I got there.'

'Did he know she has the orchid?' Edmund said.

'It's nothing to do with the orchid,' Dick said, his breathing now under control again. 'It's still safe. His fever returned; he came to Wing Yee for more medicine. She thinks he's been in hiding, but the fever came back. When he ran away from his uncle's house he wasn't completely recovered; without medicine it returned, but she has no idea how he found her.'

'So, where is he now?' Edmund said.

'I've no idea, but we need to find him. He jumped – I think he was trying to reach one of the boats, but I can't see him anywhere.'

'You mean the splash we heard, the cry for help – that was him hitting the water?' Edmund said.

'Can he swim?' James asked.

'Even if he can swim, the clothes he was wearing will drag him down – and those waves look pretty rough to me,' Edmund said. 'Surely, he doesn't stand a chance?'

'We need to look anyway,' Dick said. 'Even a scoundrel like him doesn't deserve to die like that. He may have managed to climb aboard one of the boats. Visibility is so poor now; he could be anywhere. We'd better start searching. I'll go to the far end of the wharf; you and James can cover the remainder between you.'

They walked up and down for another half-hour. They peered into the waves and out into the middle of the choppy river. Whenever they spotted a lighterman or a fisherman who had remained on board his vessel, they asked if any of them had noticed anything untoward; they asked the same of a group of coolies who sat huddled under a sheet of canvas, but no-one had anything useful to tell them.

Finally, the rain stopped. 'Will you take us out in your boat; we need to find someone,' Dick spoke to several fishermen in Malay but each one shrugged his shoulders, pointed to the sky and shook their head. No-one was prepared to take any risks until they were sure there was no more rain on the way. Eventually, when the sun broke through the clouds and it seemed certain that the storm had burned itself out, Dick began to ask again. The fishermen had busied themselves, but a Malay boatman, used to ferrying passengers between the quay and ships at anchor in the harbour, agreed to accept the money they had to offer.

They began by circling around the area where the loud splash and the cry of distress had been heard, but there was nothing to be seen. The tide was already pulling the water out towards the mouth of the river and pieces of debris, churned up by the storm, followed swiftly behind.

'If he's survived,' Edmund said, 'he could be hanging on to a piece of flotsam, a piece of wood dislodged from one of the boats. I think we should go out into the harbour and search that area where the river joins with the deeper waters.'

They spent another hour criss-crossing between the shore and the area where the bigger ships were anchored. Dick scrutinised the churning waters the small boat left in its wake whilst Edmund and his brother examined the waters on each side of the vessel. Their oarsman painstakingly followed Dick's directions, often pulling against the strong current, until the point came where the sun began to sink over the horizon. There was no point in continuing to search now it was dark.

When they returned to the quay, Dick thanked the boat-man and gave him some additional coins for his trouble. Baba Tan was waiting for them and after he'd assured them that Wing Yee was in the safety of his home and fully recovered from her ordeal, they gave a brief resumé of their investigations.

They all walked along together until they reached Hill Street, then parted to go their separate ways. Baba Tan returned to Wing Yee and his family. Dick, James and Edmund turned in the direction of Beach Road, but each step they took became more laboured as exhaustion took hold of all three of them in turn.

Nothing further was said until they reached the house; they hurried to change into dry garments and then flopped down into the comfortable chairs on Alexander Johnston's veranda. 'It looks as if the sea has claimed justice for your friend, Lam Qua,' James said.

'And for all the others he's cheated along the way,' Edmund added.

'Yes,' Dick said, 'Pierre Volande's luck has finally run out, it seems.'

CHAPTER 28
Singapore, 9th June 1826

As soon as it became obvious that Dick and Baba Tan were unlikely to return to the school, Abdullah offered to escort Chin Ming and Soong Heng back to their house. Even though Baba Tan's warehouse could not be seen from the entrance to the school, they all stood gazing along the road for several minutes before starting off in the opposite direction.

Soong Heng invited Abdullah to stay for a while and was relieved when he agreed. Abdullah provided a calming influence; Chin Ming had great respect for him and Soong Heng knew his presence would create a diversion from the drama of the afternoon. No further mention was made of Edmund's proposal.

Abdullah told Soong Heng about the early days of the Settlement; when the south bank of the river, where Commercial Square now stood, was mainly jungle leading to marshland and was totally uninhabited. He related stories of bullocks pulling large guns for the soldiers and being astonished when the animals remained unperturbed by the noise the guns made.

'As soon as an officer shouted an order to move at the double,' Abdullah said, 'the bullocks broke into a run. When the officer said "halt" the bullocks stood completely still, and when a soldier changed direction, the bullocks did likewise. It was all very strange.'

'I think you should write all your stories down,' Soong Heng said. 'Not many people have been here from the very start of the Settlement and have witnessed the challenges as well as the triumphs. Even Dick has only been here for the last four years.'

'Maybe I will,' Abdullah said, 'but my first priority is to see the completion of the Singapore Institution.'

He reminded Soong Heng about Raffles' plan to establish a school for older pupils; Chin Ming joined in the conversation, though her concentration faltered from time to time. She couldn't let go of the last words uttered by Dick as he hurried away from the school. He was correct – Wing Yee was never late; all sorts of possibilities filled her mind. It was now several hours since Dick had dashed away, thinking Wing Yee might be in danger, but no further information had been forthcoming.

When Abdullah rose to leave, it was already dark. Chin Ming asked if Chang might walk with him as far as the bridge so that he could make enquiries about Wing Yee and Dick; she needed to know that both her friends were safe.

*****

Chang had to go no further than Mr Johnston's house to ascertain answers to Chin Ming's questions. While Dick told him to assure her that neither he nor Wing Yee had come to any harm, Edmund scribbled a note. He described the broad outlines of their afternoon, he told her that Baba Tan had returned to take care of Wing Yee, that he, Dick and James were unscathed and the only person who had in any way suffered was Pierre Volande. He said he hoped to visit her soon, but decided not to risk any declaration of his affection. He simply signed it with his name.

*****

Chin Ming was glad to receive the note, but seeing Edmund's handwriting unsettled her. It was what he'd left unsaid that made her feel edgy. She tried to read a book that Father John had delivered at the beginning of the week, but the words swam before her eyes and made no sense. When the oil lamp sputtered and its light dimmed, she announced that it was time for her to retire. Soong Heng nodded and wished her goodnight.

She lay awake, listening to the house creaking and the crickets tuning up for their usual nocturnal recital. Sometime later, she heard the soft tread of her father's footsteps as he mounted the stairs and proceeded to his room at the back of the house. A bird screeched somewhere far away and then the leaves of a casuarina tree began to rustle outside her window. Her mind went back to the meeting at the school; she wondered what else might have been said had not Dick and Baba Tan rushed off to rescue Wing Yee. She was sure her friend would have understood the dilemma she now faced; after all, Wing Yee had given up all her own ambition for the sake of her younger sister. Chin Ming was sure she would have been sympathetic ....

Sleep eventually arrived, but it came with difficulty and was full of interruptions. Dreadful images came to torment her; she tossed and turned, turned and tossed until the light sheet covering her body became so tangled that it might have strangled her. She woke up with a start, struggled to remember the dream, then fell back into a deeper sleep.

Before long, the ordeal started all over again. She was standing on a wharf; sometimes she was alone, sometimes Wing Yee was standing beside her. One minute she recognised the familiarity of Boat Quay, with coolies hurrying back and forth; then the image switched, changed its perspective. She was sitting in one of the bumboats with Wing Yee, it was heading out into the harbour, then the image changed again.

Now, they huddled against each other in a sampan, it was dark and they were leaving the lights of the town behind; a shadow fell across her face and the vision faded.

She felt lost; she tossed about on the bed and then the nightmare began to repeat itself. This time, she was in a boat with two other women; it was the day they'd arrived in Singapore; someone was pushing, prodding her back with a pole, hurting her – Wing Yee was disappearing out of sight and then a shutter came down, cutting her off from the memory. She writhed about, desperate to escape the anguish, but the final trauma was yet to materialise.

Initially, the setting appeared not to have changed; small boats bobbed up and down on the water, but the wharf was bigger, much bigger; an enormous crowd bore down on her; she was no longer in Singapore, she was in Guangzhou. Standing beside her, her father tried to protect her from the crowd. It surged forward; there was a cacophony of noise – cymbals, drums, bells. Images of dancing lions changed from red, to gold, to black. Her father's hands let go; she started to fall; she could no longer see him.

As his image disappeared, she called out. She woke up, crying out 'Papa, Papa!' Once again, she was tangled in the sheets and drenched in sweat. Then she felt Soong Heng's hands link with her own. They were warm and soothing; they made her feel safe.

Chin Ming opened her eyes to find Soong Heng sitting on her bed; his smile was unfocused and his eyes filled with tears. He squeezed her hands in his and they gazed into each other's eyes for a long time. There was a fleeting moment when she recognised the pain behind his eyes; he shuddered and, without saying a word, they each understood that he had remembered the day he was abducted. Soong Heng took his daughter in his arms and pulled her close; it was as if she was eighteen again. Slowly, he let go, setting her back against the pillows, continuing to stroke her hands.

'It is over,' he said. 'We have a new life now and we must grasp each opportunity that comes our way.'

Instinctively, she knew he would never disclose the details of his abduction, but she was happy that her Papa had returned to her – that was enough. He remained sitting on the bed until exhaustion finally took hold and she sank into a more peaceful sleep.

*****

Saturday 10th June

It was almost midday when Chin Ming woke up. She wrapped a robe around her body and wandered through the house, into the garden. She found her father sitting in his usual spot, with Wing Yee for a companion. They didn't notice her for a while and Chin Ming wondered whether anything had happened overnight regarding the Frenchman.

'No news,' Wing Yee said in response to the interrogation. 'Some see remains of medicine I give him floating in water, that is all.'

Chang brought lunch out on trays, and they continued their conversation throughout the afternoon. Chin Ming wondered whether Wing Yee would mention Edmund, but the subject was not raised. A small part of her would have liked to retreat into a corner with her friend, where she could seek her advice, but as she wasn't even sure what to ask, she remained silent. Maybe Wing Yee and her father had already discussed the matter while she was still asleep and it would be embarrassing to raise the subject again.

'Do you remember your birthday, when we meet for picnic in our *Talking Place*?' Wing Yee said, interrupting her thoughts.

'Of course, I do,' Chin Ming said. 'It was a lovely day, but it seems such a long time ago.'

'We should do again. We meet tomorrow – same place. I bring food, you bring Papa.'

Chin Ming laughed; she did so enjoy the way Wing took charge of things – but in the nicest possible way. She looked at her father to see what he was thinking.

'We'll be there,' he said. 'I've heard so much about Bukit Larangan, but we've not had an opportunity to visit since I arrived in Singapore. I am really looking forward to seeing that famous view.'

*****

That evening, instead of retiring to his room immediately after they had eaten, Soong Heng suggested they take a stroll in the garden. Chin Ming was delighted with the prospect, she always enjoyed spending time breathing in the many distinctive scents and listening to the sounds that pervaded the garden at night. She held onto Soong Heng's arm, enjoying a new kind of closeness as they strolled along the path towards their favourite spot. Neither of them said a word, each immersed in their own particular deliberations.

Chin Ming lifted her head, closed her eyes and filled her lungs with the soft perfume floating across from the frangipani and oleander trees. Soong Heng had eyes only for the dark, velvety sky, dappled with tiny points of bright light.

'Look, daughter!' he shouted. 'Over there!'

Chin Ming clutched her father's arm, thinking something untoward had happened, but he detached himself quickly, spun her around and pointed to the southern sky. A handful of small silver beads, each attached to a long shiny tail, shot across the sky one after the other as if they had been thrown by a group of athletes such as those often hired to entertain the emperor.

'What is it, Papa? It looks like a fireworks display, but I

can't hear a thing. What's happening?'

Soong Heng told her about the small pieces of debris that break free when a comet flies too close to the sun. 'That is what you can see; most are no larger than a grain of sand,' he said, 'but they create a streak of light when they come close to earth. Some people call them shooting stars, but they're not really stars at all.'

'They're still very pretty, and we can see them so clearly from here.'

'You would be able to see them just as well in England,' he said.

*****

Monday 12th June

Dick and Edmund had arranged to meet Wing Yee at the place where the track from Hill Street led to the top of Bukit Larangan. As soon as she arrived, they hurried along without saying a great deal; the need to reach their *Talking Place* well ahead of Chin Ming had already been agreed. The terrain, which had been so rough and hazardous when Dick had first arrived in Singapore, was now well-trodden and familiar to all three of them; they climbed the slope in no time at all.

Wing Yee spread a cloth on the ground and placed the picnic basket in the centre; there was no point in removing the contents until they were ready to eat. 'While we wait, Dick can tell us about new friend,' she said.

Dick was confused, he wasn't sure what she meant.

'You paint Javanese family,' she said. 'Eldest daughter, they say she very beautiful.'

'Sujana is attractive,' he said. 'She's also clever – and help-ful with the smaller children; she keeps them amused when they get restless.'

'You say she talk about Bali.'

'The family has recently settled here from Batavia,' Dick

explained to the others. 'Sujana once visited Bali with her father; she described the places she stayed, but I'm afraid I no longer have any memories of the place.'

'But you have nice talk with her?' Wing Yee persisted. 'You like her?'

Dick was saved from further embarrassment when they heard the sound of a vehicle on the track below. Alexander Johnston had offered his carriage to Chin Ming so that Soong Heng would not be tired when they reached the summit. They heard the cry of an animal, followed by the blowing sound only horses make; then, the noise of wheels crunching on the track below became louder. This was Edmund's signal to move out of sight.

*****

'Now I know why this place is so special to the three of you,' Soong Heng said. 'The view is quite remarkable.' He let his gaze travel across the whole panorama, from the older buildings clustered along the sides of the river to the more recent additions which spread out in all directions, and beyond that to the magnificent harbour which had now become the focus of the entrepot trade.

'It is always lovely here,' Dick said. 'That's why Raffles chose to build his house here rather than in town. He used to walk along the ridge every morning, breathing in the subtle perfume and listening to the sounds of everything waking up again. That's the house, over there,' he said, pointing in the direction of the bungalow. 'That's where we all lived together before he returned to England. Mr Crawfurd lives there now.' Turning back to face the sea he said, 'This is the view that Edmund wants me to paint for him.'

Chin Ming could feel her cheeks warming; she was sure everyone was gazing at her, expecting her to say something, but all she could do was bite her lip and busy herself by smoothing out the creases in her tunic. She too was staring out to sea when Edmund appeared from nowhere, but she was unaware of his presence until he spoke.

'Yes,' he said, 'I've walked along the side of the hill to examine the aspect from other places, but this is definitely the one I prefer. When I'm back in England, I will look at the painting and remember everything I love about this place; the scenery, the food – and – the people.'

Dick coughed. 'Perhaps you'd like me to show you the path where Raffles liked to walk,' he said to Soong Heng. 'You can see the Spice Garden from there too – and Wing Yee can tell you all about it.'

Before anyone had a chance to comment, Edmund and Chin Ming had been left alone. They made polite conversation for a while, both feeling awkward and aware that their friends had deliberately contrived to leave them to spend some time together. Neither knew where to begin. He stole a sideways look at her and wished he could find some way to change her mind about marrying him.

'I shall miss this place so much,' Edmund said.

Chin Ming surprised him when she said, 'Tell me about England.' She patted the ground, inviting him to sit beside her and waited for him to begin.

He told her about the village in which he'd been born, the place where his father was the local vicar. He described the view from his rooms in Oxford and how he'd come to love the Physic Garden more than his studies. She delighted in his passion when he talked about his plant collections and the possibility of introducing new species into English gardens.

'Would I like living in England?' she said.

Edmund's lips parted. He looked dazed. He tried to speak, but all he could do was stutter meaningless nonsense. He took a deep breath, 'Do you ... dare I hope ... that you've changed your mind?' he said, in a tone somewhat higher than normal.

'Papa has made it quite plain that he thinks I'm being foolish. The other day, he arranged for Baba Tan, Dick and Wing Yee to come to the school to persuade me to think again. It didn't work out – but you know all about that. Last night, we had a long talk; he convinced me that I was making a mistake. I believe he knew you would be here today – and I'm glad.'

'I'm glad too,' Edmund said, 'but are you sure – England can be very cold.'

'Have you changed your mind? You no longer wish for us to marry?'

'Nothing could be further from the truth,' he said.

'There's only one thing I have to ask, before I finally agree,' Chin Ming said.

The colour drained from his face. All the optimism he'd felt a moment ago faded in the fear that he would not be able to fulfil her request. He waited for her to continue.

'I cannot leave Papa in Singapore,' she said. 'I know that his memory is almost completely restored and his general health is also so much improved, but I want him to come to England too.'

'Of course, Soong Heng must come with us,' Edmund said. 'I never imagined anything else.'

'The night that the Frenchman drowned I had dreadful nightmares,' she said. 'The very last thing I remember before I woke up was a flashback to the day we got separated, the day I lost sight of him. I woke up screaming only to find Papa sitting on my bed. When I realised I was no longer dreaming – that he was real, – all the unpleasant images that had tormented my dreams faded away.'

Edmund took her hands in his; he continued to listen.

'We looked into each other's eyes and I knew, at that moment, that Papa had remembered. He didn't say so, but there was something about the way he looked at me; I knew. You were correct when you said he may never want to discuss it, and that's alright now. He wants to put the past behind us, he wants to come to England ...'

He put his arms around her and lightly kissed the top of her head. When he looked up, he could see Wing Yee waving excitedly and encouraging the others to join her. Before Chin Ming had time to look up, Wing Yee, Dick and her father had gathered round. Everyone was smiling and applauding the outcome of the gathering.

'I'm starving,' Dick said. 'Can we have the picnic now?'

*****

James too was delighted with the news but pointed out that their ship would be leaving in just under three weeks. There was much to do if Chin Ming and Soong Heng planned to travel with them.

The remaining plants, collected during their travels in Sumatra, had already been packed in moss and placed in barrels; the seeds had been labelled and stored in small, airtight boxes. This meant Edmund was able to help Chin Ming and Soong Heng plan their own departure.

The house would be looked after by Alexander Johnston until a new tenant could be found. Chin Ming spent more time choosing the books she wanted to take with her than thinking about which items of clothing were necessary. Soong Heng, on the other hand, had very few personal possessions and even fewer items of clothing. Now that he was feeling stronger, he took pleasure in visiting a number of the tailors in town and choosing fabric for several tunics, trousers and other garments. Edmund tried to instil in both of them the need to have some warmer items of clothing made. It would be autumn when they arrived in England and the temperatures would be several degrees lower than those they were used to.

*****

At last, everything was ready; the ship was due to arrive the following day. All the passages had been booked and the ship would depart in four days from now – on Thursday 29th. Once again, Alexander Johnston – with the help of Dick – delighted in arranging a farewell dinner for their friends on what was to be their last night in Singapore.

*****

There was a sombre atmosphere at the beginning of the evening, each of them being all too aware that it was unlikely they would meet again for a long time.

'We must not be gloomy,' Johnston said. 'We have enjoyed each other's company and we have many happy memories of our time together. From now on, we will tell each other about our lives – our sorrows and our joys – by writing to each other. Letters may take a while to travel between England and Singapore, but eventually we get to know the news. Only last month I received information telling me about the great strides being made, using steam power instead of relying entirely on the wind. One ship has already crossed the Atlantic using steam for part of the journey. Maybe, one day, they will build a ship that will use steam to get all the way to Singapore and arrive here considerably sooner than it takes under sail.'

The idea seemed so preposterous that everyone burst out laughing, but it lightened the mood and everyone began to relax. The food was, as ever, delicious. Dick had made sure that all Chin Ming's favourites were served: *beef kway teow, foo yong hai, poh pia, kuah ladah* and *ayam kleo* with a variety of rice dishes and other accompaniments. The wine flowed freely, together with all the usual fruit juices for those who had not acquired a taste for alcohol.

Towards the end of the meal, Wing Yee excused herself and went out onto the veranda to collect the mysterious package she had brought with her from Baba Tan's house. It was wrapped in a fine white muslin, and she carried it with great care.

'Time to go home with you,' she said, placing it beside Edmund. He unwrapped the delicate layers of fabric to reveal William's orchid; it had produced new leaves and two new shoots, each of which displayed several flowers. When William had first shown them the plant, the light had been poor and only one bloom remained before it went into a period of rest. Edmund could have sworn that it had white petals, but the specimen Wing Yee had placed before them was displaying cream-coloured flowers, tinged with gold.

'It's magnificent,' he said. 'I had no idea it would be so beautiful.'

'Like Chin Ming,' Wing Yee said. 'Her name mean shining gold. She like orchid.'

Everyone except Chin Ming laughed. She covered her face with her hands and squirmed around in her seat; then she pulled out a pale blue fan, decorated with butterflies to hide her embarrassment.

Edmund came to the rescue. 'I know how fond the two of you are of each other,' he said, 'and I know how much you'll miss each other. You've nurtured the orchid all these months – I would like you to have it, Wing Yee.'

'But Dick say you take to England to look after, to make more plant.'

'That was the original idea, but it will be better off here, besides it could probably do without another long sea voyage. You've taken such great care of it and as you say, it is like Chin Ming. I want to leave it with you so that you can think about her often.'

'It does look incredibly healthy,' James said. 'Where have

you been keeping it?'

'I keep in workshop, good light there but not too much. I talk to orchid every day.'

'Wait a minute,' Dick said, 'that means, ...'

'That means Volande ran straight past it!' James and Edmund chorused.

'All those months of harassment, all his efforts to acquire it and in the end, he didn't even recognise what he'd been pursuing. What a waste of a life.'

*****

The others continued talking over coffee and brandy. Edmund asked Chin Ming to join him on the veranda. 'I want us to remember the warmth of a tropical night, the sound of the crickets and the rich perfumes wafting through the breeze,' he said. They linked hands and strolled into the garden.

'We must also remember the sky,' she said. 'Papa and I saw shooting stars the night before our picnic; he said the sky would be the same in England, but I think he is wrong. The moon will still appear and the constellations will be the same, but I think the colours will be different. Here, the sky at night looks like velvet covered in tiny diamonds; sometimes I think I could touch it and I know exactly what it would feel like. In England, I think the cold may change all that.'

'When we reach my father's house, I will wrap you in a blanket and take you into the garden to look at the stars. You may be right, it may well not feel the same, but it will still be beautiful – and we can think of our friends here, looking at the same stars and the same moon ...'

Chin Ming smiled; she knew now that she had made the correct decision. She was confident that Wing Yee would continue to prosper and delighted to discover that Dick might now have a new friend too.

Edmund took her by the shoulders and studied her face. 'We will go to England,' he said. 'I will introduce you to my father and we will be married in his church. We will spend some time in Oxford and visit Raffles in London, but one day we will return to Singapore.'

Chin Ming put her arms around his waist and smiled.

'I love this place,' Edmund said, 'and I'm beginning to feel that it will always remain your spiritual home; it is the place where you've thrived and been happy. It is where our friends will be, waiting to welcome us home. I love you, Chin Ming.'

She swallowed hard, there was a lump in her throat but she no longer felt shy or awkward; she was completely at ease with him. 'I love you, Edmund,' she said.

GLOSSARY

Ah Ku: A polite term of address in Cantonese for a Chinese prostitute.

Attap: The attap or nipah palm (Nypa fruticans) has long, feathery leaves and is traditionally used as roofing material for thatched houses or dwellings. The leaves are also used in many types of basketry and thatching.

Ayam buah keluak: Chicken and pork ribs braised in a local variety of nuts.

Ayam kleo: Chicken prepared in a creamy coconut gravy.

Bakwan kepiting: Ground pork and crab meatball soup is a dish that is delicately flavoured, relying almost completely on the stock and meat balls to provide flavour. It is a must-have in many Peranakan households during Lunar New Year.

Beef kway teow: Beef noodle soup.

Chi fan le ma: Roughly translated as 'Have you already eaten?'

Congee: A thick porridge of rice, prepared by boiling rice in a large amount of water until it softens significantly. It is most often served with side dishes such as meat, fish and flavourings which are added during the preparation. It is eaten primarily as a breakfast food or late supper.

Foo yong hai: Crab meat, egg and bamboo shoot omelette.

Gambier: A climbing shrub native to tropical Southeast Asia. Gambier production began as a traditional occupation in the Malay Archipelago. By the middle of the seventeenth century, it was established in Sumatra and in the western parts of Java and the Malay peninsula. It was initially used as medicine and chewed with betel nut. Local Chinese also began to use gambier to tan hides.

Gutta-percha tree: Long before gutta-percha was introduced into the Western world, it was used in a less processed form by the natives of the Malaysian Archipelago for making knife handles, walking sticks, and other purposes. The first European to discover this material was John Tradescant, who collected it in the Far East in 1656. He named this material 'Mazer wood'. The mature trees are five to thirty metres tall and up to one metre in trunk diameter. The leaves are evergreen; glossy green above and often yellow below. The flowers are white and are produced in small clusters along the stems, The fruit is an ovoid berry, containing one to four seeds; in many species, the fruit is edible.

Kajang: A traditional wooden boat, similar in design to a sampan, which has been used as a means of transportation in Sumatra and other islands in the region for centuries.

Kantan: Torch ginger lily that has showy pink flowers; different parts of the plant are used in cooking throughout Southeast

Asia, especially in fish dishes. The leaves are used in traditional medicine as an antioxidant, anti-inflammatory, for respiratory allergies and to help reduce blood pressure.

Kuah ladah: Fish prepared in a thin tamarind and pepper gravy.

Kueh: Traditional sweet or savoury cakes. These bite-sized colourful snacks are usually made with rice flour and coconut milk; they can be steamed, baked, fried or boiled.

Laksa: Noodles in a spicy coconut soup.

Lancha: A light sailing ship largely used for trading in the East Indian Archipelago and the Philippines.

Mee soup: A Hokkien dish made with fresh wheat noodles and vegetables.

Otak otak puteh: Spicy fish cake in banana leaves.

Ould Jenever: Originally invented around the middle of the eighteenth century, Jenever is a blend of two ingredients, malt-wine and neutral spirits. It is the ancestor of modern gin and is produced in Belgium and the Netherlands, where it is extremely popular. There are three main types: jonge (young), ould (old), and korenwjn (corn wine).

Pak muk huang: Meaning whitewood – one of the species of the Aquilaria genus that are great sources of resin used for perfume and incense. It is a tropical evergreen that grows up to fifteen metres tall.

Paphiopedilum superbiens: Found on the islands of the Straits of Malacca and Sumatra in leaf litter within coniferous forests and on rock ledges at elevations of nine hundred to thirteen hundred metres. It has solitary, dark purple flowers with brown-purple spotting on upright stems. The dorsal sepal is white with green and purple stripes.

Parang: A type of knife used across the Malay Archipelago. It is an excellent chopping tool and is something that you can use for prolonged periods of time without tiring.

Peranakan: A Malay word that means 'local-born'. The Peranakan community is unique to Southeast Asia. It has its origins in the interracial marriages that took place between immigrant Chinese men and non-Muslim women such as Bataks, Balinese and Chitty (descendants of old Hindu families) from Malacca, Penang, Terengganu, Burma and Indonesia in the sixteenth century.

Poh pia: Straits Chinese - style spring rolls.

Qing guo: Chinese white olive is also known as *Fructus canarii*. It is a famous subtropical fruit tree native to southern China and has at least two thousand years of cultivation history. In traditional Chinese medicine, it is often used to clear heat and remove toxins, and to promote fluid production.

Qipao: Evolved from a tubular-shaped garment that was originally worn by both men and women. During the Qing dynasty it had become a loosely fitted garment and hung in an A-line. It covered most of the wearer's body, revealing only the head, hands and the tips of the toes. Most of them were made of silk, and embroidered, with thick laces trimmed at the collar, sleeves and edges.

Queue: A plait of hair, worn at the back.

Sambal(s): A variety of prawns, vegetables, etc in a spicy gravy, to accompany other dishes.

Tek Sing: A large three-masted Chinese ocean-going junk which sailed from the port of Amoy, bound for Batavia, Dutch East Indies (now Jakarta, Indonesia) laden with a large cargo of porcelain goods and 1,600 Chinese immigrants. After a month of sailing, on 6th February 1822, the ship's captain decided to attempt a shortcut through the Gaspar Strait between the Bangka-Belitung Islands, and ran aground on a reef. The junk sank in about thirty metres (one hundred feet) of water. The next morning, February 7th, the English East Indiaman *Indiana*, sailing from Indonesia to Borneo, passed through the Gaspar Strait. The ship encountered debris from the sunk Chinese vessel and was able to rescue about one hundred and ninety survivors. Another eighteen people were saved by a small Chinese junk which may have been sailing in tandem with the *Tek Sing*, but had avoided the reefs.

Temenggong: An old Malay title of nobility. The Temenggong was traditionally responsible for the safety of the raja or sultan as well as overseeing law and order within his area of responsibility.

Terima kasih: Meaning 'thank you', an expression of gratitude.

Tuan: (in Malay-speaking countries) sir or lord; a form of address used as a mark of respect.

Youtiao: A long golden-brown deep-fried strip of dough. Conventionally, it is lightly salted and made so it can be torn lengthwise in two. Youtiao are normally eaten at breakfast.

ACKNOWLEDGEMENTS

I would like to thank the following people and organisations for their help and support in producing this book.

First of all, there is the group of writers with whom I shared the manuscript chapter by chapter, and who gave me encouragement as well as invaluable feedback: Sandra Horn, Valerie Bird, Penny Langford, Jan Carr and Carol Cole. Also, to Catherine Avery Jones for her proofreading skills.

My gratitude goes to Nick Courtright and his team at Atmosphere Press, especially Asata Radcliffe, Ronaldo Alves, and Erin Larson-Burnett.

For comments on the history and culture of Singapore in the 1820s, I thank all the local people I have talked to during the drafting of this story. For guidance about maritime events, I am indebted to Tim MacMahon. I am grateful to Philip Norman at The Garden Museum for providing information about the transportation of plants from China to Europe in the early nineteenth century. My thanks also to the British Library for access to the India Office Records, other archives, maps and online support.

I would also like to thank Peter Varney, who first introduced me to Southeast Asia and lit the spark that has become a lifelong infatuation with the history, culture and people of the region.

Finally, I thank my wonderful husband who has continued to show interest and support, has lifted my spirits and has believed in me throughout the creation of *Hope Dares to Blossom*.

Read an excerpt from Elisabeth Conway's first novel

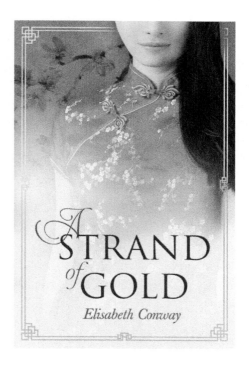

"This is a novel firmly rooted in the historical truth of the times and features slavery, sexual exploitation and a society ravaged by corruption and misogyny. Having said that, this is not at all a depresing novel. The friendship between Chin Ming and the more worldly courtesan Wing Yee is sensitively drawn, and I like both of these women and was rooting for their survival. Elisabeth Conway clearly has a great knowledge of Singapore and its history and it's a pleasure to read a book featuring this unusual setting."

- DEBORAH SWIFT, AUTHOR OF *THE LADY'S SLIPPER*, *THE SILKWORM KEEPER*, AND MANY OTHER HISTORICAL NOVELS.

PROLOGUE
23ʳᵈ January, 1822, Guangzhou

'Hurry, Papa, we'll miss the Lion Dance.'

'Patience, daughter.' Li Soong Heng smiles as he guides her ahead of the crowd. The procession will move in their direction soon enough. But now he needs her to focus on the entertainment whilst he scrutinises each face for any sign of recognition.

He lifts Chin Ming onto an old abandoned wooden crate and is amused when she protests. He realises that at eighteen, she wants to be treated as an adult, but he knows she will enjoy the spectacle more from this vantage point. He wants her to relish every moment, knowing the dangers they are about to embark upon.

A moment later the first creature, mimicking a yellow lion, leaps into the air and begins to prance towards them. Chin Ming claps her hands together; she beams at her father as flashes of yellow and white sway before her in time to the music. He feigns interest, but his main concern is to find the man he's arranged to meet here today – when will he make himself known?

'What's wrong, Papa?' he hears his daughter ask, but is saved from answering by the arrival of a band of drummers. Two men, who strike their cymbals loud and strong, join in to demand her attention. There is still no sign of the man who has promised to meet him. How much longer will they have to wait? They must leave Guangzhou behind and start a new life. Today, amidst the turmoil of the spring festival celebration, is the perfect opportunity.

The cymbals accompanying the yellow lion are now muted in the distance. They will be joined shortly by the red lion. Soong Heng's heart misses a beat as a small group, anxious to follow, bumps into Chin Ming's platform. He helps her regain her balance and is relieved to hear more drums, heralding the appearance of the third lion. Gongs begin to sound as it comes into view.

'Oh look, Papa,' she says. 'It's the one who loves to fight - the black lion, His ears are tiny and his beard is as black as his face. Can you see?'

'I can indeed daughter,' Soong Heng says as the vibrating bells on the creature's body reach a deafening crescendo. He is pleased that Chin Ming is so delighted with the spectacle; happy also that she is unaware it may be the last time she sees such a performance. When the time comes, how will he explain everything to her? How will he persuade her to move quickly and not ask any questions?

He keeps looking over his shoulder, searching the crowd for a clue. How much longer? he asks himself.

All of a sudden, a new group begins to bear down on them; they wave banners and shout in a dialect with which he is unfamiliar. The other spectators become agitated. They know instinctively that these people are nothing to do with the celebrations.

Soong Heng sees Chin Ming look towards him for reassurance. He smiles, but beyond her, he recognises one of the men he has accused of being involved with the opium trade. It is not the man he is expecting; his blood runs cold. He steps closer to Chin Ming.

'Take this,' he whispers, sliding a tiny scroll tied together with fine gold thread into her hand. 'Keep it safe for me,' he says quietly. 'You must get it to the man called Raffles in - Singapore.'

'What is it, Papa? Why are you looking so troubled?'

A foul-smelling cloth is held against his mouth. There is no escape from the man his enemies have sent to silence him. The crowd surges forward like a great tsunami. People begin to scream, the sound of gongs and cymbals assaulting their eardrums.

As he is dragged along, Soong Heng sees Chin Ming through a blur, fear on her face. Her arm is raised up above her head as if she is reaching out to him. The last image he has is seeing her fall; she is being carried along in a sea of bodies. Helpless now, he hears her scream, 'Papa, where are you Papa?'

ABOUT ATMOSPHERE PRESS

Atmosphere Press is an independent, full-service publisher for excellent books in all genres and for all audiences. Learn more about what we do at atmospherepress.com.

We encourage you to check out some of Atmosphere's latest releases, which are available at Amazon.com and via order from your local bookstore:

Dancing with David, a novel by Siegfried Johnson

The Friendship Quilts, a novel by June Calender

My Significant Nobody, a novel by Stevie D. Parker

Nine Days, a novel by Judy Lannon

Shining New Testament: The Cloning of Jay Christ, a novel by Cliff Williamson

Shadows of Robyst, a novel by K. E. Maroudas

Home Within a Landscape, a novel by Alexey L. Kovalev

Motherhood, a novel by Siamak Vakili

Death, The Pharmacist, a novel by D. Ike Horst

Mystery of the Lost Years, a novel by Bobby J. Bixler

Bone Deep Bonds, a novel by B. G. Arnold

Terriers in the Jungle, a novel by Georja Umano

Into the Emerald Dream, a novel by Autumn Allen

His Name Was Ellis, a novel by Joseph Libonati

The Cup, a novel by D. P. Hardwick

The Empathy Academy, a novel by Dustin Grinnell

Tholocco's Wake, a novel by W. W. VanOverbeke

Dying to Live, a novel by Barbara Macpherson Reyelts

Looking for Lawson, a novel by Mark Kirby

Yosef's Path: Lessons from my Father, a novel by Jane Doyle

Surrogate Colony, a novel by Boshra Rasti

ABOUT THE AUTHOR

Elisabeth Conway grew up in the Worcestershire countryside, but has spent a considerable part of her life in Southeast Asia, which she first encountered as a student of social anthropology.

Her career has included documentary filmmaking and working in the voluntary sector. She now lives in Salisbury with her husband, but returns to Malaysia and Singapore whenever an opportunity presents itself. Her very thorough research takes her to museums, libraries and any other avenue of knowledge that helps her writing.

Elisabeth has previously published non-fiction and short stories. Her first novel *A Strand of Gold*, was published by Atmosphere Press in 2021.

Printed in Great Britain
by Amazon